SON OF SONG BIRD

By
Dale Denney

PublishAmerica
Baltimore

© 2005 by Dale Denney.
All rights reserved. No part of this book may be reproduced, stored in a retrieval system or transmitted in any form or by any means without the prior written permission of the publishers, except by a reviewer who may quote brief passages in a review to be printed in a newspaper, magazine or journal.

First printing

At the specific preference of the author, PublishAmerica allowed this work to remain exactly as the author intended, verbatim, without editorial input.

ISBN: 1-4137-6156-9
PUBLISHED BY PUBLISHAMERICA, LLLP
www.publishamerica.com
Baltimore

Printed in the United States of America

*To my beloved wife,
a mixed blood Cherokee by birth
whose family embraced the white culture
by choice*

To Sonja

Dale Denney

Author's Note

Like all kids raised during the so-called Golden Age of motion pictures—20s, 30s, 40s—my concept of the natives of North America, whom we called Indians because Columbus thought he had sailed around the world and landed in India instead of the Caribbean Islands, was pure Hollywood.

The natives were wild savages who rode in circles around a wagon train shooting at the poor white people. They became the perfect villain for western lore.

While it was not the film maker's intent, I am sure, to so denigrate an entire race of people, he did so anyway.

Of course, I knew better—somewhat. I loved the stories. And everybody knows all stories have to have a villain and a hero, else there would be no story. But in Oklahoma where I was born, grew up in, was educated in, and have lived in most of my adult life, Native Americans were some of the neighbor kids I played with, perhaps the pretty dark haired girl I was secretly in love with in high school, or maybe the dark skinned politician who could make as grand a speech as anybody you ever heard at a rally.

Still, stories are a part of our culture. I, like others, simply made no connection between the savages in the movies and the neighbors whose ancestors were here when my ancestors sailed across the Atlantic ocean and overran them.

Native Americans are reclaiming their heritage, their dignity, their history. But, in truth, they are having a difficult time because they, themselves, are not one people.

There is as much difference between some Native American cultures and languages as there is, for example, between the Germanic people and Japanese.

Oklahomans perhaps understand this better than most because before Oklahoma became a state it was called Indian Territory. Congress had set aside a large portion of the Louisiana Purchase with the intent of bringing peace to the frontier by separating the white settlers and natives.

They would move all the natives living east of the Mississippi River to a designated area west of the Mississippi. That way, there would be no more Indian Wars.

However, Congress nor anyone else was able to stop the westward flow of the white man. While it was a struggle to move the natives and keep them within the boundaries of Indian Territory, it proved impossible to keep the whites out.

To accommodate the white pioneers moving westward, Congress kept shrinking Indian Territory until finally all that was left was an area roughly where Oklahoma now is.

This seemed to be a workable compromise for the last half of the nineteenth century. Oklahoma remained Indian Territory until statehood in 1907, an island in the flow of white migration westward.

Unfortunately, the history of our state which we had to study in school did not tell us about the contributions of the natives.

There was a little about Indian Territory, just to let us know there was something there before statehood. The rest of the book was about politicians, agriculture, industry, and the usual activities of the white people.

It so happened I married a beautiful girl with blue eyes and blonde hair. I suppose I knew she was one sixty-fourth Cherokee, but so what. It seemed all Oklahomans, especially those living here in the early days of statehood, had ancestors from both the whites and natives.

And, of course, not once did I ever connect my beautiful bride with the savages of Hollywood.

It wasn't until I retired and could use my time any way that I wanted that I began educating myself about the natives, especially those natives—the Cherokees—living in my area of "Indian Territory" and who were, incidentally, my wife's ancestors.

I was fascinated by Cherokee history. Despite how hard historians tried to link them with the generic native—especially the Hollywood variety—I saw them differently.

They began intermarrying almost immediately with the Europeans when the two races came in contact in the sixteenth century.

They welcomed missionaries from the New England states who established schools. And accepted their religious teachings which were, after all, not too much different from their own.

The Cherokees did not, as a general rule, war with the whites. Instead, they were more inclined to accept the good of both cultures as a way of bettering their own life.

Many became—especially the mixed bloods—the typical southern plantation owner, complete with ownership of slaves.

They saw the white man banding together to create states which then would later be folded into the new United States of America.

So they wrote their own constitution in 1827. And, you guessed it, the document called for a Principal Chief (President), a National Committee (Senate), a National Council (House of Representatives), and a judicial system. They divided their nation into 8 administrative districts. In each would be a judge, a marshal, and local council whose responsibilities would be to keep order locally according to written law.

They accepted, too, the white man's manner of dressing. So by the time the Cherokees moved to Indian Territory, they were indistinguishable from the whites, except in genetic physical characteristics.

The Cherokees were also prime movers in arranging a coalition of native tribes (they called themselves nations instead of tribes) and sought statehood. It worked. They came within a single vote in Congress of becoming the state of Seqouyah, the 46th state of the Union.

But politics forced the natives living in the eastern half of Indian Territory to join with the whites living in the western half, which was now called Oklahoma territory, to form the 46th state. And it was to be called Oklahoma.

I enjoyed writing Son of Song Bird, the first in a series of six novels, which is my own way of "Hollywoodizing" my birth state's history.

CHAPTER 1

The deep, early morning shadows of the forest gave the motionless Indian all the protection he needed from being seen as he watched the man and boy at the cabin saddling their horses.

He was a large, powerful-built man, his oval face smeared with war paint. His head was shaved except for a scalp-lock, from which dangled a single feather, dyed red with a glistening white tip.

His ears lay close to his head. He pulled thoughtfully at the one which was partially gone, bitten off in a fight. Dressed only in a loin cloth and moccasins, his weapons hung loosely; his bow from a shoulder; his quiver of arrows strapped to his back; his tomahawk—its steel blade shiny from much use—punched beneath his waist thong.

Another member of the War Party appeared, ghost-like at his side. He carried a flintlock musket. He took one look and spat.

"White Cherokee." His deep anger showed in his gutteral Osage.

He leveled the musket, cocking the hammer in the same motion. His companion's arm shot out, his hand pushing the gun down.

"No. Man and boy pack heavy. Go on long trip. No need to kill."

The man with the musket did not like the order. The leader scowled.

"I want only the woman. She carries my child. A son, perhaps. I will train him well. Make him brave Osage warrior to fight the Cherokee from the east."

"We kill man and boy. They are Cherokee."

"No. We do that and the Cherokee will come. They take our land. White man soldier on their side. I take woman. She will come. Cherokee will not know what happened. They will not come to take our land."

He glared down the man with the musket then returned his attention to the cabin below.

I ask first. If she does not come, I carry her away. I have that right.

He settled back to wait.

The boy was too excited to eat breakfast. Besides, there was still a chance his mother wouldn't let him go. She had been acting strange lately. He watched in silence as she removed the pan of biscuits from her new cook stove. She just barely made it to the table before having to let go, dropping the pan onto the planked table with a loud *plop*.

"Mercy!" she said, angry at her own foolishness and relieved to get the hot pan out of her hands. Then she turned on the man, still flipping her fingers and said with mock anger, "You two are more trouble than you're worth. I don't see why you have to have breakfast before you go. I'll be spending half the morning cooking and cleaning up. I won't have any time for myself."

Then she wanted to be alone, the boy thought, relieved. Suddenly hungry, he reached for one of the hot biscuits.

The man read the woman's words differently. She was afraid to be alone. He scowled. "There's nothing to worry about. Nobody's seen any Osages for a year now."

The woman turned away quickly, returning to the stove. The man and boy exchanged glances. The man shrugged.

The boy hoped his mother wouldn't start in on him again to stay with her; scolding his uncle like she did yesterday for letting him go, saying that if he wasn't old enough to choose a name, he certainly wasn't old enough to be going to town.

They'd be gone only one night, and she'd stayed by herself a lot of times when he and Uncle Daniel had gone on trips, hunting, helping neighbors with their harvest and haying. He furrowed his brow, puzzled. His mother seemed to have changed lately. For a while there, she acted unusually happy when they returned home from a trip, humming to herself or singing aloud as she hung the washing on the clothesline outside…living up to the name she'd chosen for herself, Song Bird. Lately, however, she seemed depressed about something. The boy liked her a lot better when she was singing.

He worried that his uncle might change his mind, seeing the way his mother was acting. Dressed the way he was for the trip didn't help matters any. He simply didn't feel comfortable in his homespun woolen trousers and a too-large dingy white shirt that had belonged to his father, his mother said.

Their cabin deep in the mountains of northwestern Arkansas was well built, its log walls thick and well chinked. The young man's sleeping room was a lean-to addition to the original structure. Its roof sloped so sharply that he could no longer stand erect near the outside wall. It was barely large enough to accommodate a bed, a trunk that his mother had stored all her possessions in when she had moved here from Georgia, and a wash basin stand skirted with bleached sacking material to hide shelving below. The room's only source of heat during the winter months was from the opened doorway into the cabin's interior. But the young man preferred privacy and kept the door closed, burying his head under a pile of hand-stitched quilts until time to get up, then he'd bounce out of bed and dress in a hurry, his toes curling from the cold flooring. He'd grab his boots and run to the fireplace in the other room before pulling them on. Most of the year, however, the heavy log walls kept it reasonably comfortable inside regardless of the outside temperatures.

There were two bedrooms on the other side of the large living room-kitchen area, one where his mother slept and kept her personal belongings, and the other his uncle's. These two rooms had been included in the cabin's original design and were more spacious than the boy's lean-to. His uncle had even built a two-way fireplace in the bedrooms' shared wall which could be used to heat the two sleeping areas with a small fire during cold nights.

The boy shared his mother's bedroom until he was seven, then moved in with his uncle. There he stayed until he was twelve when his uncle agreed to build him a room of his own. That had been five years ago. His uncle tried to bribe him on the sly when they were building the lean-to, contending that by rights a boy should choose his name before he got a place to sleep for his very own.

The boy came close to telling him that he had already chosen a name for himself. Tahchee. But he felt everybody would make fun of him when he made the announcement, for the name meant a powerful leader, a strong warrior. He was neither, and would probably never be, now that the Cherokees had taken up the ways of the white man by living as the white man lived in log homes, raising stock, cultivating land, spinning wool, building schools, and worshiping the white man's God whose son Jesus lived on earth and was able to turn water into wine and bring people back from the dead.

But many things they kept doing like they had been doing forever. Like choosing a name. Why not? Especially boys? His uncle did, selecting a Christian name. Daniel Taylor.

He'd toyed with the thought of taking his father's name. Thomas. But he preferred a Cherokee name. Besides, he hadn't known his father. He might not have liked him. He liked Daniel. That's why he used it in school.

He felt a vast sense of relief when his uncle Daniel pushed back from the table and said, "Let's go."

With one last, fearful glance toward his mother, the boy hastily gathered his things and followed Daniel out the door.

Song Bird felt good standing in the cabin entrance with hands on hips watching the two riders disappear into the forest. She was accustomed to being alone, actually relishing the freedom. And her son, she knew, was more excited over making the trip into town with Daniel than he let on. She was proud of the way he looked up to her brother, like a father. Daniel was, in fact, the only father her son had ever known. Then her proud feeling was crowded out by a worry. She frowned.

What will my son do when I give birth to his half brother? How will I explain it to Daniel? And the neighbors? What will they think? That she and her brother...??

The thought was too horrifying to complete. She shuddered involuntarily. There was another possibility. She could kill herself. But she didn't want to die; not yet, anyway. Her life was just beginning, especially so since her son was almost grown. I'm not yet thirty-five, she thought, and, at the same time, knowing she was still a beautiful woman, despite the years of harsh living in the Arkansas wilderness. Now this, she accused herself placing a hand on her stomach, which, while still flat, held the growing form that would destroy her and her family.

There was yet another possibility. Invite Roy Vann to come spend the night. He would come. Come in a minute. Later, she would tell him she was pregnant. He would marry her. He'd already been hinting at it. Even if he refused, she could tell Daniel and Daniel would make him do it, for her brother was a strong Christian man.

Why did she do it? Why, oh, why? To keep from being taken by force, that's why. The first time, yes. But how about that next time . . and the next...and all the times after that? She wanted him as much as he wanted her. Until she missed her monthly time.

Now she hated him for destroying her life, and her son's. Daniel's, too.

She stared with unseeing eyes at the chickens scratching for seeds just beyond the porch, her frown deepening. How old was her son now? Sixteen? No. Seventeen. Five in Georgia when they lived with her parents and twelve since she and Daniel had moved to Arkansas. She sighed, a heavy, helpless sound in the human stillness.

What's done's done. She'd ask Roy to marry her; beg him, if necessary, she thought, chewing worriedly on her underlip. Then she forced herself to relax. *Get busy*. She lifted her eyebrows to untangle her frown and shifted her thoughts to things which needed to be done around the cabin. She glanced at the sun. The morning was half gone. Taking one last look at the spot where she'd seen her two men disappear, she turned to go inside.

She purposefully left the cabin door standing open, for she loved having the warm sunlight splashing across her plank flooring. She studied the room, a finger to her lips, trying to make up her mind where she should start first. Or should she take time redoing herself? she questioned and pulled at her uncombed tresses. She'd dressed hurriedly to help get them packed and on the way; her black hair was still tousled, hurriedly piled on top of her head.

No. Do the dishes first, she decided, then she could take her time working on herself. She began scraping scraps from the three plates into the bowl of congealed gravy.

She actually enjoyed working in her large combination kitchen, dining and living area. Daniel had said she'd have more space than she'd know what to do with when he built the lean-to for the boy out back. He was right. Now, each of them had private bedrooms. The boy—she simply *had* to stop calling him boy, even in her own thinking! But what else *could* she do? He still hadn't selected his name. Biting her lip, she set a pan of water on the stove and trimmed soap shavings into it.

She hoped her son would continue using her brother's Christian name, as he was doing in school, instead of choosing a Cherokee name. But she had no intentions of interfering, for name selection was a very private matter. She could never forget the thrill of finding her own name. She'd gone for a walk that beautiful morning, pausing for long intervals listening to the birds singing. She was particularly fascinated with the exuberance of a mockingbird who combined all his imitations into a song of his own. He sang from the pure joy of singing.

She sat on a rock, listening, trying to identify the many different bird calls the mockingbird had in his melody before repeating himself. She could detect no beginning nor ending, and his delightful tune prompted her to leap to her feet, throw her hands in the air and begin singing all the songs her mother and grandmother taught her.

She skipped through the forest, singing loudly, singing all the songs she knew over and over, imitating the mockingbird. By the time she reached home, she was so out of breath she could barely tell her mother how she was to be called.

"My name is Song Bird!" she announced, proud, happy.

From her own experience, she wanted her son to know the joy of finding his own name. But at seventeen! Would he ever? Perhaps she could have taken her husband's advice when the boy was born.

"Call him Bill," he'd said. "It's a nice, neat name. He'll like it when he grows up."

She'd resisted. That was the white man's way. They...strange how she thought of whites as being different, especially since she had married one! She shook her head in disbelief as she scrubbed the dishes in the soapy water.

However, her white man *had been* different. Love had a way of lifting people over racial fences. Remembering him still filled her with a deep sadness.

"Please don't go," she had begged that night. "I'll be all right. You'll be here to help. Besides, Cherokee mothers have babies all the time without a doctor."

He ignored her pleas as he pushed his arms into his heavy coat, grabbed up his long rifle and headed for the door.

"Didn't I promise you I'd always see to it you had the best of everything?" he said. He gave her a quick kiss. "Now don't worry. I'll be back before you know it."

"But, Thomas! In this ice storm—?"

"I've been out in worse," he said and was gone.

He'd fallen through the ice, crossing the river; didn't even bother to change clothes until he had returned with the doctor. She delivered so easily, the doctor said he was more concerned about Thomas catching his death of cold than he was about her and the baby.

The doctor's joshing prediction had come true. Within two weeks, Thomas—big, strong, lovable Thomas Anderson—was dead, drowned in his own fluids, the doctor said. He called it pneumonia.

With a heavy, reluctant sigh, she pushed away the memories. Dishes done, she banked the fire in her new cook stove, making sure there'd be enough live coals to start her noon meal.

Out of habit, she reached for her damp washcloth and wiped her finger smudges from the stove's door handle. She loved the stove's shiny newness even more than its work-saving efficiency as compared to the open fireplace. She could never quite shake the guilty feeling for owning such an extravagant convenience. But it had been Daniel's doing. He hadn't asked whether or not she wanted one—of course, all women did—he'd simply brought it home from Fort Smith one day.

The sudden cackling of the chickens outside meant nothing until the room darkened and she became aware of someone standing in the doorway, blocking out the sunlight.

They forgot something, she thought. She turned, expecting to see Daniel and her son, her wash cloth dripping water. She gasped.

"You!"

Anger, churning with fear, gripped her in a frozen moment as she tried to decided which could she get to first, the butcher knife on the table or the long rifle standing in the corner beside the fireplace? Or was there any need to do either?

The big Osage stared, his dark eyes steady, his handsome face impassive. He still stirred deep feelings in her. His voice was strong when he spoke.

"White man give Osage land to Cherokee. They say we must go north and live in a place they call Kansas. I come to take you with me. Make you my wife."

"No! My son—"

"Forget boy!" he exploded. "He a man now."

"Never! I hate you!"

His face darkened. Having experienced results of his quick temper before, she broke for the rifle, knocking the table aside. She grabbed the weapon, her hopes surging as she whirled. But the Osage's huge hand closed over the gun's breech. He yanked, his brute strength almost pulling her arms from her shoulder sockets before she could let go. He threw the gun aside and reached for her.

"You come."

"No!" she screamed, recoiling into a corner. Tears of angry frustration blurred the vision of his painted face. When he made another grab for her, she leaped on him, grabbing a handful of his scalp-lock with one hand and clawing at his face with the other.

He let out a savage grunt and swung an open hand. She tried to duck. The sting of the slap was lost in the force that knocked her backward against the wall. Her breath went out as her head whiplashed against the logs. Crazy lights spun, bringing with them an eerie numbness. She fought to keep her knees from buckling.

Anger kept her from blacking out. She gulped in huge drafts of air and felt a sense of partial victory at the sight of blood mixing with the paint on the Osage's face, dripping from his chin. She wanted to hit him with something. Anything. But all she had in her hand was the feather she'd pulled from his hair. He must have felt the smeary mess running. He swiped it away. When he saw his own blood in the palm of his hand, his rage exploded in a wild yell as he lunged.

Desperate, she kicked, felt her foot sink into his private parts under the loin cloth. With a cry of pain, he doubled over. She seized the chance to escape. But his huge hand closed on her arm. His grip was slippery with his own blood. She struggled, beating at his face with the fist still clutching the feather. Just as she was about to pull free, he yanked out his tomahawk and, with an angry snarl, swung.

In her mind, she screamed, but the only sound made in the cabin was a sickening thump of a steel blade slicing into a skull.

The boy rode close to his uncle entering the town of Fort Smith, his constantly shifting gaze missing nothing—even noticing the various colors of the dogs which came running from the homes to bark at the heels of their horses. He also heard the loud laughter coming from a couple of soldiers lounging near their horses in front of the mercantile store. A wagon needing all four hubs tarred squeaked down the street. A woman stepped out onto her porch and called to her kids.

The raucous sounds made the young man nervous, even made his skin itch more underneath his wool trousers. He glanced at his uncle's face and wished he could be more like him, seemingly unconcerned, unperturbed. They jogged through town to the grist mill and dismounted.

Even at seventeen, the boy was taller than his uncle. Although slender built, he moved with an eye-catching grace. His lithe suppleness often proved deceiving to his playmates back home on the White River, for he could out-wrestle any of them, including some who were many years older. His eye-hand coordination was so acute, he could catch a hummingbird in mid-air instead of waiting for it to bury itself deep into a hollyhock bloom. His "V" shaped face made his dark eyes appear to be wide-set, especially since his nose was so small. His broad forehead swept back slightly from his dark brows and ended in a mass of black hair which he kept cropped short just below his ears, white man style. There were times he threatened to shave his head, leaving only a scalp-lock like the Osage, but his mother warned that the day he did that, he could just go live with the ignorant savages in Indian Territory. While he laughed at her angry threat, he never dared to test her will.

The youth carried no firearms. His only weapon was a big-bladed knife, its bone handle protruding above the knife's sheath within easy reach. In contrast, his uncle, a barrel chested man, wore a pistol, carried a long rifle and kept a small knife strapped to his leg inside a boot.

The boy made one final sweeping glance of the town's main street before following his uncle into the two-story log building which housed the grist mill. He stopped just inside the door, resisting an urge to turn and run away from the gloomy interior. The cavernous room seemed to swallow all the light coming in from the doorway and a single window, leaving only a dusk-like glow.

The boy swept the area with a quick glance and saw the two men and a girl at the rear of the room. One of the men, his long whiskers branding him at once as a white man, appeared to be trying to adjust the mill's grinding stones. The other man and girl watched, their backs to the front.

Daniel leaned his long rifle against the wall and called politely, "Anybody here?"

"Yo!" the whiskered man answered, turning his head to squint in their direction. Then he left the other man and the girl and came to greet them.

But the young man's attention remained on the girl still standing near the stones. Sunlight coming through a crack high on the log wall lay a bright line along the floor from his feet to hers, seemingly tying them together. A sunshine rope. He lifted his gaze from her moccasined feet, up her long and perfectly shaped legs to the point where her thighs disappeared into a white deerskin skirt.

The dress was the most beautiful female Indian garment he'd seen. Instead of hanging loose from her shoulders as most deerskins did, this one was cut low at the neck line, lay tight across her chest and fit snug at her waist and hips.

He was unable to take his eyes off her, unaware that he was staring until she turned slightly, on purpose, he knew, to let him get a better view. Then, suddenly embarrassed, he tried to make himself look away, but couldn't. The snug fitting garment sloped out sharply in front and fell from the tips of her breasts in a tumble of diminishing wrinkles to her waist line.

He could hear his heart beats pounding in his ears as he dragged his gaze from her bosoms up her long, swan-like neck. Her straight black hair spilled down each side of her face to her shoulders and beyond, some tresses lying forward, most behind. He got only a glimpse of the oval face, her full lips, and straight nose before his gaze locked with hers.

Suddenly, he felt hot, fearing that she was able to read his wild thoughts. When he noticed her own gaze appraising him, he wanted to run away and hide, for he was acutely aware of how sloppy he must appear in his loose fitting shirt, trousers, wide-brimmed hat. But his feet seemed to be anchored securely in a pair of his uncle's worn boots. She smiled and reached up with one hand to toss all her hair behind her shoulders. He swallowed heavily, forced a nervous smile .

Then he glanced away, hating the weak and foolish feeling inside which was making it hard for him to breathe. He shifted his attention to the approaching man, squinting hard to make out Daniel's features.

"Well, if it ain't old Daniel Taylor!" he said when recognition did come. The boy could tell the way the man kept glancing his way that he was not quite sure who he was. "What brings the Taylors to town?"

"We need that cornmeal in the worst way, Sam," Daniel said. "We're flat-dab out. Song Bird told me if you didn't have our corn ground, to stay with you and your misses until you did."

Then the boy remembered the man's name. Samuel Johnson. Only he didn't have whiskers the last time he'd seen him. The man grinned and waved toward sacks piled near one wall.

"You're lucky," he said. "I just finished doing yours in the last batch before my stones jumped out of alignment. Ruined the cutting edge on one pretty bad, it looks like. No telling how long it'll take to get another pair shipped in from Cincinnater."

"In that case, you won't have to give us room and board until you get our corn milled," Daniel said, chuckling.

The whiskered man laughed with Daniel, then gestured. "This Song Bird's young 'un?" he asked.

Daniel nodded. "That's him." He said it like he was proud. "He's kind of growed up on us, ain't he?"

The white man measured a height about four feet from the floor by holding out a gnarled hand, palm down.

"Last I seen of him at your place, he warn't no bigger'n this," he said. "What do you call him now? Or has he picked a name for hisself yet?"

Daniel shook his head. To the boy, it sounded as if his uncle was apologizing when he explained, "Around our place, there's not but the three of us. Me and Song Bird and him. No need to use names until you get mad. Then you just cuss the woman and kick the boy!"

Both men laughed again. The boy felt a sudden flush of anger. He clenched his teeth. No need for him to apologize for me! Ashamed, he glanced at the girl, knowing she heard. He stiffened proudly.

"I'm Tahchee," he blurted, loud and forceful; as if everybody in the whole world should know, and if they didn't, they damn sure did now.

The white man's eyebrows shot up and his jaw dropped, making a dark hole in his beard.

"Dutch?" he asked, surprised. "Why Dutch?"

It took a second or two before the boy realized how near the Cherokee pronunciation of Tahchee was to the English word Dutch. Daniel guffawed at the white man's sorry attempt to repeat the name.

"Not Dutch, Sam. Dahtch. You forgot your Cherokee? Our Ta's are D—"

"Tahchee!" the young man broke in, angry over their light hearted banter. He glanced at the girl, and felt a deep need to explain. "It means great leader."

The white man shook his head, smiled and winked at Daniel.

"Well, it still sounds like Dutch to me," he said.

Daniel threw up both hands. "Call him what you want, Sam," he said. "Him selecting a name's a big relief to me. I'm tired of saying, 'Hey, you!'"

The two men laughed again, over nothing, the young man thought. He fought a strong urge to spin around and stalk out of the mill and get on his horse and ride away, fast. But his sense of honor was stronger. He'd been taught early and very forcefully that you didn't walk away from your elders without a proper dismissal, either overt or covert. And Daniel, always onto him for being too impulsive anyway, said being rude showed emotional immaturity. Tahchee resisted the temptation to leave and kept his boots planted to the floor, stiffly erect, still scowling.

In a sense, Tahchee felt more angry at himself than at the white man. He should have waited until they returned home, share the moment with his family. Now embarrassed, he glanced at the girl again, still standing with the other man at the back of the room.

It's your fault! he accused silently. *You being here made me do it!*

The girl ducked her head, then peeked at him from under her long lashes with a slight smile on her lips.

And she knows it, too! Damn her!

Sam motioned for the man and the girl. "Come on up here, William," he called. As the man and the girl neared, Sam said, "I want you all to meet the Taylors. They're a fine Cherokee family. Been living here since…'15, warn't it, Daniel?"

"About then, I guess it was."

"This is William Rogers and his daughter. William just brought his family out here from Tennessee. William, this is Daniel Taylor and his nephew. The boy just now named hisself something—Dutch, I think."

All three men chuckled again over the mispronunciation as William Rogers shook Daniel's hand.

"Glad to know you, Daniel," William said.

"Likewise," Daniel responded. "You folks found a place to build on yet?"

William nodded at Daniel even as he extended his hand toward Tahchee and said, "You, too, son."

Tahchee, seething inside at being made fun of, hesitated, then relaxed when the older man added softly, "Tahchee," pronouncing it correctly, the tone of his voice carrying an understanding sympathy.

Tahchee grasped the extended hand, feeling awkward doing so, for he'd never been introduced so formally before.

Then William Rogers placed his hand on the young girl's back. "This is my daughter, Laura. She's our oldest. The wife and I have five. Laura here and four boys. She insisted they all have Christian names. Like their white cousins. All right by me, I tell her. Got one of them myself. Christian name. You know how it is."

Daniel understood. He touched the brim of his hat respectfully. "Glad to know you, Miss," he said.

The girl nodded politely. Daniel gestured toward Tahchee. "My sister's boy. There's just the three of us. We have a place up north, on the White River."

"Really?" William asked. "Where about? We're camping in Bull Hollow. Kind of like it there. Good flat land along the White river bottom. We're thinking strongly about building there and staying. Know where that's at?"

"Sure do," Daniel said with a wide grin. "We're neighbors. Bull Hollow's not more'n seven or eight, maybe ten miles from our place. Depending on whether you follow the river or cross the mountain."

"Well, I'll declare. It's a small world, ain't it?" William said laughing.

As the older men turned and walked toward the damaged grinding stone, Daniel was saying to William, "You'll need help clearing land and raising a cabin. Just let us know when. We'll be there."

"Thanks, Daniel. We..."

Their conversation turned into unintelligible echoes in the large room as they moved farther away. Tahchee, now alone with the girl, kept glancing at her, then away, not knowing what to do or say. She was even more beautiful standing close. He could even smell her, a sweet odor that, somehow, filled him with fear. Her slight smile made him feel inside like a butterfly he'd seen once trying to land on a flower but not quite knowing just where to grab hold.

He forced a long sigh and wrinkled his brow, feigning disinterest. She kept her eyes fixed on him, driving the discomfort deeper. He finally yanked his hat off and extended his a hand awkwardly, white man style.

"I'm Tahchee," he said firmly and with excessive emphasis on the proper pronunciation, in case she couldn't speak Cherokee either. Lots of kids of mixed parents didn't. Like him. He'd picked up what he knew listening to his mother and Daniel talk. His mother wanted him to use English. Claimed it would go easier on him by the time he grew up.

When she grasped his hand, she had a foxy look on her face. Her touch thrilled him more than he expected. He was surprised by his sudden urge to pull her closer, an urge that compounded itself when she returned the pressure of his grip meaningfully.

"I know—" she said. She studied his face intently for a long moment before adding, "—Dutch."

Her deliberate tease infuriated him. He flung her hand away, jammed his hat on, and turned sideways to her, stretching tall, trying to make her smaller. He crossed his arms and rested them resolutely on his chest, pretending to ignore her. She reached out to rest a hand lightly on his arm.

"I'm sorry," she said, then added, "I think Tahchee is a beautiful name."

He melted inside. But he was too proud to let his feelings show. He hung onto his deep frown as he eyed her.

"The white people have done enough to us without making fun of our names," he growled, knowing his philosophical remark was out of place even as he spoke.

"Oh, don't be silly. The joke's on them. They'll never understand us, no matter how hard they try."

She was certainly right about that, he thought. And when he considered the matter from her viewpoint, Sam's misunderstanding was funny. He relaxed.

"And don't go jumping on white people," she continued. "My mother's a white woman. Dad claims he's full blood Cherokee, but I doubt it. He doesn't know where the Rogers name came from. There has to be a white man in the family somewhere. Which makes me—I don't know what. Half Cherokee, I suppose. And you?"

He shrugged. "Me, too. Mother's a full blood...I think. She said Dad was a white man. He died just after I was born. I never knew him." He uncrossed his arms and gestured toward the men. "Uncle Daniel has been my father."

He wanted to know more about her, to be alone with her and hear every detail of her life. She was different. She was so...so...well, *different*. He stood before her, feeling awkward and ugly in his white man's clothing and her being dressed so beautifully as a young Cherokee woman.

Should he leave her and rejoin the men to prove he really was grown up? Or should he invite her to go outside and join him in a walk around town. He hated inaction. Even so, now, with her, he felt as if he were tied to a tree and unable to break the ropes to get away from it. She motioning toward the opened door.

"It's a beautiful day outside, isn't it?" she said, then brushed by him, close, on her way toward the front entrance.

He followed, as if he were tied to her with a string.

"Yes, it is," he stammered to her back. "Would you like to go for a walk around town?" It sounded stupid since she was already on her way.

She said over her shoulder, "I'd love to." Then she turned and, walking backwards, looked around him at the men in the back of the room. She called to her father, "I'm going outside—"

Tahchee, fearing he might say no, glanced over his shoulder in time to see her father give his permission with a wave of his hand.

Relieved, he shifted his gaze back to her in time to hear her add, for his ears only, "—with Dutch."

"You—!" he blurted in playful anger and made a grab for her. She dodged away from him and, laughing, ran out the door, her long legs carrying her deer-like. He stumbled happily after her, boots thumping, clothes flopping...the happiest he'd ever been in his life.

CHAPTER 2

Their day's business in Fort Smith done, Daniel led the boy—Tahchee, now—to a cool running stream near the edge of town. He handed the boy his rifle.

"Go get some meat for supper," he said. "I'll build a fire and get the coffee going. How does a roasted rabbit, beans and sourdough sound?"

"Sounds good to me," Tahchee said, hefting the rifle.

"Remember, you get only one shot," Daniel joked.

Daniel grinned at the way Tahchee swaggered into the timber, acting proud. Had a right to be. Now he was somebody, complete with his own name. *Song Bird will be proud, too.* He dismissed those thoughts and got busy preparing camp. It was several minutes before he heard the rifle crack. He had the roasting spit ready by the time the boy returned, grinning from ear to ear, carrying a rabbit.

Daniel skinned the furry creature, gutted it, washed it in the creek and skewered it on the spit. In a short while it was done, roasted just right—crusty on the outside, juicy inside, cooked through. They ate in silence. When the best peices of the rabbit, the small of the back and thighs, were gone, Daniel poured himself some coffee from the badly chipped, porcelain lined pot sitting against the coals of the fire.

"So it's Tahchee, is it?" he asked with a mixture of amusement and pride as he sipped his coffee and looked across the campfire into the boy's dark eyes, the wavering flames making shadows dance on his face, a face that appeared more mature now. "And you even know what it means."

The expression in the boy's face was one of disgust. He nodded curtly. "Yes. I know. It means great leader, proud warrior."

"You act ashamed."

"Well, I'm not."

"Don't be," Daniel said. He felt he had to say this with care…"Your mother will be disappointed that the choice was made in public. It should be a family affair."

Daniel could tell the remark hurt. He meant for it to, yet not devastating. He sensed that he'd said it just right by the look of agonized resentment he saw in Tahchee's face. He gave the boy a reassuring smile.

"Oh, she'll be pleased, now that it's done." he said.

The boy's face brightened. "You really think so?"

Daniel laughed. "Your mother means a lot to you, doesn't she?"

Tahchee nodded, then challenged, "She does to you too, doesn't she?"

He took another sip of his coffee before admitting, "Yes…"

He let the acknowledgement hang and stared into the dying fire. *More than you'll ever know, boy. She made me a man.*

"You're not mad at me, are you?"

"What for?" Daniel asked, surprised.

"For not going on using your name in school."

He shrugged, chuckled, displaying a feeling he did not feel. No, he wasn't exactly angry. Just a little disappointed. He stretched out on his side, propping himself up on one elbow while still holding the tin cup in his hands. He made no effort to comment one way or the other. The boy wouldn't understand, and it would only hurt his feelings.

He had resigned himself to the fact that he would probably never marry and would not have any children to pass his chosen name on to. When Song Bird got married and left home, it was up to him to look after their father and mother. Their father had never gotten around very good after the horse fell on his leg and broke it in about three places. Their mother had never been a strong woman. He stayed home seeing after their needs and working the farm. He'd come close to marrying only once, but decided against it because he felt he couldn't be both—a devoted son and loving husband. When Song Bird's husband died and she asked if it would be all right for her to come home and "stay awhile" until the baby was older, Daniel didn't give it a second thought even though according to Cherokee custom—the old ways—surviving males of a family were responsible for all debts of a deceased member. But since Thomas was a white man, there was some doubt about Daniel being committed to this responsibility. With Song Bird living at home, however, there would be many of Thomas' creditors who would be expecting Daniel to pay.

"Don't be silly," he'd told her. "This is as much your home as it is mine."

"But—well, you know what I mean—" she apologized.

"I don't want to hear no more about it," he told her, and that was the end of it.

He thought Song Bird would be married again in a few years. But she hadn't. Didn't seem interested. Lord only knows, she had plenty of chances. Even now, out here in Arkansas and her still a beautiful young woman, she had more than her share of suitors. Personally, he favored Roy Vann. Daniel knew for a fact that Roy'd marry her in a minute, if she would have him. He did what he could to help the one-sided romance along with subtle hints and other remarks which weren't so subtle. And once, just the other day in fact, when he was not so subtle, her anger flared.

"Will you leave me alone? I'll get married when I feel like it. Roy's nice. But I just—"

She broke off and he noticed the tears in her eyes before she turned her back on him. He was still puzzled over why she acted the way she did, as if she were keeping some sort of shameful secret from him.

He heard Tahchee say something and, embarrassed at being caught with his mind wandering, asked, "What?"

"I asked what do you think of our new neighbors?"

"The Rogerses? Seem like nice people to me."

He saw the dreamy-eyed look in Tahchee's eyes and smiled to himself, knowing what caused it. He decided to egg it on by asking, "Now what was the girl's name? I clean forgot."

"Laura, wasn't it?"

"What do you mean 'Wasn't it?' You was with her all afternoon. If you didn't find out what her name was in that length of time, I'd say there's something wrong with you."

Tahchee tried to stifle a laugh, and it came out a sputtering giggle. Daniel pressed his tease further. "What'd she call you? Tahchee or Dutch?"

"Dutch, mostly. When she wanted to get my goat."

"Sounds to me like you two got mighty familiar in mighty short time."

"She was fun to be with."

"Not to mention being a real looker."

Daniel thought the boy was actually blushing. He pushed on. "Now I don't want you to go chasing off to the neighbors all hours of the day and night borrowing this and borrowing that. First thing I'm going to do is tell Song Bird. How you got moon-eyed over some little girl moving in only ten miles down the river. She'll put a stop to you sneaking off—"

"Oh, cut that out, will you, Daniel? You know I'm not going to be doing that."

"Well, all I got to say is, if you don't, you wouldn't be much of a man."

"Ah—cut that out," Tahchee said and picked up a twig and flung it at him. Daniel knocked the twig aside, laughing.

They lapsed into silence. Tahchee sat staring into the fire, and Daniel knew he didn't need but one guess as to what was on his mind. He sipped on his coffee and left the boy alone. Soon Tahchee murmured, "I think I'll turn in. I'm getting sleepy."

"Yeah. Yeah, you go ahead. I'm going to finish this cup of coffee and do the same myself."

Tahchee spread his blanket and stretched out on his back with his hands under his head. After several minutes, he said, "Uncle Daniel—?"

"Yes?"

"Is there anything to that, about turning into a star when you die?"

Daniel knew the boy knew better than that and chuckled softly. "It's a beautiful Cherokee story. Why not believe it? It doesn't hurt to believe in beautiful things. Makes no difference whether they're true or not, does it?"

Tahchee was silent a long time and pointed to the star-filled sky. "That's my Dad."

"Which one?" Daniel asked, craning his neck.

"That bright one. I know it's him because every time I look up at night, that's the first star I see."

"Could be," Daniel acknowledged.

"Did you know him very well? My Dad, I mean?"

"Yes. I knew him. He was a good man."

"Mother said he was a white man."

"That's right."

"Did you hate him?"

"What makes you say that?"

"I thought Cherokees hated white men."

This was going to take some doing, Daniel thought before answering. "People don't hate people they know. It's a way of life people hate, not the individual people living it. Another thing, hate has a way of building on itself. It always destroys the person it's in, not the person that's hated."

What he said seemed to satisfy. Or was it his "lectures," as the boy called them, become too boring to be listened to anymore?

"You're a good uncle," Tahchee murmured and rolled himself in his blanket, his back to the fire.

As if pulled by some unseen force, Daniel's gaze drifted back to the night sky. He found the two stars he had picked out for his own mother and father. Odd, there was another one between them; one he hadn't noticed before. He felt a chill and shivered involuntarily.

Could it be a bad omen of some sort? Song Bird. He pushed the dreadful thought from his mind, sat up and reached for the coffee pot. As he refilled his cup, he noticed his hand was trembling.

He sipped the hot liquid in silence, trying to get a grip on his emotions. He forced his thoughts back to the lumpy form under the blanket on the other side of the fire.

Tahchee. That sounded strange. Not that he had anything against Cherokee names, but the boy could have at least chosen one which couldn't be mistaken for an English word. He was amused remembering how old man Johnson "translated" it—Dutch. He made a silent bet with himself that in a few years the boy would be called Dutch by everybody, including that girl. People had a knack for taking the easy way out.

He could tell by the boy's steady breathing that he was already asleep. It was a wonder he could sleep at all, the way he carried on all afternoon with that girl.

What a great thrill it must be to name yourself and find love all in the same day.

He knew for a fact that Song Bird wanted her son to grow up being a white person, for there seemed to be no escaping living with white people—not in Georgia, not here in Arkansas. They'd talked about it often, nights, after the boy had gone to bed.

"It'll be an easier world for him," she said. "In a few years, there won't be any full blood Cherokees left. Half the tribal members have white blood running in their veins now. Our blood mixing with theirs is like a stream flowing into a river..."

She hadn't finished the sentence, but he knew what she meant, knew also that what she was saying made a lot of sense. As for him, he simply liked the name Daniel Taylor. It had a nice flow to it. He'd picked it because he liked it, and that was that. He never gave a second thought to growing up in a "easier" world. There were enough precedents to pave the way for Cherokees to use Christian-type names: the Vanns, the Adairs, the Callahans, the Hamiltons, the Pattersons, Turnbulls, Fraziers, Lewises, Rileys, even Joneses and Smiths. And how about John Ross? Their esteemed Principal Chief—of the Eastern Cherokees, that is. Mix these with truly Cherokee names like Iskitee Homa, Itse Yahola, Chitto Tustenuggee, Tuscooner, Po ki tee, Esmut Eye, Chustullee, Ther wi key, Che par ney...and what have you got? A hodgepodge, that's what—especially when some of those with Christian names dressed like Indians and some with Indian names dressed like white people.

He hadn't meant to fall in love with Song Bird's baby when she came back home to live. In the first place, he didn't have the time for loving it. And in the second place, it was another man's child. But before he realized what was happening, the child ceased being an "it" and had developed a personality of his own. When he learned to walk, he followed Daniel everywhere he went, and when he didn't, Daniel went to find him and they'd go off together holding hands.

He thought he was simply having fun with a playful child, using him as an enjoyable diversion from the hard work on the farm. He was fascinated by watching the boy learn, could almost see the boy's thought processes at work, and he never ceased to experience a thrill deep inside when he saw the little face light up with understanding. He was content being a doting uncle.

The first time he realized that what he felt for the boy was love was the time the Georgia militiamen came out to the old home place and blustered their way around, demanding stock for "taxes." When he stood up to them, one of the soldiers snatched up the boy and held a knife to his throat.

"One more smart ass crack out of you, Injun, and I slit your boy's throat from ear to ear."

He had never known fear before, but he knew it then. It was a deep fear, one that made every hair on his body stand on end. Somehow, he managed to hold himself in check, showing no emotion whatsoever, until the soldier put the boy down. Then he sprang like a cat, oblivious to any fire he might draw from the other soldiers, and had the knife-wielding soldier by the neck, choking the life out of him until the officer in charge spurred his horse forward and smashed his rifle butt over Daniel's head.

When he came to and the pulsating fire ball inside his skull had eased somewhat, he was deeply grateful to find his "family" still alive and unharmed. Especially Song Bird and the boy. His parents had lived their lives and didn't matter as much. But the boy—and Song Bird, for she was still a child herself in her late teens, had a whole life to live.

The soldiers took only a couple of horses for "taxes" and left a whole basketful of threats behind. It was the typical happening which the Cherokee farmers were experiencing more and more lately, especially since the white riffraff's actions were being sanction by the the state legislature which seemed to take a delight in passing laws designed to make life hard for Cherokees.

He and Song Bird talked it over that night. They decided to join the volunteers moving west into Arkansas Territory, try to find a new life beyond the influence of white encroachment.

"What about mother and father?" Song Bird asked. "They would never survive such a trip."

"We'll wait until they're gone," Daniel said in a matter-of-fact voice.

They were gone before the boy was five, and the three of them packed all their belongings in a box wagon, hitched their team to it, tethered a milk cow behind and headed west. Since all land was held in common by the Cherokees, they left nothing of value behind except a sturdy log cabin, a barn, and one or two outbuildings. These would be easily replaced, he knew, when they found another place to live. A few day's hard work and with the help of neighbors, you could have a new home up in no time at all.

They had made it to a choice spot on the White River just in time. Their one remaining horse was on its last legs, and he had rigged a sapling drag pole to support the left rear corner of their wagon after a wheel had broken a few miles back. They had butchered their cow when it stumbled and broke a leg within a week after crossing the Mississippi.

That first winter was tough. With the help of neighbors, the young "family" managed to get their cabin up before the cold, rainy days came. Fortunately, it had been a mild winter—only one dusting of light snow—and he was able to earn enough working for others to replace his team and buy enough tools to break ground and put in a crop the following spring.

The boy, then five and going on six, went everywhere Daniel went, within reason. In a couple of years, he insisted that the boy move out of Song Bird's room into his.

"It don't look right, you keeping a big boy like that under your wing all the time," he told her.

She wept a little over it, but, in the end, conceded he was right.

"It's just that…he's still my baby," she moaned,

"He'll grow up to hate you, if you don't let him go," he argued.

While the boy's schooling had been erratic, considering the shortage of school teachers and the distances they had to travel to and from school when they were able to find one open, he was satisfied the boy was learning enough to read and write and do his ciphers. The only thing about the boy's education that was lacking, Daniel regretted, was Cherokee history and Cherokee language. Most of the teachers the Cherokees could hire were white women, wives and daughters of missionaries.

So far, they had managed as a "family." In a way, he really didn't want Song Bird to get married. She was, for all practical purposes, his wife, except for sharing the same bed. They had even done that once. He liked to think about that night, and did a lot, for it made him feel proud.

It was not long after the boy had left her room and moved in with him and it turned bitter cold that night and he kept trying to make himself get up and add more wood to coals in the fireplace but couldn't because he hated to and excused himself by arguing that he'd only wake the boy and Song Bird stumbling around in the dark and suddenly she was there beside the bed like a ghost in the night and said she was cold and did he mind if she got under the covers with him and the boy and the boy was asleep and Daniel thought she meant on the other side of the bed with the boy and he said no he didn't mind and was surprised when she slid shivering under the covers against him and he moved over next to the boy to make room for her and they could not see one another's faces in the faint red glow from the fireplace so they weren't who they were but she a woman and him a man when she scootched her back against him with her legs pulled up and he curled around her and put his arm across her and pulled her close to help get the shivers out of her and he couldn't help getting hard like he did but she didn't move or anything just let him pull her tighter against him and she squirmed tighter against him which told him she knew her close contact was making him that way but didn't care and she even took his hand and pulled it to her bosoms and he could feel her heart beating through the firm softness of her breasts and when he thought she went to sleep he moved his hand slowly until one of her bosoms filled the palm of his hand but when he felt her nipple harden and felt the ever so slight increase in pressure of her butt against his own hardness he knew she wasn't asleep and he wasn't her brother for sure any more just a man wanting and the man wanting told him it didn't make any difference if he was her brother and she was his sister that now there in the dark like that he was a man and she was a woman and she was probably wanting to, too.

No. He willed himself into becoming a log, immovable, unresponsive. He did not want them to be ashamed to look one another in the face in the morning and the mornings forever after that. She was his sister and was relying on him to help her stay alive and he had to give himself to her as a man and not take from her a satisfaction.

In a while, he felt her nipple soften and he softened too and they lay warm together through the night, all three in the same bed. When he heard the first rooster crow the next morning, he managed to slip from under the covers without waking either of them. He brought in wood and built up the fire in the fireplace and was getting a fire started in the cook stove before she came in. He was not ashamed to look at her and he could see the happiness in her face. He felt good too, and felt even better when she stood on tiptoe and kissed him.

"I love you, Daniel," was all she said, but he knew what she meant and he loved himself a little more for being a man in in control of that other thing in him instead of it being the other way around.

He tossed the dregs in his cup on the coals, enjoying the soft hissing sound of liquid hitting the hot embers. He lay back on his cover and let his gaze wander across the sky.

It was a beautiful story, that about becoming a star when you die.

He closed his eyes, smiled, and drifted off to sleep.

A man, proud, in control of himself.

CHAPTER 3

Tahchee's little mare kept trying to break into a jog, anxious, as always, to get in the barn and get unsaddled. He lost patience with the animal and jerked on its reins repeatedly, scolding it with harsh words. Daniel laughed at his futile efforts to control the animal and said, "I swear I don't know who wants to get home the fastest—you or the horse?"

"It's her, can't you see?" Tahchee blurted, hiding his own eagerness under a curse. Once again, he fought to control his mount and slapped its withers hard with the loose ends of the reins, shouting, "Ho! I said."

The horse jumped sideways and laid its ears back, but did settle down for a few minutes before it began trying to pick up the pace again. Finally, he let it go, for he *was* anxious to get home himself. He had a lot to tell his mother; that he'd chosen a name; that they had new neighbors. She'd want to hear everything about their trip into town, who they'd seen, who they'd talked to.

When they topped a rise and the house and outbuildings came into full view, he let the feisty mare have her head. She broke into a full gallop, leaving Daniel, laughing, behind.

Tahchee's darting gaze raked the cabin, the smoke house, the barn, and the garden. He saw no sign of his mother and was disappointed at not seeing her outside waving her usual happy greeting. She's busy, he told himself. He riveted his eyes on the open doorway, expecting her step out into the sunlight at any moment. When she didn't, he frowned, concerned, and urged the horse into a faster pace. At the cabin, he leaped from the saddle even before the animal came to a complete stop.

"Mom!" he called. He ran to the door.

He bounded into the room and froze, immediately sensing something was wrong. Instinctively, he moved to one side so as not to be framed in the door until his eyes became adjusted. He held his breath, listening, his hand closing over his knife handle.

When he saw the disorder, the curtain ripped from the pantry shelving, the food scattered, the over-turned table, even the new stove standing askew, his heart bounced into his throat and stopped beating. Then his eyes came to rest on the limp form on the floor and he knew instantly that she was dead.

His world exploded. Fighting to find air for his lungs, he tried to look away, but couldn't, even when Daniel's large body darkened the entry.

Tahchee pointed a shaking finger.

"Oh, goddamn!" Daniel cursed and ran to her, kicking a chair aside on his way.

Tahchee followed, numb. Daniel knelt and turned her over onto her back. A look of horror still frozen on her face, her eyes open, staring.

Tahchee's senses skewered; his eyes not wanting to see, his balance teetering; heart beats thundering in his ears. His knees wanted to buckle. An icy fire burned inside as he stood behind his kneeling uncle, clenching his fists so tight his fingernails cut flesh.

"White or Indian?" was his hoarse demand, only barely aware the words came from his own throat.

Daniel pried open the clenched fist and held the feather up to the light for closer examination.

"Osage," he said, a taut bitterness in his voice.

Blinded by white hot anger, Tahchee whirled without a word and ran out the door. He raced to the barn where he knew he'd find his mare waiting for someone to strip the riding gear from its back. He vaulted into the saddle. By the time he could turn the reluctant animal around, Daniel was standing in the doorway, spreadeagle, blocking the exit.

"Where do you think you're going?" Daniel snapped.

"I'm going to get them!"

Daniel stood fast, blocking the doorway.

"Get out of my way, or I'll run you down!" Tahchee shouted, meaning every word of it.

"Don't be stupid! She's cold. They've got at least a day's start on you."

"I don't care! I'll find them!"

"We don't know how many—"

"I don't give a goddamn! I'll kill them all!"

Daniel edged closer. Tahchee didn't understand.

Confused, Tahchee blustered, "Don't try to stop me, or I'll—!" His voice broke as frustration overrode his anger. He glared helplessly as Daniel reached out slowly and grasped the bit shank.

"Get down, son..." Daniel spoke softly, then added, "Song Bird needs tending to before we do *anything*. There'll be plenty of time for killing later."

The words 'tending to' ripped through him like a cold wind. He suddenly felt weak. His hands trembled. 'Tending to' meant a funeral and a burial. 'Tending to' meant she was dead, an irrevocable fact. His heart ached. His vision blurred as tears formed and raced down his cheeks. Ashamed for Daniel to see, he lay forward on the little mare's neck, hiding his face in folded arms.

"No! No! No!" he cried, trying to hold it back, to be a man. The confusion tore at his guts.

Daniel patting his thigh. The sympathetic touch helped. He knew Daniel was hurting, too, and he sniffed the tears back inside. He sat erect in the saddle, finally, and smeared the dampness from his cheeks with the heel of his hand.

"I should have stayed home with her," he said and slid to the ground.

"Now don't start talking like that," Daniel said, gripping his shoulder. "We can't blame ourselves, you hear? We've left her lots of times and nothing happened. You get that kind of thinking out of your head right now, this very minute!"

He knew that what Daniel was saying was right. Even so, that didn't chase away the feeling that this might not have happened if he'd stayed home.

"Come on. We've got work to do," Daniel said.

When they headed back toward the cabin, Tahchee felt as if he were having a bad dream. Things would be different when they stepped inside again. His mother would be cooking something on her new stove and would be surprised when she turned to see them coming in. She would—.

The overpowering presence of death when they entered the cabin demanded respectful silence, total reverence even from his thoughts. It wasn't a dream. He fought against weeping again by busying himself straightening the furniture, with an occasional, worried glance at Daniel examining the limp form.

"One thing about it," Daniel commented, more to himself than to Tahchee. "She sure gave them one hell of a fight. She must have clawed all the hide off the face of whoever did it, from the looks of her fingernails. Bet he has scars the rest of his life." Then Daniel searched for the wound in her hair and found it. "Damn! Oh, damn!...She never knew what hit her...Tahchee, go draw a fresh pail of water. We'll clean her up the best we can. We'll dress her nice and lay her out before calling in the neighbors."

The moral support of their neighbors until and during the day of funeral helped lessen Tahchee's grief—at least diverted his thinking enough to make the tragedy seem less like the end of the world and more like an unwanted part of day to day living; especially when Laura showed up with her family.

He hardly recognized her, for she was dressed in a conventional gingham, ankle length gown with a starched white collar. He felt confused when she introduced him to her mother.

"Mama, this is that nice boy I was telling you about," Laura said. "Tahchee, this is my mother—Ellen."

He mumbled a hello, and immediately liked her stern smile. She seemed such a nice lady that he found himself wishing his mother could have known her. They would have been great friends. It was easy for him to visualize his mother and Ellen canning peaches together, talking, laughing, fussing at the children, one a white woman, one a Cherokee, but both, first and foremost, mothers.

Laura's younger brothers certainly needed fussed at, he concluded later. They were a rowdy bunch and the oldest brother, an arrogant imp about twelve named Clancy, was the worst of the lot. But, all in all, they did fairly well. Most of their discomfort, he guessed, came from the clothes they had to wear. He hated being dressed up in fresh pressed pants and starched white shirt himself. Worst thing of all was having to wear the loose fitting suit coat his mother had made over from one of Daniel's.

So many people showed up, they had to hold the service outside, in the shade of a gigantic elm. Tahchee found it a comforting ceremony. Reverend Westfall would speak a few minutes in Cherokee, then in English. He liked the hymns better when they were sung in Cherokee, for the words seemed less harsh and more spiritual. He liked, too, the sound of Laura's voice, standing tall and slender beside him.

After the burial on a rise behind their cabin, people milled about, laughter returned, kids chased other kids, their clothes awry. Some of the people began taking plates of food from the long table Daniel had set up in the yard, some gathered in the shades of the nearby trees to talk, others just stood and watched the kids play. During the rest of the day, Laura stayed close, not saying much, but always there, bringing him a plate of food, keeping his cup filled with hot coffee...touching him. Once when he sat in a chair pretending to listen to some older men talk, Laura walked behind him and laid her hand on his shoulder. He reached up and seized her fingers, holding tight.

Her responsive grip was reassuring. She waited, holding the steaming coffee pot with a calm patience until he released her. She gave him another pat and moved on. Later, as he watched Laura supervising the play of smaller children, he could hear her laughing and wondered if he would ever be able to laugh again.

Although he heard some of the quiet talk during the day about the men needing to organize a War Party, he paid little attention, for he'd already made up his mind to go after the Osage, War Party or not. He assumed Laura had heard the talk, too. Her knowing that the men might be riding off to fight the Osage made him feel oddly heroic. Would she cry over him if he rode away into the wilderness and got killed fighting with the savage Osages?

Even as he watched Laura with the children, he noticed Mr. and Mrs. Rogers carrying their belongings to their wagon. Finally, Ellen began calling to her children. Their actions started the homeward movement of the others. Laura broke away from her game and came toward Tahchee, tossing her long hair over her shoulders, a sympathetic smile on her lips as she reached out to touch his arm.

"We're leaving, Tahchee," she said. "Goodbye—for now."

He nodded, hating to hear the words. "Thanks for coming."

"I wanted very much to see you again, but certainly not under these circumstances. Will you—?"

"Laura!" Ellen called, waving impatiently from her seat on the wagon.

Will he, what? Tahchee thought as he sought the answer in her face. Then she turned and ran to join her family.

He watched the Rogers' wagon pull away and began pacing the yard, impatient for the others to leave. He and Daniel needed to get going.

When the last family left, Tahchee hurried to his bedroom and struggled to get out of his good clothes and into his close fitting deerskins. He slapped his floppy brimmed hat on his head, and was belting his knife about his waist as he reentered the living area. He stopped short at the sight of Daniel sitting at the table staring into space.

"What's the matter?" Tahchee asked. "Hadn't we better get going?"

Daniel's dark eyes shifted to focus on Tahchee's face. He shook his head. Tahchee stomped to the table, angry.

"They already got three days on us!" he said, his voice rising. "We wait any longer, and we'll *never* catch them!"

Daniel held up a hand. "Just settle down now—"

"Settle down! An Osage put an axe in my mother's head, and you expect me to settle down?...Are you going with me, or not?"

"The trail's cold, Tahchee. It'll take a good tracker—somebody like Johnny Jumper. We can't do it ourselves."

Tahchee leaned on the table, bracing himself with clenched fists.

"You don't have any intentions of going after them, do you?" he accused, trying to keep control of his raging emotions.

Daniel's face flushed. He rose slowly from his chair, his burning look fixed on Tahchee's face.

"When are you going to grow up!" he said, his tone menacing. "You're always running around like a chicken with its head cut off! A thing like this takes planning."

Tahchee opened his mouth to snap back with something hateful, but he could find no hate inside him for his uncle. He'd never seen that look on Daniel's face before and knew his uncle's anger was deep, more dangerous. Tahchee's mouth still hung open as he sank into a chair across.

"What—what do you mean?" he stammered.

Daniel folded his powerful arms across his broad chest and stared down. "Song Bird's death will be avenged. But we have a problem. Things aren't like they used to be in the old days. We have laws—"

"But—"

"This is a matter for the Cherokee General Council to decide. Chief Cahtateeskee is away. I am Assistant Principal Chief. I've asked for a special meeting. If everybody's agreeable, we will form a War Party and go after the Osages. Before we go, we have to discuss—"

"To hell with discussing! There's nothing to discuss! A man killed my mother and I'm going to get him! That's all there is to it!"

"Will you just shut up and listen?" Daniel snapped.

Facing Daniel's forceful will, Tahchee dropped his gaze to the table top and sat in sullen silence as Daniel went on.

"If we vote to go, I'll ask if they'll let you join us. There'll be some who say you're too young. But under the circumstances—" Daniel shrugged, then added, his tone softer, "If we do go and do find them, you'll get your chance."

He felt helpless. What good were laws when one side doesn't abide by them? Laws didn't stop the Osages from killing his mother.

"We both loved Song Bird, Tahchee. But the people's rights, the people's safety—the end of the Osage-Cherokee war—are all bigger than the way you and I might feel over what happened to Song Bird. Chief Cahtateeskee has been working hard to stop the killing between our people and the Osage. He's on a trip right now to meet with delegations from the federal government and the Osage—"

Why listen? Tahchee felt as if the whole world had turned against him. His thoughts shifted to Laura and wondered if she, too, would turn against him.

Daniel was worried when he entered the council chamber with the thirty-two other delegates. Chief Cahtateeskee was back. Daniel hadn't had a chance to talk with him yet, but he had picked up from the conversations with other members that the Lovely Treaty had been signed. Would this kill the formation of a War Party? Worse, would it prohibit individual revenge? If it did, he doubted he would be able to control Tahchee. And if the boy defied the Council's will and went on his own, Daniel knew he had no other choice but to go with him to keep him out of trouble.

Chief Cahtateeskee stood, signaling the beginning of the debate. He was a large man, long arms dangling loosely from powerful shoulders. A perpetual, mean look on his oval face hid the wisdom behind his squinting, smouldering eyes.

"As we all know, we're here at Daniel Taylor's request to discuss forming a War Party to go after the Osages who killed his sister. But before we get into that, I have an official announcement to make." He paused. When his dark eyes settled on Daniel for a long moment, Daniel attempted to read favoritism for his cause in them, but couldn't.

"As some of you already know," Chief Cahtateeskee droned on in that deep voice of his, "I have just returned from a meeting with Agent Lovely in Fort Smith. The Osage leader, Chief Clermont, was present. We signed the treaty which Agent Lovely has been wanting. I think it's a good treaty. We give up our claim on land here in Arkansas for a like amount across the line in Indian Territory. In addition to the seven million acres we get, the federal government threw in another eight million acres—"

There were whistles of disbelief. Chief Cahtateeskee grinned and continued, "I took it, of course. But I don't know what we'll do with it. It's a strip of land fifty-some miles wide laying against the Kansas line and extending two-hundred miles westward."

Daniel heard the murmur of approval roll around the room. And rightly so. This more than doubled the amount of land they had sought.

"What was that for?" a suspicious sounding voice asked.

"Yeah," another voice warned. "What's it for? They want something to take away from us later on?"

Chief Cahtateeskee's grin widened. "You won't believe this: Agent Lovely explained the strip of land would give us access to go hunt buffalo on the high plains out west."

Guffaws romped around the room and Daniel joined in halfheartedly for everybody knew Cherokees did not hunt buffalo for a livelihood, never had, never would. The same suspicious voice, now full of ridicule, boomed, "Did Lovely give you any instructions how to hunt buffalo?"

More laughter. The ridicule was on the mark, Daniel thought, shaking his head in disbelief. There was no understanding the federal government and its peculiar ways. Cherokees hunted buffalo like the white man did; take your rifle and go hunting. You see a buffalo, you bring him down like you would a deer or any other big game. Then you cut off a hindquarter or whatever you wanted and leave the rest to the wolves. It was the plains Indians like the Osage who hunted buffalo. They had to. The animal provided them not only food, but both shelter and clothing from the hides, and tools—including sewing needles—from the bones.

When the laughter died, Chief Cahtateeskee said, "I saw nothing in the treaty that said we *had* to use it for going west to hunt buffalo. The only thing I could figure out was that the people in Washington was so tickled to have some Indians *volunteering* to move into Indian Territory that they threw in the strip just to make sure we didn't back out."

"What happens now?" another voice asked.

"Agent Lovely says the federal government will have to move the whites out first."

"How're they going to do that if they won't go?"

"They're going to buy them out. Give them money to relocate back here in Arkansas. He says if they don't leave, they'll get the army after them and make them go."

"What about the Osages?"

"Same deal. The government is going to pay them for their land, plus the cost of moving all their people to a reservation in Kansas, plus annuities of some sort."

"Where's the government getting all that money?" someone in the crowd asked, the tone of his voice sarcastic.

"They print it," another shouted, "Maybe that's what we should start doing," he joked, and everybody laughed. A more serious voice criticized, "Looks to me like you should have got some of that money, the way they're throwing it around like that."

Chief Cahtateeskee nodded in the critic's direction and told him, "I did. I asked for fifty thousand dollars to buy a printing press and all the fixings to get a newspaper going. I got it. Then I asked for annuities so we could set up a school system and build new school houses. They gave that to me too."

When the murmurs of approval and amazement died, someone asked, "When we going to start moving? I got crops to harvest before I go anywhere."

Chief Cahtateeskee shrugged. "A year. Two years. It depends. Chief Clermont told us he was having trouble with his brother, Black Dog. He says Black Dog keeps wanting to stay, and he has a lot of followers."

"Are they going to get the army after the Osages too?"

"That's what Lovely says they'll do."

"When the army goes after the Osages, they'll blame us for it, like they always do."

Chief Cahtateeskee held up a hand to bring the meeting back under control. When he got the silence he wanted, he said, "We'll just have to be patient. Let the government work. We certainly don't want to do anything to give Black Dog an excuse to stir up trouble."

"You suppose it was Black Dog who led the raid on Taylor's place?" somebody asked.

Chief Cahtateeskee looked in the direction of the voice. "That's possible. Which brings us back to the purpose of this meeting: Do we go after the Osages who killed Song Bird, or not?" His dark eyes drifted back to Daniel. "Daniel?"

Daniel stood, trying to hide his nervousness and apprehension. "I asked for this meeting because it is the way we have decided to live. Some say it is the white man's way. Some say it is good. Some say it is bad. I'm not here to say one way or the other. It's hard to live by the new rules when it is the one you love who is killed. Right now, I wish it was like the olden days...when it was the right of the family to avenge the death of the one he loves."

Daniel paused, and the unusual silence disturbed him. Was he embarrassing them? Had he been wrong requesting the meeting? Did the signing of the new treaty change things? He let his gaze wonder over the crowd. Some looked away. In other faces he saw sympathy. He settled slowly onto his seat.

"What happens if we go after the Osage?" someone asked. "Does this violate the new treaty?"

Chief Cahtateeskee nodded. "Yes. In fact, the Osage would have grounds to declare the treaty void. We would stand a chance of losing a claim in Indian Territory twice the size of our claim here."

Another voice entered the debate. "It appears to me the Osage violated it first by killing Song Bird."

Chief Cahtateeskee broke in. "This was one point Agent Lovely tried to get across to us—retaliation only brings about retaliation. He asked both sides to report all treaty violators to him. He promised that he would get the U.S. Army to find the perpetrators and bring them to justice."

"Song Bird was killed before the treaty was signed," a belligerent voice sang out. "The way I see it, we got a right to go after the killers on our own. We wait for the army to act, we'll never find them. They've been gone three days now. I say let's get Johnny Jumper and track them down. We can settle this our way."

There was a muttering of approval and nodding of heads. Daniel's hopes rose. He could tell he had support, perhaps more than he thought.

"Just because the Osage broke the law first is no sign we have that right," a cautionary voice piped.

Daniel leaped to his feet again, angry this time. facing the objector. "No, but it would certainly justify our actions."

The approval-sounding mutterings rose again, this time louder and stronger. Daniel turned slowly, spoke slowly, "I found signs in the woods behind the house. Many men had stayed there for several hours that morning. I have reason to believe this was no ordinary raid by a bunch of young bucks out having a good time. They were there when my nephew and I were packing to leave. They waited until the boy and I were gone to attack Song Bird. She fought them alone. These big strong Osages defeated this woman by sinking a tomahawk into her skull." Daniel paused and finished by emphasizing every word..."They...did...not...steal...a single...solitary...thing."

He sat down. He had his say. Let the message sink in. He kept his gaze fixed on Chief Cahtateeskee as more mutterings began, swelling finally into a chorus of angry shouts.

"I say let's go get them."

"It's time the Osage learned a lesson."

"We whipped them once, and we can do it again."

"Damned women killers."

Chief Cahtateeskee held up a hand. The comments died down.

"Does any here object to forming a War Party to go after the Osage women killers?"

Daniel pulled in a nervous, relieved breath after a few seconds when no one objected, at least aloud. Chief Cahtateeskee nodded.

"So, it has been decided. We will go. Those who object to violating the new treaty—for whatever reason—are free to leave." He paused, waiting. All thirty-two Cherokees remained seated. With a curt nod, he continued. "We will leave at dawn. We will not return until those killers of women are caught and punished. They will pay with their lives. It is the way of our people. I hereby declare this Council closed."

Relieved to have won his point, Daniel worked his way closer to the front as the men filed out of the crowded cabin in noisy anger. Cahtateeskee was in deep conversation with another man. Daniel stopped a respectful distance away, waiting to be recognized. When Cahtateeskee finished his conversation with the other man, he gave Daniel a nod.

"Come," he said.

Daniel stepped forward. "One request?"

"Speak."

"The son of Song Bird who now calls himself Tahchee wishes to join the War Party."

Cahtateeskee shook his head. "He is too young."

"Song Bird was his blood relative. He must have revenge for his family," Daniel insisted, angry.

"You are a blood relative. You have volunteered to go. It is enough."

"Tahchee says he will go—with the War Party or without it."

Daniel thought he detected a faint smile on Cahtateeskee's stern face as the man folded his arms and studied the floor. He waited, breathing slowly, but feeling breathless. Soon, the leader's gaze lifted.

"I have decided. Tahchee may go with the War Party. He will have the job helping the cook."

"But—!" Daniel stammered, humiliated.

The leader raised a hand, stopping him. "Ask no more," he said. "I have granted your wish."

"I'd rather tell the boy he can't go than tell him he will be the cook's helper." Daniel argued, his voice rising despite his efforts not to let it do so.

Chief Cahtateeskee shrugged. "Do as you wish."

Daniel felt like telling him to forget it; that he and Tahchee could go after the killers themselves. Instead, he clamped his jaw shut to keep from saying the wrong thing, turned slowly and walked away.

CHAPTER 4

Tahchee's frustration grew and kept on growing the more Daniel tried to explain.

"I asked if you could go, like I promised. But Cahtateeskee said you were too young. He did say, though, that you could go as the cook's helper."

Tahchee leaped to his feet, exploding with, "But she was *my* mother! I deserve more respect than that!"

Daniel raised both hands and said, "Make the most of what you got, will you? You're going. Be thankful of that. Let's worry about fighting after we find the Osages—if we ever do. It's a big country out there."

"You said yourself that Johnny Jumper was the best tracker there is! He'll find them!"

"Jumper's good. But so are the Osages. They'll guess we won't send soldiers after them over this. They'll be expecting somebody like Jumper to be tracking them. They'll use every trick they know to cover their trail. It could be weeks before we find them."

Daniel paused, looked down as if he were ashamed, and finished quietly with, "We may never find the one with scratches on his face…So it's up to you. Go as the cook's helper or—" Daniel shrugged away the alternative.

Tahchee searched his mind frantically for a way out, peering intently into every shadow in the candle-lit room as if by doing so he would find some answers to this whole bizarre situation. True, by now the trail would be dim, at best; only experienced trackers like Jumper would have even the remotest chance of catching the Osages, but there must be something else he could do besides tagging along as cook's helper! He pounded one fist into the palm of his other hand, feeling more and more humiliated. Well, Daniel had always preached he needed to practice a little patience once in a while. He gave up and gestured helplessly.

"All right," he said. "If being a scrub boy is the only way they'll let me go, I'll do it. But if we find them—!" He scowled a warning at Daniel.

"And you'll promise to obey orders and conduct yourself with restraint and dignity at all times?"

He nodded. "I promise."

"I know that would be Song Bird's wish also."

He turned away to keep Daniel from seeing the dampness welling up in his eyes, tears of hurt, tears of frustration.

Tahchee, bare to the waist and wearing his woolen britches, boots and floppy-brimmed hat, sat his horse beside the cook's wagon when the group assembled the following morning for last minute instructions from Chief Cahtateeskee. Others were wearing deerskin outfits, some with complete white men clothes, but all heavily armed. Tahchee had only his big-bladed knife strapped to his waist. After a short speech, Chief Cahtateeskee cautioned, "Remember men, if we run into any soldiers, we are on a hunting trip—"

"Hunting buffaloes?" a skeptic cut in. The others laughed. They're acting like this is a fun thing, Tahchee thought bitterly. Somehow, Cahtateeskee's grim smile silencing the comic made him feel a little better.

"My story to the federal authorities will be: We were on a hunting trip. A bunch of renegade Osages jumped us. That is, if we find them. I don't want to lose the gains we made with the Lovely Treaty. Am I understood?"

The laughter died. Tahchee found himself wishing he had gone after the killers by himself the day his mother was killed. But no—Wait, Daniel said. Always wait. He couldn't stand waiting. If something needs doing, why not do it?

Chief Cahtateeskee motioned for Johnny Jumper, a scrawny, bow-legged man with a hatchet face, to take the lead. They headed west. Tahchee was determined to keep them all moving westward, somehow, someway. He worked at his assignment as cook's helper with dedicated thoroughness. He made sure each man's eating utensils were kept shiny clean, and he carefully bundled all the cooking paraphernalia in deerskins to mute their clanging when hung across a pack horse. The cook, a grizzled old man who seldom spoke, commented at the end of their first day, "Tahchee do good job. Make my work easy."

He took the cook's compliment as graciously as he could, but he had no intentions of becoming a good assistant cook. For, despite his lowly position in the War Party, he felt he was the one going after the marauding Osages and the thirty-two Cherokee warriors were accompanying *him*.

On the second day out as they tracked west, they crossed the Arkansas line. He overheard the men talking. This was Indian Territory, their new, soon-to-be home.

As far as he could tell, Indian Territory wasn't a lot different from Arkansas. It was hilly country, heavily forested, with clear, cool streams in almost every ravine; if not a stream, then at least a flowing spring. Occasionally, they crossed an open prairie, ringed by bluish hills. Wild flowers painted these flat lands in muted colors of reds and blues mingled with bright orange and yellow. Deep violets hid in the shades.

The War Party moved north and west, mostly west, always on the lookout for soldiers. The going was slow, too slow, Tahchee felt. But the trail *was* dim. Johnny Jumper was forced to do a lot of guesswork. Tahchee watched intently, almost holding his breath, each time Jumper would run out of signs, sit his saddle a few minutes thinking about his quarry, then head off in a different direction. And sure enough, they would cross the trail of the Osage riders several miles later.

Once when they passed what appeared to be cow droppings, Daniel pointed them out to Tahchee, explaining, "Wood buffalo."

"Wood buffalo?" he asked. "I thought there was only one kind of buffalo."

"Nope. Wood buffalo are a smaller breed than the ones roaming the plains farther west. They've been almost all killed out. When you do find them, they're in small bunches, sometimes no more than five or six in a group. The ones out on the high plains gather in herds so big, it takes all day for them all to make one river crossing."

He had never discovered Daniel telling a lie. Nor was his uncle one to stretch facts a little here and there. But it was difficult to picture a herd of buffalo so big that it took all day for it to cross a river.

"I'd like to hunt buffalo someday," he said, after accepting what Daniel said to be the truth.

"Well, maybe we can someday," Daniel said, then grinned and motioned toward the cook. "Have him teach you how to cook them," he said, laughed, and rode away to join the main body of the War Party.

On the fifth day, the riders pulled up abruptly on the crest of a timbered ridge. Tahchee heard them talking excitedly and saw them pointing. His heart bounded into his throat. He tossed the pack animal's lead rope to the cook, flanked his mount and rode forward to join the group on the ridge. Then he saw the Osages. His blood raced. He counted nine. Evidently, they were confident they were not being followed, for they were riding carelessly out in the open, across a treeless bottom toward a river which must be the one Jumper said the French traders called the Verdigris.

Tahchee resisted an urge to dig his heels into the flanks of his horse and charge. What were they waiting for? He was surprised to see Chief Cahtateeskee turn his horse and came riding toward him. The Cherokee leader held out a war club, a stout shank of hickory sapling. The weapon had a wicked looking ball on its end, fashioned by expert trimming of the young tree's root system.

"Here. Take this," Cahtateeskee said, his attitude serious, challenging. "You want to live up to your name and be a great leader? This is your chance. If you fail, you can use use the club for beating on the bodies of the dead."

Tahchee felt his face grow hot from being singled out. He tried to sit tall on his horse as he reached for the club. He could feel the power in the weapon and hefted it for balance.

"Tahchee will never be accused of beating on the bodies of the dead," he vowed. He had no idea what the phrase meant, but it sounded majestic.

"We will see," the old Chief said. Then he reined away and returned to the front of the War Party. Cahtateeskee lifted his own club high, shouted to the sky.

"The blood of Song Bird will be avenged! Die, Osage! Die!"

He kicked his horse and the animal leaped forward. In an instant, Tahchee found himself at the front of the War Party thundering down the slope. At the bottom, they leaped their mounts across the narrow ravine. Tahchee lost his seat and almost fell, but managed to right himself and hang on. However, he dropped behind. When they swept out upon the meadow, the Osages heard the muffled thud of hooves, turned for a quick look, then scattered.

Tahchee peeled away to chase an Osage fleeing to the left, obviously trying to make his escape in the timber along the river. He leaned forward, holding his war club high, strange whoops erupting from his own throat.

The Osage unshouldered his bow riding full speed as he disappeared into the timber. Tahchee, fearing the Osage would get away, threw all caution aside and rode hard at the spot where the Osage vanished.

An arrow zipped by just as he reached the tree line, narrowly missing. He leaped from his horse and tumbled for cover behind a tree, still gripping his war club. He lay still, holding his breath, straining to hear above the snorting and stamping of his confused mount.

Only then did he realize that charging into the trees like he did was a foolish thing to do. That arrow almost got him. But he overrode the fear racing along every nerve of his body, turning the feeling into a high emotion which called for action. He leaped to his feet and raced across an opening, diving into a drainage gully just as another arrow thudded into a tree over his head. He glanced up. The still-vibrating shaft pointed in the direction of the Osage. He flattened and squirmed snake-like down the gully to the river's edge.

Now what? The sandy bank of the river was not more than four feet high. If he attempted to circle behind the Osage by wading in the water, the Osage would hear and know where he was. He gathered his legs under him and ran, bent double, along the sharply sloped bank. His footing was almost non-existent, and he had to scramble with every step to keep from sliding into the water.

After covering a good distance, he stopped and popped up his head for a quick look. He saw the Osage peering intently around a tree toward the drainage gully, his bow strung, his fingers on the string.

I fooled him, Tahchee thought and took a firmer grip on the war club as he crept stealthily over the rim of the sandy bank. But he knew the Osage would have time for one more shot with the arrow if he charged him from this distance. How could he dodge that? He quickly selected a large oak between him and the Osage. It might be too far, it might not be far enough. He had to risk it. He leaped to his feet and ran straight at the man.

The startled Osage whirled, frozen by surprise for one full, precious second before he took quick aim and snapped his bowstring. At the last instant, Tahchee spun behind the oak. The arrow thudded harmlessly into the tree trunk. He continued his spin, emerging from the other side and was on the Osage before the man had time to whip another arrow from his quiver.

With a wild yell, he swung the club one-handed, his accuracy deadly. He felt the skull crunch under the impact. The Osage dropped into a crumpled heap.

He knew the man was dead by his grotesque limpness...like the robin he'd accidentally killed once. He'd thrown the rock at the bird just to have something to throw at and was both shocked and surprised when the robin exploded into a ball of feathers and fell to the earth with the rock. Now, as then, staring down at the lump that was once alive, he felt an unexplained chill, as if he were alone in the world.

A sudden release of his pent-up grief, combined with joy of victory, caused him to throw both hands high in the air. He turned his face to the sky and yelled as loud as he could, a long sustained cry meaning what, he did not know.

Then he lowered his arms, letting normalcy ease back into his being. When he glanced down at the body again, he saw no signs of any scratches across the painted face, and he felt a deep bitterness. Suddenly, his disappointment was replaced by a sense of urgency, a desire to hurry and find the one with scratches on his face. He wanted to kill him before someone else did. But he had to have proof of his kill. And there was but one way.

He whipped out his knife, stooped, seized the dead Osage's top-knot in his left hand, then froze.

How do you do it? he wondered, then answered himself with a firm resolve. *Just do it!* He gritted his teeth and cut the skin in a tight circle around the top-knot. His hand shook from a combination of excitement and revulsion to what he was doing to the dead man. The neck was so limber, the head seemed to be only loosely attached to the body. His knife slipped and cut a deep gash in the heel of his left hand.

His own blood flowed, mixing with the Osage's on the shaved scalp. He tried to ignore his wound as he peeled the palm-sized scalp from the Osage's skull. He held it high, visualizing himself as a proud warrior, boasting a kill.

But, strangely, he did not feel proud. He'd killed a man who may or may not of had anything to do with his mother's death.

He struggled to overcome a sudden empty feeling. He considered throwing the disgusting scalp aside, but finally tied it to his belt. Then he pressed his fingers on his own wound, trying to stop the bleeding.

The others would laugh at him for cutting his own hand while trying to take his first scalp. He would never live it down. They'd ignore the name he'd chosen and call him Hand Cutter, or some other such designation of ridicule.

He had to conceal the self-inflicted wound, he told himself as he kept wiping away the blood, hoping it would clot so no one would notice. But the cut was too deep. The blood continued oozing out.

He felt so humiliated that he began trying to fabricate an honorable story to explain his wound—the more heroic, the better. He could tell them he dodged the Osage's arrow and caught it in mid-air as it went by. But he was too quick and grabbed the arrow's head instead of the shaft. They would enjoy a story like that. Or he might get away with telling them he cut his hand on a sharp stone when he dove for cover into the gully.

No! He would not lie! He was a Cherokee warrior! He unsheathed the knife again and stooped to cut a piece of deerskin from the Osage's loincloth. He fashioned a crude bandage for the cut, stopping the bleeding. That done, he took the dead man's bow and arrows, his knife and tomahawk. He rounded up both horses, mounted his own and, leading the Osage's, went to find the other members of the War Party.

Daniel saw him coming and rode out to meet him.

"Are you all right?" he asked.

Tahchee pointed to the bloody scalp. "I got him. But he wasn't the one. There were no scratch marks on his face." He saw the disappointed look on Daniel's face and asked, "What's the matter?"

"Two got away. None of the others have any scratch marks."

"Then let's go after them," Tahchee said and handed the reins of the dead Osage's horse to one of the others and motioned for Daniel to follow.

"Where do you think you're going?" Chief Cahtateeskee asked, his voice stern.

"We're looking for the one with scratch marks on his face," Daniel explained. "None of these have. The one who killed Song Bird got away."

"Seven warriors for one woman is enough," the old Chief said. "The Cherokee Nation has been avenged. Let the two who escaped run to their people. They will tell how the Cherokee warriors tracked them down and killed their friends."

Tahchee felt a surge of resentment. He wanted to defy the old Chief and get on his way. He glanced at Daniel, waited for him to take the lead.

When Daniel hesitated, Cahtateeskee added, "I put my name on a treaty that said there will be no more fighting between the Osage and the Cherokee. We will return home and live in peace."

Tahchee's heart sank when he saw Daniel turn back and dismount. He followed, downcast and reluctant.

Then Cahtateeskee saw the scalp dangling from Tahchee's belt. He seized

Tahchee's left wrist and raised his arm high.

"The son of Song Bird is our new warrior! He will never beat the bodies of the dead."

Tahchee felt proud being accepted as an equal. But when the other warriors slapped their thighs, their quivers, their horse's withers—whatever was available—and chanted their congratulations, he was embarrassed and attempted to pull his hand down. Then one noticed the bloody bandage.

"I see a wound," he said, his voice grave. "Tell us how you fought and killed the Osage who drew your blood."

The thumping began again, but this time, the chants called for a story.

"The Osage did not draw my blood," Tahchee told them with a firmness that was tinged with bitterness. "I cut myself when I was taking his scalp."

His curt, unexpected reply killed the merriment. They all busied themselves with personal tasks preparing for the journey home, adjusting their equipment, mounting up. He noticed that even Daniel acted embarrassed.

He'd show them! he thought as bitter resentment surged through him. He was on the verge of jumping on his horse and going after the two that got away when Daniel, tightening the cinch on his saddle nearby, muttered a low warning, "You promised…"

And he knew his uncle was reading his mind. He clenched and unclenched his fists repeatedly to bleed off some of the anger.

"All right," he mumbled through clenched teeth. "That was for this trip. Just as soon as we get back, I'm going out alone. I'll find that…" and the best words he could think of was the white man's "son of a bitch"…"even if it takes me all my life."

He vaulted into the saddle and fell in beside Daniel following the group heading for home, angry, frustrated, and vowing to himself to go into Osage country and look at every man's face, if he had to, to find the man who killed his mother.

CHAPTER 5

Just stay out of it, Daniel told himself as he watched Tahchee gathering his things to leave. *Let him go.* He'll get killed and it'll be all over and he could get on with his own life. Maybe even find a woman for himself and get married. Have someone he could love and who would love him, who would want him nights in their bed.

Then he had second thoughts. There was the Cherokee nation to think of. He was sitting at the kitchen table, the dirty dishes from their evening meal scattered about before him. Tahchee passed by on his way to his bedroom for more things and Daniel said, "You stir up more trouble with the Osage and we'll lose over fifteen million acres of untouched land in Indian Territory."

"It's not untouched land," Tahchee mumbled sulkily. "The Osages live there."

Daniel squirmed at the gig. The truth of the matter was, they were taking land from the Osages by government decree just like the whites were taking land from the Cherokees, both here and back home in Georgia.

He watched in silent anger as the boy went to his room and was still staring sullenly at the doorway when Tahchee returned with a wad of underclothes in each hand and stuffed them into a saddle bag.

He knew that trying to appeal to Tahchee's sense of civic responsibility would be useless. The fact that they had negotiated the largest land swap in the history of both the United States and the Cherokee nations would mean nothing whatsoever to Tahchee.

Nor would he care a diddly squat about them finally having the legal authority to establish a bonafide educational system and enough money to build schools wherever and whenever they were needed.

What good would it do to tell him they would be able to buy a press and all the paraphernalia that went with it so they could publish a newspaper? And it would be meaningless to tell him they had plans to print the news in two languages, English and Cherokee, so that all Cherokee citizens would be properly informed of all laws enacted by the Council and all actions the U.S. Congress made that affected the tribe.

The helpless feeling made him feel weary. He sighed just thinking about it, leaned back in his chair and picked at his teeth with a sharpened splinter he'd cut from a piece of kindling.

"How are you going to do it?" he asked, letting his sarcasm show.

"What do you mean, how am I going to do it?" Tahchee snapped with a sharp look his direction. The impertinence the boy was showing stirred a parental desire to snuff it somehow.

"Just what I said: How are you going to do it? Got any plans? I can just see you riding into an Osage village and telling them who you are, that you came to kill all men with scratch scars on his face?"

Tahchee snorted. "Don't be ridiculous."

"I'm not being ridiculous. You are."

Tahchee whirled. "Call it what you want. I don't care. I have the right, and I'm going to get him."

"We don't live that way anymore."

"Maybe you don't. There's others who think different."

"You do that and that makes you a Cherokee outlaw."

Tahchee smirked. "What'll you do, have me arrested?"

"I just might."

"You can't before I go because I haven't done anything. I don't care what you do to me when I get back."

"So the great warrior is riding out to avenge his mother's murder in spite of everything?"

Tahchee turned his back. Daniel knew he'd touched a sore spot and was immediately sorry for having said what he did. He chewed on his underlip, trying his best to keep from apologizing.

The silence between them was the heaviest he had ever known. He struggled to understand. Why such determination? Hell-bent determination, at that? Was it really revenge? Or was it something else?

Theirs wasn't exactly a father-son relationship. Maybe that was it. Could it be that the boy was developing a feeling that this was his home now that Song Bird was dead, that his uncle was only a relative who'd come to stay? Surely not, for he was the only father the boy had ever known.

There wasn't but one thing to do. After a few more minutes of the strained silence, he spoke to Tahchee's back in a low, apologetic tone. "I promised the Rogerses we'd help with their cabin raising tomorrow. Wait 'til that's done, and I'll go with you."

He noticed the pause in Tahchee's actions. The boy turned, his face impassive. "You volunteering to go after them on my account, or my mother's?"

Daniel made a helpless gesture. "Both."

"You don't have to go on my account."

"Take it whichever way you want."

Tahchee said nothing, seemed to be staring into space. "Well...Another day won't make that much difference, I guess."

That was easy. A lot easier than he thought. It must be the girl. The thought brought a smile to his lips and he quickly hid it by rubbing a hand across his cheek and chin.

"Then it's settled?"

"Yeah. I guess so, if that's what you promised the Rogerses we'd do."

A new idea began to germinate and, feeling good about it, Daniel began gathering up the dirty dishes. "Get a pan of water on the stove and build up the fire. We can't go running around in Osage country and leave dirty dishes behind, can we?"

Daniel could tell the boy's sudden scowl was obviously forced when he asked, "How are we going to do it? I mean to keep them from killing us before we find the man who did it?"

"Why, I thought you had it all figured out," Daniel said, faking surprise.

Tahchee's scowl turned real. "Go ahead. Make fun of me all you want. Seems like that's all you do anymore." And he lifted the pan of dishes from the table and banged it down on the stove. Then he yanked open the stove door, poked at the coals furiously, spun and stalked out to get some more wood.

He's sure sensitive, Daniel thought, pressing his lips together. *Must be his age.* He'd have to be careful what he said.

Yeah, that was it. His age.

He knew for sure then that his idea might work. Get the girl after him. It wouldn't take much for a girl to make a boy Tahchee's age forget about running off into Osage country on a wild goose chase.

Tahchee sat in glum silence on the wagon seat beside his uncle, his floppy-brimmed hat pulled low over his eyes. He had no interest whatsoever in participating in a cabin raising. In fact, if it had been for anybody else but the Rogerses, he would have refused to go.

Things just weren't the same since his mother...died. He had to force the dreaded word "died" through his mind. He still was unable to say it aloud. With her out of their lives, he sensed an estrangement developing between him and Daniel. Like now. He glanced sideways at the man on the wagon seat beside him.

Daniel was just as stubbornly silent, driving the team hunched forward, his strong shoulders swaying easily with the rock of the wagon.

Tachee fretted, *Why was he so puffed up?* Hadn't he agreed to come with him to the cabin raising?

He hated the oppressive silence worse than if Daniel were poking fun at him. He felt his long frame getting more and more tense as he tried to think of a way to apologize without making it sound as if he'd been angry in the first place. Just then the wagon pitched downward where the road crossed a shallow ford, its momentum forcing the team to run down the steep slope. Daniel fought to hold them back.

"Ho up there!" he commanded in a deep, harsh voice.

The team struggled to obey. As the wagon bounced over the rocks, the two men braced themselves, stiff-legged against the dash planking. One wheel dropped into a washout rut. The sudden jolt nearly threw them both from the seat. Tahchee grabbed a rail and hung on. The horses, startled by the loud grating sound of the iron tire on the flint rocks, tried to bolt.

"HO! HO!" Daniel yelled, throwing his entire weight on the lines and dragging the prancing team to a halt at the water's edge.

Tahchee interpreted Daniel's angry glance his direction that he was blaming him for the way the horses were acting. He said nothing. Then Daniel returned his attention to the team and angrily popped the reins against the rumps of the frightened animals.

"Giddap!" he snapped.

The skittish team lunged ahead, splashing through the shallow ford. Water dripped from the wheels going up the other bank. On level ground again, Tahchee let go of the seat rail and leaned forward, resting his elbows on his knees, still worrying about his relationship with his uncle, especially since Daniel had promised to go with him into Osage country.

Going anywhere with Daniel used to be fun, he remembered as he absently scratched at the healing knife cut in his left hand. Daniel surpised him with an elbow nudge. "So you're a Cherokee warrior now?" he asked, teasing."Suppose that girl will think you're any different?"

"I doubt it," Tahchee said, relieved the strained silence between them was broken. "Getting to be a warrior wasn't what I was after."

"I know," Daniel said. He pushed his hat up, leaned back on the seat and rested his hands holding the reins on his thighs. "Earning the rank isn't important these days. But it doesn't hurt to hang onto some of the old customs. The way I see it, every society has a similar rite or ritual to signify the coming of age for its young men."

Tahchee was in no mood for another long lecture comparing the Cherokee culture with the white man's way of living.

"That was not what I was after," he repeated, too stubborn to agree.

Daniel rode in silence a long moment before he said, "What'd you do with that scalp you took?"

"I threw it away."

Daniel's laugh was a silent shaking of his shoulders. "I wondered what you were going to do with the nasty thing."

"I guess I just got carried away. I'd never killed a man before."

"Did it make you feel good?"

"Not really."

"You suppose he had a wife and family back in his village waiting for him to come home?"

The remark cut deep. Tahchee turned on him scowling. "If you think you can talk me out of going after the man who killed my mother, you can just shut up right now. I intend to go whether you go or not."

Daniel kept his eyes fixed on the road ahead. After a few minutes, he said softly, fatherly, "Let it go, Tahchee."

"I can't."

"Seven Osages died. It's enough."

Tahchee clenched his fists, trying to get a grip on the frustration inside him.

"It is *not* enough!" he snapped, his voice tense. "I want the one who killed her! I want to see him die!"

"You'll never find him. By now, the scratches have healed."

"You said there'd be scars," Tahchee countered. "I'll find him."

"And how do you figure to do that? He's an Osage, you know."

"I don't know how."

"Go live with them?" Daniel ridiculed.

"I might," Tahchee flung back.

Daniel returned his gaze to the road ahead. "Want my advice?"

Tahchee refused to answer, not wanting to open the door for another lecture.

Daniel made a kissing sound urging the horses into a faster pace, then said, "I'll give it, anyway. Don't let this thing warp your life. People die everyday, one way or another. When it's done, it's done. All you can do is try and make your own life worth something before it's your turn to go."

Disgusted over getting some more advice he didn't want in the first place, Tahchee lifted his head and rolled his eyes skyward. Daniel simply didn't understand! He felt his life was warped now. His mother's existence would not be complete until the man who killed her dies. Daniel should know that. He let his breath out slowly and leaned back in the seat. They slipped into the heavy silence again as the wagon angled across a grassy meadow. In the distance, he could see the crowd of people already at work building the cabin for the Rogerses.

Then he spotted Laura and everything he and Daniel had been discussing vanished from his mind. She was looking their way and was wearing the same deerskin dress she wore that day in the grist mill when he first saw her. She waved and came running to meet them. His heart began to pound, and he felt a deep sense of pleasure knowing she appeared to be as equally anxious to see him.

CHAPTER 6

By mid-afternoon, the older men had the walls of the new cabin up and were busy engineering the rafter poles in place. The young men had gone into the forest to cut more logs. The women had the food put away and the noon dishes cleaned and were back at their quilting racks in the shade of a tall pine.

Laura, wanting to be with Tahchee again, saw her chance when she noticed the men pouring the last drops of water from the bucket into a gourd dipper. She turned to her mother, tossed long strands of hair over her shoulder, and said, "I better run to the spring and get some more water."

Her mother frowned. "Let one of your brothers go...tell Clancy." She didn't even bother to look up from her sewing. Laura hesitated, then her mother did look up, explained, "Clancy's been told to see to it there's plenty of fresh water to drink. Go tell him."

When her mother returned her attention to the story which one of the ladies was telling, Laura slipped from the bench, stretched as if in relief from sitting too long, and sauntered toward the water bucket.

She noticed Tahchee's uncle move away from a cluster of men and head for the water bucket too. She picked it up and turned it upside down to let him know that it was empty, no need coming. He came on anyway.

"I've been wanting to talk to you," he said, his voice low. He had a conspiratorial air about him that excited her.

"Oh?"

"That nephew of mine's taken quite a fancy to you. No doubt you've noticed?"

Of course, she noticed. But she wasn't going to say so. What was he driving at? "He's nice," she said, trying to be non committal.

"I was wondering if you felt the same about him?"

This was getting interesting, she thought. Was he trying to flirt with her? She looked him over, seeing him in a different light. He was a little shorter than Tahchee, but heavier built. He was a full blood, at least as much as her own father. There were a few pock marks on his dark face that did little to detract from his ruggedly handsome features. She'd had only one older man before and found it exciting. She grasped the bucket's bail with both hands, holding it in front of her as she pursed her lips, pretending to think over his question before answering.

"Ummm. I suppose you could say that. Why?"

"I know it's none of my business. And I apologize for intruding. But this is important to me—to all of us, when you get right down to it—and I wanted to ask if you'll do me a favor?"

It sounded important. She nodded. "Of course. What?"

"Tahchee's determined to go into Osage country to look for the man who killed his mother. The chances of him finding the man is slim, at best. He'll only get hisself killed when they find out he's Cherokee."

"I see. And you don't want him to go, is that right?"

"That's right."

Now it came to her what he was up to. She felt flattered. "You're wanting me to try and talk him out of it?"

"Like I said, he thinks a lot of you. He was about ready to walk out of the house last night until I asked him if he could put off leaving one more day and come here with me to help you folks." He paused and grinned. "All of a sudden, him leaving didn't seem so urgent anymore."

She laughed lightly. "Thanks for telling me, Mr. Taylor. I'll see what I can do." She held up the bucket. "I was hoping to run into him in the woods when I went to get water."

"I should have known," he said, laughing with her.

He turned to leave and she stopped him with, "Mr. Taylor?"

"Yes?"

"What do you think I should do to make him stay?"

"Oh—whatever," he said. She could actually see him blushing despite the dark color of his skin. "Just let him know how you feel, is all."

"Ask him to marry me?" she teased.

"No need to go as far as all that," he growled. "Not just yet, anyway. Your folks'd kill me, if they thought I was suggesting anything like that."

"I'll see what I can do," she promised. She headed for the spring, feeling a happiness inside she'd never felt before. She held her head high to let her long hair flow behind her shoulders. Somehow, her conversation with Tahchee's uncle made her even more conscious of how she looked with her shoulders back and her breasts prominent beneath the close fitting deerskin.

"Hey!" someone called...Clancy. She turned to face her younger brother as he came toward her, a deep frown on his face, the ends of his cotton colored hair damp with sweat.

"Where do you think you're going?" Clancy demanded.

"None of your business," she answered and returned her attention to the path ahead. Clancy ran to catch up. He grabbed the bucket's bail and tried to yank it away from her.

"Getting water's my job!" he shouted.

Embarrassed by the attention he was attracting, she angrily slapped his hand and made him release his hold on the bail.

"You certainly can't tell by looking! All the men are half starved to death for water, and you off playing!"

Clancy made another angry attempt to get the bucket. Laura shoved him away. He almost fell, but recovered to shout, "I know why you want to go!" When she didn't respond, he raised his voice. "You just want to sneak off in the woods and get with that Indian!"

She whirled, jabbing a finger at Clancy. "You little snot! It's none of your business what I do, or who I see. Besides that, you better watch what you say. You're as much Indian as he is!"

Clancy stuck out his tongue. "Oh yeah! Maybe so, but I don't look like one! And I certainly don't go around acting like an one!"

"You let Daddy hear you say that, and he'll make you leave home so fast it'll make your head swim!"

Clancy ducked his head, glared at her sullenly through his eyebrows. She had enough of him and spun to continue on her way, swinging the empty bucket defiantly. She flung one last remark over her shoulder. "I don't even know where he's at!" she lied.

She glanced over her shoulder again just before entering the timber to see if he were following. He was standing where she'd left him, glaring. *Would he try to follow?* she thought as she worked her way deeper into the woods. To make certain he wasn't, she paused, listening, waiting. No Clancy, nor any sounds of his footsteps. She moved again, slipping quietly toward the chopping noise coming from her left.

When the sounds became louder, she slowed. She glimpsed Tahchee and the other two boys working to bring down a tall tree. She halted, hiding behind a bush, feeling intense pleasure watching Tahchee work.

He was stripped to the waist. His olive skin glistened with sweat. His lithe body whipped the axe with unbelievable power, making the shiny blade bite deep into the wood with each stroke. Wood chips fluttered through the air from the bite of the ax.

Heart beats pounded in her ears. She knew Tahchee was strong, but she'd never felt his strength—*really* felt it, as she was wanting to feel it now. She thought about what she and Daniel talked about. A curious fear nagged at her, giving her a sinking feeling; she felt as if time were running out...not for just today, but forever. Would she ever see Tahchee again after today? Not if he goes after that Osage. How could she change his mind? Offer him something he would want more? The thought made her shudder, a delicious, thrilling shudder.

She left her hiding place and headed for the spring. She had to walk across the edge of the clearing, but pretended to ignore the boys at their work as she strode along swinging the empty water bucket.

The chopping stopped. Pleased, she felt their eyes following her until she dropped over the edge of the limestone bluff, following the narrow path down its face. The large spring at the bottom gushed from a gaping hole in the rock and spilled over a low ledge before pooling below on the gravel bar.

She stooped to fill the bucket, lingering to enjoy the feel of cool air coming from the black hole in the rock above the stream of water. She shivered in the chill and remembered the story her Indian grandmother once told. Cold winds from holes in the earth were made by the breath of a lost warrior. The warrior entered the earth to find the North Wind and kill it so all his people and all the plants and all the animals of the earth would not have to suffer winters anymore. A beautiful story. She loved the legend, proud of her heritage. And to think Clancy hated being an Indian, would even fight when another boy called him one.

She straightened, lifting the now heavy bucket. A sweaty hand closed over hers on the bucket's bail.

"Here. Let me help you with that," a strong voice said.

Startled, she tried to pull away before she saw who it was.

"Tahchee!" she scolded. "You scared me half to death!"

Tahchee, still stripped to the waist and his smooth olive skin wet with his own body fluids, laughed. She noticed how his his dark eyes seemed to be devouring her. She welcomed his open examination and tossed her hair over her shoulders and stood straight so he could get a better look.

"Don't you dare sneak up on me like that again!" she said, doing a poor job, she knew, of feigning anger.

His warm smile crumbled what little anger she was able to muster as he gently pulled the bucket from her grasp and said, "Well, fair's fair. You sneaked up on me back there in the woods."

"I did not!"

"I saw you hiding behind that bush."

"You didn't either see me. You were working."

"I see everything," he said matter-of-factly and without a trace of boastfulness.

"Oh—" she said, showing her disgust. "Nobody can see everything all the time!"

"Except me."

"Well, look at Mr. See-It-All! I suppose I'd better stop going swimming. You might—*see* me!"

Her taunt did what she hoped it would do. She felt her nipples harden when his intense gaze traveled down her body, then up again. Had he ever seen a naked girl? The thought fueled the warm feeling. She had to get him to touch her. She reached for the bucket.

"Let me have the water. The men'll be wondering what's keeping me."

He stopped her, inadvertently placing his strong hand directly over one of her breasts to hold her off.

"I'll carry it for you—" he said, then broke off as she was unable to contain the gasp from the thrill of feeling the pressure of his hand on her. He jerked his hand away.

"I'm sorry!" he apologized, his olive coloring unable to hide the deep blush.

She smiled at his innocence. She calmly reached for his hand and brought it back, replacing it where it had been and held it there.

"I'm not sorry," she said softly. She searched his face for some sign of desire. Instead, she saw the flash of panic and knew this *was* his first time, deepening her own desire. She pushed closer, her face up, inviting. He swallowed heavily, then lowered his face cautiously to touch her lips with his own, just a quick brush.

She noticed how his hungry gaze searched her face, questioning. Her mouth felt dry. She licked her lips.

"Would you like to—go swimming?" she asked, mildly surprised at the huskiness of her own voice, the unusual tightness in her throat. She pressed his hand tighter against her breast, felt his strong fingers respond, feeling. The thrill was so intense, she could hardly stand it. Through half-closed eyes she could see the rapid beat of his heart in a neck vein. She slid her hands up his chest, enjoying the feel of his hot skin made slippery by the sweat.

"Tahchee," she whispered, barely able to find enough breath to speak. "You thrill me so..."

He dropped the bucket of water, seized her hand, whirled and ran, dragging her after him. She stumbled and almost went down, but he kept going.

She clung to him, her elation giving her a feeling she was soaring, birdlike, high in the sky. She had no idea where he was going, or why, nor did she care. She knew what was going to happen, and that was all that mattered.

Brush limbs slapped her long legs. She leaped over rocks to keep up, his pull on her arm at times so strong it hurt her shoulder. They ran, splashing through the creek's shallows. Water sprayed her face, unable to cool the raging fire inside her. The heavy foliage along the banks kept closing in until he was forced to stop. They stood in the middle of the shallow stream, both breathing heavily. He glanced around, his desperation showing.

His helpless look alarmed her. Afraid she was going to lose him, she glanced around frantically searching for a place. She felt her own sweat running down her cheeks. She was only vaguely aware of the world they'd run away from, the bucket setting beside the spring, the thirsty men working on the cabin, the women quilting and talking. She saw a place.

"Here," she breathed softly and pulled him under the overhanging hanging branches of a redbud tree where its thick, heart-shaped leaves drooped, almost touching the water.

While the small space underneath the tree seemed secluded enough, half the floor area was covered with shallow water, the other half a sloping mud bank. Laura didn't care. More anxious than she'd ever been, she slipped her deerskin dress over her head, and tossed it carelessly over a limb. When she faced him, she saw he was frozen, staring at her, eyes wide.

The thrill deepened, for she knew for certain now this was his first time. To enhance her own raging passion, she moved all her long hair behind her shoulders with measured deliberateness, enjoying to the fullest the way his dark gaze jumped from one nipple to the other, now bare and so turgid they ached. She held her arms out, still breathing heavily.

"You want to kiss me?" she asked.

He uttered a little cry and threw his arms about her, pulling her tight against him. When he lowered his face to kiss her lips, she placed her hand over his mouth, stopping him.

"I mean down here," she murmured and cupped a breast with her other hand.

He hesitated, then lifted her bodily, lowering his head at the same time. She closed her eyes and moaned as his eager lips covered her nipple, the thrill stabbing through her. She rubbed her hands on his broad back, felt the supple muscles working beneath his wet skin.

She floated on a sensation she never knew existed. She wanted to watch him press his hot, anxious kisses on her breast, but at the same time she wanted to close her eyes to enjoy his new-found eagerness. When he attempted to take her entire breast in his mouth, she pressed against him to help. The tingle of his wet tongue plunging excitedly onto and around her nipple was almost more than she could bear. She felt his teeth pressing high on her and, unable to breathe, she pulled away slowly as he closed his soft bite, his teeth sliding on her skin until they clamped gently on the nipple itself. She continued pulling. He refused to let go. The combined pain and ecstasy was too much. She gasped.

"Tahchee—!" she cried out.

He let go and jerked away.

"I'm sorry," he panted. "I didn't mean to hurt!"

"No!" she breathed huskily. "You didn't hurt! It's so thrilling. I—I want you to do it some more."

He did and made clumsy attempts to unbelt his trousers. She helped, her own hands trembling with as much nervous anticipation as his. Finally, they managed to slide his trousers down. The sudden sight of his erection took her breath away. Before she could stop herself, she dropped to her knees to stroke the the beautiful manliness, unable to resist one soft touch with her lips. She glanced up at his surprised, emotion filled face.

"He's so beautiful, Tahchee."

He acted stunned, only stared. She returned her attention to the beauty in her hand. Dare she? No, she decided. Another time. This was his first experience. It might spoil everything. She wanted him to fill her with his pulsating strength.

She took his trembling hands and pulled him down. Pressing him backward onto the mud bank, she slid her wet body across his.

She rocked on him gently, then placed both hands beside his shoulders, arching her back, pointing her breasts at his passion filled face.

He cupped a breast in each muddy hand, thrilling her to her toes when he gingerly fingered her, smearing mud and water over her smooth skin. Moaning without any inhibitions whatsoever, she began pulling back and pressuring forward. She closed her eyes, each gritty feel skyrocketing to a higher emotional level.

When she felt his strong arms pulling her upward, she responded, sliding higher and higher, knowing what he wanted. She eased off his hardness and spread her legs.

He probed for entry as he took one of her breasts in his mouth and washed its nipple clean with his darting tongue. She almost climaxed watching him swallow the mud as he moved to her other breast and washed it clean also.

She felt herself falling into a flooded river, rushing madly to the sea. She lowered herself to kiss his mud-smeared lips. She forced her tongue into his mouth, felt of his strong teeth and wet tongue. She paused and breathed hot words into his mouth.

"Open me with your fingers and put him in," she whispered.

He eagerly sloshed his hands in the water to clean them before reaching over her buttocks. His touch parting her damp folds caused her to lose all reason and she froze, suspended between heaven and earth, as he felt her, obviously curious. His nervous fingers were wet from her own fluids as he ran them ever so gently over her most sensitive areas.

She closed her eyes, not even conscious of her low moans as she moved her pelvic area, helping him probe, thrilled by his curious examination.

"Now," she begged, her own voice sounding eager and strange. She lifted, squirmed to help him find the right spot. Then she felt his strong beauty entering her. She sank both hands deep in the mud bank and she pushed onto him, hard.

She heard him gasp as his strong body surged against her, driving himself deeper. Her entire being centered on him filling her. She felt as if she were tumbling through a night sky, bouncing from one star to another. Soon, the pulsating sensation came alive and froze every fiber in her body. She couldn't move, couldn't breathe, but he still kept plunging into her, deeper and with increasing force. She threw her head up, wanted to cry out and tell him of her love, but "oh-o-o-!" was all that came out.

He raced on, faster and faster, lifting her high. She felt his fingers digging into her cheek bottoms and his violent thrusting action shoved her over a precipice of joy.

Never...oh, never...never had it felt so wonderful as this.

The raging flood waters washed from her, left her limp, unable to respond. Odd sounds, pleading sounds, from his throat brought her back. She knew what he was searching for. She tried to take control of his wild rhythm. She felt his body tense, then began jerking spasmodically as it fought against immobility. She rolled her hips, pressing her pelvis tight against him.

She heard his breath catch, explode, then catch again. She lifted her head to watch the rapture flood his face, watch with deep love as his eyes glazed and widened. She felt him filling her as little sounds gurgled from his throat, culminating in an unrestrained cry of joy.

When he went completely limp, she collapsed on him, totally exhausted. She lay there filled with a satisfaction she'd never felt before in her life.

This was her man and she was determined to have him for the rest of her life. She would never want again. And she would teach him new ways, do things to him to make him want her the rest of his life.

She found herself wishing they could lie like this forever, their wet, naked bodies melded by the exhausted passion. Would she be able to excite him enough to do it again? But he was so quiet, she raised herself to look at his face. Her long hair spilled down on each side of his head, its ends lay loose on the muddy bank. She lifted a hand to brush the strands aside, but stopped when she saw how muddy her hands were.

"Would you look at that?" she said, faking anger, as she held a muddy hand up for him to see.

When he laughed, she retaliated by threatening to smear mud on his face. He kept twisting his head to dodge her efforts, but she managed to smear some of the mud on his face.

"There!" she panted. "That'll teach you to make fun of me."

He spluttered and wiped his lips clean with the back of his hand. "I wasn't making fun—"

She kissed him hard on his mud-smeared lips, a long kiss made even more exciting when she felt his arms circle her and squeeze her tight against him.

When she took her lips away, she whispered in his ear.

"Say you love me."

He pulled in a long, shaky breath.

"I—I love you."

"I love you, too. I want to live with you forever and ever and ever..."

He did not respond. She lifted her head to look him in the face.

"Did you hear me?"

"Yes."

"Don't you want to?"

"I can't," he sighed. "I have to go away."

Her heart plummeted. She tried to smother a sense of panic. "What do you mean?"

He shifted his gaze aside. She grasped his chin with a muddy hand.

"Isn't this—" and she rolled her hips with him still inside her meaningfully before finishing with, "—better than anything else in the whole world?"

He pushed her from him and sat up in the shallow water. Furious over the rejection, she faced him on her knees, both hands on her hips, her body streaked with muddy water.

"Tahchee—?" she demanded.

He reached for her, tried to pull her to him, but she resisted. He pleaded, "Let's don't spoil this moment, Laura. It—it was more wonderful than I ever imagined. I'll never forget—"

She flung his hand aside. "You haven't answered me." she said, her tone cold and hard. She sensed a sudden coolness in him as he avoided her gaze and began sloshing his hands in the shallow water to wash away the mud. Then his dark eyes focused on her again.

"If you must know, I'm going after the Osage who killed my mother," he said.

The hurt stabbed deep. Daniel had said he was determined. But this—! After what she'd shown him! "How can you—?"

He looked away. "It's something I have to do."

She couldn't lose him. She felt the loss piling up inside and resorted to begging, "Tahchee—? Doesn't this mean anything to you?"

"More than you know. I'll never forget it."

"You don't love me. You lied."

She saw the anger in his sharp look and knew she'd pushed him too far. She watched, full of instant remorse as he stood, reached for his trousers.

"We'd better wash off and get on back before somebody comes looking for us," he said, his voice level, unemotional.

Did he know? Could he tell that he wasn't the first to enter her? Had she demonstrated too much experience? She watched him closely, trying to read him as he pushed through the canopy of foliage. She hesitated a long moment, thinking what to say next, before retrieving her own dress and following.

They sloshed downstream in silence to deeper water. Tahchee tossed his pants on a bush and dove in. She followed.

As the cool water washed over her, she debated about telling him; try to explain the way it was with her. Would he—could he—understand?

She bobbed to the surface, blinked water from her eyes. Watching him wade toward the shore, she felt the tingle of desire trying to come alive again as he rubbed himself down to get rid of excess water.

There must be *some* way to stop him from going. She sloshed toward the bank, wringing water from her long hair.

They dried and dressed in silence. She had a thought. Would he know what made a woman have a baby? She could claim what they did would make her have a baby and they would have to get married. It was a long chance, but worth a gamble.

"Tahchee—" she began, but he silenced her with a quick hand motion.

He was listening intently, then whispered, "You better run back to the spring. I heard somebody call you."

She didn't believe him, for she hadn't heard anything. She wondered what he was up to. He scowled and motioned again.

"Go!" he commanded. He turned and disappeared into the brush.

She stood where she was, perplexed and unmoving. The sounds of Tahchee scrambling up the foliage-covered bank faded. Perhaps he had heard something. She hurried downstream toward the spring, heart pounding. Had they been seen? She heard somebody calling her name. She slowed to a leisurely walk, fashioning the lie in her head. She'd gone for a swim to cool off.

It was Clancy. When he saw her coming, he frowned and picked up the bucket.

"Where've you been?" he demanded. "The men are all wanting a drink of water!"

"I went for a swim," she said, too quickly, she knew, but Clancy wouldn't notice. Or would he?

He spun away to head up the path. "A fine time for that," he grumbled.

"Swimming! When everyone else is working to get us a house built, she goes swimming!"

Relieved that her lie hadn't been detected, she paid little heed to his fussing. She followed him up the path, her thoughts drifting back to Tahchee. She had failed to do what Daniel wanted her to do, but it wasn't over yet.

At the top of the bluff when they headed across the meadow toward the cabin raising activity, Clancy turned his head to squint up at her.

"I looked for you for a long time," he said. She ignored what he was leading up to until he added, "I found you, too. And I watched."

Aghast, she seized his arm, jerking him to a stop in his tracks. "You did no such thing!"

"I did so! You was on top!"

She shook him, feeling both frightened and angry at the same time. "You had no right to spy on me like that!"

He grinned. "You're lucky it was me looking for you. You two sure was carrying on. I could hear you for a mile!"

She felt her face flush and let go of his arm. She knew she was at his mercy now, totally.

"You wouldn't tell, would you?" she said, using her sweetest older-sister-to-little-brother tone.

He lifted his head airily and said, "It all depends on how you treat me from here on."

He stalked away toward the cabin, leaning to one side to adjust for the weight of the water in the bucket. She followed, trembling with anger, an anger tinged with a strange combination of frustration and fear over what the little imp might do.

CHAPTER 7

Time to go. Daniel's thoughts drifted more and more away from the conversations going on around him and more and more to the going.

Where in the world was Tahchee? Finally he spotted him, under a tree some distance away. And with that Rogers girl. They appeared to be arguing. Was she still working on him like he asked her to do? He tried to catch Tahchee looking his way so he could signal to him. No luck. He began working his way through the crowd toward the young couple.

Nearing them, he called, "Tahchee?" his voice barely above an undertone.

Tahchee heard, jerked his head around, a surprised look on his face. Daniel motioned toward the grove where the horses were tethered, sleeping and awakening occasionally to stomp away flies, jangling their harnesses.

"Hitch the team. We have to go."

"All right," Tahchee said; much too quickly, Daniel thought, as if he were anxious to get away from her. He was unable to hear what Tahchee said to her and, when he left. Daniel moved closer to the girl. He noticed the moisture in her eyes, even though she was smiling.

"Did you do any good?" he asked.

She gasped, "What do you mean?" with a shocked look on her face.

"About what we talked about—you talking him out of the idea of going after the Osage."

"Oh," she said, as if she'd forgotten. She was acting flustered for some reason. He silently castigated himself for not only intruding but also for conspiring with her against Tahchee. She shook her head, and it was then that he noticed how damp her long hair was. He guessed she'd been swimming. With Tahchee? In the old days, Cherokee girls and boys went swimming together. The missionaries changed all that.

He decided to drop the subject, coming to the conclusion that he might be pushing them into a situation worse than going after an Osage with scratch marks on his face. An unwanted pregnancy. Tahchee was too young for that. He didn't know about the girl; they had a way of being able to cope with motherhood several years sooner than boys were able to handle family responsibilities.

He had never discussed sex with the boy. Why should he? His own father had never discussed sex with him, nor his uncle, not anybody. It was something you grew into, like becoming aware your family loved you, and you them. You saw sex in the natural order of things; saw it producing kittens, puppies, wobbly-legged calves, and baby chicks squirming wet-feathered out of eggshells. Young girls had babies within a year or two after getting married and sleeping with a man. It didn't take much intelligence to figure things out by matching your own strong urges with the foolish antics of a half-crazed bull mounting a cow, and on her terms.

He'd never talked sex with Tahchee for the simple reason there was no need to. Nobody grows up oblivious of the bodies in which he is imprisoned for life. You experiment with playmates, in secluded places, studying the wonders nature has allotted you; learning that, indeed, men and women are different. As you get older, there grows in you a sense of wanting to possess, a desire to have a different person for your very own with whom to share these things inside you which you know about but don't understand.

He sometimes wondered, however, if Tahchee ever had problems during his awareness development with the fact the man and woman of their house— he and Song Bird—slept in separate beds, never kissed, never touched. Would he feel he had no beginning? True, Tahchee had always known he had a father, but did the knowing ever really *mean* anything to him? If the boy had had sisters of his own, he would have been able to understand, to realize the difference between family love and the flowering of passion.

What the hell was his own problem? he asked himself in a fit of bitterness as he busied himself gathering his tools; axes, saws, his adze and sledge. He carried them to the wagon. No man ever had all the correct answers, so why search for them? Even when you find the correct answers, somebody changes the question and there you are, caught running around with a truth nobody's interested in.

"Daniel?" somebody called.

It was William Rogers coming toward him, hand extended, a chewed twig in his mouth.

"Thanks for coming," he said. "We really appreciate your help—and the boy's, of course," he added motioning in Tahchee's direction as Tahchee guided the team into position at the wagon tongue.

Daniel waved aside the comment. "No bother at all, William. More than glad to help out. We haven't done any more than the others."

William resumed picking at his teeth with the sharpened twig. "It's not easy to get your life rearranged after you lose the woman of the house."

The reminder hurt, just a little. He disguised the feeling the best he could. "You have to go on," he said.

"All the same, the misses and I wanted to give you and the boy a special thanks before you got away."

"Tahchee and I haven't forgotten how you folks came to help out at the funeral. You didn't even have a place to live yet."

Then he nodded toward the finished cabin and added, "It's still not much of a place to live. But not bad for one day's work."

"I'm proud. Thankful *and* proud. We can sleep the kids on the floor. We'll make do just fine until I get time to add on another room or two. I don't plan on doing too much, with all the talk going around about all of us moving to Indian Territory."

Daniel frowned. He was in no mood to talk politics, but it seemed none of them could escape the unpleasant subject anymore. He'd never had a chance to talk with William about the tribe's situation back in Georgia. He asked, "What's the talk back east now? Are the rest of the Cherokees coming out here or not?"

William threw out both hands in a helpless gesture. "Some say they should, some say they hadn't ought. They've even started fighting amongst themselves. That's why we decided to leave. Got so you dasn't say anything to anybody, else you'd get jumped on for having a thought. It's especially hard on those of us who married a white person, like my Ellen. Personally, I think they'll all be here sooner or later."

Daniel shook his head, disagreeing. "I don't see it happening. It's hard to leave a good home and a good farm and start all over again. I know from experience."

William removed the sharpened twig from his mouth and pointed it at Daniel, saying, "That's exactly the point. Nobody really wants to leave. But the whites in Georgia have the whites in Washington scared to death they're going to secede from their precious union if they don't push all Indians west. That's why Congress set up Indian Territory."

"It's a mess, if there ever was one," Daniel said, his thoughts on the obvious problem of what would happen if the eastern Cherokees did move out here. "It's bad enough helping even one family get set up and going—like you folks. I hate to think what it'd be like having all the Cherokees back there coming in on us at once, especially since it looks like we're going to have to move again ourselves. I can just see it. Us pulling up here in Arkansas and moving into Indian Territory, trying to clear land and get crops in and fighting off Osages. Then here they come from back east... It'll be more than a mess, if you ask me."

"It would be quite a problem, wouldn't it?"

"How many's back there now? Ten thousand?"

"More near twice that, last count I heard."

"Good God! They'd outnumber us four to one! We could never handle them! We'd *all* starve to death before they could get settled in and raising their own crops. Almost as bad, what'll we do about our government? If they have the right to vote, they'll literally take over. We can't let that happen! It wouldn't be right. If they're coming, whyn't they come a thousand or so a year and spread it out? We could take care of them that way."

"Maybe it won't come to that," William Rogers suggested, then added, "However, us living in and governing our own legalized Territory is not a bad idea, in my opinion. There wouldn't be any state overlapping us anywhere. Like it is in everwhere back east."

"No. But there's another side to it."

"What?"

"No matter what the politicians in Washington say, those damned Osages say that country—" and he waved to the west, "—is theirs. Even if Washington gives it to us on paper, we've still got to fight the Osages for it."

"I hear the army—"

"The army, my ass!" Daniel spat contemptuously to one side. "The only thing I see the army doing is arresting Cherokees for fighting Osages. Then they shake a finger at the Osages for doing the same thing. As if we should know better, and as if they had a right doing what they do, but shouldn't be doing it."

In the silence which followed his unplanned outburst, Daniel regretting exposing his strong feelings on the subject. He searched for something to say which would bring the conversation back to the sociable level where it belonged. But that brought on an even worse feeling when Laura came to stand beside her father. Daniel touched the brim of his hat with a finger.

"Miss," he acknowledged respectfully.

Laura didn't seem to hear for her attention was fixed on Tahchee as he snapped the last piece of harness in place. When Tahchee came to them, she smiled at him and said, "I hope you enjoyed your day with us."

Her demeanor seemed pleasant enough, but Daniel detected a trace of cattiness in her remark. He noticed, too, the sudden flush in Tahchee's face and how tongue-tied he appeared to be.

"We did, Miss," Daniel said, answering for Tahchee. And to William, he said, "You folks come see us soon's you get settled in. There's no misses of the house around anymore, but I bet Tahchee and I could fix up a meal that'd do justice for any company."

"We just might do that, Daniel. Thanks for the asking."

Laura broke in with, "Tahchee tells me you're going to be away for awhile."

"We talked about it," Daniel said quickly. "Nothing's been decided on when. But don't let that stop you folks from coming over. You'll probably be the first to know if we do leave, being our nearest neighbor. I'd like to think I could ask you folks to sort of keep an eye on our place."

"We'd be more than happy to," William said.

Daniel sensed Tahchee's nervousness and, with another touch of his hat brim to Laura, he climbed to the wagon's seat. He gathered the reins as Tahchee mounted the wagon from the other side.

"Good luck," Daniel said to the William and his daughter then flapped the leather lines against the horses' rumps. The wagon moved forward, its seat springs squeaking under them.

"I thought you promised we'd go soon as the cabin raising was over," Tahchee said when they were out of earshot.

"I said we'd go, but I didn't say exactly when. There's things that need tending to first."

Tahchee's head swiveled, an angry look on his face. "I knew it! You were lying to me, weren't you?"

"No, I wasn't lying to you."

"It sure sounds like it."

It seems like that's all they did anymore, Daniel thought. Argue. He clamped his jaw and stared straight ahead, seeing nothing, thoughts churning. Song Bird was the knot in his and Tahchee's relationship and it was no longer there. Perhaps he should turn the boy out. Let him go tearing around in Osage country on an impossible chase by himself. He could see no benefits in putting up with a sassy teenager who wasn't his. The memory of Song Bird checked him, however. He heaved a sigh and said, "I can see you'll never be free until you find this man."

"There's no need for *you* to go!"

"Listen to the big, brave warrior talk."

He could feel Tahchee bristling, then was thankful for the sudden silence that fell over them. He'd never backed out on a promise before, but he was getting close to doing it on this one. To go would be the same as saying, "Whyn't we go out behind the barn and shoot ourselves in the head?"

How he managed to stall Tahchee from going after the Osage for two more days, Daniel wasn't quite sure; he was able to convince him they had to make arrangements for somebody to see after the stock and prepare the the cabin for an extensive stay away. He noticed Tahchee's determination weakening and racked his brain for other excuses. He felt if he had more time, he might be able to crowd the idea out of the boy's head completely.

He was busy in the barn repairing a crib door when he thought of the Rogers girl. Why not invite them to come over? Get them to spend the night, maybe. If he could get those two young kids together somehow and let nature take its course, it might solve his problem. He stepped outside to get a board when he saw William Rogers riding up the lane. His first thought was: I wish the girl'd come with him. He laid his hammer aside and hurried to greet his new neighbor.

"Get down," he called. "I didn't expect—"

"I don't have the time." William snapped, pulling his mount to a halt. Puzzled by the obvious anger, he stared, mouth open, not knowing what to say. William demanded, "I want to talk to that boy of yours."

"You mean Tahchee?"

"I don't care what his name is. I need to talk to him."

He racked his brain for some cause for the anger, found none. But one thing for sure, he didn't have to put up with it unless there was a reason. He tried to keep himself in check and said, "Sounds to me like you're not looking for a friendly visit. Suppose you tell me what this is all about before we get ourselves all balled up in such a way we can't get out."

"Where's he at?" he asked, looking around.

"He's not here right now," Daniel said and started to tell him he'd sent Tahchee looking for a cow that had a habit of hiding out when she calved, but he decided it was none of his neighbor's business, especially with him acting the way he was.

William seemed to be thinking something over before he said, "My Clancy let something slip that bothers me, Daniel. I had to drag the whole story out of him. He told me he seen your boy making my Laura have a baby. I want to talk to your boy and find out if there's anything to it. If it's true, you and me's got some mighty serious things to talk over."

His first impulse was to laugh. So what? Then he put himself in William's shoes. What if she did have a baby, and Tahchee was off on a trip? She'd have to grab up any man she could find and get married. Curious, he asked, "How come you don't ask her?"

"You ought to know the answer to that...It's easier to talk man to man."

Then he remembered how he'd put the girl up to trying to make Tahchee change his mind and not go after the Osage. But he certainly hadn't meant for her to go that far. What if she told her parents he'd put her up to it to try and get Tahchee to stay home?

"Yeah," he said, uneasy. "Yeah. I guess you're right."

"Where's he at?"

"Out looking for a cow. He might be gone all day." When he noticed the frustrated look on William's face, he suggested in as calm a voice as he could muster, "You're welcome to spend the night...Or you can let me talk to him. Man to man."

William screwed up his face as he considered the alternatives, finally nodded and said, "That might be the best way to handle it, you talking to him. We don't want to be unfriendly neighbors, Daniel. But we got responsibilities. If it did happen and my Laura does turn up pregnant, I'm expecting your boy to do what's right. We're Christian people."

"I'll talk to him."

"Not that we got anything against your boy—"

"My nephew," Daniel corrected, just for the record.

"Oh, yeah. I forgot...You understand the spot me and the missus is in, don't you?"

"I understand."

"It's not that we want to be unfriendly, or anything. Fact is, if it has to be, we wouldn't have any objections whatever to having your boy—your nephew, I mean—as our son-in-law. Why, the misses and me was talking about the boy the other night, saying what a fine looking young man he was."

He squirmed inside. Sounded like they had already picked out Tahchee to marry their innocent little girl. He'd bet his last dollar that she wasn't near as innocent as they thought. He sensed it when he talked with her. Parents were the last to know.

Then a shocking thought crashed into his brain. What if she was already pregnant by someone else? And they were just looking for a way out?

"Yeah," he mumbled finally to break the awkward silence that lay between them. "Tahchee's a fine boy...more near a man now, you might say."

"Well, I guess I'll be getting on back," William said and reined his horse around. He said over his shoulder, "You find out anything, let me know."

"Sure—" he promised, giving William a half-hearted wave, his mind elsewhere.

This little bit of news changed everything. He returned to his carpentry work, deep in troubled thought. Which did he want: Tahchee chasing off to Osage country and getting killed, or staying here and getting married to a girl who may or may not be carrying his baby?

By late afternoon, Tahchee still wasn't home and he still hadn't answered his own question. Before starting supper, he walked up the hill behind the house and spent a few minutes standing at the foot of Song Bird's grave.

Which would *she* want? Her son dead with honor, or living a life he didn't want to live?

He was still wrestling with the problem when Tahchee came home just before dark. He'd thrown a rope over the cow's horns and was pulling her in. The cow was bawling angrily and throwing her weight back against the rope. Sometimes she would almost win the tug-of-war with Tahchee's little mare, but never quite made it. Daniel held the corral gate open so Tahchee could get the cow in the pen. When he was able to flip his rope from the cow's horns, he came riding back to the gate.

"I see you got the cow, but where's the calf?" Daniel asked.

"Looks like it was born dead. Either that or the wolves killed it. Liked to never found them. Rode right by where they were twice. The last time I rode by I heard her. Down in a gully. She didn't want to leave what was left of her calf." He held up the now coiled rope. "This was the only way I could get her to come."

"Well, you got her, and that's that. Now go wash up. Supper's ready. You can put your horse away later."

They ate their supper in silence. Daniel watched the boy eat and was on the verge several times of asking him about the girl, but backed off every time. Tahchee'd either lie about it, or tell him it was none of his business. He didn't want to hear either answer. Before the meal was over, he'd made up his mind what he thought he had to do.

"I've got it all figured out," he finally said. "We'll go pretending we're mixed blood Delawares on a buffalo hunt. That'll be disguise enough to cover our looks. We'll spend a couple winters in Osage villages, and who knows…"

Tahchee glanced up, an excited, surprised look on his face. "You're going with me?"

"I let you go by yourself running around in Osage country asking questions about a man with scars on his face, you wouldn't last two days. This way, we might be able to visit a lot of villages and look at a lot of men without anybody getting suspicious."

"Won't they kill us, if they find out?"

"Probably," he said, his tone matter-of-fact. Then he went on. "But, then again, maybe not. All Osages aren't bad. Only those who go looking for trouble. It's the same everywhere. We'll go in peace. If there's a man out there who's face is marked by Song Bird's fingernails, we'll find him."

He hoped the statement sounded inspirational, for he didn't feel uplifted inside. This was the best way out of the mess, he figured.

"When're we leaving?" Tahchee asked, obviously the happiest Daniel had seen him since…since they'd come riding home that morning only to find Song Bird dead.

"In a couple of days," he heard himself saying without enthusiasm. "I need to find someone to take care of the stock and see after the place—"

"How about the Rogerses? They said they would, didn't they?"

"They have their hands full, getting settled in. I'd better talk to Roy Vann…"

CHAPTER 8

General Matthew Arbuckle was a tall man, appearing even taller than his six feet because of his skinny build. His cheeks were sunk in, his ears too large, and his long nose had a very pronounced hump. His owlish eyes belied the dominant will that kept him going despite his chronic bowel condition, a condition made even worse out here in this godawful wilderness of western Arkansas. One thing about it, the Fort Smith army facility had a good hospital, and he was thankful for that.

He disguised his weakened feeling when the Indian Agent was ushered into his office by standing stiffly erect to shake the visitor's hand before motioning toward a straight-backed chair.

"Have a seat, sir," he said, his voice deep and strong.

He was disappointed. The Indian Agent was a mousy looking bureaucrat. Not at all what he had expected. The Agent's accomplishments in the short time he'd been on the frontier was so great that he had expected to see a more forceful personality and an energetic physic to go with it. He found it hard to believe this sandy haired, unimpressive looking little man was able—almost single handed—to negotiate a treaty with the Osages and get them to *voluntarily* vacate seven million acres of land and confine themselves to

Kansas Territory, leaving the abandoned land for exclusive use by the Cherokees. Of course, Lovely had to offer to pay reparation claims to the Osages for all damages they had suffered in their border wars with the Cherokees during the past decade. But the cost to the government was well worth it, in the General's opinion.

There was only one thing wrong with the treaty, the General noted in his reports to Washington; it wasn't working and its terms were unenforceable. He had decided to talk to Lovely personally and tell him what he was recommending to his own superiors to help solve the problem. He sent word for Lovely to come to his office in Fort Smith for a conference…not a conference, actually; more of an informational meeting, a courtesy.

He waited until Lovely was seated before sitting down on the edge of his own chair, disdaining the use of the chair's back support. He picked up a piece of paper from his desk and handed it to the Indian Agent.

"This is the official order I mentioned in the note I sent you," he said.

Lovely found some wire rimmed spectacles somewhere in the loose suit jacket he was wearing, slipped them on and studied the information on the piece of paper. Growing impatient with Lovely's meticulous reading, he explained, "As you can see, I'm instructed to initiate the construction of a new fort somewhere out there—" and he waved to the west "—to position the United States Army between the Osages and Cherokees. In my opinion, this is the only way to bring this guerilla warfare to an end!"

Lovely ignored the comment as he continued reading. When he was through, he removed his glasses and carefully placed the paper on the desk.

"Peace on the frontier will never be accomplished militarily," he said, his voice soft, a tone fitting his mousy look. "The use of soldiers to enforce terms of the treaty will arouse the Osages to new heights of anger. They'll think the United States Government has joined forces with the Cherokees."

General Arbuckle stifled an urgent need to make a sarcastic remark; forcing himself, instead, to return a compliment for criticism.

"No man will take exception to your work out here," he said, hoping his tone reflected none of the bitterness he felt. "The schools you've established for Indian children, your orphanage here in the Fort Smith civilian settlement—even your method of—" he almost let the word 'pampering' slip out before he could finish with—"counseling recalcitrant treaty violators…Such tactics are commendable, and we all appreciate your efforts to maintain peace on the frontier. However, that one Osage Chief—" He hesitated, searching for the Chief's name.

"Clermont," Lovely filled in.

"Chief Clermont has no intention of vacating the Territory. His braves—"

"Warriors," Lovely corrected.

"—his warriors are still running loose, harassing the Cherokees."

"Chief Clermont wishes to live in peace, but he has a problem," Agent Lovely explained. "It's his brother, Black Dog. Appropriately named, I might add. He's difficult to handle right now. He's got his own following, a group of young rowdies."

The General disdainfully waved aside the explanation. "Indians are Indians. They're like soldiers. What one does, the uniform gets the blame."

"But, sir—"

"I have my orders," he said, keeping his voice stern, and, he hoped, carrying a note of finality in it.

He spread a map across his desk, turning it upside down for the Agent Lovely's benefit. He touched his finger to a spot. "This is the place we propose to build the new fort; near where the Grand and Verdigris Rivers empty into the Arkansas. There's an excellent spot right here—" he found the exact spot with his finger tip. "It's on a bluff overlooking the Grand River valley, about five miles above the river's mouth."

He watched the Indian Agent carefully perusing the crude map and braced himself for an argument. When none came, he tapped the proposed spot for emphasis.

"I'm naming it Gibson. Fort Gibson. Not only will troops stationed there be in a position to capture and punish offenders of your treaty, that area will be conveniently located for westward and southwestward traffic."

"Traffic?" Lovely questioned, showing alarm when he glanced up from the map. "What traffic? I believe one of the stipulations in the Congressional Act creating Indian Territory was that it be for the exclusive use of Indians. There shouldn't be any traffic through it. None. I would even question the legality of troops being stationed in the Territory."

"That's just the point, Mr. Lovely. Washington officials are having trouble getting eastern Cherokees to move out here because of these wilderness wars."

He paused for emphasis, then rapped his desk with his knuckles to emphasize his final words. *"These disturbances have got to be stopped! By hanging the violators, if necessary!"*

The Indian Agent stood and fingered the brim of his hat nervously.

"I can't stop the military from building a fort," he said, his own voice reflecting irritation. "But I warn you, this action will only add a third irritant to an already unstable condition. For the record, I hereby officially request authority to review cases of treaty violations before any drastic punishment is meted out."

"I have no such authority to do that, Mr.Lovely," he said, struggling to keep his own irritation from showing. "According to long standing military protocol, that decision lies with the Commanding Officer who, for the time being, at least, will be me."

He felt a certain degree of satisfaction when he saw the flush creep into Lovely's face. At least, he had let the agent know who was in charge. And as far as he was concerned, it was going to stay that way. He noticed the angry way Lovely set his hat on, jerking it firmly in place, before he said, "My final word to you, sir, is this: If you go ahead with these plans, you must show no favoritism to one side or the other."

He stiffened at the implied insult. "Let no man accuse the U.S. Army of ever showing favoritism to *any* tribe!"

Lovely nodded. "I'm glad to hear you say that, General." he said, turned to leave, then faced back, adding, "Since you were kind enough to inform me of your plans, I'll reciprocate. My plans are to go through Congress and get this military foolishness stopped. The Indians are quite capable of governing themselves. They've been doing it for thousands of years, and I see no reason they can't keep doing it for another thousand—provided we stop trying to tell them how."

Such incompetent arrogance! The General clamped his jaw shut to hold back his words, his burning gaze following the Indian Agent as he stalked to the door, opened it, then closed it softly.

He made a great effort to bring his anger under control, for he had work to do. He called in his executive officer and dictated orders to begin construction of a new army post immediately. It's primary mission: To bring peace between the Cherokees and the Osages—He paused and said, "Make that the Cherokee Nation West and the Osages. We need a new designation for the Cherokees out here. Many of our honorable congressmen still find it confusing trying to distinguish between the Cherokees here and the Cherokees remaining in the east. And the Cherokees here will cease to be Arkansas Cherokees when they move into Indian Territory. I suppose we could call them Indian Territory Cherokees. But that doesn't sound right. Let's use the nomenclature Cherokee Nation West."

"Yes, sir," the young executive officer said. He was a young, handsome captain, very efficient, very effective.

"Ah—now where was I?" General Arbuckle muttered.

"To bring peace between the Cherokee Nation West and the Osages, sir."

"Oh, yes…by relentlessly pursuing, arresting and punishing those members of either tribe who persist in perpetrating acts in violation of the Lovely Treaty." Then he added, "Off the record, Captain. I intend to take command personally, and I will not fail. I'll keep the peace, or burn up the frontier trying."

"Yes, sir," Captain McCall said. "I'll see to it at once."

He felt better, except for the constant ache in his guts. He dismissed his young Exec with a wave of his hand and returned his attention to the map for one last look before hurrying to get on his chamber pot.

This was the first time he noticed the rather large island at the junction of the three rivers and, curious, he studied the skull-shaped island for several minutes, scowled, and muttered aloud, "I wonder if that's an omen of some kind?" Then he frowned thoughtfully as he refolded the map and put it away in a desk drawer.

Laura was so filled with curiosity she paid little attention to the usual family squabbling on their way into town, her father and mother on the seat and her mother constantly onto the boys romping around in the bed of the wagon. She sat on the tailgate, dangling her long legs over the edge.

She felt good for a change. There were some mornings recently she didn't want to get out of bed. And there were certain food smells that made her vomit for no reason at all. Her mother kept making her take large doses of Epsom salts, which only made matters worse. Just then, a wagon wheel jumped over a rock and the jolt she took was so hard it caused her teeth to pop together.

She glanced down at her stomach, wondering. Does it feel hard jolts like that? No, of course not. It? She wished she could think of it as a him or a her. An 'it' just didn't seem right, somehow.

She hardly realized they were at the church until her father pulled the team to a halt. She slid from the tailgate and the boys came tumbling out behind. Ellen kept snapping her fingers.

"Here! Here!" she warned, trying to calm her four rowdy boys.

Normally, Laura would help her mother bring the boys under control. When she made no effort to do so, Ellen frowned worriedly and asked, "Are you feeling all right?"

"Yes, Mama. I feel fine."

She turned away from her mother's skeptical look. She heard her father say, "I don't know how long this meeting will last. You and the kids will have to wait here."

"I still don't understand what business you have in the meeting," Ellen said. "We haven't lived here long enough to know what's going on."

"They told me it's an open meeting. Since Chief Cahtateeskee died and Daniel Taylor's gone on a trip, there's no official leader for the Council. They want to talk about making the move into Indian Territory, in case we have to take some sort of action before Daniel gets back. That's about the size of it, I guess."

"I don't see what good you'd do."

"Me neither. But I'll do what I can." He held Ellen's hand as she climbed down. "I'll be back as soon as the meeting is over."

"Daddy, why can't I ride into town with you?" Laura asked. He looked up, his brow wrinkled.

"What would you do all day in town, for heaven's sake?"

"I could spend a lot of time at Webber's store looking for something to wear. I can walk back here when I get through. It's not all that far."

He glanced at her mother, an unasked question on his face. Her mother waved a hand and said, "For goodness sakes, let her go. You know what a time I've had getting her into something besides that skimpy thing she wears all the time. Maybe if she finds a dress to her own liking, she'll wear it."

Her father patted the seat. "All right. Hop up here and let's go. I'm late already."

Tickled to get out of spending the day at the church with other wives and their kids, she scrambled over the wagon wheel and slid onto the seat beside her father. He whipped the team forward.

She felt good getting away. She flipped her long hair behind her shoulders and said, "I sure wasn't looking forward to sitting around the church all day. A quilting party to raise money for new song books might be a fine day's entertainment for some people, but not for me."

He chuckled softly, but made no comment and, after a few more moments of silence, she had a feeling he knew. She remembered seeing him talking to Clancy not long after...that day. He appeared to be asking Clancy a lot of questions and they both kept glancing her direction. Later, her father had gone to visit the Taylors. He hadn't told her mother why, even when her mother had asked him straight out. He made up some flimsy excuse which nobody believed. She braced herself for the worst, tried to ease around the subject by asking, "If I find something I like, can I buy it?"

"You know we're short on cash right now, sweetheart."

"Can't we buy it on credit? Lots of people do at Webber's. He same as told you we could the last time we were there, didn't he?"

"I know. But I just don't trust white store owners."

"Oh, Daddy. You love Mama, don't you? She's white."

"She's different. She's not like the others."

"White people out here seem different."

"I guess maybe they are."

"Then can I? If I find one I like?"

He sighed. "I suppose so, seeing as how bad your mother wants you to have one." Then he looked directly at her. "Laura, mother and I have to know—your morning sickness and all—Are you—you know—in a family way?"

His gaze was boring into her. A dozen responses flashed through her mind in a second, all little lies that would explain away her pregnancy. She rejected them. Now she knew that was what her father and Clancy had been talking about. For that matter, Tahchee might have told him what they did that day on the creek. There was no way out, she finally decided, except to tell the truth.

"I—I think so," she said, barely above a whisper and looked down at her hands in her lap, ashamed.

The last thing she expected was for him to put his arm about her and pull her tight against him. She went limp and lay her head on his shoulder.

"I'm sorry, Daddy—"

"Hush," he said. He patted her shoulder. She wanted to ask him if mother knew, but she already knew the answer to that. She wanted to cry. She wanted to get angry at them for intruding. She wished it hadn't happened. She wished Tahchee was there. She wished a thousand things...

"Was it Tahchee?"

"Yes."

"So that's why they run off," he said aloud to himself.

"No, it wasn't, Daddy. He doesn't know."

"Maybe he doesn't, but *Daniel* sure knows. That's what I went to talk to him about. Clancy said he saw you."

"I know."

"That's enough right there to make him marry you whether he wanted to or not."

How simple that would be. But she knew Tahchee wasn't coming home until he found the Osage he was looking for. Maybe never. She decided it was time to lie, for her parents' sakes. "We talked about getting married. He said we would just as soon as he got back from his trip. Of course, neither one of us thought this would happen. I don't think he would have run off if he did."

He patted her shoulder again. They were pulling into the main part of town. She sat up, flipped her long hair over her shoulders, and said, "If it wasn't for you and Mama, I wouldn't care. If Tahchee doesn't come home soon, I'll try to find another man—"

"Stop that kind of talk. You'll do nothing of the sort."

"Oh, Daddy. That's fine for you to say. But Mama's a white woman. That's the way white people are. Most everything is a sin, especially if it's fun. But I love Mama and wouldn't hurt her for the world. That's why I said that. It would save her—and you—from a lot of embarrassment, especially since we're new here."

He said nothing as he pulled to a stop in front of Webber's General Store. She leaned over and kissed him on the cheek. "Bye, Daddy," she murmured and started to get down, but he stopped her.

"There's another way," he said. "You could go stay with Aunt Ishta in Texas. They say in their letters it's nice there. The government in Mexico City is so far away the politicians don't pay any attention to Cherokees living Texas, she said. They say there're no whites there and never will be because whites don't like to go outside the boundaries of the United States. That's why Aunt Ishta tried to get us to move to Texas with them instead of Arkansas. We almost did, and would have except your mother wanted to raise you kids in the United States. But there's lots of our people around here moving down there. I could arrange for you to go with another family. You could tell Aunt Ishta you got married shortly after we got here and your husband was killed fighting Osages."

Somehow, his little speech had a sense of urgency about it that depressed her. She could only assume they definitely didn't want her around, now that she was "in a family way." At least, not being married. The rejection hurt. Her throat felt restricted. She was afraid to say anything. Only nodded, swallowed, and forced out, "Yes, I could do that."

She turned her face away quickly and hopped nimbly down from the wagon. She forced a smile and gave her father a little wave before turning and going into the store.

She struggled mightily to hide her tears of hurt and was thankful that Mr. Webber was busy at the pay counter arguing with a funny looking man wearing a bowler hat. She began looking at dresses hanging on a clothes rack, but her mind wasn't on clothes.

What could she do? Would Tahchee even marry her if did come back soon? She'd like that, for he was so quick witted, he would be a real challenge to live with. That time at the creek was so wild and exciting, she wanted more of him. She felt goose bumps and shivered thinking about it.

There seemed to be a greater sense of pleasure sharing with Tahchee that she hadn't found in the others. Most men lost control, acted like animals, anxious only in getting it in hurrying to satisfy themselves without once thinking about the woman. She sensed that with Tahchee they could experiment, try other things. Her mouth felt suddenly dry again. She licked her lips and swallowed heavily.

Oh, Tahchee—!

Or was her desire real love? She felt confused. What *was* love? Certainly, sharing was love. And she wanted so much to share with Tahchee—share everything.

She simply had to force Tahchee from her thoughts. To distract herself, she held a bright red dress up against herself, trying to get some idea how she might look wearing it. It was too long, she decided, even for her. She didn't care for white women dresses. Besides, she liked having her legs free, enjoyed the way men looked at her.

The arguing at the pay counter climbed to another level. She couldn't help but shift her attention to Mr. Webber and the man dressed in funny looking clothes.

A traveling salesman? He'd make a good husband. They didn't stay around long...I don't care...All I need is a marriage ceremony and one or two nights with him.

She studied her prospect in more detail. He was good looking. Not as tall as she, but well built. He wore a brown bowler hat, a fluffy red tie, a vest, and a brown suit. His coat was too big and his trousers too short, exposing his cream-colored high button shoes. He had a sharply chiseled face, small ears and a square jaw which he jutted out at Mr. Webber.

"I say, sir," he said, his voice high pitched and his words oddly clipped. "You're a ha' pence short."

Mr. Webber, a gangly man with wispy gray hair, showed his irritation by alternately looking at the change in the man's hand through his bifocals and over the top of his gold rimmed glasses at the man's face.

"I damn sure don't know what a ha' pence is," Mr. Webber said, his voice breaking at every two words. "But I do know good old American money, and that's the correct change!"

"'Ere now, mate," the man said. "'Tis not my purpose to be unfriendly traveling through your country, but right's right, I always say!"

Mr. Webber's frustration showed as his mouth opened and closed wordlessly. When he glanced her direction, she motioned for him, pretending she needed help. Mr. Webber brushed aside the man to come to her. His feisty customer trailed along, still holding out his handful of coins. Mr. Webber smiled pleasantly and asked, "Find something you like, Miss Rogers?"

"How much is this dress?" she asked and stepped from behind the clothes rack holding the red dress up. She hoped the stranger would look at her instead of the dress. He did and came to a dead stop. His mouth fell open.

Pleased by his reaction, she turned sideways as she discussed the price with Mr. Webber and let the stranger gawk at the shape of her breasts. His lustful stare was thrilling, but not as thrilling as Tahchee's.

She paid no attention to the prices Mr. Webber was quoting, for she was too amused at the sight of the man in the bowler hat, still frozen, standing with his hand extended. She replaced the dress on the rack, suppressing a desire to laugh.

"Thank you," she told Mr. Webber. "I don't believe I'd look good in that color, do you?"

"I—"

"Excuse my impropriety, Miss," the stranger cut in, coming to sudden life. "I think it would be such a tremendous loss to the world if you dressed yourself in any other garment other than what you are wearing."

She gave him a grateful smile. Then, feigning innocence, she said, "Why, thank you, mister—" she paused, glancing at Mr. Webber's scowling face for help.

"Some Englishman's all I know," Mr. Webber said, and made a couple of harumphing sounds before explaining, "Says his company sent him to do some trading with the Indians." Then he added with a distasteful tone, "He don't even know how to count our money! Some business man, I say!"

The stranger tipped his bowler. "David Gentry, Miss. At your service."

Just then, a woman came in, tugging two children.

"I'll be right back," Mr. Webber said and hurried away to see what the lady wanted. Laura, glad to be left alone with the man from England, kept her gaze fixed on his pale blue eyes and asked, "Did you bring your family with you to America, Mr. Gentry?"

He hesitated a fraction of a second before shaking his head. "No. Fact is, I have no family."

She knew he was lying. But that was all right. If he did have a wife in England, that'd be more of a reason for him leaving her after they got married. Then she'd be free when Tahchee came home. She lifted her brows to express her sympathy.

"You poor man. I bet you're lonely, aren't you?"

He nodded, his smile changing subtlety before he said, "Very lonely, Miss. Are you married?"

"Daddy says I'm not old enough to get married."

"Now, how old would that be?"

"Almost twenty," she lied.

David cleared his throat. "I'd say that's plenty old, Miss—ah—I didn't get your name."

"Laura. Laura Rogers."

"What a lovely name for an—"

She finished for him, "An Indian?"

He flushed. "Please forgive my crudeness. Those of us still living in the old world find you natives both perplexing and enlightening. We never know if your way of life is one step above the stone age, or the next step above our own brutal civilization. In either event, what we read in our newspapers across the sea is nowhere near what you are really like."

"What are we really like—" she asked and lowered her voice to add a soft, meaningful, "—David?"

The intimate emphasis she put on his name had the predictable effect. She could see the lust surge into his expression.

"That, Miss Rogers, is something I'd very much be interested in exploring further."

"Oh?"

"May I be so bold as to ask if I may call on you at your home?"

She frowned, hoping she'd appear thoughtful. And she was, to a degree. She'd rather marry Tahchee. Her parents—especially her father—would approve of Tahchee much quicker than he would this Englishman. On the other hand, her mother would probably think an Englishman would be better for her than a Cherokee. If and when Tahchee did come back, she could get a divorce according to Cherokee custom, which was to simply take her belongings, including all livestock they may have accumulated and go home to her parents.

The Englishman fidgeted at her delay. He swept his bowler from his head, revealing his heavy shock of tousled black hair.

"Please don't get the idea I'm rushing you, Laura. If you need more time—"

She shook her head. "I don't need more time. I'd love to have you call on me whenever you feel like it."

Mr. Webber returned in time to catch the tail end of her remark.

"Feel like what?" he asked her with a suspicious look toward the Englishman. David popped his bowler on, grinning broadly.

"I don't believe this is a matter of your concern, sir," he said, now in an obvious jocular mood. Then he asked Laura, "if you'll give me directions to your home—?"

"Now see here, young man—!" Mr. Webber broke in, leveling a finger at David Gentry.

"It's all right, Mr. Webber," Laura interrupted. "Mr. Gentry is a perfect gentleman. He only asked to visit me at my home. I see nothing wrong in that, do you?"

Mr. Webber's mouth opened, then closed. She slipped her arm around Mr. Webber's, then slid her hand down to clasp his as she often did with her father when she wanted something he didn't want her to have. Mr. Webber instinctively lifted her hand, patted it, and smiled.

"No," he sighed. "I guess there's no harm in that."

Then he frowned at the Englishman and said, "I'm warning you, Mister Foreigner. We're proper folks around here. Her father's a full blood Cherokee, and Indians have ways of making you wish you hadn't when you did. Do you understand what I'm saying?"

David Gentry answered with a frown of of his own, "You still owe me a ha' pence, sir. Now, if we might run over that bill of goods one more time—"

"I'm telling you for the last time! We ain't got no pences in America! Can't you get that through your thick head?"

David was already on his way to the counter. Mr. Webber followed, mumbling angrily.

Laura, pleased over what she accomplished, made her way quietly to the front entrance. She supposed the Englishman would have enough sense to find out where she lived and how to get there.

When she stepped out onto the street, she saw the soldier—a captain—dismounting at the hitching rail. Not only was he much younger than the Englishman, he was handsome! Tall, blond haired, blue eyes, a thin, but strong face with a wide mouth. His movements were graceful and easy. She decided suddenly that he'd make a far better father for Tahchee's child than the Englishman. She hurried toward him, shamelessly, excited by the prospect of meeting him.

"Excuse me, Captain," she asked, still not knowing what to say next, then thought of something. "Is there a private Benjamin Smith on the roster at the army post?"

The young man glanced up, a surprised look on his face. She regretted being too near when his gaze appraised her with a look more discreet than either the Englishman or Tahchee. Would he be able to see her legs?

"Haven't heard of a Benjamin Smith, Ma'am," he said, touching the brim of his hat politely. "We have two other Smiths, though—a Peter Smith and a Carl Smith. But no Benjamin. Sorry."

She hoped her disappointed look appeared sincere. It did, for he gave her a slight bow and announced, "Captain George McCall, Ma'am. I am the Post Executive Officer. May I ask why you are making the inquiry? If you have a complaint to make against one of our men, I will do all that I can to make it right."

She watched his cool gaze travel down her body, then up again slowly. When their eyes met, she felt a delicious thrill. She affected a worried look. He scowled.

"Has one of our men taken advantage of you, young lady? If he has, I'll—"

"Oh, no! I mean—well, yes. In a way…" Her mind was racing madly to keep plausible thoughts ahead of her words. "He promised to—" she ducked her head and lowered her voice—"marry me if I—"

She didn't finish. When she looked up at him from beneath her brows, she caught him blushing. She knew what he was thinking and wanted to laugh, from the sheer joy of being able to affect him the way she knew she was doing. She watched the furious scowl form.

"You needn't say more, Miss—?"

"Laura. Laura Rogers."

"Miss Rogers. I have to pick up a couple of things in the store. I'll only be a minute. If you care to, you can ride with me out to the post. I'll have the men fall out and stand at attention. You can look them all over."

"Oh, my, no. I wouldn't want to do that. Perhaps if I could just go out there and look around. I might be able to see him. No need making such a big to-do out of it."

"You stay right here. I'll only be a minute."

"I can't be gone long. My family will go home without me if I'm not here when they get ready to leave. I wouldn't have any place to stay tonight, if they did that."

"Don't you worry about that, Miss Rogers—"

"Laura."

"Laura. If that happens, we have guest quarters at the post where you could stay."

"Oh, how nice."

She watched him hurry into the store and waited patiently for him to come out...a mantle of contentment settling over her even as an exquisite thrill raced along every nerve of her being in anticipation of the new adventure she faced.

She felt a twinge of sorrow for her mother and father. But she knew they would be relieved to hear she'd rode away with and married an officer in the United States army.

CHAPTER 9

Daniel had an uneasy feeling as he and Tahchee rode into the small Osage village, their long rifles balanced across their laps. He kept glancing around trying to find some reason for feeling the way he did. What he saw appeared no different than dozens of other Osage villages they'd lived in during the past two years; a few teepees, a few domed huts that once belonged to the Wichitas, curious men staring—some with scowls of suspicion, some with expressions of open friendliness—women cooking over open fires or scraping and curing buffalo hides, children playing, dogs barking. Always dogs barking.

He guided his mount closer to Tahchee's and muttered a low warning, "I'm changing our story here. We're Pawnees instead of Delawares."

"Why?" Tahchee asked. "It's worked everywhere we've been so far...just so long as you don't slip up and call me by my Cherokee name like you did that first village we stayed in."

"Yeah," Daniel admitted. "That was a close call. Good thing the Osages have as much trouble pronouncing it as the white man. Dutch is not hard to live with, is it?"

"I don't mind. Like you always said, names don't mean anything until you put the person behind it."

"Well, well," Daniel mused. "One thing good about this little outing—appears you've been listening to things your old full blood uncle's been telling you."

"Had to," Tahchee quipped. "It was listen to you or listen to the bullfrogs croak. Least I could understand some of the things you said…though I admit there was times I'd sooner you shut up and let me listen to the bullfrogs."

Daniel laughed quietly. Then, still worried, fell silent. Tahchee, also looking around, said, "Everything looks normal to me. What makes you so up tight?"

"Just a hunch." Daniel said. "Word has a way traveling ahead of you out here. Two mixed blood Delawares out buffalo hunting for two years could be wearing thin. Let's change it to Pawnees on our way south to visit our relatives in Texas."

"Why Pawnees? Aren't they up in Nebraska somewhere? That don't make sense. Why not Wichitas or Cheyennes?"

"Can't be Wichitas. See those huts? That's the way Wichitas build their shelters. The Osages ran the Wichitas out and took over their land. They're still using their huts. And they wouldn't like any of them coming back. I don't know what they think of Cheyennes. Pawnees should be far enough away not to have had any run-ins with the Osage."

Tahchee's only comment was a shrug. Daniel could tell he'd already lost interest in the story about who they were and where they were going by the way he was searching every man's face, looking for scars. A tall warrior stepped out and blocked their path. He was stripped to the waist, wore only deerskin trousers and moccasins and had his head shaved the traditional Osage way—leaving only a scalp lock two inches wide running from his high forehead to the nape of his neck. A single feather dangled from the loose strands behind. He was unarmed except for a big-bladed, bone-handled knife strapped to his waist. Daniel pulled up and made the universal peace sign, uplifted hand, palm outward.

He'd managed to learn a little of the Osage language, enough to carry on a decent conversation. He'd tried to get Tahchee to do the same, telling him the more languages he knew the better off he was. Especially if you're out traveling across the plains. But Tahchee's hatred toward the Osages for killing his mother seemed to extend to every aspect of their culture. He hadn't bothered to learn their language—just bits and pieces.

"You don't need to talk to a man to tell if he's out to kill you," Tahchee had said contemptibly. "I heard you say a thousand times a man's body language speaks a lot louder than words."

He had grudgingly admitted the boy was right, especially with him throwing his own philosophy back in his face. He was beginning to get a good feeling that his two years on the high plains with the boy wasn't a total loss after all. Even so, he'd argued weakly, it didn't hurt to learn as many languages as you could.

"Strangers come?" the Osage grunted, his words both fact and inquiry.

"We come in peace," Daniel said, pronouncing his Osage words as carefully as he could. "Our way has been long. We have far to go. Other Osages have opened their villages and given us rest. We will pay with good buffalo hides."

"Strangers dress like white man."

Daniel interpreted the comment to mean they didn't want anything to do with white men. A bad sign. He attempted to calm his concern with a friendly smile, explaining, "Our ancestors are both white and Pawnee. We go to Texas in land called Mexico to visit relatives."

The silence about them seemed to deepen. He heard all kinds of warning bells going off in his head. Maybe they hated the white man more than most do, he decided. But there was no way taking back what he said. Best to pretend they weren't offended. He removed his hat and wiped his brow on his shirt sleeve.

"It sure is hot. We could do with a drink of water," he said, trying to keep his voice as normal as possible. "The name's Daniel. My young friend here is called Dutch."

His words were no sooner out than the Osage's demeanor changed. His face brightened and he laughed, saying, "Strangers welcome. Get down. I'll have my men take care of your horses. Come to my lodge. Eat. Drink."

"What made him so happy all at once?" Tahchee blurted in English, suspicious.

"Beats me. He wants us to get down and come to his lodge—"

"I don't like it. Let's get the hell out of here."

"Just simmer down. And let's keep our conversations in English to a minimum. I'll bet most of them can understand English as well as you or me. We got no choice now. Let's bluff it out."

To the Osage, he said, "Sounds good to me." And he dismounted, handing his reins to another Osage who stepped forward to take the horses. Tahchee, after hesitating, dismounted also.

Another Osage offered to take their long rifles. That was being a bit too friendly, Daniel thought. He shook his head.

"Come," the tall Osage said and turned to stalk away.

They followed, Osage children running alongside, their curious jabbering unintelligible. The tall Osage ducked through an entrance into one of the domed huts. It was more spacious inside than Daniel thought. Although they had been in other huts like this during their travels through Osage country, this one was larger than most, better constructed, better maintained. In fact, on closer inspection, this hut seemed to have been just recently built. The supporting poles arching overhead still retained much of their green-wood characteristics. The skin covering was stretched tight, not an age wrinkle in it anywhere. The sticks used to frame the hole in the roof where smoke from the interior fire escaped were not blackened as deeply as in older huts. It was obvious that the Osage liked the Wichita huts better than their own traditional teepees, since they had started building them themselves.

An older woman was busy at the small fire in the center of the hut's floor area. Once inside, the tall Osage turned to face them.

"Pawnee strangers do not need guns in Osage home. You leave by the door."

He told Tahchee what the man was asking them to do. Tahchee said, "Like hell I will. Tell him—"

"Will you shut up! I wouldn't be surprised if he doesn't understand every word you're saying. Let's do what he says. Show our friendliness. Hell's bells, Dutch, we have just as much chance to get to them as he does."

He turned and leaned his long rifle against the wall. Tahchee seemed reluctant, but finally did the same. The Osage ordered the old woman to bring water for the strangers. She hurried away. Then he indicated the buffalo robe bed nearby.

"Sit," he said and sank slowly to the floor himself, crossing his legs. Now his face was dark and he fixed his intent gaze on Daniel's face. "You lie," he said, his voice harsh.

The unexpected accusation caught Daniel by surprise. He searched the Osage's face, trying to recall. Had he been at one of the other villages where they'd stayed? If he had, their story now wouldn't jibe with with their story then. He shouldn't have changed it—like Tahchee warned.

"Osage friend insult guest. We—"

"There are no Pawnees in Texas. They afraid to pass through Osage land."

Uh-oh, Daniel thought. He picked the wrong tribe to be one of. He admitted quickly, "We never lived with our Pawnees ancestors. We live with our white ancestors."

The Osage's face remained impassive. He could only hope he'd planted enough doubt to at least stall any actions the Osage might have in mind.

"Pawnee no good," the Osage said. "They raid Osage villages when Osage lived in land white man call Kansas. They kill women and children. Pawnee will be Osage enemy forever."

"I didn't get all of that," Tahchee cut in, speaking English. "What'd he say?"

He had to laugh and answered Tahchee in English. "He says Pawnees are enemies of the Osage and will be forever."

"I don't see what's so damn funny. Looks to me like you've got us in one hell of a fix."

Daniel patted him on the shoulder. "Relax, relax—"

Tahchee shrugged his hand away. Daniel returned his attention to his Osage host. He'd learned this much about the Osages—they respected courage.

"I said we come in peace. If Osage wish to fight Pawnee guest because of what our ancestors did, Pawnee ready."

The tall Osage's dark eyes shifted to Tahchee. "You call young man Dutch. You not Pawnee. Dutch is Delaware buffalo hunter. Word comes. Dutch is great fighter."

So, Daniel thought with a certain degree of amusement, Tahchee's reputation had run ahead of them. Stories of the wrestling matches the boy'd been in with young Osage bucks during the past two years had grown to no telling what. Of course, his accuracy in shooting and knife throwing could have added to the story. Plains Indians seemed to like telling tall tales even more than the Cherokees, Daniel had noticed.

"He's using my name," Tahchee said. "What's he saying about me?"

"He's saying Dutch is not a Pawnee. He's a Delaware. He knows, because he's heard of you."

Tahchee scowled. "I told you not to change our story."

"Just simmer down, son. We're getting too close to the real story here," Daniel cautioned. Then, thinking fast, he said to the Osage, "I apologize. I did not want to frighten your people by bringing the great fighter Dutch to their village."

A slight smile spread across the Osage's face. "There's talk that Dutch is Cherokee, not Delaware."

"Oh, no," Daniel assured him, shaking his head for further emphasis. "He's—"

"I fight Dutch."

"What?"

"I better warrior than Dutch. I prove it by killing him. People will then say Cheho is greatest fighter of all."

Just then the woman returned, and Daniel was glad for the interruption, for he had to have time to figure out how to get out of this one. The woman was carrying the water in a tightly woven basket. Evaporation of the dampness of the liquid seeping through the basket's minute openings cooled the water. A gourd dipper floated on the surface. He helped himself to a cool drink as Tahchee asked, "What's he saying now?"

"He wants to take you on in a knife fight. To prove he's the best man."

To his surprise, Tahchee grinned and said, "Bring him on. Nothing would suit me better than to stick a knife in an Osage's gut."

"Are you serious?"

"That's why I came out here. It's beginning to look like we're not going to find the man we're looking for. One's as good as another."

Daniel didn't like it. He recalled the feeling he had when they rode in. Could it be the word was already out who they were and who they were looking for? He sized up the Osage. He just might be more than Tahchee could handle. But to back down now could be even more disastrous.

"I don't like it," he told Tahchee.

"You mean you don't think I can take him."

"I didn't say that."

Without warning, Tahchee got to his feet, standing tall and proud. He pointed to himself and said, using the few words of Osage he knew, "I am Cherokee. You are woman killer. I kill you easy."

"For Christ's sake! What're you doing—"

"He's telling me he is a Cherokee," the Osage said in perfectly good English, a grim smile on his face. Then he, too, got to his feet. "Osage hate Cherokee more than we do Pawnee. We fight."

He spun, slipped his big-bladed knife from its scabbard and stalked through the entrance. Tahchee followed. Daniel scrambled to his feet and hurried after them, blood racing, heart pounding in his ears, fear for the boy gripping his heart. And he knew, too, that his own life was on the line since Tahchee told the Osage they were Cherokees.

Outside, a ring of people began forming rapidly as men, women, and children came running from every direction, jostling one another for better positions. Cheho, knife blade glinting in the sunlight, turned to face Tahchee.

Tahchee slowly stripped to the waist, handing Daniel his worn mackinaw and woolen shirt. He kept his floppy brimmed hat on, however, and Daniel wondered about his fascination for wearing it. The boy did have sense enough to remove his boots.

The two men began circling one another, warily looking for an opening. Daniel's own fear mushroomed. Wrestling for fun, even in anger, was one thing—fighting to the death with knives was another.

The Osage lunged. Tahchee sidestepped quick as a cat. He was able to slash a deep gash in the Osage's side as he went by. But before Tahchee could get on him from behind, the Osage whirled, knife ready to slice Tahchee's stomach open.

Tahchee backed away. The Osage ignored the blood gushing from the ugly cut in his side. A murmur of concern swept through the crowd. Daniel's palms began to perspire so much he kept rubbing them on his pants legs, only vaguely aware of what he was doing.

Sun beams bounced off the mirror-like surfaces of the knife blades; Tahchee's now streaked with red. The Osage lunged again. Tahchee deflected his thrust and, at the same time, wrapped his arm about the Osage's, trapping it against his body and pressuring the elbow to bend backward. The Osage countered to immobilize Tahchee's knife hand by seizing his wrist.

Both men strained to get their knife wielding hands free while keeping their opponent's locked. The monumental test of sheer strength had its effect on the crowd. Every spectator, it seemed, was holding his breath. Only the quick bursts of sucking air and grunts of the fighters could be heard as they staggered back and forth.

Daniel saw the Osage's move to hook one of his legs behind Tahchee's.

"Look out—" he shouted, but too late. Tahchee lost his balance and fell over backward, the Osage's knife hand underneath his back.

The scream of pain cut through Daniel's insides before he realized that it was the Osage who screamed and not Tahchee. Then he saw why. Tahchee had applied so much pressure to the Osage's arm that he snapped the bone. The Osage's elbow was bending backward. The grotesque sight made Daniel's guts crawl.

The Osage released his grip on Tahchee's wrist to try and free himself. Tahchee plunged his knife into the Osage's side, twisting the blade into the man's heart.

The Osage grunted, went limp. Tahchee rolled him aside and rose to one knee, the Osage's blood splattered across his bare chest. He panted heavily. His eyes glaring down at the Osage's twitching body still showed hate.

Daniel, weak from the high emotion, went to the boy. "You hurt?" he asked, surprised at the nervous shakiness in his own voice.

Tahchee stood and drew in a full breath. He shook his head. He didn't appear nearly as wound up as Daniel was inside. He noticed the ring of people around them was pressing closer, many of the men with ugly knifes already drawn, others gripping wicked looking tomahawks.

"Here. Put your clothes on, and let's get out of here," he said in a low, urgent voice.

Instead, Tahchee turned slowly, brandishing his bloody blade at the men closing in.

"Come on," he snarled in his garbled Osage. "Who wants to be next?"

This is it, Daniel thought. He dropped Tahchee's clothes and whipped out his own knife and began circling back to back with his nephew.

Just then a woman's voice shouted a warning. The ring of Osages began dissolving. Riders appeared from beyond the teepees and huts.

Soldiers! Daniel went limp with relief, especially when he noticed the effect the approaching soldiers had on the Osages. The men quickly put away their weapons, most began sneaking away with the women and children.

And wonder of wonders—Johnny Jumper was riding up front!

"Man are we ever glad to see you," Daniel said to the officer in charge, a young lieutenant who was desperately trying to grow a beard but had managed only a stand of limp, blond fuzz. Then to the expert Cherokee tracker and long-time friend, he said, "Johnny Jumper! You old son of a gun! You're a sight for sore eyes. You working for the army now? Or did they conscript you?"

Johnny laughed, a cackling, happy laugh. "Both, you might say. But the pay's good and the work's easy. All they want is somebody to get them there and get them home again."

"Well, good for you," Daniel said, and meant it. Poor old Johnny Jumper never was much good at feeding his family. Good trackers never were needed much; and when they were, the pay was skimpy, to say the least.

"What's going on here?" the lieutenant demanded.

"Me and him just settled a little argument," Tahchee said, gesturing with his knife at the dead Osage. "I won. He lost. It was a fair fight."

The officer looked skeptical. "Who're you?"

Daniel spoke before Tahchee had a chance, saying, "We're Cherokees. We've been out west hunting buffalo. We were on our way back to Arkansas. Rode in here peaceable. My name's Daniel Taylor. This is my nephew, Tahchee. Some call him Dutch."

The lieutenant eyed Tahchee a full minute before saying, "So you're Dutch?"

Daniel's heart leaped. Unbelievable how a reputation spreads. He started to deny it, but Tahchee spoke first.

"Whatever," he grunted as he stooped to clean the blood off his knife in the grass. "Who're you?"

"Lieutenant Colson…You Cherokees have no business here in an Osage village. Don't you two know there's a war on?"

"What're you talking about?" Daniel asked.

"The Osages and Cherokees. How long have you two been gone?"

"A couple of years," Daniel said. "We've been staying with the Osages, off and on. Course, we didn't tell them we were Cherokees. Had more sense than that. As for the war, Lieutenant, we've been fighting Osages ever since we moved to Arkansas. I'd say near before you were born."

The Lieutenant frowned and said, sounding a bit miffed, "You two had better get your gear and come with us. We've been escorting a survey crew marking the new boundary of the Cherokee Outlet and are on our way back to Fort Gibson."

"Fort Gibson?" Daniel asked. "Never heard of it. Where's it at?"

"We had to build a new post near where the Grand River empties into the Arkansas. We've been stationed there to keep the peace. And, I might add, sir, trying our best to keep men like you two out of Osage country until we can get them all rounded up and moved north."

Daniel laughed. "I thought the Lovely Treaty was a done deal—two years ago."

"Some of the details haven't been worked out yet," the officer explained.

Daniel turned to Tahchee. "How about it, Dutch? You ready to go home?"

"I suppose we might as well."

The Lieutenant scoffed. "It's a good thing you decided to volunteer."

Daniel bristled. "Or what?"

"Or we'll take you by force, Mr. Taylor. Is that clear?"

He returned the Lieutenant's glare and debated telling him to go to hell. Only Tahchee's agreement to go home kept made him keep his silence. He said to Johnny Jumper, "Johnny, they took our horses when we rode in. A roan. A chestnut and a black pack horse. Get them for us, will you?"

They were several miles east of the village before Daniel had a chance to talk at any length with Johnny Jumper. He was curious about home.

Johnny was happy to answer all questions and brought them up to date on what different people had been doing before he mentioned politics.

"Chief Cahtateeskee died," he said. "The Council's been running things until you got back."

This news made Daniel feel sick. Not because of Chief Cahtateeskee's death, since that had been expected, but because he had been gone at a critical time when his people needed him. And, as it turned out, gone on a wild goose chase. However, he was consoled by the thought that he at least kept Tahchee from having to marry too young to a girl of questionable virtue. He tried to think of an excuse to inquire about the Rogerses, but could think of none. Maybe they had moved.

Tahchee beat him to it. "What about the Rogerses?" he asked. "They still there?"

"Oh, yes. They're doing just fine."

"Their girl—?" Tahchee asked.

Johnny's dark eyes looked sad. "I didn't mention them because everybody knew how you felt about her. She just up and left home, they say. Wound up getting married to an army officer. George McCall, I believe was his name. I guess she's doing all right. She lives there in Fort Gibson. Got a kid now. A girl, I think."

Daniel felt a chill. Tahchee's? He wanted to ask if it looked like an Indian. But then the chances were it would anyway, even if it did belong to the McCall feller, with her being at least half Indian herself. His heart ached when he saw the hurt in Tahchee's face. And he knew why…even if he didn't love her, she was, as far as he knew, his first and only experience with a woman. Daniel knew it would be a memory that would live with him the rest of his life.

"Did you two ever find that man who killed Song Bird?" Johnny asked.

Daniel shook his head. "We've been in about every Osage village we could find. Haven't seen anybody with scratch scars on his face. Personally, I'm glad we're on our way home."

"I'm not," Tahchee said. "I know he's out here somewhere."

"Have you been to Pasuga yet?" Johnny asked.

"No," Daniel answered. "Where's that at?"

"It's just about due north of here, across the Cimarron. It's where the Chief of the Osages lives. Clermont."

Daniel wasn't too interested in continuing the search longer. "Aw, I—"

"I'm going to take a look," Tahchee cut in.

"You crazy?" Daniel blurted. "Everybody out here knows you. What happened back there in that last village proves it. Especially Chief Clermont. He's as smart as they come. I've led battles against him, and he whips us every time. He'll know who you are the minute he hears your name."

"So what? You go on home, if you want to. I got no reason to now. I'm going to Pasuga."

Daniel heaved a heavy sigh, understanding. "All right. One more village. Then will you go home?"

"I said you didn't have to go with me."

"I heard you. But that doesn't change things."

Daniel hoped the boy appreciated his loyalty. After a moment, Tahchee nodded. "I promise," was all he said.

Daniel turned to Johnny. "Will you help us sneak away from these soldiers tonight. No use causing a big uproar over us doing what we have a right to do."

"Oh, I think we can manage that without too much trouble," the tracker said. "You want me to tell them at home you'll be coming soon?"

"Yeah. Tell them that. But also tell them not to wait too long. If I don't show up, tell them to elect someone else Chief."

CHAPTER 10

Tahchee, puzzled over the sound of the muted booming, like distant thunder, kept glancing at Daniel, waiting for him to hear and say something about it. He'd been accused so many times of imagining that he was hearing or seeing things that he'd learned to wait, let someone else mention it first. The underbrush thickened, and he dropped back, tugging at their pack animal's rope.

The heavy rumbling sound increased ominously. He swept the sky with a quick look. No clouds, even on the horizon. Apprehensive, he fixed his gaze on Daniel's back, knowing he surely must have heard by now. He guessed right for Daniel suddenly twisted in his saddle to ask, "What the hell kind of noise is that?"

"Sounds like thunder away off," Tahchee suggested.

Daniel shook his head. He pushed on. Soon, they broke into the clear on the brow of a boulder-strewn hill. Daniel pulled up sharply.

"Good God!" he said, raising his voice over the booming roar. "Would you look at that!"

Below, the Cimarron River, which they had crossed and recrossed many times the past two years, normally a peaceful trickle of rich brown water winding lazily back and forth over a wide expanse of gleaming white sandbars, was a raging torrent, bank full, throwing up sprays of white foam as it pushed against trees and boulders in its path.

Filled with wonder, Tahchee could only stare, fascinated by the power. "Where'd it come from?" he asked. "It hasn't rained a drop in a month."

"Must of rained plenty on the high plains out west," Daniel explained. "A real toad strangler."

They rested their mounts several minutes, both hypnotized by the awesome sight. Tahchee could see the river come charging from the low hills to their left, twist and turn as if it were a great, angry brown snake crushing its way through the forest below, and slither madly away around the bend to their right.

Whole trees, nine-tenths submerged in the muddy water, bobbed along helplessly. Occasionally, one would snag bottom and the water would pile over it with a renewed fury, boiling high, turning a raging white at the tree's impudence. The tree would try to hang on, but the pounding water would tear it loose, roll it over and carry it away, out of sight around the bend.

Daniel shook his head, emitting a long, low whistle. "Forget about going to Pasuga. It'll take days before we can cross this!"

"We can wait. We've been out here two years now, what's a few more days?"

"That's just the point, Tahchee. We've wasted two years looking for a man with scratch scars on his face. Maybe there were no scars. Maybe that Osage you gutted was him. It's time to bring this foolishness to an end. Head for home. Our people need us."

"You promised," Tahchee insisted, a trifle irritated.

Daniel made a sweeping gesture at the flood below. "We could be home before we'll be able to cross this river. I think somebody's trying to tell us to stay away from Pasuga, don't you?"

Who? God? There was no God. God would never have let an Osage kill his mother.

"We can wait," he repeated stubbornly, noticing also the signs of Daniel's growing impatience. The older man shifted in his saddle, the damp leather creaked.

"Damn it to hell, Tahchee!" Daniel exploded, pounding the saddle pommel with his fist. "It's time to go home! Can't you get it through your head you're never going to find the man who killed Song Bird? Why waste your life trying? The only reason I came in the first place was to keep you from having to marry that Rogers girl. Now that she's married and got a kid, we don't have to worry about that."

"What the hell are you saying?" Tahchee asked, dumbfounded.

Daniel appeared repentant, as if he'd said something he regretted. When he avoided looking him in the eye, Tahchee felt betrayed. How could his uncle have known? Besides, there was no way Laura could know she was going to have his baby between the time they'd...and the time he and Daniel left home. Suddenly, the beautiful memory became ugly. Anger rising, he nudged his mount closer to Daniel's and demanded, louder this time above the roar of the flood below, "I said, what're you saying? Can't you hear?"

"Yes. I can hear."

He waited, wanting to know, but not wanting to hear. Daniel's reluctance to explain pushed his irritation deeper.

"She blabbed around about us, didn't she?"

His uncle's stubborn silence was infuriating. "Didn't she?" he exploded.

"No, Dutch. It wasn't her," Daniel said, his voice low, the words barely distinguishable above the sound of the booming river. "Her old man told me. Said his son saw you and her doing it that day of the cabin raising. He wanted to ask you if it was true. If it was and she come up pregnant, he was expecting you to marry the girl. I put him off talking to you. I told him I'd ask you myself."

Before Daniel finished talking, Tahchee remembered hearing someone that day at the creek. He should have found out who, instead of running away like he did. What Daniel was saying was beginning to make him feel uneasy.

"I decided I'd rather see you dead than throwing your life away fathering a kid which might not even be yours."

"Just what is that supposed to mean?"

"She could have already been pregnant and looking for somebody to marry. It's as simple as that."

Frustration overrode his anger. Could it be true? She certainly acted like she knew what she was doing. In about ten seconds, he ran every detail of what they did through his mind. Like he'd done a thousand times before, but before it was always late at night and he was able to re-live the incident second by lingering second. Now it was all exploding in his head. He'd been treated by everybody like he was a little boy, ignorant, stupid, naive. Everybody. Including this man he'd trusted all his life. He turned away, unable to look him in the eye any longer.

"I'm sorry, Dutch," he heard him say.

He wouldn't even call him by his right name any more. What should he do? He stared at the raging river below, only vaguely aware that Daniel was urging, "Let's go home, son. Forget this madness. Forget the girl. Start over—"

"*You* forget!" he flung back. "Forget me! Forget Song Bird! Forget everything and everybody!"

"Now just simmer down—"

"Simmer down hell! What's to simmer down? Go on home, if you want! I never asked you to come in the first place. Remember?"

"Aw, shit!" Daniel spat, making a get-away-from-me gesture. "Do what you want. I'm going home. I've got better things to do."

He pulled his horse around to leave. Frustrated, angry, and hurt, Tahchee sat his saddle trying to decide whether to follow Daniel home or let him go. He took one last angry look at the river. A movement on a toppled tree with its roots still clinging to the bank far below caught his attention. He stiffened.

"Hey!" he called after Daniel. "Look at that boy down there!" He pointed.

"Where?"

"On that tree...the one that's fallen over and laying in the water. See him?"

"I see the tree—. Oh, yes! What's he doing?"

A rising sense of fear for the boy filled Tahchee as they watched. "Looks like he's trying to snag one of those floating melons!"

"I don't believe it! That tree could be ripped loose any second!" Daniel said, a worried look on his face. "Can you see anyone else around close? A grownup?"

He searched for some sign, saw nothing. He shook his head, then tossed the pack horse's tow rope to Daniel.

"I'm going after him...!"

Daniel shouted a warning which he ignored as he flanked his tired mount into action. The horse balked at the crest of the hill.

"Hi yah!" he shouted, angrily popping its shoulder with loose rein ends.

The horse, wild-eyed, leaped into space and landed on its forefeet and haunches. The animal stumbled, recovered and dropped down the hill in a series of running leaps and slides. Tahchee reined furiously from side to side to avoid the larger boulders. He ducked from overhanging limbs reaching out to knock him from the saddle. An avalanche of dead leaves and loose rocks built up behind the plunging horse.

He turned his mount at the river's edge to ride toward the boy, only to face backwater poking up into the ravines and over the low benches, forcing him to make repeated detours into the forest. He wasn't going to make it, he thought. He urged the stumbling horse faster.

His hopes surged as he broke into the clear and saw the tree still clinging to the sandy bank with its roots. He jerked his horse to a pounding stop.

"Hey!" he yelled, his voice lost in the thunder of the flood. He cupped his hands around his mouth and yelled again, louder. "Hey! Get off!"

The boy heard, turned his head, obviously startled. Tahchee motioned, repeating the command in Cherokee, then again in English. He searched for an Osage command, couldn't find the words. Instead, he frowned and increased his motioning action.

The boy—about seven or eight, he guessed—wore only a loin cloth. A colorful band about his head kept his long hair from his face. An Osage, probably, from a village nearby. The tree shifted, yielding to the push of the river, its roots loosened. Chunks of the sand bank plopped into the swirling water.

It could go any second! He shouted again, louder, with more authority, motioning with more emphasis. Instead of coming his direction, the boy scrambled further away, into the branches.

Crazy kid! He had to get him off. He swung from his saddle, bounded to the tree, fought over the wad of roots and ran along the wet trunk toward the tree's branches. A surge of water caused the tree to make a slight roll. Tahchee's boots slipped on the wet bark. He leaped, caught a branch, his legs dangled in the rushing water. The current dragged at him as he struggled to pull himself up. He worked his way through the branches toward the boy. The youngster, wide-eyed and afraid, kept inching farther away, balancing himself on limbs so limber they sagged under his weight, almost touching the water. Realizing now that he was scaring the boy, he paused and held out a hand.

"Come!" he begged. He forced a smile, trying to show friendliness. The frightened youth glanced around wildly, then his eyes focused on something upstream.

Tahchee took advantage of the diversion, whatever it was, to work himself closer. The sagging branches threatened to dunk him, but he was almost there.

Then he noticed the boys eyes, even wider with fright and still riveted on something coming at them. Tahchee took a quick look and saw the huge log which the river was shoving straight at them.

Save yourself! a thought screamed. Instead, he made one last lunge for the boy, grabbing a handful of hair the instant the log plowed into the tree. Water boiled over them, foaming with anger as it ripped the tree loose from the sandy bank.

They went under. Blind now and holding his breath with a booming in his ears, he tightened his grip on the boy's hair and whipped an arm about a big limb. The muddy water he'd swallowed wanted to come up, but he held his breath, hoping the boy would do the same. When the tree stopped tumbling, he struggle toward what he thought was up, dragging the boy with him. Moving with the current now gave him an eerie feeling they weren't moving at all.

He had to have air. Another second and his lungs would win, pulling in water. The big tree's lower limbs scraped bottom, the current churned, giving the tree another half roll before it broke free.

Suddenly, they were in daylight again. He sucked in huge gulps of air, then lifted the limp boy and shook him violently. The boy coughed, spewed out water between pitiful cries, his eyes wide with fright. Then the boy's tiny arms whipped about his neck in a lock-tight hug.

"That's it! Hang on!" he shouted above the thunder of the flood. "We'll ride it out!"

He glanced around. They were in mid stream, both banks flying by, faster than a horse running. The tree seemed stable now. As long as no limbs touched bottom, he concluded, the tree would not roll again. He threw a quick look upstream, hoping to see Daniel coming, riding hard along the bank to keep up.

Nothing, only the forest charging by and disappearing behind them. They swept around a bend. Daniel probably thought he drowned. Forget Daniel. The boy began to cry, his wiry body jerked with huge sobs. Tahchee patted him.

"It's all right," he said. He hoped his voice, even not understood, would have a calming effect. He wasn't sure just how calm he sounded himself. His own hands shook from excessive exertion and fear.

They rounded another bend and the bobbing tree headed straight for a half submerged boulder in mid stream. Tahchee tightened his arms around the boy.

The tree smashed into the rock, hung there. The water piled over them. He knew they would both drown in the heavy wave unless the tree broke loose.

The force of the water pulled at the boy. He felt his own arm around the tree limb weakening. That ugly thought came back—let the boy go and hang on with both arms.

But he couldn't. He stiffened his back against the weight of the crashing water. His strength was going, fast. Then he felt the tree turning. The water caught it broadside and they were free, bobbing up in daylight again, both gasping for air. The force of the rushing water was once again reduced to zero as they rode along with the current.

His belt—a white man's belt. Why not use it to tie himself to the tree? No. If the tree caught and made a half roll, he'd get pinned under water.

He considered trying to swim for shore. One look at the tumbling brown water between him and either bank told him he could never make it.

His only hope was to stay with the tree and fight the river. Somewhere, sooner or later, the tree might be driven into a bank, or an island, and he could scramble off. But suppose they floated all night? Already the sun was low, so low that at times they rode the current in the complete shadow of the trees lining the bank.

The boy shouted something. He was able to understand only a word or two. Tahchee patted him again, trying to reassure him everything was all right.

How ironic! An Osage sinks a tomahawk into his mother's head, and here he is, risking his own life to save one of their sons!

But a man always does what he has to do, Daniel always said, for he can never hide from himself. Daniel? He'd find the horse and see the tree was gone. He'd search downstream a day or two, then give up and go home.

Laura. That lovely long hair, her long legs, her beautiful face, and the way they shared their bodies. No longer his now. She belongs to another man. Even has his kid.

No time for that kind of thinking. He jerked his thoughts back to the present. The river swept them around another bend. The land on either side flattened. The water spread out, seeming to slow its pell-mell pace. Then he saw the village ahead on higher ground. The boy pointed, screamed something. Tahchee guessed it might be where the boy lived.

It was a slim chance. He climbed as high in the branches as he dared, stood, balancing himself with each foot on a slippery limb. One bump in the raging current and he'd be gone.

As the tree bobbed past the village, he waved and yelled at the top of his lungs. Then he tore the boy from his neck and held him high. The boy waved and screamed.

People in the village began pointing in their direction. Grim relief flooded through him when he noticed men running toward their ponies. The river carried them out of sight. He dropped quickly down among the branches, renewing his grip. He'd cut his luck thin, standing up like that.

The thought that the Osages might help renewed his determination to hang on. But how could the Osages from the village help? He had to believe they must have something in mind, the way they broke for their horses. Maybe the river made a loop here. The riders would cut across and be waiting somewhere ahead.

He kept searching both shore lines hopefully. He noticed they were, indeed, making a wide loop, for the low sun moved almost completely around them.

Whatever the Osages had in mind, he knew he'd have to be ready.

But he wasn't ready for what he saw dead ahead; the river piling into a high sandstone bluff. Evidently, the spot was one of those place where the river normally nudged against the bluff's base, pooled, then slipped away to the right, making a harmless ninety degree turn. Now, however, the enraged river tried to climb the rock, flinging up sheets of white foam spotted with all kinds of flood-driven debris.

Even as he watched with mounting horror, he saw a tree smash its roots against the bluff. The water stood it upright, then just as quickly swallowed it out of sight.

The thundering roar increased as they rushed toward the rock with seeming increasing speed. This was it! He tightened his grip on both the boy and the tree, determined to fight the river to the end.

Then he saw them—Osages lining the top of the bluff, dangling ropes down its face.

His heart leaped. One chance in a million! He scrambled forward in the tree's branches. Once again, he balanced himself, disregarding caution, for he would have only one chance. He held the boy in the crook of his left arm.

"Hang on!" he shouted, but his voice went nowhere in the tremendous roar they were rushing into.

He saw the Osages above trying to position at least one rope at a spot where they guessed the tree might hit.

The rock came at them with breathtaking speed. He knew he had to time this just right. Leap too soon, and he wouldn't make it. Wait too long, and the jar of the tree smashing into the rock would throw him off. He focused his eyes on a single rope, concentrating all his thoughts on the brown strand laying against the water-lashed bluff.

A split second before the tree hit, he leaped. His fingers closed on the rope as their bodies crashed into the rock. His air went out, his body numbed, his grip weakened. The tree's branches speared into the rock all about him. Limbs snapped and leaves flew. A jagged end of a broken limb stabbed into his side, pulled at his clothing, trying to knock him loose. He threw all the strength he had into his grip on the rope.

The river raged with more fury as it spun the tree and slapped its trunk against the rock. Water piled over the tree, reached up to get him and the boy.

It was too much. As he slid down, he fisted the rope with even more strength. He felt the hide peel from his palm. Then he hit a knot and his arm nearly separated from his shoulder as the rope began dragging him upward with increasing speed.

They broke free of the river. The rock's jagged surface tore at his knuckles as the men above pulled them upward. Could he hold on? He looked up, loved every single one of the Osage faces peering anxiously at him over the edge. They were pulling him up swiftly, hand over hand. He welcomed the eager hands snatching at his wet shirt, pulling them, finally, over the edge.

Somebody pried the crying boy from him. He let go and lay panting on the rock, thankful to whomever. Every muscle in his body ached. He began to wretch and shake violently. He could actually feel the rock's tremors as the river continued to throw its fury against the bluff below. The noise drowned out everyone's words as the Osages examined the boy and talked excitedly.

Then some of the men turned their attention to him. He sat up, coughing water. His hand was bleeding, both from the rope burns in his palm and from his lacerated knuckles. The painful throbbing in his arm dove deep into his shoulder. He tried not to, but he was unable to keep from vomiting.

When he was through retching, the Osages helped him to his feet. His knees were so weak he would not have been able to stand without their support. Most of the men had their heads shaved with a single feather dangling from their top-knots. He knew how easy it was to grasp the hair and take the scalp. He had done it once…a very, very long time ago. His first kill.

He heard someone mention the word "Cherokee." They knew. So? He pushed free from those supporting him and stiffened proudly.

"I am Cherokee," he admitted.

One of the Osages pointed and spoke in barely distinguishable Cherokee.

"You Cherokee," he said, then turned the finger on himself. "I Old Hop. I know Cherokee talk. You tell Old Hop how you save life of boy."

He studied the old man, curious most of all over how he learned to speak Cherokee. Old Hop, as he called himself, was a scrawny man, bow legged, and bony. His head was too big, making his long face the most dominant part of his appearance. His hair, splotched with gray, lay flat and strung down to his shoulders. Why didn't he keep it shaved like the others? Was he even Osage? The old man acted quite comfortable in his position as the one in charge of the group. His strong voice carried well over the booming noise of the flood, but Tahchee's did not. Old Hop led the way to a spot some distance from the cliff's edge where they could talk.

After a quick, furtive look at all the faces, checking for scared scratch marks and saw none, he explained how he spotted the boy on the tree reaching for floating melons; how he had ridden hard to get him; how he had gone onto the tree when the boy refused to come off.

Old Hop listened, nodding when he understood and frowning at words he didn't understand. He kept repeating those words until Old Hop would nod and smile. When he finished the long story, Old Hop said, "It is a good story. I tell others."

As the Osage talked, the others listened with rapt attention. By the time *this* story made the rounds, Tahchee thought, he would be a mighty hero who swam the river to get to the boy, fought off giant water dragons, and leaped twenty feet through the air to grab the dangling rope.

He smiled to himself when he saw the boy, clinging tightly to the neck of an Osage, listening with wide-eyed wonder at the story's telling as if he hadn't been a participant in it himself. When Old Hop finished, Tahchee pointed to the horses.

"I need a horse. I go find my uncle."

Old Hop shook his head. "You come with us."

Now what? Did this mean he was their prisoner? He squelched an urge to walk away. Then the boy leaned toward him, holding out his arms, a deep love written all over his face.

He was unable to resist. He took the boy and was thrilled by the tight squeeze of those small arms around his neck. The boy said something. The men laughed and nodded at one another. Tahchee glanced at Old Hop for an interpretation.

"He say he want you for his father," Old Hop said, grinning.

He knew the remark was only the boy's way of saying thanks. But, all the same, he felt embarrassed, wondering if any of these men might be the father. Old Hop motioned for him to follow and led the way to their horses. He obeyed, for he had no choice.

They all remounted, except one. The man held his pony and gestured for Tahchee to mount up with the boy. He nodded his appreciation and understanding and set the boy on the horse's bare back, seized a fistful of mane and tried to vault on. He was weaker than he thought and nearly fell. The Osage caught him, gave him a boost. He felt weak and ashamed.

At a word from Old Hop, a couple of men rode away at a fast gallop, evidently to tell others in the village the boy had been saved. By the time Tahchee's group entered the settlement, people streamed from their lodges and pressed close.

He began scrutinizing each and every face, hoping. Hungry dogs barked at the horses' heels. These dwellings seemed more permanent than those of other Osage villages in which he and Daniel had lived. The dome-like structures were scattered everywhere in the bend of the river. Most were about head high if you were standing on a horse, and about ten steps across from front opening to rear wall. Some even had rolled up skins over the entrances which were obviously used as drop down doors, giving occupants privacy.

He saw no scratch scars on any of the faces and, although disappointed, relaxed. The men who participated in the rescue rode proudly, shoulders back, as if they were the heroes. Old Hop led them straight toward the largest lodge, located in the center of the village. A tall man emerged, stooping to get through the opening.

He had a round face—with no scars—a long nose and thick lips. His heavy eyebrows seemed heavier because of his shaved head. He was bare to the waist. Several necklaces dangled from his neck, some were made of glass beads strung together and some were made of bear claws, some brightly colored stones, and some of polished pieces of wood. A gaudy medallion dangled from the longest necklace. Bands of shiny metal circled the man's arms above each elbow. He wore tight fitting deerskin pants with elaborate thonging down the seams. Each moccasin carried identical patterns of stitched-on glass beads.

When the man neared Tahchee's horse, the boy leaped into his outstretched arms and clung tightly to his neck. The man spoke and Old Hop interpreted.

"He say for you to get down. He say you come in his lodge."

Tahchee hesitated, wary, then shrugged. He slid from the horse and followed the man into the lodge, with Old Hop trailing behind.

Inside, it was gloomy, almost dark. He caught a whiff of burned fat. He could make out a buffalo robe bed beyond the dying fire. The man lay the boy on the bed, then sat cross-legged beside him. He motioned for Tahchee to sit. Still apprehensive, he settled down, duplicating his host's posture.

"How are you called?" the man asked through Old Hop.

There was something about the man that made Tahchee want to trust him. Perhaps it was because of the way the boy hugged him. "Tahchee," he admitted. Then after Old Hop translated and he saw no particular reaction from his host, he added, "Some call me Dutch."

The Osage's eyes opened wide in surprise, then narrowed.

"Dutch? I have heard of you. Then it is true. You are Cherokee and not Delaware?"

"It is true."

"You are dressed as a white man."

"Many Cherokee's dress like white man."

"Why? Do you love white man?"

Tahchee had no answer. Silent, he searched for one, going back to his earliest memories. Why did they dress as white people in their home? Daniel never told him the answer to that. All their neighbors did. There were the Billingtons who lived in Round Springs Hollow; they were white. Did he love them? Hate them? No. Daniel always said neighbors were neighbors, people you lived with, people who helped at haying time, sat up with when someone was sick, ate dinner with on Sundays after church.

The man, impatient, said, "Osage at war with Cherokee."

"I know."

"I have just returned from a trip to try and bring peace between our people. My son drown in river, my people say. But Old Hop send word. Cherokee save my boy from drowning."

The Osage stared, his dark gaze burning into Tahchee. He tried to see behind those dark eyes. He waited, thinking, *They will kill me.* The man appeared to arrive at some sort of a decision.

"I am called Clermont."

Tahchee's quick intake of breath was audible before he could smother it, but he knew Chief Clermont noticed his unconcealed surprise. He nodded, respectfully recognizing his host's rank.

Apparently satisfied with the proper respect, Chief Clermont launched into a lengthy speech, pausing frequently to allow Old Hop to translate.

"Clermont is grateful to you for saving the life of my son. Even though you are Cherokee, Clermont say you earn right to become Osage. You are free to come or go, as you please, but Clermont would consider it a high honor for such a brave man to live in his village."

Tahchee was able to control his emotions better this time, showing no surprise over learning Clermont was the boy's father. That had been obvious, thinking back. Becoming an Osage was another matter. He chewed on his underlip, giving the offer deep thought. They knew he was a Cherokee. And if this Clermont was as smart as Daniel said he was, what would he be up to?

Chief Clermont patted his son's wet hair before explaining through Old Hop.

"Clermont wants his only son to grow up and be brave Osage. But Clermont also wants him to learn white man ways. The old days are gone. Our children must live in a world with the white man. They are too many. Many Cherokees already live like the white man. You would be a good teacher for my son. You stay?"

His initial reaction was: Why should I saddle myself with such a responsibility? He glanced at the boy. The lad crawled across the buffalo robe and snuggled onto Tahchee's lap.

Aw, hell! How can a man turn away a boy's love? Before he could restrain himself, he responded by wrapping his arms about the little life in his lap. When he looked up, he saw Clermont grinning.

"I will make brave Cherokee my brother," he said. "No Osage will harm Clermont's brother. All Osage respect the bravery of the one called Dutch."

How do you plan to find the man with scratches on his face, Daniel had said. *Go live with the Osages?*

This was a perfect set up. He could hardly contain his excitement when he said, "Two moons. That is all. Then I must return to my people."

"It is agreed. When two moons are gone, we talk again."

"Agreed," he said and slid the boy from his lap and stood. "Now I must have a horse. I must go find my uncle. He will think I drowned in the flood."

When Old Hop related the request, Clermont scowled, shook his head.

"The sun is gone. I will send men with you at first sunrise. We find your uncle and bring him here."

Tahchee wrestled with an inner impatience, but knew the Osage Chief made sense. Besides, he was beginning to feel the effects of complete exhaustion. He settled slowly onto the buffalo robe bed beside the boy, feeling aches and pains in every muscle and bone of his body. He resigned himself to do as they asked, ate what they brought and accepted a place to lie down on the buffalo robe beside the boy as men gathered around the fire to talk again about how the brave Cherokee fought the flood and saved the Chief's son from drowning.

Soon, he fell into a deep sleep, listening to the dull roar of the raging river in the distance and the muted talk of men close by.

It was late when another man entered the lodge, a powerfully built man with features resembling Chief Clermont. The angry look on the man's face brought the talking to a sudden halt. Chief Clermont rose slowly to his feet.

"Black Dog has returned," he said, the statement simple, but the tone cool. He waited for a reply. When none came, he asked, "What is it my brother wishes?"

Black Dog scowled, then fixed his dark eyes on the Cherokee asleep on the robe beside the boy. Firelight glinted off the scratch scars angling down his left cheek.

CHAPTER 11

Daniel moved without thinking, his mind troubled, tormented, and focused on self abuse as he built a small fire. When the blaze had burned long enough to make a bed of coals, he set a porcelain coated pan filled with water against the coals. Soon the water began to boil and he dropped the last of his coffee grounds into the bubbling liquid. He set the pan aside to let the coffee cool, not wanting to drink any right now. Then he dug out a piece of dried deer meat and sat staring at the food in his hand, not wanting it, either.

He may as well accept the fact Tahchee was gone. He lay the unwanted food aside. His nostrils stung. He blinked moisture away to clear his vision.

He knew from the beginning this foolish search was going to come to a no-good end. Before ever leaving Arkansas two years ago, he'd made up his mind to die for the boy, if he had to, to save him from being killed by a savage Osage. But this—! There was no enemy to fight. He stared across the pitch black void covering the thundering flood racing blindly by in the night. He pulled in a deep, shaky breath.

Wasn't that just like Tahchee? Jumping on that tree to save a child without giving it a second thought? He pounded his clenched fist on his knee in a frustrated, helpless anger.

Goddammit! He should have known better! I *tried* and *tried* all of his life to get him to stop leaping before he looked! What good did it do?

He ground his teeth in frustrated anger. He could feel the force of the river shaking the earth where he sat, taunting: *No man can withstand my mighty power. Not you, nor Tahchee, not even God.* Daniel lifted his tear-streaked face to the starry sky.

"I'm sorry, Song Bird!" he cried aloud. More tears stole from the corners of his eyes. His attention centered on the star between the ones he'd set aside for his mother and father. Now he knew it was her.

"I send your son...Forgive me...I tried to be a good brother to you...I tried to be a good father to your son...I tried...I tried..."

He was afraid to look longer, afraid he'd see yet another star there; one brighter than all the rest, for it is the young ones who make the brightest stars. Eyes closed, he let his chin descend slowly to to rest on his heaving chest.

"I tried...and I failed."

He let himself slide into a trance, let his inner turmoil join with the rampaging flood, with the blackness of the night, with the vastness of the universe, with the stars of the dead.

His communion with nature brought an inner peace. Nothing changes in a constantly changing universe. Children come from you know not where. We live to do we know not what. In the end, all die. Nothing has changed since the creator of all things sent his divinity to live in water and fire and give fertility to earth and man. The twinkling stars are equally bright for everyone lost in the dark. Tahchee had tried to bridge both worlds—his mother's, a people devoted to living with nature; his father's, a people dedicated to conquering nature. Such a bridge can never be built, for neither race understands the other, nor will they ever.

His mind slowly edged into reality. He stared at the smouldering sticks, their red-coal ends busy making more ash. He could feel the power of the flood coming from the ground, climbing his spine. You don't try to fight nature, for you can never win. Time is on its side. The root of a tree can split a rock. If man sees himself as a part of nature, he will live forever. If not, he is forever doomed.

Tahchee! Oh, Tahchee!

He crossed his legs, grasped his ankles and inhaled several deep draughts of the night air, letting them out slowly. Soon, he was in control. He reached for the porcelain pan, blew on the steaming fluid several seconds and sipped cautiously.

He made his decision. He would return home and lead his people against the Osages. There was but one way to make this country safe for women and children, families like the Rogerses. They would whip the Osages like they did at Three Forks when they chased them out of Arkansas. Since Clermont was too stubborn to go back to Kansas like the treaty said, the Cherokees had every right to attack Pasuga and wipe them out. Every man, woman and child. They were nothing but savages and they understood only one language.

He felt mean and ugly inside thinking like that. But he'd lost Song Bird, and now Tahchee because of the Osages. It was a mean and ugly world. He lifted his eyes again to the bright star. This time, he searched for Tahchee, but found nothing.

He scowled into the blaze at his feet, uncomforted, and took another sip of coffee.

Foolish legends!

Tahchee led the search party along the north bank of the flooded river, unable to cross and knowing Daniel would still be on south bank. It was hopeless. All he could see across the wide expanse of water were tall trees and wooded hillsides. Trying to spot a man on a horse from that distance was time wasted. By mid-afternoon, he pulled up and sat astride the Osage pony, staring across the flood as Clermont's escort grouped behind him, waiting his decision.

"It's hopeless," he said to Old Hop. "We might as well go on back to the village and wait. He'll come across when the river goes down."

Old Hop shook his large head. "Uncle think you drown. He no look long."

"You're probably right. He was wanting to go home anyway."

He turned his horse around and headed for the village. His escort strung out behind. And Daniel was probably right about me, he thought, winding up being dead. So what? What else is there? Laura? Not even her. He'd like to have her again. Love her? Perhaps. Only he did not know what love was. Did anybody? Old Hop was talking again.

"Your Uncle. He a white man?"

Tahchee shook his head. "No. He's a full blood Cherokee."

"You dress like a white man. You know white man talk?"

"Yes. I—"

"I know white man talk, too," Old Hop announced proudly.

"You do?" he said. "Then let's talk white man talk. It's easier for me."

Old Hop nodded and switched languages to ask, "If you're not a white man, why do you dress like white man?"

He shrugged. "I don't know. Some Cherokees do. Some don't. They teach us in our schools that our people were among the first to meet the white man when he came to this country from across a great sea. That was two hundred years ago. Our people and their people mixed. My mother married one of the white men."

"Then you're a white man and not a Cherokee?"

"I'm both."

Old Hop chuckled. "You the best of both or the worst of both?"

A good question. He forced a smile but did not join in Old Hop's mirth. But Old Hop had left an opening. He decided to explore it, by using one of Daniel's favorite phrases, "There's bad people everywhere. Bad white men. Bad Cherokees. Bad Osages."

Old Hop nodded his huge head. "Half-white Cherokee speak the truth."

"I saw a bad Osage once. He had scars across his face—like he'd been scratched in a fight. Do you know of such a man?"

Old Hop's surprised look told him the old man did, indeed, know something. Old Hop touched one of his ears.

"Did he have part of his ear bitten off?"

His heart jumped, filling his throat. This was better than he hoped! He had no idea about a missing ear.

"Yes. That's the one," he said quickly, nodding.

"You speak of Black Dog. He's Clermont's blood brother. He's our number one warrior. You know Black Dog?"

He'd found his man! He resisted an urge to wipe his suddenly damp palms on his trouser leg which would expose his feelings. He pretended to cough dust from his throat.

"No," he said between his cover-up coughs. He tried to think of a good story, how he came to know Black Dog. He made the story purposefully vague.

"I just saw him once—" and added more vagueness "—when I was a boy."

He felt uneasy at the old man's silence. He tried to ease away from his knowing Black Dog by encouraging Old Hop to tell a story.

"How did Black Dog get scratches on his face and an ear bitten off? He fight with lion or bear?"

Old Hop kept his eyes fixed on the trail ahead when he answered.

"He did not have any scratches on face when you were a boy."

Damn! Trapped with his own words. He tried not to show any reaction.

The less said, the better, he decided.

Old Hop continued in a matter-of-fact tone, "Black Dog said he got scratches on his face when Cherokee War Party sneak up on him when he asleep with his friends. Black Dog said he fought Cherokee War Party single handed. He said he killed them all. His only wound was when one of the Cherokees fought like a woman and scratched his face."

Then his burning gaze swung on Tahchee. "How did you know about the scratches?"

His gaze locked with the old man's. Let him guess. What difference did it make? He'd be facing the lying son of a bitch as soon as they returned to the village anyway. Old Hop's level gaze never wavered as he continued talking.

"Black Dog is angry at Clermont for making Cherokee his brother. He take warrior friends and leave last night. He said he was going to collect the treaty money from soldier. He tell his brother that Cherokee better be gone from Pasuga when he comes back."

Another jolting surprise. From what Old Hop was saying, the man with scratch scars on his face had been there last night while he lay sleeping on Clermont's bed!

"What did Chief Clermont say?" he asked, bracing himself for the wrong answer.

"Nothing."

So? Now what? Anything could happen. One thing for sure, he thought, he'd found his man. He urged his mount into a faster pace, anxious now to get back to the village.

Neither of them spoke for a couple of hours. Then Old Hop asked, quite suddenly, "How many moons is two hundred years?"

Tahchee, surprised at first, laughed. He searched his mind for a simple way to explain the time span, then gave up. He shook his head, still laughing. Old Hop joined in the fun.

"Is Old Hop more than two hundred years?"

He saw that he had to make a stab at explaining. "Your father's father was a boy one hundred years ago. Two hundred years is..." As he talked, he realized how much he missed the long talks he'd had with Daniel; that time really didn't exist outside of one's self. Just when he thought he might be getting through to the old man, they were back at the village.

When Clermont's son saw them, he came running. Tahchee leaned down and swept the boy up, rested him on a hip. The boy jabbered excitedly, pointing at himself.

"Honekahsee! Honekahsee!"

Tahchee shot Old Hop a questioning look, unable to make out the boy's meaning. Old Hop translated.

"He's telling you his new name. Honekahsee. It means Pretty Nearly Drowned."

Tahchee had to laugh, for to reasons; the name's meaning and because the incident reminded him of his own foolishness when he blurted out his own name. Still holding the boy, he slid from the pony and started to reenter Clermont's lodge where he'd spent the night. But Honekahsee tugged on his hand, wanting to go another direction.

"Honekahsee say he want to take you to your new lodge." Old Hop explained.

Feeling honored, but undeservedly so, he let the boy lead him through the village to a lodge. He hesitated before entering. This wasn't right. He knew some poor family had to give up their home to make room for the Chief's new brother. And he doubted if he'd ever find out which family made the sacrifice. He glanced around. A few of the younger people in the village were watching, but none of the older folks.

Still, he hung back, resisting Honekahsee's pull. He finally decided: *This assignment to his own home could be Chief Clermont's answer to Black Dog's ultimatum.* Perfect! He let the boy drag him through the opening.

It wasn't a large lodge, but neat. And standing just beyond the cooking fire was a young girl. He froze, surprised and puzzled, studying her. She was slender with long black hair framing a beautiful oval face. Her dark eyes were large and luminous. The customary deerskin dress she wore hung loosely from her shoulders, further concealing her age beneath its loose folds. There was a slight smile on her full lips, a smile that, somehow, seemed sensuous. His face suddenly felt hot and he knew he was blushing. Honekahsee let go of his hand and ran to the girl, talking excitedly. The girl answered, then returned her level gaze to Tahchee's face—and the smile broadened.

"Who are you?" he asked in English, scowling, then changed quickly to Cherokee and asked again. Her unaltered expression told him she understood neither language. Somebody stepped through the opening behind Tahchee. He turned, saw Old Hop.

"Who is she?" he demanded, jabbing a thumb toward the girl.

"It was decided last night. Brave Cherokee who saved Clermont's son and become Osage deserves a lodge of his own. Little Tassel is an orphan. She will take care of woman work in your lodge."

Stunned, he studied the smiling girl. Or was she a girl? Just how old was she? An Orphan? His woman? What did that mean exactly?

If it meant what he thought it meant, he told himself, it wasn't right. To honor him by furnishing him a place to live was one thing; to force an orphan girl—.

"I—" he stammered, intending to tell Old Hop he wasn't having the girl. On the other hand, was he assuming the wrong thing? After all, she was just a girl...wasn't she?

He gestured helplessly and mumbled what he thought was the Osage word for "Thanks."

CHAPTER 12

Sporadic rain drops thumped on the domed roof of the lodge. Tahchee, restless from being cooped up, stood in the entrance and stared into the rain. His emotions ranged from deep fear to deep hate. Wanting to kill a man and doing it were two different things. The runner that morning brought the message he'd been waiting to hear—Black Dog was returning, with soldiers.

He fidgeted, trying to bleed off hyper energy. It did no good. He turned from the entrance and went to the fire. He warmed hands which didn't need to be warmed, then turned his back to warm his buttocks which didn't need to be warmed. Although the temperature had dropped since the spring rain began, it still wasn't what you would call cold.

The unusual chill reminded him how long he had been in Pasuga waiting for the return of Black dog. Since April. Now it was late May.

What would Black Dog be doing bringing soldiers here? The unanswerable question was worrisome, to say the least. Surely, Black Dog would not be using the U.S. Army to get him out of Pasuga. Then, again—

The lodge darkened. Already tense and nervous, he whirled, then just as quickly relaxed when he saw it was only Little Tassel. She carried a bowl of steaming food.

"Where is Honekahsee?" she asked.

He was proud how much his understanding and use of the Osage language had improved. He had learned fast with almost non-stop coaching from the the two of them, Little Tassel and Honekahsee. Old Hop had been a big help too, along with what he'd already picked up the past two years.

"I haven't seen him today," he told her.

Her long hair was wet from the rain, its strands clinging together on the ends.

"Here. Let me have that," he said, offering to take the heavy bowl from her.

"No."

She hurried past him to the fire. She set the bowl on a rock and used a gourd dipper to ladle some of the contents into a smaller, shallower bowl. She faced him holding the smaller bowl in her hands, waiting patiently for him to sit.

Exasperated over her slave-like antics, he put his hands on his hips and demanded, "Will you stop doing that?"

Her face remained impassive. He reached for the bowl. She pulled it back.

"You sit. I serve."

"Look, Little Tassel. I've told you and told you I don't want you to come in here treating me like a slave. Cherokee women don't treat their men like that."

"I no Cherokee. I Osage."

He threw up his hands in a helpless gesture. "We're alone. Nobody can see us. Why can't you just relax for a change?"

"Sit. I serve."

"All right. I'll sit and you can serve. But will you eat the same time I do?"

"If you wish."

He flopped onto the well-swept dirt floor, crossing his legs. He took the soup from her.

Stew again. He waited until she filled her own bowl and sank to her knees, sitting on her legs across the fire from him. He slurped from the bowl, making a loud noise to show he enjoyed the taste. Little Tassel smiled.

"You like?"

He nodded. "It's great." He swallowed more of the greasy liquid. He had no idea what the chunks of meat were. He knew it could be anything from bear meat to snake. It made little difference, for their stew tasted the same, regardless of what meat they used.

He watched her take a delicate sip from her bowl. She kept her eyes lowered respectfully as they slurped their way through the meal.

Just how old was she? he thought studying her closely. When she tied her hair up, she appeared quite a bit older. When she let it fall loose about her face, she seemed but a child. Her deerskin dress was heavily ornamented, and he could only make wild guesses about whether her breasts were large or small, whether her legs were long and lender, or short and chubby. There were times he felt bold enough to demand she remove the dress so he could make an accurate determination, especially when she worked around the lodge with her hair up. He still wasn't certain how she was supposed to "serve" him; to keep his lodge clean, or share his sleeping robe...or both.

Thinking back, he knew what Laura had wanted the first time she looked at him. Little Tassel was different. Besides, he forced himself—one more time—to think: *She's just a child.*

She had the moon-faced features of an Osage; large round eyes, smallish chin and nose; a broad forehead. Her ears, when he'd seen them the times she'd worn her hair up, were oddly attractive, delicate. He'd decided it was the smoothness of the folds in her ears which excited him. Excited? He squirmed in self embarrassment because of the thought, and glanced away to kill the temptation.

After a few long seconds, eyes averted and listening to the raindrops thumping on the taut skin roof, he felt her looking at him. He tried not to yield, but had to. His gaze locked with hers.

There it was—the silent invitation. No doubt about it this time. Like Laura did in the grist mill when he first saw her. When it happened with Laura, there had been no other woman in his life, no experience to guide him. With Little Tassel, there was the remembrance of Laura. Laura was so beautiful, you couldn't keep your eyes off her. Little Tassel was beautiful, too, he decided; but in a different way. A child-like beauty that you knew went all the way down to the core of her being. Child-like? Still...what did it hurt to be friends with a young girl? He set the empty bowl on the ground. Little Tassel made a move to refill it, but he stopped her with a curt wave of his hand.

"No more," he said. Little Tassel, on her knees, settled back on her folded-under legs.

"I go find Honekahsee. We need to take bath today." she said.

"In the rain?"

"Rain will stop. Sun shine soon. You will see."

He shrugged his doubt.

"Will you come with us?" she invited.

"No—"

"Then I will wash you."

When it dawned on him that she was offering to give him a bath, he felt his face flush. He scowled, cleared his throat and said, gruffly this time, "No!"

He considered giving her a lecture. He should be an expert at that, listening all these years to Daniel. Since Little Tassel was an orphan, so he was told, he was experiencing a growing sense of responsibility toward her. But he still had doubts about the orphan story. He'd never bothered to find out which lodge she lived in, or who with. She came and went, sometimes being there in the morning before he awoke. And there were times when he'd have to order her to leave at night before he stripped and crawled into his buffalo robe bed. She was very thorough with her work, which he appreciated. She kept the fire alive with ash-covered coals on warm days, and with fresh sticks feeding a tiny flame as the nights brought in the chill. She brushed the floor, leaving the dry earth so clean he could walk on it barefoot and not carry sand grains to his bed. And once a week, she'd hang his sleeping robe over a pole outside, letting the bed sun and air.

She irritated him, too. He had to keep a close eye on his clothing, for she'd snatch up his spare trousers and shirt and be off to the river with them before he could stop her. He tried to explain his woolen garments were not the same as deerskins. Drying wool shrank, deerskins did not. And every time when it seemed he had worn his clothes long enough to where they felt comfortable, he'd come in to find she'd been to the river with them again. He wondered at times what she would be like taking care of a real home—like theirs back in Arkansas. Would she be as proud of that shiny new cook stove as Song Bird was?

Song Bird.

The memory hurt and hate surged through him again. He would kill Black Dog slowly—after he told him who he was. Slowly. Very Slowly. Bare handed.

"You need a bath," Little Tassel told him, jerking him back to the present.

Stunned by her blunt remark, he stared, his chin sagging as he tried to think of something appropriate to say. He knew communal bathing was a way of life with the Osage, but had never participated since he'd been living among them. Now might be a good time to give it a try. However, she made him feel as if he were a little boy, standing over him this way. Then anger seeped in.

"I'll take a bath when I feel like it," he growled, frowning up at her.

"You smell. 'It is those white man clothes. They smell like a wet dog. I will make you new clothes out of deerskins."

He scrambled to his feet, glowering down at her. She stood her ground before him, a slight smile on her lips. He shook a finger in her face, saying, "I'm damned if I'll run around with nothing but a pair of britches on, half naked—like your men do!"

Her dark eyes shifted from shoulder to shoulder.

"I would like to see you that way sometime. You are a beautiful man."

"You get on out of here!" he said angrily, pointing at the doorway. "Go on! Get!"

She turned away with an amused look on her face. At the entrance, she paused and said over her shoulder, "If Honekahsee come, bring him to the river. You both need a bath."

He made an angry motion. "Get!" he commanded.

She gave him a teasing smile, then disappeared. He felt frustration piling in on top of his anger—anger which wasn't anger at all. Just a show, designed to frighten a recalcitrant child. He began pacing, worried. Then, to soothe his feelings, he sat down and commenced sharpening his knife, the stroking actions and steady sound of metal against stone a pleasant sensation, the feel of the steel's sharp edge filling him with a desire to plunge it into Black Dog's guts.

The room grew lighter. He glanced toward the entrance. She was right—the sun was coming out. Remembering what she had said, he lifted an arm to sniff. Right again. He did smell. Maybe he should try to find Honekahsee and go take a bath.

Just then he heard voices. The hubbub increased. He heard creaking leather. Saddles meant soldiers. It was him! His blood raced. He sheathed his knife and stood.

At long last, he was going to meet his quarry face to face. He was sorry that Daniel couldn't be with him, to share in finding their man. He hurried to the lodge doorway, hesitated, and drew in a deep breath. He felt strange, elated yet fearful, knowing exactly what he wanted to do, yet not knowing how to do it. Or, worse, when. He stepped outside.

The first action which caught his attention was a soldier dismounting in front of Chief Clermont's lodge. Nearby, a huge Osage slid off his own mount to stand beside the solder. Other Osages in the arrival party remained on their horses in a semi-circle behind the two. Chief Clermont came out with Old

Hop following.

Chief Clermont exchanged smiles and nods with the large Indian. Tahchee could see the resemblance. Black Dog. He felt his scalp tighten, a tingling sensation raced up his spine. He squinted, trying to see scratch scars on the man's face, but was unable to make out any from this distance. He did see, however, the mutilated ear, which told him enough.

The soldier extended a hand and Chief Clermont responded, acknowledging the greeting, white man style.

He was unable to hear and edged closer, stopping at the edge of the crowd now gathering. Now he could get a good look at Black Dog's face, and he saw them. Three long scars down his left cheek...*Song Bird's mark!*

A peculiar feeling stole over him as he studied the man who killed his mother. He was a big man, broad shouldered and strong. Although he had his head shaved Osage style and looked like a savage, there was air about him that made him stand out from all the rest.

As from another world, he heard the soldier saying, with Old Hop translating, "I come in peace, representing my government. I come to discuss the terms of the Lovely Treaty, which you signed. You gave up this land. Our government will pay much money. Yet you have not moved. What are your plans?"

Chief Clermont waved, using both arms to make a grand motion. "Why move? This a big land. We at peace with the Cherokee. I show—" and he craned his neck looking around until he spotted Tahchee. He motioned. "Come, my Cherokee brother."

Tahchee, feigning a look of total innocence, elbowed his way through the ring of people and stood beside Clermont. He caught the surprised look on Black Dog's face. He could not take his eyes off the scars. His heart thumped, too hard, he knew. He fought to bring his feelings under control and was only vaguely aware of Clermont putting his arm across his shoulders.

"See?" he said through Old Hop. "Cherokee my good friend. He save life of my only son. I make this brave Cherokee my brother. Now he is Osage."

The army officer's blue eyes burned into Tahchee.

"Do you speak English?" he asked, his voice sharp.

Tahchee nodded, not intimidated. "I do."

"What the hell's going on here?" the soldier snapped.

"Who wants to know?" Tahchee asked, matching the officer's irritating demand.

A suspicious look crept across the soldier's face as he studied Tahchee, repeatedly slapping his loose rein ends in the palm of his gloved hand.

"I think that should be obvious. I represent the United States government," the soldier answered. "But for your personal information, the name's George McCall. Captain George McCall."

CHAPTER 13

Tahchee's mind leaped from the hate of Black Dog's world into the hurt of Laura's. Filled with curiosity, he stared at the handsome army officer with a certain degree of bitter jealousy. How could she have done this to him? Didn't that day at the creek mean anything to her? He wanted to hate this man, her husband, the father of her child. But how could he? He was innocent of any wrongdoing. He wanted to invite him into his hut, introduce him to Little Tassel, and ask him about Laura. It was with a sudden shock that he realized the captain was waiting for him to say something.

"And why are you so interested in me? Why I'm here, a Cherokee?" he finally asked.

"There's talk, ugly talk, among the Cherokees. They claim the Osage is holding one of their people captive. A man called Dutch. If you're here against your will, now's the time to say so. Otherwise—" He broke off and shrugged.

Tahchee glanced at Black Dog, caught the dark eyes boring through him. What had Black Dog told the U.S. Army? He shifted his attention back to the soldier.

"What Chief Clermont told you is true," he said.

Captain McCall nodded. "I'll take your word for it, for now. But I warn you, if I find out your presence here is the cause of this war, I'll have you arrested and removed by force."

Hot anger flowed through him, but before he could tell the Captain to go mind his own business, Black Dog spoke to Chief Clermont in Osage.

"Why is the Cherokee still here?"

"Cherokee is my friend," Chief Clermont said, his tone cool, but firm.

"He is Cherokee! Cherokee do not belong in Pasuga!"

Chief Clermont's face darkened. "It is I who decide that!"

"The Cherokee is the enemy of all Osage people!" Black Dog's own anger rose. "How can we destroy them if we make them our friends?"

"That might be the best way to stop the war!"

Black Dog was silent a moment, then leered. "My brother fears the mighty Cherokee. He make treaty. Give up our land for money. I go get money treaty say is ours. White man does not have money. White man make fool of my brother. Cherokee come live in Osage village and make fool of all Osage! I do not like being made a fool!" He motioned in the direction of the warriors behind him. "My friends do not like being fools!"

"If you don't like what I do, you can go live somewhere else!" Chief Clermont said, slicing the air with a hand. His voice was bold and authoritative. "Young Cherokee save my son from drowning in flooded river. I honor his bravery by making him Osage. I make him my brother. He will stay. I have spoken."

The aside conversation in Osage and in obvious anger brought a questioning look from the Captain. He asked Old Hop, "What are they talking about?"

Old Hop pointed Tahchee's direction. "Black Dog does not like to see Cherokee in Osage village. He wants him to leave."

Captain McCall returned his attention to Tahchee and said, "The government has spent a lot of time negotiating with the Osage. We are trying to get them to move north and open this land for your people. You don't seem to be helping matters being here. I think you should go."

Tahchee scowled. "You can go straight to hell! I have as much right here as Black Dog!"

McCall's tight smile turned into a sneer. "Bull shit!" he spat. "These honorary tribal memberships don't mean a damned thing!"

"Not to a white man, because that's exactly what they are—honorary! But to an Indian, honorary relatives are just as valid as the birthright."

Chief Clermont demanded of Old Hop. "What do soldier say to my brother?"

"Soldier tell Cherokee brother to leave Pasuga."

Chief Clermont's face clouded. "Tell soldier this is Osage village. He have no right to insult Clermont's new brother," he said, his words to Old Hop were harsh and to the point.

When Old Hop translated, Captain McCall's face reddened. He swallowed nervously before replying, "Tell Chief Clermont I apologize. Tell him I come in peace. I come only to inquire why the Osage people have not moved north as they agreed."

Old Hop translated and Chief Clermont's reply through Old Hop was hostile.

"Soldier's apology not good. My brother, Black Dog, go to Fort Gibson to collect money from soldier for white man part of the agreement. Has Black Dog returned with the money?"

"The money will come," McCall said lamely. "White man government in Washington must vote on money first. This takes time."

A sly smile spread across the chief's face. "Osage people live here long time. If white man government want more time, Osage wait."

Captain McCall threw up his hands, then glared at Tahchee as if he were the cause of the government's treaty problems. Tahchee turned aside, letting the soldier know he could care less about the army's troubles. Black Dog spoke to one of his mounted men.

"Take soldier to my lodge."

The Osage slid from his pony and escorted Captain McCall away. Black Dog watched until the two were out of sight, then faced Clermont.

"I take soldier back to Fort Gibson," he said. "Many Cherokees move on Osage land from Arkansas. I take warriors and chase them back. I keep Osage land free of Cherokee until white man government send money."

"The money will come, my brother. There is no need for war."

"Black Dog men want war. I will lead them."

"If brother make war, Cherokee will make war."

"Then we will kill them," Black Dog said darkly. He shifted his burning gaze to Tahchee and said, "When enemy attack Osage, will new Osage brother be brave enough to fight?"

The insult stung. Tahchee wanted to ask, "Brave enough to fight men or kill women?"

But before he had a chance to say anything, Black Dog turned and stalked away. The mounted Osages followed.

Chief Clermont, watching them leave, said, "My brother is angry. Be careful."

"If Black Dog attacks, I will defend myself."

Clermont appeared uneasy, shifted his weight from one foot to the other, then apologized.

"Black Dog is a good man. Something happened two snows ago. He is not the same brother."

The Osage's words brought a strange chill. Until now, he suddenly realized, he had been motivated by a desire to reverse time, to convert a horrible reality into a bad dream. The image he'd been searching for had no feeling, did not bleed, did not suffer, knew no pain. In contrast, Black Dog was real. He was big. He was strong. He could fight...He could also kill.

The thoughts stirred his emotions, his senses focused. The element of danger added a new dimension to his two-year search. Revenge, sweet revenge, was the only possible way to right such a terrible wrong.

A tug on his sleeve distracted him. It was Honekahsee.

"Let's go play ball," the boy begged.

The simple request seemed so out of place at the moment that he had to laugh. Honekahsee was a spoiled brat if he ever saw one. He knew if he'd interrupted talk between adults like this when he was Honekahsee's age, Daniel would have given him a tongue lashing he'd never forget. He shifted his attention back to Clermont, sought unasked permission to leave. Chief Clermont's indulgence was written all over his face. He waved them away. Tahchee yielded to the boy's tug and allowed him to drag him away.

They found a boy's game already in progress at the edge of the village. He was thankful, for now he would not have to play himself. The boys welcomed Honekahsee, each side wanting him on their team. Tahchee had to laugh when he noticed that Honekahsee chose the team which offered him the best stick.

He was content to watch. It was a brutal game when grownups played. Each side could have any number of players. They scored by carrying a tight leather ball in a netted pocket on the end of a heavy stick across their opponent's goal line. The defense used any means to stop a scoring threat, including breaking the bones of the ball carrier with their heavy sticks, before he could pass off to a teammate. When younger boys played, however, the game was nothing more than a contest of keep-away, with just enough action to create a lot of yelling and screaming. Tahchee stood with arms folded, remembering when he was their age and the many times his nose was bloodied playing the game…also the times he had drawn blood from his opponents. The point was to win…and he was on the side that won most of the time.

He saw a couple of young girls emerge from the timber beyond the ball field. They circled the players on their way back to the village. As they walked, they kept running fingers through their wet hair trying to dry the strands. Obviously, they had been swimming…bathing? With Little Tassel? Was she still at the river? Curious, he skirted the playing field and headed for the timber lining the river bank.

He could hear feminine laughter, heard water splashing. She had told him to bring Honekahsee, hadn't she? Why not? Besides, Little Tassel was his lodge woman, wasn't she? It would be a good opportunity to see how old she was, once and for all; give him some idea how to treat her.

The game behind him had deteriorated into a shoving and shouting match. When Honekahsee threw his club down in disgust and came to Tahchee, he said to the boy, "You look hot. How about a swim?"

"Yes! Will you go with me?" the boy panted.

He hesitated, then said, "I'll go with you, but I don't think I'll go in."

He draped an arm across the boy's shoulder and they made their way through the stand of timber toward the water. The laughter grew louder. He slowed, having second thoughts, but Honekahsee tugged harder.

"That sounds like Little Tassel and Gray Mouse. Let's hurry."

When they reached the 10-foot high rock ledge overhanging the water, they could see two girls in the clear water. One was, indeed, Little Tassel. He could see the shimmering underwater image of her naked body. She was older than he thought. He felt hot.

"Dutch! Honekahsee!" Little Tassel called, motioning. "Come on in."

His throat felt tight and his voice pitched a little too high when he explained, "Honekahsee's been playing ball. He's sweaty and dirty. He needs to wash off." Then before he could stop himself, he lied, "I—I didn't know you girls were here."

Honekahsee was already kicking out of his britches. "Come on, Dutch," he said and tugged on Tahchee's hand. He held back, suddenly embarrassed.

"You go ahead. I'll get on back to the village. The girls might not want me—"

"Come on in with me. Little Tassel and Gray Mouse won't care. I want them to see how good you can swim. Like the time you saved me from the flood."

Tahchee found it hard to believe how the rescue story kept growing. He tried to relax, but still resisted Honekahsee's pull, wanting to look at the girls, but still afraid to do so.

"Come on in, Dutch," Little Tassel called again. "It's nice." She settled slowly into the water until everything but her long hair was part of the shimmering image. She resurfaced and wiped the water from her face with her hands. "See?" she said. Her innocent laughter made him want to strip and dive in.

Honekahsee let go and ran across the rock and jumped in feet first, holding his nose. He made a big splash, spraying water on the girls. He came up coughing and spitting. The girls splashed water on him in retaliation, and the water fight was on.

Looking down on their play, Tahchee could not help but visualize himself standing naked before them, aroused. An ugly image, like some rutting buck.

Just then, more boys materialized out of the timber. Their stickball game was over and they began stripping for a fun bath. Some of the boys were not so young, Tahchee noted. Well, if it was the custom…

He discreetly turned his back as he removed his white man's clothing. Then he spun quickly and dove into the water behind four or five of the boys leaping and diving from the overhanging rock.

He welcomed the icy chill. It cooled his hot blood. He stayed under, swam to the bottom, and turned lazily to put his feet down. The gravel tickled his toes.

The water was so clear, he could see for several yards in all directions, naked bodies everywhere. Surface waves broke up the sunlight, distorting gyrating arms and legs. Bright spots danced across the gravel bottom. Then he saw Little Tassel make a surface dive and come swimming toward him, a smile on her face. Tiny bubbles were stringing from one corner of her mouth. Her breasts were much larger than he first thought. She swam close, then reached out to put both hands behind his neck, suspending herself upright before him, unashamed.

His lungs fought against his will not to breathe, for he wanted to stay forever in this underwater wonderland. He placed his hands on Little Tassel's waist, enjoying her youthful beauty. Then he could wait no longer. He kicked against the bottom. They floated upward together. Their heads broke the surface at the same time.

He gasped, pulling in great lungfuls of air. Gray Mouse and Honekahsee swam to them. The boy, tired now from treading water so long, grabbed Tahchee's arm and locked his legs around his waist. Gray Mouse nestled against his back, holding on also. He had to paddle furiously to stay afloat.

"Hey!" he said, spitting water. "I can't hold all of you up! Let go before you drown me!"

Little Tassel took a deep breath, let go of his neck and went under. He felt her hand sliding down his body and fondle him gently, almost as if it were a caress, sending a strong tingling sensation throughout his groin and racing up through his chest. His breath caught. It was no accident, he knew. Or was it? He had to know. He reached up to take Gray Mouse's arms and pull her loose from his neck. Honekahsee kicked free and swam for shore to join in a game of tag the other boys had going.

Tahchee sucked in a couple of deep breaths and settled underwater again, sinking slowly to sit on the gravel. He saw Little Tassel surface for air, then dive again. Gray Mouse followed. Both girls played about him, the dancing sun rays adding delirious highlights to their beautiful young bodies. He felt himself beginning to swell, wanting Little Tassel.

This is wrong! Angry at his lustful thoughts, he pulled his feet under him and pushed toward shore, swimming underwater away from the girls. He surfaced at the rock ledge.

Honekahsee had not joined in the tag game after all. Instead he was standing on the rock hugging himself and shivering.

"I'm cold," he said, his teeth chattering.

"Me, too," Tahchee said and worked his way to where he could climb out. The girls followed, climbing the bank. He kept his back to them and hurriedly pulled on his trousers. He wrapped his wool shirt around Honekahsee and held the boy close to keep him warm.

The girls struggled to get into their deerskin dresses. He trued to make his glances their way appear casual.

"We're going to go on," he said to them. "See you at the village."

Leading Honekahsee away, he found himself wishing—but for what? More like a yearning.

One thing for certain, he knew there was no way he would ever forget seeing Little Tassel in his arms underwater, a floating dream in the broken sunlight.

CHAPTER 14

Daniel rode at the front of the column of Cherokee soldiers heading west. It was a loose formation, but a formation nevertheless. He was proud of each and every man. They had laid aside their axes and awls, unhitched their teams from their plows and wagons, gave last minute instructions to their young children on how to care for their livestock, taken down their long rifles from pegs over the fireplace, kissed their wives goodbye, mounted up and rode off to war.

Yes, war. They had been more or less waiting for him when he returned home. There were those who told him story after story of being burned out, their livestock either driven off or killed...and they told him stories about those who had not lived to tell stories of their own...of entire families either being burned to death or hacked to death trying to escape.

The vote to carry the war to the Osage was only a formality, Daniel recalled grimly. What this would mean to the Lovely Treaty, he could only speculate; really didn't care at this point. There wasn't but one way to settle the score with the Osage—go whip hell out of them...again.

"Where we going to hit them first?" William Rogers had asked after the vote had been taken.

"Where it hurts the most," Daniel shot back. "Clermont's home village—Pasuga." And to himself, he added, "If it hadn't been for Pasuga, Tahchee would still be here."

Later, to the assembled militia, he briefed his men on their plan of attack. "We will use essentially the same battle plan we used at Three Forks. Those of you who were there, know what that was. For those of you who weren't: Men with bows and arrows will move in first under concealment; surround the village. But if that's not possible because of cover or any other reason, you are to get in as close as you can without revealing your position. When I give the signal—a call of the rain crow—" and he demonstrated just make sure they understood—"Every man with bows will start shooting arrows at once, and keep shooting them until I lead the charge of men with firearms. We will all engage the enemy with our knives and tomahawks, even shooting them at point blank range, if necessary...Any questions?"

"What about the women and children?"

Daniel did not know the man who asked the question. He countered with, "There's no doubt in my mind we'll find plenty of farms between here and Osage country where the Cherokee families, including women and children, have been shot, burned, or mutilated. When you look at a few of those, any feelings you might have for women and children of the savages will go away real fast, I assure you."

Silence. He took his time trying to read as many of the faces before him as he could. He saw the anger. Most, he knew, had already seen such a sight, or had heard of one.

"Any more questions?" he asked.

There was none. Then he made the usual announcement. "I want only those of you who are fully committed to make the trip. If there is any with any shred of doubt, I would prefer he turn back now. None will hold it against him."

All agreed it was a good plan, especially when attacking a village. The shower of arrows coming in from a concealed foe demoralized the enemy and hindered him from getting organized for a counter attack.

No one turned back. Daniel led the hastily organized army into Osage country, staying out of sight in low lying areas where possible. He avoided crossing over any of the rolling mountains unless their skylines were covered with a heavy stand of timber which would provide suitable cover.

Once, with William riding at his side, Daniel remarked, "I'm more concerned about being spotted by an army patrol than I am being seen by the

Osage."

"That's a possibility. They've brought more troops in since you've been gone," Williams said. "I guess you heard they've built a new fort out here in Indian Territory?"

"Fort Gibson?"

"Yeah."

"Yes. I heard. Where's it at?"

"It's near where the Grand River empties into the Arkansas."

"Well, we're a good forty, fifty miles north of there. I hope we get in and get out before word gets back to Fort Gibson. The way I see it, the army'd have a hard time pinning the attack on us if we can all be back on our farms before they come looking for us."

After a few minutes, Daniel said, "You shouldn't have come, William. It might be best if you turned back."

"What are you talking about? I got as much a stake in this as anybody," the surprised newcomer to the area said.

"I understand your daughter is married to an army officer and is living at Fort Gibson. If we meet up with a patrol and have to shoot it out…"

"The odds are, we won't. I'm staying."

"How're you going to keep it from her that you were involved when the news gets out?" Daniel asked, concerned.

"We don't see her much," William confessed. "Besides, I doubt she'd tell her husband anything about us. They don't appear to be that close, from what I've seen. I think he knows the baby's not his. My guess is, he knows she tricked him into marrying her. Seems an awful thing to say about your own daughter, but it's the truth."

What did he mean by that? He swung his gaze to William, tried to read his face. William nodded and answered the silent question. "It was one of them premature births, if you get what I mean."

There was still an unanswered question he wanted an answer to. He decided to be blunt. "You think it's Tahchee's?"

"I don't think. I know. She told me it was. That was after you and Tahchee was gone. I tried to get her to go stay with her aunt in Texas and have the baby there. Say she was married to your boy—I mean your nephew, and say he got killed fighting the Osage. If she had of, that's the way it would have worked out. Instead, she got that soldier to marry her somehow."

That made him feel bad. The Rogerses were fine people. Now that things turned out the way they did, he wished they'd stayed home and Tahchee had of married the girl. At least he'd be alive. And he could have acted the part of grandfather to Song Bird's grand—"

He had to know. "Is it a boy or girl?" he asked.

"What?" William asked, momentarily puzzled.

"Laura's baby. Is it a boy or girl?"

"Oh. It's a girl. She's a doll. Looks a lot like her mother. You can tell by looking at her she's more Indian than white. Dark hair, and the most beautiful eyes you ever saw. Light complexion. Like all mixed bloods, they seem to inherit the best of both. I ought to know. All our kids are better than either one of us, both in beauty and brains. With Laura being only half and that soldier white, the girl'd be more white than Indian. She's not. You can tell that just looking at her. I understand your boy—your nephew, I mean—was half, wasn't he? That makes the baby a half, too."

"What's its name?"

"They call her Dacy. After his mother in Philadelphia, Laura said."

"Dacy. That's a pretty name. I'd like to see her."

"I bet she'd like growing up to know you, too."

Just the thought of Tahchee having a daughter was exciting. He'll live through her. Daniel, feeling good over the thought, said, "Soon's this war blows over, I'll make arrangements to meet them. McCall's the name, isn't it?"

"Yeah. George McCall. *Captain* George McCall. Don't forget the Captain. He's a proud man. I guess he's got a right to be. He some sort of high muckety-muck at the post. Works for the General, he tells me."

Daniel dropped out of the conversation mentally, his mind conjuring up visions of getting to know Tahchee's daughter, of loving her, even telling her the truth someday. He rode on in silence, leading his men deeper and deeper into Indian Territory, which the Osage claimed belonged to them.

They crossed the Cimarron at dusk and found a place near a lagoon to bed down for the night.

"No fires," Daniel ordered. "And get a good night's sleep. I figure we'll be there early in the morning."

Each man dug into his saddle bags for food and sat silently with his friends chewing on dried meat and crusty bread. They drank water from leather bags lined with pig bladders, the containers making no sounds when carried like metal containers did, even when muffled.

They slept under light blankets, used more to keep the dew off than for warmth. Daniel lay on his back and sought out his favorite set of stars. Still only three. Where was Tahchee's? He'd have to find one for him, so he could point it out to his daughter when she got older.

Dacy. What a beautiful name. He was already falling in love with her. If only he hadn't been so protective of Tahchee. Made him do the Christian thing—be responsible for his own actions...

Troubled, he was thankful when a south breeze full of dampness pushed in a layer of clouds that blanked out all the stars in the sky. He slept fitfully, every rock and hump in the ground growing into monstrous size before he was forced to squirm about trying to find a more comfortable position.

CHAPTER 15

When Tahchee first awoke, he sat up, looked about, puzzled and confused by the amount of daylight in the lodge. Where was Little Tassel? Before, when he slept late, she was there to awaken him. He heard morning sounds outside, people busy with their daily chores, children laughing at their play. Slowly, it came to him how late he'd really slept. Feeling guilty, he scrambled from the robe bed and reached for his threadbare trousers.

They were gone. *She did it!* He cursed, kicking off his buffalo robe cover. Just then she came in with a proud smile on her face and carrying a new pair of deerskin trousers draped over her arm. Although angry, he instinctively snatched the robe to cover himself.

"What'd you do with my pants?" he asked.

"I have you a new pair. I throw the old ones away. They stink."

He heaved a sigh of resignation. "Well, let me have them so I can get out of bed." He tried to make himself sound angrier than he really felt. She was right. His worn out white man clothes did smell sort of rank. The only washing they'd gotten in two years before coming here was when he was caught out in the rain or crossing a river holding onto the tail of his horse as it swam across. She handed him the trousers, then stepped back to watch.

"Turn around," he demanded.

She giggled. "You are a funny man," she said, but did what he told her to do.

When her back was turned, he slipped from his bed and pulled on the deerskins.

"They fit perfectly," he said. "You can turn around now." She did. "How do they look?"

"Gray Mouse mother say they too big when I was making them. Your legs are bigger than I thought." She felt of his thighs. "Are they too tight?"

"No. They feel good. A bit snug, maybe. But that's the way I like them."

"I finish top tomorrow."

"You mean I'm supposed to run around like this all day? I look like an Osage, if I had my head shaved."

She clapped her hands and laughed. He chided her with, "That's what you been wanting to do all along, wasn't it?"

She circled behind him and gathered his long hair. "Not all Osage shave heads. I tie yours back here. Then you look like Osage."

He threw up his hands. "All right. Dress me up any way you want, if that makes you happy."

She pulled a thong from a pocket and tied his hair behind his neck. When she finished, he reached for his boots. In their place was a pair of moccasins.

"Where's my boots?" he said, anger rising. "I hate moccasins. I've always hated moccasins. I'd rather run around barefooted than wear a pair of these!"

She acted frightened. "I trade boots for enough deerskins to make pants and shirt."

"Well, you can just trade back, girlie. Tell whoever you traded them to I want them back. I'll swap him something else for his deerskins."

"You tell," she said, wide-eyed.

"Show me who he is, and I'll durn sure do it," he said as he strapped his knife about his waist and slipped his feet into the moccasins."

She appeared about to cry and he put his arm across her shoulder. "You did good, Little Tassel. I'm going to like these deerskins. But I have to have my boots. I'll pay him well to get them back, all right?"

She gave him a nervous smile and an impulsive hug with her arms about his waist.

They left the hut together. It had been over a month now since bathing with her, and he sensed their attraction for one another was growing; in little ways, the touch of her hand; their exchanged, often lingering looks—not to mention her soft for-him-only smile.

She was young, yes, he had concluded, but not too young. For some odd reason, he felt a need to protect her instead of scheming to take advantage of their relationship.

But just what were his feelings? Was it a father-daughter relationship? Sister-brother? Or...was it love?

He was even more mystified by his own actions. What was he doing? Waiting for Black Dog to return? Or staying in Pasuga because of Little Tassel? Clermont himself had said yesterday, "Black Dog make bad things happen to my people."

"What makes you say that?" Tahchee had asked.

"Word comes. He burns homes of the Cherokee. He kill women and children. This is not Osage way."

He came within an inch of telling Chief Clermont why he was there, that he had reason to believe Black Dog murdered his mother and he intended to kill him...or be killed by him.

"Can't you order him back to Pasuga?" Tahchee asked hopefully.

"I send word. Tell him to come back. He does not come back. I fear for him. The soldiers will capture him. They will hang him. Then they will say we do not get money like the treaty says. They will drive us north anyway."

Before dropping off to sleep last night, he was overcome with remorse. He should be home helping his own people, for Black Dog might not ever return. He could be killed, or captured and hung. Perhaps the best thing for him to do was leave Pasuga for good. Not tell anybody. Not Little Tassel. Not Clermont, nor Honekahsee nor Old Hop. Just leave.

Daniel had tried to tell him. He wouldn't listen. He'd go tomorrow, he told himself as he drifted off to sleep.

Now it was "tomorrow." Walking along beside Little Tassel, he felt comfortable being "half dressed," as he put it. He noticed that people didn't pay any attention to him, as they had been doing.

Men strolled about, gathering in clumps for casual conversation before drifting apart and moving on. Women busied themselves around open cooking fires, yelling commands at their children and chasing slinking dogs away from prepared food. Some of the older ladies sat in the sunlight repairing clothing, scraping fresh hides, or patiently kneading fat-oil into curing skins to make the furs soft and pliable for family use.

A peaceful scene, he thought. He was finding it more and more difficult to believe it was an Osage who killed Song Bird. He finally concluded that it wasn't an Osage who killed his mother, just a man who happened to be an Osage. Like Daniel always said. To the Osage, Cherokees are invaders; invaders from the east, just as the white man had pushed from the east against the Cherokees in the lower Appalachians. Cherokee pioneers moved west and settled in Arkansas, cleared land, planted crops, built permanent homes—just as the white man had done to the Cherokee back east. Today, Daniel said, Cherokees think the Osage attacks on Cherokee settlements nothing more than a primitive love for savagery, just as the white man thought of the Cherokees back east. Here, we want the Osages to move so we can have this land. The comparisons Daniel had made were beginning to make sense and they gave an uncomfortable feeling every time he thought about it.

What was the answer? He shook his head, trying to push the curious and troublesome thinking from his mind. He made a mental note to suggest to Little Tassel that they go swimming today—somewhere away from a crowd, just the two of them. That would help him forget.

He heard a rain crow calling and wondered why it was calling so early in the morning.

Just then a whispering sound descended from the sky. A shower of arrows spiked into teepees, huts, the ground all around.

"What...?" he froze, filled with disbelief. He searched the sky for an answer. Then saw the puzzled fear in Little Tassel's face.

A woman screamed and he saw her attempting to pull an arrow from her daughter's chest. The little girl coughed blood and collapsed. People scrambled. Women caught up their children and ran for cover. Men dove for weapons.

Then it hit him. They were under attack! Who or what, he didn't know, nor cared. He grabbed Little Tassel by the arm and ran, dragging her back to his lodge. Inside, he shoved her toward his robe bed.

"Stay here!" he shouted above the rising clamor outside. He snatched up his long rifle and bolted outside. He saw the knot of men gathering near Clermont's lodge, and ran to join them. One was pointing in the direction of high ground to the west.

"Over there! In those trees!" the man yelled.

"Pawnees?" another suggested.

"Clermont? Where's Clermont?"

"We need Black Dog and his men!"

To hell with them, he thought. Somebody, anybody, had better do something. And damned fast. Just then, another shower of arrows came hissing from the sky. One pierced a man's throat, others fell. Guns cracked. Tahchee saw the smoke fingering from a stand of trees on the hill.

"Let's go get 'em!" he yelled, his Osage words still awkward, but effective. Without waiting for an answer, he ran toward the trees. The men hesitated for only a second, then whooped and followed.

He could see the shadows in the timber now. He saw, too, the guns pointed at them, saw the fingers of flame and smoke. Hot lead cut down two men. He kept running, thoughts churning as he estimated the time it took for the enemy to reload. When that time was up, he yelled, "Down!" and hit the dirt, belly first. The others followed his example an instant before the guns cut loose again. The hot lead balls whistled harmlessly overhead. He leaped to his feet.

"Now!" he shouted, waving them on as he ran up the hill. They made it to the timber, crashing into the underbrush before the attackers could reload.

Under cover of the brush, he froze, listening. How many were there? Had he led the Osages into an impossible situation? He'd heard the talk...The Pawnee was tough to beat when it came to hand to hand combat.

His tension increased at the sounds of battle going on all around. Death grunts. Victory yells. Bodies crashed through the underbrush. Gunfire. Tahchee tightened his grip on his rifle, moved cautiously, gaze searching. He heard Old Hop whoop.

"They run!"

"After them!" he heard another Osage shout.

Suddenly relieved that they had won the skirmish, he raced through the forest, eager to join the rout. He caught sight of a fleeing figure. He pulled up, took quick aim and fired. He began reloading on the run.

Suddenly, he sensed danger from behind and whirled. A figure exploded from the brush with a raised tomahawk. Tahchee reacted instinctively. He whipped out his knife, sidestepped the lunging figure, and plunged his blade in the man's belly.

The force of the man's charge carried him past Tahchee, even jerking the knife from his grip. He fell belly down in the tall weeds. Tahchee leaped, rolled him over to get his knife. Not until he had yanked it free did he look at the man's face.

"Daniel!" he gasped, horror choking the word from his throat.

Daniel's pain-filled eyes tried to focus as his uncoordinated hands fumbled aimlessly to find the wound in his lower chest.

"Dutch?" the voice gurgled, a disbelief showing in his face.

Tahchee nodded, swallowing. His mind screamed, "No! No! No!" He flung his weapons away, knelt and cradled his uncle's head in his arm. Blood pumped from the wound. The world blurred. He hugged the only father he ever knew, crying uncontrollably.

"Why?" he sobbed.

The sudden silence filled him with a sense of helpless panic. He shook the dying man.

"Daniel?" he begged, desperate.

Daniel's eyes were closed, his breathing stopped, then started again with a jerk. Tahchee felt his own heart being ripped apart with unbearable grief.

"Oh, God. Don't die! Please, don't die!"

Daniel's eyelids fluttered open, his gaze searched wildly, then became fixed on Tahchee's tear-streaked face.

"Dutch?" he whispered, as if he were seeing him for the very first time.

He leaned close. "Yes," he answered softly, his eyes filling. "It's me."

There was no answer as the eyes closed again. Choking back sobs, he shook his uncle gently.

"Uncle Daniel—?"

With a seeming great effort, Daniel opened his eyes again. This time, they did not focus as he groped for Tahchee's arm, found it. He began feeling, his grip weak. Then, seemingly satisfied, he smiled and relaxed.

"Thank God, my son. You're not dead after all. I'm glad I found you," he said, each word fainter than the last. There were more, whispers, "Dacy is your…"

The final word that came out was followed with a long sigh, what was left of his last breath.

"Dacy? Dacy is my what?" he asked completely mystified and hoping against hope he would answer. But he knew there would be no answer—ever. Although Daniel's eyes were still open and his jaw kept working as if he were trying to talk, Tahchee had felt the life go out of him. He hugged the limp form to his chest and began rocking to and fro.

"No!" he moaned, shaking his head. "Oh, God! No!"

A thousand futile thoughts crashed through his mind. *Why did I have to know he was coming at me? Why couldn't I have taken his tomahawk in my own skull instead?*

What kind of man am I?

The answer that came told him he was nobody, a being without form.

Dacy? Dacy is my what?

Someone laid a hand on his shoulder. He was still too numb to react.

"You hurt?" It was Old Hop asking.

He showed Old Hop Daniel's face.

"He's a Cherokee," he mumbled, wanting so desperately to blame somebody else for this terrible mistake.

"We know," Old Hop answered. He settled to one knee beside Tahchee. "They gone. But they are many. They may return. We go now to village. Protect women and children." He stood to leave, then paused to ask. "Dutch come, or not?"

Without a word, he lifted his dead uncle, draped the limp form over one shoulder and headed for the village. Old Hop stared, then ran to catch up.

"Where you go with dead enemy?"

He barely heard, made no answer. Old Hop said, "We have our own dead to bury. People get angry when they see you bring in a dead Cherokee."

When Old Hop clutched Tahchee's arm trying to stop him, he flung the hand away angrily. Old Hop, a bewildered look on his face, fell behind.

In the village, returning warriors, many of them wounded and bleeding, pointed, dark scowls on their faces as he strode past lodges heading for his own, carrying Daniel, not caring what they thought. He got a blurred vision of Chief Clermont holding up a hand to stop the group of angry warriors closing in behind.

In his lodge, Little Tassel stared in shocked surprise as he lay Daniel's body on the robe and sat cross-legged by his side, silently begging forgiveness over and over and over. Why hadn't he gone home when Daniel wanted him to? Why couldn't he have drowned in the flood? Daniel had said chasing Song Bird's phantom killer was foolishness. It was worse than foolishness. It had been tragic.

He lifted his tear-streaked face to the hole in the ceiling and the blue sky beyond.

"But I found him!" he moaned, more apologetic than boastful. He rocked back and forth with hell tormenting his soul to produce a new kind of anger; anger now at a real person. He knew now what that person looked like, knew the sound of his voice, knew he needed killing if any man ever needed killing. He lowered his gaze and focused his eyes on his uncle's now pasty-white face, studying the peaceful expression he saw there.

"I'll get him," he spoke aloud to make the repeated vow more binding. "I'll make him die twice. I'll—"

Little Tassel placed a hand on his shoulder and dropped to her knees beside him.

"He's dead," she whispered.

"No!" he shouted, turning on her fiercely. "He will never die! I will live for him. I will make his name a great name!"

She was cringing from his anger and he was sorry he frightened her. But before he could apologize, Chief Clermont came in, his shoulder bleeding from a bad wound.

"You bring dead enemy to Osage lodge. Men angry at Clermont's new brother. I tell them I find out why you do this terrible thing."

"He's my uncle and I killed him."

He heard Little Tassel's soft gasp, felt her sympathetic squeeze on his arm. Chief Clermont's eyes reflected compassion, but his face remained stony. Tahchee saw the barely perceptive nod before returning his gaze to Daniel's body. Clermont's strong voice was soft when he said, "Osage warriors go now to chase enemy. My people understand if brave brother do not join War Party."

He shook his head. "I cannot fight my own people."

Clermont touched his shoulder. "Osage understand," he said, paused, then added, "I go now to lead my people in war. If Clermont die, will Cherokee brother see after my son?"

"Yes," he said, hardly realizing what he was promising. His own voice sounded strange and far away.

Clermont left. It seemed only minutes, but he knew it was several hours before Little Tassel said, "We should bury him."

He knew it was so. He nodded. She said softly, "Carry him to the burying grounds. I will go find Honekahsee. He will know where to find a digging tool."

He moved without feeling, hoisting Daniel's body to his shoulder. The people who had been left behind watched wordlessly as he carried his uncle to the Osage burying grounds, but none interfered.

Honekahsee brought a white man's shovel, and they were able to dig a decent grave. They placed Daniel in the ground and, before covering him with the fresh dug earth, he spent several minutes standing at the head of the grave, face uplifted, tears stealing from the corners of his eyes as Little Tassel and Honekahsee waited in reverent silence. Finally satisfied with the forgiveness he received from the great spirit above, he gripped the shovel and began covering the body. When he was finished he leaned heavily on the shovel handle.

"I will carve his name on a rock," he said. "I will say on the rock that he was a great Cherokee leader. People will wonder someday why a Cherokee is buried here with the Osages."

He took a deep breath, shouldered the shovel and reached for Honekahsee's hand. With Little Tassel holding to his other elbow, the three, a surrogate family, crossed the ball field and returned to the village.

CHAPTER 16

Tahchee sat alone in his lodge, not wanting to be with anybody, a mixture of grief and anger churning inside him. The village itself was quiet, too quiet, as if the people themselves were honoring his moment of sorrow. But he knew better. Besides himself, only a few old men had been left in Pasuga to protect the women and children. Clermont should have known better than to take every able bodied man with him to go after the Cherokees.

He heard the old men talking during the two days it had been since the attack; about how the Cherokee people being a threat to women and children. The insinuations hurt, but he said nothing. He knew from experience that people full of fear and hate do not think in term of individuals. Like when he was with the War Party chasing the killers of Song Bird, the Osages weren't individuals. Each was part of a force against him and, to destroy the force, he had to destroy its pieces.

That was another time and another place. Black Dog. The man was still free. Free and growing more powerful every day.

The lodge darkened. He glanced up. Little Tassel stood in the entry, waiting for his invitation to come in. He said nothing, dropping his gaze instead to the blank space on the floor in front of him where he'd been staring before she arrived. She came in and settled to the ground before him, on her knees, directly in his line of sight.

"Dutch—?"

For the first time, he noticed how beautiful she really was. Her hair was up, those soft folds in her pretty ears exposed. She wasn't as beautiful as Laura. Too young, probably, her full womanhood yet to come.

"Why do your people and my people kill one another?" she asked.

He shrugged. She said, "I'm Osage. Do you hate me?"

"No," he said, his voice husky from several days of disuse.

"You do not hate Osage?"

"Only one."

"Who?"

"Black Dog."

Her lips parted, a strange look came across on her face. Her reaction made him cautious. After all, Black Dog was Clermont's blood brother, probably his successor as the Osage leader. Also, he knew, in a community such as Pasuga, almost everybody is related to everybody else, either by blood or through marriage. He might be her relative.

"You act surprised," he said. "Do you know something about Black Dog I don't?"

"He offer to take me in his lodge when my mother and father died."

A cold fist gripped his heart. The vision of her beautiful young body covered by Black Dog's was maddening. Most orphan girls grew to become a second wife to the man who provides a home for them, bearing his children, sometimes a mother while she's still a child herself. He had no right to interfere, but he had to know.

"You live in Black Dog's lodge now?" he asked, his voice hard.

Her eyes widened. She shook her head. "I stay in lodge of my friend, Gray Mouse. Her father was a good provider. He say it is all right. He does not like Black Dog."

Relieved, he heaved a sigh, until she added, "But Gray Mouse's father was killed in raid. There is no provider in Gray Mouse lodge. I must go live somewhere else. Black Dog ask once. He will ask again."

"You'll stay here," he said, his command forceful.

She dropped her gaze. He detected a faint reddening in her dark-skinned face. He cleared his throat. "You take care of my lodge like always. Bring your sleeping robe and put it over there." He pointed to an area on the other side of the fire.

Little Tassel turned her face aside, peeked at him from the corners of her eyes, a faint smile on her lips.

"Dutch make good husband—"

"Don't talk crazy," he said, gruff, trying to maintain a big brother attitude.

"I talk crazy because I love you."

He cut off the small intake of air before it became a loud gasp. She was mistaken. Without looking at her, he shook his head.

"No..."

She reached out to put her hand on his cheek to stop him from shaking his head, forcing him to look at her.

"Yes," she stated with determination. "And you know I do."

"You can't! I—" he stammered to a stop.

"You already have Cherokee woman?"

Yes, he did. No, he didn't. He did once, but not anymore. She married a soldier. She had a kid. He felt confused. It had been so long, so terribly long ago. Only two years, but it seemed now as if it were a lifetime. When he said nothing, she dropped her hand from his face.

"You think I'm too young to be a wife. That's it, isn't it?"

He saw the hurt in her eyes. He cupped her chin with a hand.

"Yes," he said, gentle. "A beautiful young girl like you needs a fine young Osage warrior who will live with you always and provide well for his family." Her eyes moistened, and he raced on. "I'm no good for you. I have searched long for the man who killed my mother. That man is Black Dog. Now I must kill him...or be killed."

"No...!" she cried, shaking her head. She tumbled into his arms, circling her own about his neck. Surprised, he looked down into her upturned face, a powerful stirring deep inside. He had a sensation of falling into her dark, damp eyes. Her lips, slightly parted, waited. Slowly, ever so slowly, he moved his arms, his will fighting his reason, to circle her waist and pull her yielding body to him.

He wanted her, wanted her badly. He wanted to kiss her, but before their lips touched, a wild yell outside stopped him.

"What the hell—?" he exploded. He scrambled to his feet, pulling her up with him. He ran to the entry, holding her behind him as he peeked out.

In the dusk, he saw more than he wanted to see.

"Good God!" he gasped.

"What is it?" she pleaded, trying to look.

"The Cherokees. They're back!"

"Oh, Dutch—! What will you do?" she asked, her frightened voice trembling.

He didn't know. Somehow they must have evaded the Osage search party and returned. He knew what they were thinking. Their leader had been killed, and they were intent on wiping out the village, every man, woman and child. Even as he watched, he saw a man sweep up a toddler, swing it by its heels, and smashed its brains out against a pole.

He whirled, pulled Little Tassel to the rear of the lodge, whipped out his knife and ripped the skin wall. He shoved her through.

"Run to the river!" he shouted. "Wait for me at the rock!"

"No, Dutch! I'm afraid!" she begged, resisting his efforts to push her away. He shoved with more force.

"Go! I must find Honekahsee. If I'm not there soon, get in the water and swim downstream. They'll be everywhere looking for survivors!"

Little Tassel tried to hold onto him. He slapped her hand away. Then he turned and ran out the front entry, ignoring the fighting going on everywhere as he raced for Clermont's lodge. He saw the same blood-smeared Cherokee who killed the baby dragging Honekahsee out of the lodge.

Tahchee let go with a wild yell and covered the final yards in two great bounds. The Cherokee released Honekahsee and turned, just in time to take Tahchee's knife, plunged to the hilt under his rib cage.

The man's eyes widened. He gasped for breath. Tahchee felt him sagging on his knife and was glad he did not know the Cherokee by name. He yanked his knife free.

"Dutch!" Honekahsee screamed, pointing.

He spun, threw his arm up just in time to deflect a descending tomahawk. The numbing blow paralyzed his hand, the knife spun away. He swung his left fist, felt the man's cheek bone collapse. The Cherokee wilted.

He grabbed Honekahsee's hand and ran, leaping over the dead, dodging through the village, avoiding the killing and plundering. He tried to shut out the screams of the the women and cries of the children, also the weak war whoops of the old men dying to defend them. He headed for the river.

When he caught sight of Little Tassel through the foliage backing from two leering men, he jerked the boy to a stop, signing for him to be quiet as he forced him to keep low and out of sight. Then he lunged through the brush, hurling himself straight at the two men. Before they knew what was coming, he grabbed both around the neck, his momentum carrying them off the rock into space.

He filled his lungs an instant before they plunged into the water. Both men struggled to free themselves from his arm lock, fighting frantically to surface. He held on, turning upside down at every chance, kicking deeper. His own lungs burned for air. Their fists flailed at his face, their blows softened by the water. Some connected hard enough, however, to smash his nose, his ears, his eyes. He held on with grim determination, tightening his arms about their pulsating throats.

He felt one man go limp, revive and struggle wildly. When he went limp again, Tahchee released him and redoubled his effort to drown the second man. Even when the man was making his last feeble struggles to free himself, Tahchee feared he would never make it to the surface himself.

The instant his head broke free, he gasped for precious air. After one quick look around to make sure the other man did not surface he swam toward the rock where Little Tassel and Honekahsee were waiting.

He was so weak he had to have their help climbing out of the water. He sat on the rock, panting, sneezing and coughing water, willing his strength to return.

"Are you all right?" Little Tassel asked.

He nodded, not wanting to waste valuable energy talking. Honekahsee's eyes shone. "Wow!" he shouted, expressing his admiration.

"Sh-h-h!" Little Tassel cautioned. "I hear somebody coming!"

Tahchee struggled to his feet. He spotted a log nearby. He motioned for the two to follow.

"Quick! Help me get this log into the water!" he whispered hoarsely.

With their help, he was able to roll the decaying tree trunk down the bank and into the water. All three waded into the water, pushing the half submerged log ahead of them.

"Get on the side away from the bank," Tahchee instructed. "And keep your heads below the log. Stay out of sight, whatever you do."

When he was satisfied Little Tassel and Honekahsee were hidden from view, he gripped a snag near the upstream end of the log and kicked away from the bank. As the current caught the log and carried them downstream at an increasing rate of drift, he was able to guide the log, using his free hand as an underwater rudder.

He could hear the searchers crashing through the underbrush. He stopped paddling and let the log drift. Would the spot the signs they made rolling the log into the water?

He heard a man shout, calling a name. Did that mean they'd been seen? He quietly steered the log toward the opposite bank. If they were spotted, they could hit the bank and run for it. They probably wouldn't get far, but it would be worth a try. He could send Little Tassel and Honekahsee on. He'd stay and fight.

But the shouting took a new twist. He could tell by the conversation that the searchers had found one of the drowned men. He hoped against hope the new mystery would take their minds off the drifting log. He decided to stay with it and guided it slowly down the river and around a bend.

He kept going, keeping the log in the middle of the current until darkness closed in and the full moon climbed over the trees in the east. He pushed the log into the bank and helped Little Tassel and Honekahsee climb out.

Both the girl and the boy shivered violently in the cool night air. He pulled them to him, taking advantage of their warmth as well as giving them his. Honekahsee looked up with wonder in his moonlit face.

"You think they killed everybody?" he asked, a plaintive tone of disbelief in his voice.

"No, not everybody," he said, trying his best to console, but not knowing the truth himself. "Let's don't think about that right now. We need to find a place to spend the night, a warm place. Somewhere where we won't freeze to death."

"Then what?" Little Tassel asked, her teeth chattering so hard he could barely understand. He gave her a reassuring hug.

"We'll make our way downstream. They've built a new army post somewhere down there. We'll find it. They'll take us in," he promised, and added grimly, "This war is going to spread."

They found a place to spend the night under a rock overhang.

"It's not much of a shelter," he told them. "But it'll have to do."

"Can we build a fire?" Honekahsee asked, shivering so hard he could hardly talk.

"No," he said. "We'd be found. Here. Let's all huddle up close in this shallow ditch. Our bodies will keep us warm."

He sat down with his back to the rock, set Honekahsee on his lap and pulled Little Tassel up close under his arm.

In a little while, he could feel their warmth and knew they could feel his for they both stopped shivering.

"What's it like living with soldiers in a fort," Little Tassel asked.

"Yeah. What's it like?" Honekahsee echoed.

"It's nice. You'll like it. They have good cooks and warm cots to sleep on."

"Will we be there long?" Little Tassel asked.

"It depends," he said. He hated being evasive, but he'd already made up his mind to head back into Osage country to get Black Dog, just as soon as he got these two settled in a safe place. He'd break it to them after they got there and seen how it was. They wouldn't take it so hard that way. He could come back and get them after he killed Black Dog.

Then another problem occurred to him: Would the army let him, a Cherokee, head back into Osage country? Not likely, according to the way Captain McCall acted. He wouldn't tell them he was a Cherokee. But there was Captain McCall who knew he was a Cherokee, because Chief Clermont had told him. Chances are, however, that he'd still be out in the field, especially with the war breaking out like it was.

But Laura was there, too. Would she recognize him? Doubtful, dressed like he was. Besides, he would be in and out within a day or two. It was a chance he had to take, for he damn sure couldn't go after Black Dog with these two.

"There's just one thing you two will have to remember," he said, giving them both an extra tight squeeze. "Don't call me Dutch while we're there. All right? Can you remember that?"

He felt Honekahsee nodding. Little Tassel asked, "Who will you be?"

"I knew an Osage named Cheho. Call me Cheho."

"Why? I thought you didn't want to be Osage."

He chuckled softly. "You finally got me to be one, didn't you?" he said.

"I don't care what you are...I love you."

"Me too," Honekahsee mumbled sleepily.

"I love both of you too," he said. "Now let's all be quiet and try to get some sleep."

CHAPTER 17

"Dacy!" Laura called and hurried to stop the child before she pulled the bucket of seeds over. She was too late. The bucket tipped, spilling its contents on the planked floor.

"Now look what you've done!" Laura scolded, reaching for her. Dacy squealed and tried to run away. Laura caught her at the opened door, lifted her and set her on a hip.

"I'm sorry," she apologized to the post sutler who was already scooping up the seeds and returning them to the bucket. He was a well-fed man in his fifties with squint eyes and large ears.

"That's all right, Mrs. McCall," he said, forcing a smile, then added in that gravely voice of his, "These are just sunflower seeds. A great seller back east, they say. Have you ever tried any?"

She shook her head. "No."

"People eat them like bird seed. Not bad, either." He held out a handful. "Want to try some? You have to break the hull off."

Dacy reached to get the seeds, but Laura pulled her away. "No, Dacy," she said, and to the sutler, "We don't want any."

Dacy whimpered. She was out of sorts and Laura was wanting to get groceries get back to their quarters. While making her food selections, she kept throwing her long black hair over her shoulder. Dacy, intrigued by the hair tossing, seized a fistful and pulled.

"Stop that!" Laura snapped and swatted her hand.

The child let go and acted hurt for a couple of seconds before she swept the room with her dark eyes, as if she were looking for some other devilment to get into.

Laura returned her attention to her shopping and, frustrated over the quality of goods she was seeing, sighed resignedly. There simply wasn't much to choose from. Most of the supplies arriving at Fort Gibson, either overland from St. Louis or by boat up the Arkansas River, were in bad shape. She'd have to talk to George about it. Maybe he could do something. He could if he'd stayed on as Post Executive Officer instead of accepting a transfer to field assignment. Maybe he'd get his old job back after the General took his sick leave and the new Major assumed command.

George was a fine soldier, but a poor husband. No. She didn't mean that. He was a good husband, but a poor companion, for he was gone from the post so much lately. She examined the contents of four barrels of flour before finding one without weevils working in the yellowish, unrefined powder.

"Give me ten pounds of that," she said, pointing to the opened barrel.

The sutler gave her a condescending smile. "Ten pounds it is, Mrs. McCall. Will there be anything else today?"

"Yes. I want to look at your cured hams."

"Be right with you soon's I get your flour sacked up."

He scooped the flour from the barrel with a battered pan and weighed the purchase carefully. She knew he was probably cheating her, but let him get away with it. With Dacy as fussy as she was, she was more interested in getting back to her quarters than she was in challenging the sutler. She wandered away to look at the smoked hams hanging in a darkened corner.

"The Captain still out?" the sutler called to her across the room.

"Yes."

"Where'd they send him this time?"

"North," she answered, not wanting to talk about it.

The sutler tied the bag of flour with twine and hurried to assist her with her meat selection.

"That Cherokee raid on Pasuga was a bit nasty, I hear. Word is, they wiped out half the village."

She ignored his remarks. She heard all the ugly talk she wanted to hear about what her people did to the Osages. Despite what the gossip was, she knew her people weren't savages. You can hear anything these days. She'd learn the truth of it when George came home. Besides, if the Cherokees attacked Pasuga and did all the things people say they did, they must have had a good reason. Dacy began fussing again, wriggling to get down.

"No!" Laura said firmly, losing patience. She slapped the baby's leg. Dacy blubbered. The store manager waggled a finger at the little girl's face and made noises.

"Kootchie-koo. Kootchie-koo…She sure looks like a full blood instead of a quarter, doesn't she?"

Nosey old bastard, she thought. She refused to comment and busied herself with the hams instead. Everybody knew the child did not belong to George—including George. But was too much of a gentleman to mention it. He never made any remarks the baby's Indian features—just insisted that she be named Dacy, after his mother, who was still living back in Philadelphia.

Her non-answer silenced the sutler. She finished her shopping, retaining her cool composure until she left the commissary. Since the early June weather was so nice, she decided to walk the long way around the square to the officers' quarters. She lowered Dacy to the board walk, holding one hand to keep her from toddling too near the edge. Unusual activity near the post entrance caught her attention. She saw soldiers grouping around three Indians, a man with a boy and girl.

One of the soldiers motioned for them to follow and led the way across the parade grounds toward General Arbuckle's office. There was something about the man…

Refugees from the Pasuga attack? Her thoughts were diverted momentarily as Dacy tugged to get free. When she managed to get Dacy under control again, she returned her curious attention to the tall Indian, the way he walked…

"Tahchee!" she gasped aloud. The sudden word frightened Dacy. She began crying, causing Tahchee to look their way.

Her heart skipped a beat. She knew Tahchee's eyes missed nothing and expected instant recognition. But if he did recognize her, he gave no indication that he did. Deeply disappointed, she glanced down at herself, seeing what Tahchee might have seen. Just another soldier's wife, wearing a white woman's dress and walking a baby…typical for an army post. The disguise was too perfect, especially after two years.

But his quick look reminded her of that first day in the grist mill. She felt her face grow hot, her ears burn. She wanted him then, and she wanted him now.

Was the Indian girl his wife? The boy theirs? Impossible! She picked Dacy up and hurried home. She had to make a social call on Margaret Arbuckle as soon as possible to find out what was going on.

There was something familiar about the tall, dark haired woman he saw chasing the baby on the boardwalk, Tahchee thought and searched through the dusty memories of his mind to place a name, time, and place to the figure. But his mental search was interrupted when he was lead into the General's office with Little Tassel and Honekahsee close behind.

The Major explained to the skinny General, "The men say this Indian told them—he speaks English—that he was in Pasuga when the Cherokees wiped them out. He said he escaped and brought this Osage girl and boy with him. He says they don't belong to him. The girl is an orphan and the boy is Chief Clermont's son. He wants to turn them over to the army for safekeeping until the fighting is over."

"Chief Clermont's son?" the General questioned, surprised.

"Yes, sir," he acknowledged, then asked Tahchee, "Isn't that what you said?"

"That's right," Tahchee said. "Chief Clermont left him with me when he went after the Cherokees. Told me to take care of him."

"I suppose that can be arranged," the General told the Major. "We could turn them over to Mr. Lovely's Indian orphanage in Fort Smith."

"Isn't the girl a little old to be sent to an orphanage?" the Major questioned.

The General eyed her, then asked Tahchee, "How old is the girl?"

"I don't know," he said. His answer was an honest one, but deceptive. He knew she was more mature than she appeared and visions of swimming with her underwater popped in his head. However, having them placed in an orphanage was not what he had intended, and he was beginning to feel uncomfortable about what he was doing.

"I suppose temporary arrangements could be made, in any event." the Major suggested.

"That's not what I had in mind," Tahchee broke in. "Chief Clermont wouldn't want his son placed in an orphanage. I'll be back and get them in a couple of weeks at the most. I only want to go back to Pasuga and check on my parents. I doubt they survived, but I have to know."

"Very well. What's your name?" the General asked.

"Cheho. My father was a white man," he said, which was true. He added the part about being half white because he thought they would be more inclined to believe him.

The Major suggested, "We could place them under Corinne Simon's custody for a few days. She'd probably be pleased to earn the extra money now that her husband's gone."

"That's a possibility," the General agreed. "However, I understand she's making preparation of returning to her home in Ohio soon. She may not want to burdened with such a responsibility."

"I'll check it out," the Major offered.

"I'll leave it to you," the General said. Then to Tahchee, he said, "We've been hearing bits and pieces about what happened in Pasuga. Our Captain McCall tells us there is a renegade half-breed Cherokee living with the Osages. Called him Dutch, I believe. He said his presence angered Chief Clermont's brother. Do you know him?"

He was glad that neither Little Tassel nor Honekahsee could understand English. He had no choice but to admit he knew the man, since the captain had reported it. He nodded to hide a nervous swallow and said, "Yes, I know him."

"What's your opinion? Was he a troublemaker?"

"He seemed like an all right man to me. Been in some knife fights, I hear. Never did anything that I know of to cause Black Dog to ride out and make raids on the Cherokees, if that's what you're driving at."

"Hm-m-m," the General mused thoughtfully, before saying, "I dispatched Captain McCall with a troop to go break up the fight and bring in both Black Dog and this man called Dutch. This fighting has got to stop, and I mean now. Since you were there when it happened, perhaps you could give me a first hand report on the attack."

Tahchee felt a measure of relief hearing Captain McCall was away from the post. He didn't let on.

"There's not much I can tell. The Cherokees attacked without warning. We fought them off. Some of our men took out after them. Evidently, the Cherokees gave them the slip. They came back. They started killing every man, woman and child in the village. When I saw what was happening, I got these two and ran for the river. We rolled a log in the water, got behind it where they wouldn't see us and floated downstream."

"How come you stayed in the village when the others took after the

Cherokees?" the General asked, suspicious.

He had to think fast. "My mother. She got an arrow in her shoulder. I had a hard time getting it out. Since I was going to stay, that's when Chief Clermont told me to see after his son."

The General, evidently satisfied, waved a bony hand. "See what you can do for them, Major. Whatever arrangements you make, you'll have to live with. I'm turning my command over to you effective at the end of the day."

"Yes, sir. I hope your hospital stay will solve your problem, sir," the Major said, then to Tahchee, "Come with me Cheho. You can stay in my quarters until I find out if Mrs. Simon is willing to take boarders."

Tahchee motioned for Little Tassel and Honekahsee, "Come," he said in Osage.

And they followed the Major out of his office, down the boardwalk, and into his quarters.

"Doesn't she ever cry?" Margaret Arbuckle asked as she took Dacy from Laura's arms, cuddling the child to her bosum. "I've never seen her do anything but smile! Isn't she *simply* adorable?"

Indian babies aren't playthings, old woman. Laura thought, hiding her hurt behind a smile. *They are new human beings who must be taught from birth how to survive.*

But she forgave the older woman. She was sweet. If there was an ounce of racial feelings in Margaret Arbuckle, she had never experienced any.

The General's wife was a tall, slender woman—a perfect match physically for her husband. Her ever-present smile forced tiny wrinkles in each sunken cheek and at the corners of her large brown eyes. Seemingly, Margaret Arbuckle had no concern over her graying hair, for it always appeared unkempt. But the hair's short, bushy growth softened the sharp lines of her face. It was months before Laura had come to realize the hair style was more intentional than neglect.

She forced herself to respond to the generous compliments with, "You should be around when she's hungry! You'd see plenty of crying then!"

Margaret poo-pooed the disclaimer and continued with her baby talk to the child. Laura searched for a feeling of pride inside as she watched, but found none. Margaret glanced up suddenly and said, "She certainly doesn't look a thing like George, does she?"

Laura opened her mouth to respond with something that would hurt the old woman as badly as she was being hurt. Instead, she held back, unable to believe Margaret was being catty. No. That wasn't the old woman's nature. She filled her position as the post's first lady well. No need to take offense when none was intended. She had been trying to discipline herself against imagined prejudicial remarks since marrying George and moving into the officers' quarters on the post. How many times had George patiently explained to her that a seeming racial innuendo wasn't that at all? She finally said, "You better not let George hear you say that. To hear him tell it, Dacy is the spitting image of his mother."

"Oh, fiddlesticks!" Margaret laughed. "She looks almost like she's full blood Cherokee."

Not quite, old woman. Only half. Like me and Tahchee. When Margaret put Dacy down to let her run about the room, Laura asked, trying to make her inquiry sound casual, "I saw one of the men escorting some strangers into the General's office yesterday. What's going on?"

"You haven't heard?"

"I don't hear anything when George is away."

"They're a family of refugees from the Pasuga massacre."

Family? Her heart sank. Then it's true. Tahchee was married to that…that…She only half heard what Margaret was saying.

"Matthew is very upset over the man's report. Some of the things the Cherokees did were horrible. He sent a messenger to instruct your husband to pursue and punish the Cherokee renegades. Something simply must be done to stop all this bloodshed, don't you agree?"

"Yes," Laura agreed, her voice subdued, her mind still on Tahchee. Who didn't hate war? But she hadn't come to talk about the turmoil going on in Indian Territory. She came to find out why Tahchee was here and what his plans were.

"That man they brought in—" she began. "He looked familiar. What was his name? I might know him."

Margaret frowned, as if she were attempting to recall, then gave up. "Matthew mentioned his name, but I don't remember. He claims he's an Osage. But if you know him, he would have to be a Cherokee, wouldn't he? I never knew of a Cherokee living with Osages, have you? You don't suppose he's not telling the truth, do you?"

"I don't know—" Laura said.

Margaret snapped her fingers. "I've got it! If you think you know him, I'll take you to meet him. Maybe you can help us solve the mystery. They're boarding with Corinne Simon. Matthew thought the responsibility would do

Corinne good—help her get over her grief losing her husband to the fevers."

"Are you sure it will be all right for you to do this?" Laura asked, trying not to show her mounting excitement.

"Certainly! I don't see why not. They're not prisoners, or anything like that. They seem to be such a nice young couple. It's a shame how these border wars make more living victims than they do dead ones."

The older woman's philosophical statement didn't make good sense the way she said it, but Laura knew what she meant. She wanted very much to see Tahchee; and for him to see her, to know she was here; his, if he wanted her. She would even tell him Dacy was his. She lifted the baby and set her on her hip, ready to go, anxious. Remembering, she could actually feel the thrill of having Tahchee against her naked body.

She often thought of him that way, and could never figure out why he was so different. It wasn't as though she hadn't enjoyed physical thrills with George. She had. Almost every night when he was home, sometimes more than once. Tahchee was just...just...different, was all. Even his running away to chase after the ghost of his mother's killer was different. Certainly not a wise thing to do to her own way of thinking, but different all the same. Now with Tahchee's child, she would be a part of him forever. She waited in high anticipation as Margaret adjusted her shawl and fluffed her hair before the hall mirror.

"I'm ready—finally," Margaret said as she opened the door. She laughed. "I know I'm forgetting something. Last time I was at Corinne's, there was something she wanted me to bring the next time I came. Now, I can't think what it was to save my soul. Oh, well—"

"If the man is who I think he is," Laura said when they were on their way along the board walk. "I might ask him to spend the night with us when George returns...To talk over old times."

"Of course. Of course," Margaret agreed. Then she said a few words to the baby. Dacy goo-gooed playfully and hid her face in Laura's long hair.

The hollow sound of their heels striking the planking echoed from the buildings in the mid-afternoon quiet. The perimeter walk touched every barrack, the hospital, the stable entrance, the empty powder magazine—which was often used for a jail because of its heavy construction—and all living quarters within the stockaded area. Individual entry overhangs blocked the sun in splotches, giving the walkway a checkerboard look.

"How is the General feeling these days?" Laura asked, being polite.

"Not too well, I'm afraid. He can't seem to hold anything on his stomach.

If I don't get him to the hospital in Fort Smith soon, he's liable to dry up and blow away, he's lost so much weight. But now that that new Major is here to take over, he'll go. Benson. Was that his name?"

"Benefield, I believe. Tom Benefield."

"Oh, yes. He seems to be quite capable, don't you think?"

"I haven't had a chance to meet Major Benefield yet," she commented. "I've seen him though. He's quite a handsome man. Does he plan to bring his family out here?"

"He's moved into the bachelor quarters, so I assume he's not married. Or perhaps his wife refuses to come out here, if he is."

And when he takes over, she thought, feeling better, George will probably get his old job back as Executive Officer. He was hurt when the General demoted him to field officer to make room for Major Benefield because of his rank. Life with other army wives was more pleasant when your husband is the second man in charge. It didn't make any difference what people thought of you, they didn't want you to not like them if your husband outranked theirs.

Margaret rapped on Corinne's door and Laura bounced Dacy nervously, unnecessarily. Had Tahchee forgotten her? Her thoughts tumbled over one another. Her heart pounded. She was only vaguely aware of the black piece of cloth still draped over the door. She didn't want to look at it, even think about it, few army wives did. The door opened.

Corinne, a proud looking woman with wavy black hair, deep blue eyes and a long, angular face, smiled with instant recognition.

"Margaret! Do come in!" she said, opening the door wider. And to Laura, in a cooler, detached tone, she asked, "And how's the baby, Laura? Does she still have her constipation problem?"

"No," Laura answered and followed Margaret into the room. "She's just fine, Corinne. I stopped feeding her pork like you suggested. It worked."

Margaret removed her shawl and said, "Laura thinks she knows the Indian man who came in yesterday. We ran over to take a closer look. Are they still around?"

Corinne motioned with her head. "Yes. Out in the kitchen. But if he's a Cherokee, I find that hard to believe. Him living with an Osage woman and dragging an Osage boy around."

Laura felt herself trembling as Corinne led them to a double door which opened into the combination kitchen-dining area. Her breath caught and her heart skipped a beat the moment she saw Tahchee seated at the table with the girl and boy. She flashed him a nervous smile.

"Laura!" he said, leaping to his feet.

His instant recognition and the sound of his strong voice washed away all fear, left only sweet excitement. She hurried across the room.

"So it is you?" she said, holding out her free hand. He seized it as his dark eyes searched her face, melting her inside.

Margaret laughed and clapped her hands. "Now isn't this a delight? You two really do know one another."

"Yes, we do," Laura admitted, still keeping her attention on Tahchee's face. "In fact, we're childhood sweethearts, you might say."

"How nice! Come, Corinne. Let's go in the other room and leave these two alone. They'll have a lot of visiting to catch up on."

As the two older women were leaving, Laura sneaked a quick glance at the girl, a sharp pang of jealousy making her want to find some flaw. She found one—she was too shy to be any serious competition; besides being a full blood Osage, a savage. She felt better, and doubly so when she determined the boy was far, far too old to be Tahchee's.

"Who was that woman who came in with you?" he asked, his voice low, conspiritorial.

"Margaret? She's General Arbuckle's wife."

"You didn't tell her who I was, did you?"

"No. Not really. I just told her I thought I knew you. Why? Are you in some sort of trouble?"

"I don't know. I don't think so. I told them I was Osage—"

"You certainly look it," she said with a short, cynical laugh. "I thought you and Daniel went hunting for Osages. How come you wound up being one of them?"

"We didn't. I mean Daniel didn't. I did. We got separated when I saved the boy here from drowning in a flooded river. He was Chief Clermont's son. The Chief made me his brother. I stayed. I thought it would be a good way to find the man who killed my mother."

What a strange turn of events, she thought, then asked, "Did you?"

"Yes. Black Dog. He's Chief Clermont's real brother."

"So you killed him?" She couldn't keep the cynicism out of her voice, while at the same time feeling glad that it was over.

"No. The time wasn't right. Matter of fact, when I first saw him, he came riding into the village with your husband."

"George?" she blurted, surprised. "How'd you know?"

"We ran into Johnny Jumper a few months ago. He told us you'd married an army officer named George McCall. Looks like you made a good catch. He seems to be a fine man."

"Really?" This was exciting. "Did you tell him...?"

"That I knew you?" he asked, then answered his own question. "No. I didn't have the chance. We weren't on very friendly terms at the time, you might say. He didn't like me being in Pasuga because I was a Cherokee. He tried to get me to leave." He laughed lightly. "Chief Clermont didn't like a soldier telling one of his brothers to get out of town. It made him mad and he told your husband to leave instead."

"They didn't harm him, did they?" she asked quickly.

"No. He and Black Dog rode out together."

"So now, what? You giving up your foolish chase?"

"No. I want Black Dog more than ever now." He fell strangely silent, as if his mind was far away. The question popped into her mind: Was this the same Tahchee she...? Then he was talking again, as if lost in a world of his own.

"When the Cherokees attacked, we thought they were Pawnees at first. I led the Osages out against them. We got tangled up in hand-to-hand fighting in the woods. One of the Cherokees jumped me from behind. I killed him. It was Daniel."

"Oh, Tahchee..." She didn't know what to say. She wanted to take him in her arms and comfort him. Then she found herself struggling to keep from saying, *I told you you would destroy yourself, didn't I?*

"I was holding him in my arms when he died."

She reached out with her free hand to touch him, let him know she was truly sorry. Her touch seemed to bring him back to the present. His eyes focused on Dacy and he smiled.

"So this is your baby," he said. "Johnny Jumper told us about her, too. She's a little cutie."

Laura, pleased, brushed the squirming girl's hair back. She wanted so very much to tell him that she belonged to him, but felt it wasn't the time nor place especially with that—that Osage girl staring at them.

"So the boy is the Osage Chief's son?" she asked, curious.

"Honekahsee. It means pretty nearly drowned in Osage," he explained, laughing.

She didn't understand the humor, didn't try. "How come he's with you?"

"Chief Clermont left him with me when they went out after the Cherokees. When the Cherokees gave them the slip and came back, I grabbed the boy and escaped."

She nodded toward the girl. "Who's she?" she asked and couldn't help herself from using the most derogatory term she could think of when she added, "Your Osage squaw?"

"No, Laura, she's not my Osage squaw!" His voice sounded cold and hard. "Her name is Little Tassel. She means nothing to me. Chief Clermont assigned her the job of keeping my lodge clean—"

"Oh, how convenient."

He glared. "Will you stop that? Can't you see she's just a girl?"

She thought: He may think she's just a girl, but she and I both know different.

She sensed his mounting anger was building a wall between them, a wall she did not want. She'd pushed him too far. She decided to try a new approach. She held Dacy out, inviting him to take her.

"Want to hold her?"

He hesitated, then extended his hands and waggled his fingers. Dacy turned away bashfully. But with Laura's urging, the child finally leaned to let Tahchee take her. He juggled her awkwardly.

"What's her name?" he asked.

"Dacy."

The stunned look on his face startled her.

"Dacy?" he gulped. "Is that—the baby's name?"

"Of course, silly. I said it was, didn't I?"

He didn't seem to hear. Still staring at the baby, he sank slowly into his chair, as if he were too weak to stand.

"Are you all right?" she asked, concerned.

She saw his adam's apple bounce as he nodded. Then he studied the baby again. "She sure looks more Indian than a quarter, doesn't she?"

It would have been a good time to tell him, to say she was more than a quarter because he was her father. She held back. Later, perhaps. Wait until the feeling between them was like it was before he went away.

"That's what everybody says," she said, affecting an amused disposition. "But you know how it is with us mixed bloods. Sometimes one of us will look more Indian than others who actually are more."

"Yeah," he mumbled as if his mind was in another land. "I know."

Then he turned his back on her and began showing Dacy to the boy and girl, talking excitedly to them in Osage. It sounded as if he were bragging on her.

She resented being left out. What was he telling them? The look on the Osage girl's face changed quickly from surprise to motherly. And when she held her arms out to take Dacy from Tahchee, Laura's resentment boiled over. She quickly stepped in between and jerked Dacy from his arms.

"I have to go," she said, curtly. "I'm expecting George home today. I have a million things to do."

As she turned away, he leaped from his chair and seized her arm, spinning her about to face him. "Why did you marry him?" he asked, angry. "You knew I'd be back."

The unexpected force of his anger startled her. What right did he have saying that? Especially, since he had obviously been enjoying himself with a—a squaw.

"Back? Back from where? The dead?" she said cynically.

She wanted so desperately for him to put his arms around her, hold her close. She felt a stinging sensation in her nostrils and knew she was going to cry. She didn't want him—or that other girl—to see. She pulled free of his grasp and hurried into the other room. She announced, "I'm ready to go, Margaret, if you are."

"Are you finished visiting with your friend?"

"Yes."

Laura kept going toward the front door. Margaret followed, talking all the while, asking Corinne to come over more often and inquiring when she planned to return to her home in Columbus.

Laura fought against a rising sense of failure, choking back tears. She had been petulant. Vindictive. She had tried to hurt Tahchee for no reason. No reason at all! Why? It was that girl, that's why! She was older than she looked, that's for sure. Tahchee belonged to her. He had no right being with that savage! Her vision blurred. She blinked her eyes clear, was able even to smile her goodbye to Corinne.

On their way to their own quarters, she paid little attention to what Margaret was saying. She did have enough presence of mind, however, to make decent replies. She was more composed by the time she left Margaret at her door and continued along the board walk alone, carrying Dacy.

Despite all that happened, despite her marriage, she knew she had to have Tahchee again. With George gone, she could have him over for dinner or something and they could...No. That wouldn't look right. She could offer to feed and bed all three of them for a few days on the pretense of giving Corinne some relief—just be doing her duty as a good officer's wife. Then they could get back to where they were before he went away...and she could tell him Dacy was his.

But what good would that do? She was a married woman now. Damn it! Why did she ever get married? Everybody knew why she did it, even her own parents. So why the cover up? She'd messed up her life, not to mention George's. She wished he'd get killed—

Laura Rogers! What in the world's come over you, thinking things like that? Then she consoled herself with the thought that nobody ever knows what a person was thinking. So what's wrong with a little harmless thinking? What did it hurt? Why not arrange a world in your own mind where you can enjoy all the pleasures and not have to suffer any of the hurts? Your thoughts do not make it real, do they?

When she neared her living quarters, she saw the new man—Major Tom Benefield—standing at her front door, apparently waiting for her. She paused in mid-stride, unable to breathe. Something was wrong. And the look on his face told her that whatever was wrong, it was something she did not want to hear. Not now, anyway. She continued walking toward him with hesitant steps and stopped a few feet away, waiting.

Major Benefield, a square-built man with a stern face, took two steps to be at her side when he said, "Are you Mrs. George McCall?"

"Yes," she answered nervously.

"I'm sorry, Mrs. McCall. I have some bad news. We just received word Captain McCall was killed by the Cherokees."

She stared at the Major's face, her eyes focusing for some reason on his square jaw, drained of all feeling. She noticed his jaw muscles working and felt the same tension she knew he must be feeling. Dazed, she heard herself mumbling, "It's all his fault."

"Who?"

"Him. The Osage with the boy and girl."

"You know him?"

"Yes. I know him. Tahchee. They call him Dutch. He—"

"Dutch?"

She nodded.

"He's the one who started this whole mess."

She shifted Dacy on her arm. "I know."

"I have to go. Will you be all right?"

"Yes."

"I can send someone—"

"That's not necessary. I'll be all right."

And she watched him hurrying across the parade grounds toward the Post Headquarters. A strange sense of release flooded over her and she hurried inside before she broke out into a fit of hysterical laughter.

CHAPTER 18

Tahchee lay awake most of the night staring into the darkness, the enormity of the situation growing and growing. Him a father! Had been for near a year and a half. Song Bird would be a grandmother, if she were still alive. Impossible! Only old women are grandmothers, and Song Bird would be young forever. Life was certainly confusing when you thought about it too much.

Strange, he didn't feel any different. And he had made her a mother. She hadn't changed much since he had last seen her...that day at the creek. He brought up the memory once again, as he had so many thousands of times during the last two years, re-experiencing each thrilling moment.

Why didn't she tell him Dacy was his? He'd never tell her he knew, if she didn't want him to know. As far as that went, he may never see her again!

By daybreak, he made up his mind to leave. Laura showing up like she did yesterday, saying she knew him, pretty well destroyed his story that he was Osage.

When Corinne offered to pour him more coffee, he shook his head.

"No, thanks, ma'am," he said, getting to his feet. "I'm going to run over and have another talk with the General."

"That messenger last night said you were under house arrest, didn't he? That means you're not supposed to leave this house until further notice," Corinne cautioned. He noticed she'd been a little testy ever since Laura came. Supicious, would be the best word to describe her, he thought.

"House arrest doesn't mean much inside an army post, the way I see it," he said. "Besides, I've done nothing to be arrested for. If they don't make up their minds soon, I'm leaving—even if I have to climb over the stockade wall"

Corinne waved the subject aside. "Do as you like. It's none of my affair. I'm not a part of the army anymore." Then she nodded toward Little Tassel and the boy. "What about them?"

"I'll be right back."

He picked up the hat she'd given him. "Thanks for the hat," he said. "This shirt, too. I don't feel so out of place now. Wish your husband's boots had been big enough to fit me."

"Take all you want out of his trunk. He won't be needing them anymore. I've got too much to pack as it is."

He noticed the tears welling up in her eyes and reached out to pat her shoulder sympathetically. He sensed she appreciated his gesture and no words were necessary. Speaking Osage, he told Little Tassel, "I'm going to talk to the General. You two wait here."

Little Tassel had a concerned look on her face. "Are you coming back?"

"Yes. I'm coming back."

"We want to go with you."

"You can't. We're not supposed to leave this house."

"Why? What are they going to do to us?"

"They're not going to do anything. It's just the army's way of making sure everything is proper before they take the next step. Whatever that is."

Honekahsee blurted, "I want to go home."

He gave the boy what he hoped was a reassuring smile. There was a strong possibility he had no home. Nor a father, for that matter. And if Clermont was dead, Honekahsee would, according to custom, be taken into the lodge of his nearest relative...Black Dog. And he was going to kill Black Dog. Which would make Honekahsee homeless, for sure.

He'd think about that some other time. He patted Honekahsee's head. "They'll turn us loose. Probably today. That's what I want to find out from the General."

Corinne interrupted with, "What are the children saying?"

He shifted to English. "They asked if it would be all right to help you clean up the breakfast dishes. I told them I was sure you would welcome their help. So put them to work. They need something to do."

He left. Outside, he noticed the unusual activity, soldiers hurrying back and forth across the parade grounds. There was a solid line of men leaving the stable leading their mounts. Organizing a search party, he guessed.

When he entered the General's outer office, the sergeant at the desk looked up, surprise on his face.

"What're you doing here?" he demanded.

"I came to see the General. Is he in?"

"He ain't the commander no more. Major Benefield is."

Then Tahchee remembered. "Oh, yes. I forgot. Is the Major in?"

The sergeant got to his feet, keeping his eyes on him as he moved to the opened doorway leading to the General's office. He said, "That Indian is here to see you, sir."

"The hell he is!" boomed the voice from the other office. "What's he doing out running around?" Then the Major appeared in the doorway, scowling. "You're under house arrest, Mister. General's orders...and mine."

"I'm not military," Tahchee stated curtly, then added. "I'm not even a citizen of the United States."

The Major appeared confused, then became stiffly angry.

"It makes no difference what you claim to be, you're under arrest."

"Arrest? What for?"

"For suspicion of inciting a massacre, for one thing. Mrs. McCall says she knows you. You're Dutch. The man we've been looking for. I'm holding you until I complete my investigation on exactly why you were with the Osages and what you're doing here with those two young people."

"I told you—" he stammered, not knowing what to say.

"You lied about who you are, and you could be lying about how you got those kids. Among other things, I have just received a report that it was a renegade Cherokee called Dutch who killed a Cherokee chief named Daniel Taylor. This was what precipitated the massacre at Pasuga."

Stunned by this interpretation of events, he could only glare back into the Major's pale blue eyes which was boring into him. He could hear his own heart beats thundering. What did this mean? Was he some sort of an outlaw? Should he admit that he did, indeed, kill Daniel? But that it was only an accident of war, that Daniel was his own uncle?

"Sergeant, take this man and lock him up. Put a double guard on the door around the clock."

"Yes, sir."

The sergeant reached for Tahchee's arm. He jerked away, thinking fast, trying to make up his mind whether to make a run for it. But there was Honekahsee and Little Tassel.

"You can't do that."

"The hell I can't. You're going to have more charges thrown against you than you can shake a stick at, not to mention out and out murder—"

"It was not murder!" Tahchee exploded as a chilling anger swept through him. "They attacked and we fought them off!"

"Then you admit fighting with the Osages?"

"Yes. I did fight with them, but—"

"And now half the population of an entire village has been killed. Chief Clermont himself is dead. He was the one person we were depending on so heavily to help us bring peace to this part of the frontier. Now his brother, Black Dog, is leading the Osages. They have gone on a rampage—burning, looting, raping the countryside. He is responsible for the death of one of our finest officers, Captain George McCall."

More stunning news...Laura's husband. Dead. Honekahsee's father. Dead. Black Dog, alive and running wild. And here he was, about to be jailed for causing all of it. The Major was still talking.

"I intend to put an end to this blood letting once and for all. I am hereby placing you under detention as a rogue Indian. In my opinion, you should be hanged. Among them could be causing the death of Captain McCall, the latest victim of the uprising. Sergeant, take him away."

"Yes, sir!" the sergeant said. This time his grip on Tahchee's arm was more firm. Tahchee resisted.

"You can't. The boy and girl—"

"I'm sending the boy to the Lively's Indian Orphanage in Fort Smith. The girl is old enough to be returned to her own people."

"You can't do that. You'll be giving her to Black Dog."

"That's none of my affair, nor yours." He waved a hand. "Take him away, Sergeant."

This time Tahchee yielded. He was suddenly weak and, for once in his life, undecided what to do. If he broke for it, he'd risk being shot. He was no good dead to Little Tassel and Honekahsee. He simply could not let Black Dog get his hands on her.

Even more dazed by the realization it was Laura who had turned him in—

probably blaming him for the death of her husband—he offered no resistance when the sergeant guided him across the parade grounds toward the empty powder magazine. It was a solidly built building with iron straps across the windows. He noticed how that it had been built with its rear wall against the fort's perimeter pilings, its peaked roof almost as high as the sharpened stockade logs.

Somehow, someway, he had to get away…get to Black Dog before the army did, and get to him before he could get to Little Tassel.

The sergeant forced him to wait until the guard unlocked the chained door. They shoved him into the long, dimly lit bare room. He heard the heavy chain being dragged through holes in the door and jamb, and heard the loud, metallic click when the heavy lock was snapped shut outside.

CHAPTER 19

Three weeks! Tahchee surveyed the gloomy, empty room for the hundredth time, fighting to keep his hopes from bottoming out. He'd been better off to have made a break for it, taking his chances on getting killed, rather than being locked up like this.

He still found it hard to believe any human being had a right to cage another human being. He walked to the close fitting door, fingered the links of the heavy chain draped from a hole in the door to a hole in the wall. Once again, he tested the chain, pulling on it gently, successfully slipping a couple more links from the holes before it stopped sliding through the hole. He could visualize the lock outside, its hasp hooked securely through the chain's rusty links.

Now he knew what Daniel meant when he said a man's word is more confining than four walls? The instant a man is confined physically, his mind begins immediately trying to find a way to escape, he said. But when you tell a man you won't run away, that ends it. What you say is the ultimate confinement.

Unless, of course, you never mean what you say, Daniel had said. Which was one of the basic faults of the European philosophy. Consequently, they cannot trust one another and are, therefore, totally incapable of believing a Cherokee would not run away if he said he would not; even when it means facing his own execution, as often happened.

Now here he was. Caged. Like some wild animal, totally void of all sense of reason. He ran a hand along the wall. Daniel was right. It is the Europeans who are the barbarians; their sense of humanity distorted—on both sides of their law. Violators did not violate through a sense of honor. Nor did the enforcers enforce honorably. With us, Daniel had lectured, when a man kills someone, he is to be killed himself—the punishment meted out by those whose grief is the greatest. The matter ends there. Honor restores dignity to the human being. Strange how Daniel talked that way, but still acused him of wasting his life trying to live it.

He heard someone talking outside. He faced the door expectantly, saw the chain wiggle, then slide from one hole to the other until the last link fell through. The door creaked loudly on its metal hinges.

Laura's tall figure filled the opening. She was wearing black, from veil to long flowing skirt. His spirits soared. Why? He didn't know. He tried to read her smile when she lifted her veil and turned immediately to put her hand on the chest of the soldier following her into the room.

"No. You wait outside," she said and pushed firmly against the guard's chest. "My business with the prisoner is personal."

"But, Mrs. McCall—"

"Do as I say. I'll only be a minute."

The guard resisted. "I have my orders, Ma'am."

Laura dropped her hand from his chest and stiffened. She stood as tall as the army private, looked him in the eye.

"You have my permission to search me if you think I'm carrying a concealed weapon," she said, her voice crisp.

The soldier's gaze dropped to her breasts, then bounced up again. His face reddened.

"It ain't that, Mrs. McCall. It's—It's—"

"It's what?"

The soldier glanced nervously over his shoulder to the empty parade grounds outside, then swept his gaze back to Laura. He licked his lips.

"You—you say it's all right if I feel—" he swallowed, "—if I search you?"

The poor bastard. Tahchee suppressed a smile when Laura held out both arms.

"Certainly. Go ahead. Search. Feel of me anywhere you want."

The soldier hesitated, then pocketed the key and felt down Laura's sides, his hands puffing the long black skirt to a point below her knees. He brought his hands up, patting her front and rear this time. He let one hand linger on her rump as he fondled each breast. Laura watched him with an understanding smile on her face.

"Satisfied?" she asked. "Or would you like me to undress?"

He jerked his hands away. "Oh, no, Ma'am!" he said. He stepped back and saluted smartly. "No need for that. I'm satisfied. Just doing my duty, is all, Ma'am. But make it quick, will you? They find out I left you in here alone with him, they'll court martial me for sure."

"Oh, I wouldn't let them harm you. I'd be more than happy to describe how you felt—I mean how you searched me."

The young man's face turned a sick white. He backed through the entrance, pulling the door closed behind him. Laura turned, then ran across the large room in a shameless hurry.

He was just as eager as she and caught her in his arms; her own circling his neck. He held her tight, the press of her body against his awakening forgotten desires, desires further inflamed by her sweet smell. Her lips brushed his cheek. He felt her hot breath across his ear. He wanted her, wanted her worse than he realized. Their tight embrace spoke a thousand words, bridging the chasm separating them.

"I'm sorry," he whispered around the emotion-filled lump in his throat.

She pulled back, dark eyes studying his face.

"About what?"

"Your husband—"

She covered his mouth with one hand. "Don't! It's past. Done. I came to talk about us." She removed her hand and brushed his lips with hers. "I've missed you, Tahchee. More than you'll ever know."

He was unable to tear his eyes from her lips, wanting more than a light touch. They pulled him like a magnet and he felt himself falling into her willing response. He closed his eyes to get the fullest pleasure from their lips pressing together. So warm. So tender. So alive! His emotions churned, his raging desire on the verge of breaking away from all restraint.

She pulled away, leaving a hungry void.

"I don't have much time," she said. "They found out who you are. Instead of turning you over to the Bureau of Indian Affairs for killing another Indian, they're going to take you to Fort Smith and try you in the federal court. The charge is inciting a disturbance with intent to abrogate the treaty—or something like that."

"Ridiculous!"

"Of course, but you know how it is. Cherokees aren't allowed to testify in their own behalf or have another Cherokee testify for them. The trial would only be a show. Your hanging would be used to send a signal to other Cherokees. To keep them from having any notions about violating the treaty."

"What about the Osages? Men like Black Dog?"

"They're after him, too."

"I hope to hell they catch him! I hope they bring him here and lock him up with me! I'll kill him with my bare hands."

She turned sideways, stared out the barred window, as if she were debating something.

How had he angered her? He waited, tried to figure out why she came. To taunt him? Whatever, he needed her—more ways than one. He touched her arm.

"Laura—?"

She faced him. He said, "I'm sorry. It's just that I feel so damned frustrated at times."

"You're letting hate destroy you, Tahchee. Can't you see that? You've already wasted two years of your life—and mine—because of what happened to your mother."

"You don't understand. It's more than that now. There's Little Tassel and Honekahsee and...Daniel."

"Look at you! Talking as if you got a whole family to take care of! When will you *ever* stop this foolishness?"

He squelched a surge of resentment, and managed a shrug of indifference.

"Let's drop it. You didn't come here to argue. Or bring me news that I'm going to hang."

Her lips parted slightly. She hesitated before saying, "If I help you escape, will you take me with you?"

He noticed she didn't mention their child. He started to tell her he knew, decided not to. "What about your baby? Dacy?" he asked, curious.

"I plan on taking her home to Mother and Father. If they won't take her, I'll send her to her grandparents back east. There'll just be the two of us."

While her plan had a certain amount of logic to it, he didn't like it—made her seem cold, somehow.

"I don't know," he mused. "The army's everywhere. Even if I got away, it'd be tough hiding all the time. Doubly tough on you and—" He didn't add, "Dacy."

"We could go to Texas. That's out of the United States. The army can't touch you there."

"I can't do that."

"Why not? Many Cherokees are doing it. I have an aunt and uncle living there. We could find them. They would help us."

"I have Little Tassel and Honekahsee to think of."

Her eyes flashed. "Them again! What do you see in her? And that boy's nothing but a little savage!"

"I feel responsible for them," he said. He resented her unwarranted attacks and fought to keep his voice calm.

"That's nonsense," she snapped.

He said nothing, not wanting to get into another argument. After a few moments of silence, she seemed more in control when she added, "You may as well forget them. The girl is already gone, back to her people. The army is sending the boy to Lovely's Orphanage in Fort Smith. They'll be taking him when they take you."

So it was true. The Major was doing what he threatened to do. He was crushed. But he knew that any further discussion about those two would only irritate Laura. Right now, she represented his best chance to get free. And he had to be free before he could help anybody. He put aside his concern for Little Tassel and Honekahsee and started giving Laura's proposition serious thought.

He had no desire to live in Texas. His mother was buried on the banks of White River in Arkansas. He owed Daniel's memory…a lump came in his throat when he thought about the man he killed. On the other hand, he would never get a chance to go home again or do justice to Daniel's memory if he were hanged. He gestured helplessly.

"How do you propose to get me out of here?" he asked, unconsciously evading her question about taking her to Texas with him. "Slip me a gun? A lot of good that would do on an army post. I'd get shot before I went ten steps beyond that door."

"You haven't promised."

She wanted to bind him with his own word. Should he? It was the best choice he had at the moment. He nodded.

"All right. I'll take you to Texas…"

She smiled her relief, then turned and headed for the door. He stopped her with, "But I think we should take Dacy with us. She should be with her mother, don't you think?"

He felt good, somehow, seeing the bewildered look on her face when she looked at him over her shoulder. He waited for her to tell him Dacy was his, and then agree that taking her was a good idea.

Instead, she said, "We can send for her later, if that's what you want; when we find a place to live and you're sure you want to raise another man's child."

Why was she keeping the baby's fatherhood from him? He began to see her in a new light. More hard hearted than he thought. When she reached to lift the door latch, he called, "Hey, wait a minute. How're you going to get me out? Don't you think I should be in on the plan?"

She paused, her lips set with that peculiar, bewitching smile.

"I don't have a plan yet. But I'll think of something."

Then she was gone before he had a chance to say anything. The soldier threaded the chain through the holes. Tahchee heard the lock snap, plummeting his hope once again into an even deeper, darker hole.

He whirled and rammed a fist into the wall as hard as he could hit without breaking a knuckle. It hurt anyway, and he limped about in a tight circle nursing the damaged fist in his other hand.

Damn her! Making him promise the impossible in return for his life. She didn't even have a plan for his escape. But the more he thought about it, the more he liked the idea.

He and Daniel had talked about moving to Texas themselves. More and more Cherokees were doing it—especially since the Lovely Treaty was forcing them to leave their homes in Arkansas to resettle across the state line in Indian Territory. They were tired of having the U.S. Government interfering in their lives, Daniel had explained. Across the Red River in Texas, they were farther from Mexico City than they were from Washington. And the Mexican Nationals, a new race of people arising from a blend of Spanish and Indian blood lines, viewed the North American Indians as people, not as if they were some sort of primitive animals to be caged and manipulated.

Still, he did not want to go to Texas. Not just yet, anyway. He wanted to find Black Dog first and kill him.

He stopped pacing suddenly and smacked the palm of his hand with the aching fist. Of course! He hadn't promised Laura *when* he'd take her to Texas. Fudging on a promise was a white man's ruse. But, under the circumstances, he found the fudge acceptable. Besides, he was half white, wasn't he? He had to smile, thinking of what Old Hop had asked, "Are you the best of both, or the worst of both?"

"The worst, probably," he mumbled aloud.

The following day, Tahchee stood at the barred window watching a troop escort forming up on the parade grounds. Soldiers helped Corinne into the lead wagon. A burly sergeant dragged Honekahsee from Corinne's quarters and attempted to lift the boy over the tail gate. Honekahsee fought back. Tahchee laughed silently, rooting for the boy to win. Honekahsee knocked the sergeant's hat from his head, revealing a balding scalp covered with long strands of thinning, white hair. Another soldier came to the sergeant's aid, then another when Honekahsee seized the edge of the covered opening and refused to let go. Tahchee gripped the window bars, trying to help.

"Hang on, Honekahsee. Don't let go!" he muttered aloud, knowing all the while that it was a losing cause.

Two of the soldiers managed to pry Honekahsee's fingers from the canvas hoop, but the boy extended both arms and legs and all three soldiers struggled to get him pushed through the opening. The escort, not yet mounted, gathered around to watch the struggle. They cheered, hoo-rawing the sergeant and the two men fighting with the boy. When they finally succeeded in pushing Honekahsee into the wagon, the sergeant barked a command and the men scattered.

The sergeant picked up his hat and dusted it off. He smoothed his wispy hair and set the hat on his head, squaring it neatly. Just as he started to move away, a tiny fist shot out from the canvas opening and knocked the hat off again.

"Give it to him!" Tahchee laughed.

Then he sobered when he saw Laura leave her quarters and head for the wagon. She was dressed for traveling, long skirted dress without a bustle. She did not have the baby. Bewildered, he watched her climb the front wheel, with the sergeant's assistance, and seat herself beside the driver.

What's she up to? Where was Dacy? If she is leaving the baby here, that means she is coming back. Or was she? When he saw men coming his direction, he backed from the window, gaze centered on the door.

The chain rattled. He saw it slide through the holes. Major Tom Benefield stepped in, flanked by two soldiers.

"We're taking you to Fort Smith, Dutch," the Major said. "Give me your word you won't try to escape and you can ride free. Otherwise, you make the trip with your hands tied behind your back and your feet lashed beneath the horse's belly. Which will it be?"

He knew Laura must have a plan of some kind. He could not give his word. He shook his head.

"I'm not saying, one way or the other, Major."

Major Benefield motioned. "Secure the prisoner for travel, men."

The two soldiers advanced, one carrying leather thongs, the other a rope.

CHAPTER 20

Tahchee counted fifty soldiers in the escort. Half a dozen ahead of the wagon carrying Laura, Corinne and Honekahsee, and the rest strung out behind in a column of two's. He was somewhere in the middle with his hands tied behind his back and a noose around his neck. A corporal kept the other end of the rope tied to his saddle pommel. A fine arrangement, he thought bitterly. If either horse bolted, he would be strangled; or if he was lucky, his neck broken on the first lunge of either animal.

Why him? The Osage-Cherokee wars were not his doing. The U.S. Government forced the Cherokees to come west. Congress should have made arrangements with the Osages first—moved them somewhere else, particularly since the U.S. Government was in the Indian moving business.

The column of soldiers wound upward from a deep ravine and strung out across a small prairie. A faint road had been beaten out through the stand of wild flowers, their reds, blues, oranges and pinks stunted and crushed where wagon wheels had rolled.

In the open like this, he could easily see the wagon up ahead. He smiled grimly. Black Dog would feel honored if he knew the army was using such a strong escort to deliver three adults and a boy to Fort Smith,

Whatever...He knew he had to escape, somehow, before they jailed him in Fort Smith. Laura's plan had better be good, and it had to be tonight or never.

In the wagon ahead, Laura flirted with the driver, a garrulous old coot from South Carolina, he said. He talked so much he hardly took time to spit, letting his tobacco juice trickle from one corner of his mouth. Old or young, married or unmarried, she knew what men wanted most and she enjoyed provoking them into mental rape.

She disagreed with Corinne who thought it was shameful for a widow to stop wearing black so soon after her husband was killed. Laura felt three weeks was long enough. She had her own life to live. And now that Tahchee had come back, she was looking forward to living a very exciting life. The only reason she hadn't gone back to her short deerskin was because she needed the long cotton dress on this trip to hide the knife.

At sunset, the cavalry column curled back on itself, assembling in an area where one small stream emptied into another.

"Typical army," the old South Carolinian said, cackling, then gagging on his own tobacco juice before finishing with, "One crik for the people, t'other fer the animals."

"How thoughtful," she responded, smiling sweetly. She waited for him to climb down then held her hand out inviting him to help her from the wagon. When he allowed one hand to slip, getting a quick feel of her breast, she gave him a knowing smile to let him know she knew what he was doing and didn't care. She'd never had an old man, and wondered what it would be like.

She watched dispasionately when Honekahsee made a break to get to Tahchee, but a soldier dragged him back. The little savage kicked at the soldiers as they tied him to a wagon wheel. He needed a slap in the mouth, she thought. She knew Indians didn't use physical force punishing their young, but she had experienced it on many occasions from her white mother and knew such punishment was effective. Not that she cared one way or the other whether or not the boy was taught to respect his elders, it was Tahchee's affection for him that she resented.

She affected a grieving widow attitude and sat apart from the group while the men prepared an evening meal. Sure enough, Major Benefield came to join her carrying a plate of food in each hand.

"Here," he said holding one of the plates out for her.

She lifted her appreciative but sad, she hoped, eyes and shook her head.

"I'm not hungry."

"You must eat," he insisted. "You can't just stop living. I know. I lost my wife two years ago."

She sighed and took the plate from him, dragging her fingers across his hand. "I'm sorry," she said. He smiled, gestured toward the spot on the log beside her and asked, "May I?"

"Oh, yes," she gushed. "Do. It's so quiet and lonely out here, don't you think?"

"Yes. Yes, it is," he said, glancing around. "But it's a good spot for a camp."

She tasted the food. She was hungry as a bear, but she forced herself to act dainty as she ate. She answered his manly attempts to cheer her up with increasing friendliness. At one point actually laughing delightedly over one attempt he made trying to be amusing. She reached out to push him lightly on the shoulder.

Her touch had the desired effect, she noticed, as he seemed to relax and become more sociable. She let him talk. She kept nudging the conversation toward more personal subjects until she was sure he had a sincere interest in her well being. Finally, she handed him her empty tin plate when and said, "I need a few minutes alone with Dutch. He'll have some requests for his family."

"I'm sorry, Mrs. McCall. He's—"

"Laura. I'm not Mrs. McCall any longer," she said looking deep into his pale blue eyes. "I'm just a lonesome girl called Laura."

The way he stared gave her a good feeling. She knew he would think it was some sort of veiled invitation. She saw his adam's apple jump when he swallowed.

"As you wish. Addressing you 'Laura' is more comfortable. But I cannot let you go near the prisoner. He is under maximum security. He refused to give his word not to attempt an escape. I must keep him tied and not let anyone go near him."

"Oh, pshaw! What could he possibly do to me with his hands and feet tied?"

When he hesitated, Laura hiked her skirt above her knees and crossed her long legs, letting him get a good look.

"Well—" he began, and paused, apparently debating with himself whether he should or not.

"It'll only take a couple of minutes, Major—"

"Tom," he corrected with a beaming smile.

She returned his smile and continued, "I won't be long, Tom. You can tell your guards to keep their eyes on us. Just have them stand back a ways so we can talk in private."

He pulled in a deep breath. "You Indians!" he said awkwardly, trying to disguise his acquiescence under a blanket of exasperated bluster. "I never know what you're up to next." He stood. "Very well. Come along. But only for a few minutes. All right?"

"Thank you...Tom," she said taking his arm and letting him escort her through the camp to the fire where the sergeant and three men stood guard over Tahchee. Major Benefield returned the sergeant's salute.

"Stand aside, Sergeant. Mrs. McCall wants a few words alone with the prisoner."

"Yes, sir!"

"Stand away and give them privacy. But don't take your eyes off them, in case he tries to harm her."

"Yes, sir." The sergeant saluted again, then jerked his thumb at his men, leading them to a spot a few yards away. They turned to glower. Major Benefield patted Laura's hand.

"Don't be too long, Laura. And keep your distance from this man. Don't hesitate to call for help if you need to."

"Thank you, Tom."

Major Benefield strutted away. Laura edged nearer to the bound figure stretched out on the ground. He attempted to sit up.

"It's about time. I'm saying here and now, if your plan don't work, forget Texas."

She laughed lightly. "You look a mess. How'd you like to stay tied up that way until they hang you?"

"All right! All right! Let's not start arguing. Just get me out of here—if you can."

She switched to Cherokee, just in case the guards moved close enough to hear.

"I'm carrying a small knife stitched to the hem of my petty coat. I'm trying to tear it loose with my foot. Keep talking."

He snickered. "Don't cut your toe," he said and continued talking. She kept working to get the knife free. Soon, it fell.

"There," she said. "When I back up, stretch your legs and drag it under you. Make it look natural."

"Is that all I get? Just a knife? What can I do with a knife against a squad of soldiers all armed to the teeth?'

"That's your problem," she said. "But knowing you, I think you'll figure out a way."

She turned, pretending to leave, then spun about, positioning herself between Tahchee and the guards. She spoke louder, and in English. "Is there any other messages for Song Bird?"

He squirmed to pull the knife under his legs. "Yes," he said. "Yes, there is. Tell her to get Uncle Daniel to help dig the potatoes. It don't look as though I'm going to get home in time."

"Anything else?"

"No…" he answered, then switched to Cherokee. "If I make it, where will I find you?"

"Go home. Wait for me there."

"That's the first place they'll come looking for me."

"No, they won't. I'll tell the Major you mentioned going to Texas. They'll be watching for you between here and the Red River."

"How long before you come home?"

"Not long."

Even in the ghostly firelight, she could see the irritation in his face when he said, "I'll be damned if I sit around waiting on you forever. And the way you've been playing up to that Major, it just might be forever. A widow who didn't love her husband makes interesting company for a man, in case you didn't know."

"I know," she answered, her laughter soft and throaty. "But we sometimes need all the friends we can get."

She turned to leave and heard him call out, "Be sure and bring Dacy with you."

She continued walking away, pretending she hadn't heard, wondering why he made such a foolish request. One of the guards emitted a low whistle as she passed and she exaggerated the sway of her hips for his benefit.

Tahchee glared at the guard who whistled when they moved back into position nearer him, two in front and two behind. The soldier leered and jerked a thumb at Laura's retreating figure.

"She's somethin, ain't she?"

He refused to answer. The man licked his lips and added, "I sure would like to be in the Major's shoes, now she's a widow. She a relative of your'n?"

It was none of the man's business. Tahchee turned his head away, stared into the fire. The guard snorted.

"I bet she's more'n that," he taunted. "You've dicked her, ain't you?"

Only the knife hidden under his legs kept Tahchee from kicking the son of a bitch in the balls.

"Cut out that crap, Silas," the sergeant growled. "You'll not be baiting prisoners on my watch."

"Hah!" the one called Silas huffed and turned aside to spit, expressing his unspoken contempt. Tahchee hoped Silas would try to stop him when he made his escape. He'd love sinking the knife into his gut.

As the night hours dragged, Tahchee never moved, afraid of exposing the knife under him if he did. The stillness of the camp deepened, the night sounds in the forest grew louder. Camp fires died, one by one. Night dew began to settle, giving everything a damp feel. A whippoorwill kept fussing at nothing. Water tumbling over a creek riffle sounded ten times louder than it did earlier in the evening.

He shifted, slowly, as if to ease a cramped leg. He felt for the knife with his fingers, found it. The two guards which he was able to see were dozing, their heads jerking occasionally as they tried to stay awake. He could only hope that the two behind him were also asleep, as he went to work sawing on the thongs binding his wrists.

They loosened suddenly. He lay still, hopes mounting. He affected a light snore. After several minutes, he doubled his knees and sawed on the ropes binding his ankles. They fell away, too. Now, he knew, surprise was his only weapon. He pulled in a deep breath, then leaped to his feet and bounded away into the darkness. He jumped over sleeping forms, stepped on others.

"Hey!" someone shouted.

"Holy shit!"

He hit the creek in a dead run, made it across in three bounds.

A rifle cracked. He heard the ball cut through the foliage. Then a fusillade followed, the hot lead whizzing all around, thudding into timber, whining off rocks. He kept going at full speed in the darkness. Unseen limbs whacked him. He ran on instinct, alert for any deep ravines which he might tumble into and break a leg. He tried to think like a wild animal. Most ran in a wide circle, never getting far from their lairs.

He stopped to listen, holding his breath. He could hear the confusion going on behind and below. If he could circle and could get over on the opposite ridge, the chances of the soldiers finding him would be remote. They would have no tracker as good as Johnny Jumper. Also, in his favor, the Major would be forced to continue his journey to deliver the women and the boy to Fort Smith as scheduled.

The thought of having to abandon Honekahsee added to his torment as he ran through the darkness. What a waste to save him from drowning only to have him grow up in a white man's institution, Honekahsee would never know the freedom he had in Pasuga. No matter how nice or how motherly his teacher or teachers might be, it wouldn't be the same. There would be no old ones around to tell him stories of bravery and conquest, of how the sun and moon and stars came to be, of how the Cherokees came across the great sea from the east on wings of eagles. No. In an orphanage, they'd teach Honekahsee science, teach him facts, teach him that the universe is, and man only an incidental part. In Pasuga, the old ones would have taught him that man is, and the universe only an incidental part.

He pushed the boy from his mind and ran on in the moonless darkness, thinking like an animal.

CHAPTER 21

It seems peaceful enough, Tahchee thought as he approached the Trading Post, his quick glances missing nothing. What they would think of him, a stranger, on foot was another matter.

He'd tell them he was a settler who had been burned out by the Osages. He'd lost everything. Needed credit to outfit himself until he could rebuild and market some of his pigs. He would probably have to let the trader get him drunk first. It was their way of cheating Cherokees, Daniel had always warned.

He saw a tall, stooped shouldered man come out the front door of the Trading Post carrying a bucket. When the man caught sight of Tahchee, he hesitated, then poured the bucket's contents into a barrel. It looked like shelled corn. The man set the bucket on the flooring and pulled a large handkerchief from his hip pocket. He wiped sweat from his face and neck, waiting.

Tahchee, still cautious, kept his gaze whipping from place to place—the coral, the barn, back to the main building, to the trees behind on the knoll—as he neared the porch. He saw no sign of any soldiers. He halted at the bottom step. The tall man gestured.

"Come on in out'n the sun, stranger. Just drawed a bucket of fresh spring water. Looks like you could use a cool drink."

"Thanks. I sure could."

With one last quick look around, he mounted the steps and followed the stooped man inside.

Brooms, mops, shovels, picks, bedsteads, hoes, axes, cross-cut saws, long rifles, and other odds and ends were stacked along the walls; some hung from pegs. Racks of clothing dominated the interior area. The trader led the way to his water bucket sitting on a wooden shelf at the rear of the room. He motioned toward the gourd dipper hanging on a peg.

"Help yourself, mister—?"

Tahchee ignored the invitation to give his name, only nodding his appreciation as he reached for the gourd and plunged it into the water. He lifted the dipper, dripping, to his lips and drank, swallowing heavily, savoring the pleasure of the cool liquid in his mouth and throat.

He knew the trader was curious. It was his business to know everybody and what everybody was doing in his trade territory. He would have to be careful how he handled the man's curiosity; being too reticent would arouse suspicions, and you could get caught in a lie trying to be too devious. Attack, he concluded. It beat being defensive by a mile. Finished with his drink, he flipped the last drops from the gourd, replaced it on the peg and glanced around the store's interior.

"Turned out to be a nice place," he said. "Last time I was through here, you'd just started up with your building. Didn't have any idea you'd be carrying this much merchandise."

The trader, although proud, eyed him curiously as if he were trying to remember.

"I don't recollect—"

Tahchee stopped him with a wave. "I was in a hurry at the time. Didn't stop to visit," he said, then brought his gaze back to the trader's face. "Got any guns?"

The trader's eyes brightened. "What'chur need?"

"A good piece. Osages burned me out. Lost everything."

The trader's face clouded. "The bastards," he growled. "They sure messin' things up around here, ain't they? You one of those new settlers up on Barron Fork?"

"Taylor's the name. Daniel Taylor," he said easily, making the most of the opening. He kept his eyes on the man's face, watching for any sign of recognition. He saw none. The trader extended his hand, saying, "Hilderbrand. Jesse Hilderbrand. My woman's a Cherokee. Polly."

They were always quick to let you know they're Cherokees by marriage. Tahchee thought. *And when the Osages come, they will say they are white.*

"The wife's away. Neighbors are gettin' together for a quiltin' party."

"A real worker, is she?" Tahchee chuckled, then added after seeing the man's proud grin, "Now about those guns—?"

"Right," the man said and led the way, still talking, to his gun rack. He lifted a long rifle and held it out.

"This'un's a nice piece," he said.

Tahchee took the weapon, turned it over in his hands, pretending to examine the gun while estimating his chances for credit. Never go in debt, Daniel had warned, especially to a white trader. Once in, you'll never get out. The trader pointed at the name etched on the gun's breech.

"It's a Henry. Ever owned a Henry?"

Tahchee shook his head and sighted down the barrel. The trader's voice indicated he anticipated a sale.

"Never been fired, so fer's I know. I'll be honest with you, though. Picked it up from a family on their way back home to Missouri. Been t' Texas, they said. They looked it, too. Their team was poor as old Job's turkey. Kids with ribs stickin' out. Near starved. I put 'em up for a couple days. Fed 'em good. Helped 'em fix a wheel and make a new single tree fer their wagon. Nice folks. He give me this gun when he left. I told 'em I didn't expect pay fer a kindness. He insisted. He was a good Indian."

Tahchee detested the way whites used the word "Indian" and doubly so whenever it was preceded by "good" or "bad." Wouldn't they ever see us as people? Outwardly, as usual, he kept his face impassive. They simply didn't know any better.

He tested the rifle, thumbing its hammer back. He kept his thumb hooked on the hammer's knurl when he pulled the trigger and eased the firing mechanism back to safety.

"How much?"

"Cash or barter?"

He looked the trader directly in the eye. "Have cash in mind. But I lost everything in the fire. If the price you're asking's not out of line, I can get you your money in a few months."

This gave the trader the option of doubling his price on a gamble. He knew he would get the piece when the trader asked, "What'chu mean by 'a few months'?"

Tahchee shrugged. "Less than six."

Then before the trader could agree, he added, "I'll need some balls and powder to go along with it...a few other things."

"Like what?"

He cradled the gun in his left elbow as if it were already his and ticked off on his fingers the provisions he would need, finishing with, "Also, a good horse and riding gear."

The trader licked his lips, tried to appear undecided as he kept making quick glances out of the corners of his eyes in Tahchee's direction. He pretended not to notice, knowing he had guessed right. The total sum, doubled, would be worth the gamble. The trader coughed.

"Taylor, huh?" he questioned. "Ain't heared of no Taylors."

"Just moved over from Arkansas couple months ago."

"One of those, huh? Lots of new folks movin' in since the Lovely Treaty. Don't see why we can't make a deal. Always glad to help out people in trouble."

He went behind the counter, reached down, and came up with a gallon jug. He worked the corn cob out and shoved the jug across the counter.

"How about a drink whilst we discuss prices and terms?"

"Sounds good to me," Tahchee said and swept up the jug, laying it across his elbow and tilting it to his lips. He plugged the opening with his tongue and faked a couple of swallows. He handed the jug to the trader, making a gagging sound, blinked, and said, "Good stuff. You make it?"

"Nah," the trader said as he wiped the jug's opening with his shirt sleeve. He lifted it to his lips, took a couple swallows and set it down. "Cheaper buyin' it from moonshiners over in Arkansas. And a lot less trouble."

He shoved the jug across the counter. They continued the ritual until a deal was set. Tahchee faked inebriation, agreeing to a price, plus twenty percent interest. He hated using Daniel's good name in such a manner, but he was desperate.

He watched the trader piling the items he'd bought on the counter to be inventoried and priced, then stiffened when he heard hoof beats. Wishing he had the Henry rifle loaded, he strolled to the front of the store for a quick look. His heart bounded when he saw the two soldiers. He studied them closely as they pulled to a stop in front of the store and dismounted.

He felt a measure of relief when he didn't recognize either man. Best to play it cool. He edged away, and tried to make himself inconspicuous among the racks of clothing by the time the soldiers came in.

"Jesse!" one called. "You got anymore of that Arkansas rotgut!"

"Now, now, boys," the trader said. "You know it's illegal to sell likker in Injun Territory."

The soldiers laughed. Jesse grinned.

"But I do have some tonic. Good for anything that ails you."

They made a deal. As the trader passed the jug to the soldiers, he asked, "What's new with the army these days?"

"Injuns. Always injuns."

"Osage?"

"Osage and Cherokees both. One's as bad as the other. Had one get away from our escort couple days ago."

"Osage or Cherokee?"

One soldier looked at the other and asked, "What was he?"

The other soldier grimaced. "Hell, I don't know. They all look the same to me."

Tahchee caught the trader's suspicious glance his direction, but he kept on pretending to be unconcerned as he studied the heavy, sheep-lined coats.

"What was the man's name?" the trader asked.

"I don't know. One of those injun monikers. Sounded like Dutch, or something like that. They say he and an Osage named Black Dog are into it with one another. Burning folks out. We're scheduled to ride out tomorrow and run down Black Dog. Up north somewhere."

The trader reached under the counter and set up another jug.

"My compliments. You boys are doin' a fine job keepin' the peace in the Territory. We let this feudin' get out of hand, they'll be turnin' on us white folks next."

One of the soldiers hooked a finger in the jug's handle.

"Thanks, Jesse. Don't you worry about them injuns. As long as they ain't botherin' white folks, let 'em kill off one another, I always say."

"Then what'er you doin' chasing after this Black Dog feller?"

"Way I hear, we got to make it look good. We catch the worst Osage and hang him. Then we catch the worst Cherokee and hang him. That settles things down a while."

The soldiers took their whiskey and left. The trader made his way to Tahchee's side.

"Let's go pick out a horse," he said. "I got some real cheap ones if you're interested. Branded U.S. Army. But it's almost growed over."

Somehow, the bold remark about having army mounts nudged Tahchee's funny bone. He had to laugh. "Give me one one of those," he said, then added, "That is, if you'll guarantee it ain't stolen."

Then the trader laughed. "Why, shore. I always guarantee everything I sell."

So Black Dog was up north somewhere, Tahchee thought as he mounted his new horse and headed that direction. After all, he hadn't promised Laura when he'd be home. Besides, she would wait...if she didn't get arrested herself for slipping him that knife.

The horse with its U.S. Army brand "almost growed over" was a heavy-boned animal, built for work. When he got out of sight of the Trading Post, he touched his heels to its flanks, urging it into a lope. He liked the feel of the horse's muscles bunching and stretching between his legs. He guided the racing animal purposefully through some timber, dodging branches and leaning into the wind when the horse leaped over logs and across ditches. A man needed to know what his mount could and couldn't do in case of trouble. After several minutes of wild riding, he straightened in the saddle and pulled gently on the reins.

"Ho, up," he called softly.

The horse's ears twisted backward to pick up the command, then pounded to a stop. Satisfied, he relaxed in the saddle and patted the animal's damp neck.

His new gear left him better than four hundred and fifty dollars in debt.

Never borrow, Daniel had always warned. *If you can't pay for it, do without.*

And he'd signed Daniel's name to the note the trader had written out. Somehow, it had made him feel good doing so, as if he'd brought Daniel back to life.

"Sorry, Daniel," he apologized aloud. "This is an emergency."

Daniel had tried to explain the white man's economy one time. It was based on land, he'd said. Acres represented dollars which you multiplied by a varying factor which, in itself, was ambiguous, depending upon how many people wanted the same piece of land. A white man could be penniless, claim he owned thousands of acres of the earth, and declare himself wealthy.

Land ownership was still confusing to Tahchee's way of thinking. Land usage made sense. You cultivate a patch of ground, raise crops, and harvest what you raise. You used land, the same way you used air or running water.

Even the U.S. Government was interpreting the Osage-Cherokee wars as a land dispute. It wasn't, Daniel pointed out. It was over individual rights, the right to occupy and use the land. When one side or the other won that right, the loser moved on to occupy another section of the earth. The U.S. Government drew boundaries around everything, regardless of who might be using the land at the time. Individual states surrounded themselves with boundaries. There were counties within the states and, of course, individual plots of land within the counties. And yet, when the white man wants to build a military road or an army post, his government declares individual ownership of all land in the road's path or where the army post is going to be null and void. Just like that. They revert to the Indian philosophy.

In the end, he justified his indebtedness by mentally estimating the old home place on White River to be worth two or three thousand dollars. So he wasn't actually in debt to the trader. He'd bartered a portion of the old home place for transferable goods. But if his home and farm were here in Indian Territory instead of Arkansas, the Cherokee government would still own it. On reflection, he doubted the two economies would ever mix because their primary sources of wealth differed so greatly.

During his first day's ride north from the Trading Post, he came across two farms. In each case, the buildings had been burned, leaving nothing but ash-covered, blackened logs. At one, he saw the fresh graves. When he approached a third farm late that evening, he saw the man and woman and their children already at work rebuilding their burned-out place. When the man noticed Tahchee, he ran to get his gun. Tahchee, not wanting to kill the man in self defense, quickly held up a hand.

"Osi-oh," he called out in Cherokee to prove his nationality. Then he switched to English. "I'm on the trail of Black Dog, the Osage." He motioned toward the destruction. "Is this his work?"

The man appeared to relax, but kept his rifle cocked and his finger on the trigger.

"All I know is they was Osages."

"It's Black Dog."

The man's face still reflected skepticism.

"Are you a Cherokee Lighthorseman?"

Tahchee shook his head. "No, I'm not a lawman. My fight with Black Dog is personal."

"That's our trouble," the man said, lowering the gun barrel. "They's too many personal fights going on. One thing always leads to another. What's our Council doing...still making treaties which nobody pays any attention to? Whyn't we get up our own army and go whip the Osages once and for all?"

He resented the man's implication that he had no business taking the law into his own hands. But he clamped his jaw shut, determined not be drawn into a political controversy. Number one, he didn't have time. Number two, the man was upset, and had a right to be. He removed his hat and wiped the dampness from its sweatband with his handkerchief.

"You need any help here?" he asked.

The man rested his rifle butt on his toe, clutching the long barrel in a gnarled hand. "I done it before and I can do it again," he said, rejecting his offer. "You got business with the Osage, you better get on your way." He pointed north, and added. "Tracks show they rode off in that direction. About a dozen or so. We was lucky. We was gone visiting the wife's kin, or we'd probably be laying here with you looking at our corpses if it wasn't for that."

Tahchee replaced his hat. The dry sweat band felt good against his brow. He glanced at the woman, touched the brim of his hat respectfully and took his leave properly, saying, "Ma'am." And to the man, he said, "Good luck."

As he reined his horse around, the man called after him, "Don't see why the Council don't do something."

Tahchee ignored the remark as he rode away, studying the hoof prints in the sand. The sun searched for a place to settle as he hurried north, wanting to ride as far as possible before darkness blotted out the trail.

He had to get Black Dog—had to, before the Cherokee National Council got into it. While there were no provisions in the Cherokee's written constitution calling for a militia—a very serious flaw in the document, many claimed—the Cherokee Nation, as a protectorate of the U.S. Government, would petition Congress for a stronger police action by the army. This would make him a legal outlaw instead of a hero if he found Black Dog and killed him.

At full dark, he stopped and made a cold camp. He took the ground for a bed, used his new blanket for cover and his new saddle for a pillow.

Song Bird was somewhere up there among the stars with Daniel... *Would Daniel tell her it was me who killed him?* He closed his eyes in shame and felt the dampness in them.

Laura. He had promised to take her to Texas. His groin ached, and for the first time in two years, he went to sleep thinking of someone else other than Black Dog.

CHAPTER 22

Tahchee awoke, his mind filled with new thoughts. Why not return to Pasuga? Black Dog would be back there sooner or later, especially if has become the Osages' new leader. Sure. Let Black Dog come to him instead of chasing all over the country trying to run him down. All you'd ever do doing that is a trail of burned out homes like those he saw yesterday.

And he would get to be with Little Tassel; see about her. What if Black Dog has taken her into his lodge? The thought chilled him, filling him with a sense of helpless rage. All the more reason to kill him, he vowed to himself. The deepening sense of hurt and resentment galvanized him into action.

He quickly satisfied his early morning hunger at a nearby blackberry patch and completed his meal by stripping bark from a slippery elm, peeling away the inner layer and chewing the succulent membrane as he saddled his horse. He swung up and headed for Pasuga.

Late that day, he rode into the village, cautious, his gaze darting everywhere. Activity appeared normal, but he kept his long rifle laying across his thighs, one hand gripping its breech, thumb on the hammer. Many recognized him, smiled and waved. And others stared, hostility in their eyes. He spotted a familiar, bow-legged figure hurrying through the crowd. He smiled and urged his horse alongside the squat man.

"Friend Old Hop! Remember me!"

Old Hop rolled his big head to look up, apparently surprised by this intrusion into his thoughts. Then recognition flooded his long face.

"Are these old eyes seeing Cherokee friend people call Dutch?"

"They are," he acknowledged, still cautious. "I heard Clermont was killed. Are you Chief now?"

Old Hop glanced around warily, as if to make sure no one would hear, then said, "Black Dog is Chief. But when he is away, people say they want me to be their leader."

"That figures, old friend. I think you should be."

"I no deserve honor."

"Old Hop would make a great leader," Tahchee encouraged. He surveyed the activity in the village again and asked, "Is Dutch still welcome in Pasuga?"

"Friend Dutch always welcome among the Osage," Old Hop said, nodding. "Many like to talk how you saved Honekahsee from flood." He eyed the gun in Tahchee's lap. " But there are some who talk of nothing but war with Cherokee."

Tahchee searched the wrinkled face for a meaning. A warning? The old man motioned.

"Come. Rest in lodge of Old Hop."

Perfect. He swung down from his squeaking saddle, relieved to get the sweat-dampened leather from between his thighs. He cradled the gun in one arm and followed Old Hop to his lodge, his gaze sweeping the village one more time. He saw no sign of Little Tassel before they went inside.

Old Hop's woman, so large she appeared to be rolling around the room, heated a quick meal over the coals. She passed the bowl of thick soup to the men sitting cross-legged at the far wall, as far as they could get from the cooking fire. Old Hop tipped his bowl to his mouth and slurped loudly before he paused to lick his lips.

"White soldier bring Little Tassel home," he began, guessing, probably, why Tahchee had come back. "We all listen to her story. How you save her and Honekahsee. How you drown two Cherokees. How you float down river behind log. We all sad that white man take Honekahsee to orphanage. Many say it is better Clermont's son be there and learn white man ways than living in Black Dog lodge. Little Tassel say white man put you in prison. She say her life belong to you. She tell her story many times since she return to Pasuga."

Tahchee shrugged and attempted to deflect the praise. "I only did what had to be done."

Old Hop sipped from the bowl again, sat in worried silence, then said, "Black Dog get angry when he hear story. He say you are cause of Cherokee attack on Pasuga. Some warriors listen to what Black Dog say."

"I'm not afraid of Black Dog."

"He has many warriors. They go fight the Cherokee. They only return to Pasuga to be with their women. They go fight again. Black Dog is powerful enemy. Each time he go out and kill Cherokee, he come home more powerful than before."

Tahchee set his bowl on the ground, thinking. Old Hop was trying to tell him something, that's for sure. And he knew what it was: If he was going to kill Black Dog, he'd have to catch him away from his many friends.

His goal was getting more and more complicated. One thing for certain, he wanted to be sure Black Dog knew before he died that it was the son of Song Bird who was killing him. He spoke into the stillness of the room, "Does Old Hop know where I can find Black Dog?"

Old Hop's large head waggled from side to side. "People tired of war. I say to Black Dog, it is time for Osage to move north. We should join other Osage brothers in place white man call Kansas. Black Dog say never. Not until all Cherokee die. When Black Dog return this time, the people want me to tell him we go live in Kansas. I will tell him like the people want me to. Then Black Dog will kill me."

Tahchee's lungs sucked in a quick, involuntary breath at the fatalistic prediction. But there was nothing he could say. After a short silence, he cleared his throat and said, "Maybe Black Dog will never return. Old Hop will live to lead his people north."

Old Hop turned his dispirited gaze on Tahchee. "Cherokee friend speaks of better things to come. Make Old Hop have hope."

Tahchee shrugged. He grasped the rifle lying by his side and stood.

"I need to have a word with Little Tassel. In whose lodge will I find her?"

"People ask about Honekahsee," Old Hop said, as if he hadn't heard Tahchee's request. "Will he ever come back some day to be great leader of Osage like his father?"

"Perhaps."

"He will go to white man school?"

"Yes."

"That is good. It is as Clermont wished. The old days are gone. Our children must learn white man ways."

Tahchee heard what the old man was saying, but he was uneasy over the way Old Hop dodged his question about Little Tassel. This time he was more direct.

"I need to talk with Little Tassel. Where will I find her?"

Old Hop waved toward the river. "Many women wash clothes today," he said, and refused to look Tahchee in the eye. Looking down at the old man, Tahchee knew he was keeping something from him and wanted more information. Instead, after a long silence, interrupted only by the loud slurping of Old Hop drinking his soup, Tahchee gave up and went to find Little Tassel.

She was at the river bank, alone, scrubbing deerskins on a flat rock. Tahchee's heart ached at the sight of her. But at the same time, he felt an inner joy. He stopped a few paces behind her, knew she was unaware of his presence. He could not help eyeing the changing contours of her body as she worked. She seemed older, much older now, and he felt a deep stirring to…to take another bath with her—just the two of them, alone in a secluded place. He eased himself into a squatting position, resting a buttock on one heel, his elbows on his knees.

Something about his quiet movement caught her attention. When she turned her head far enough to see him out of the corner of her eye, she started, falling away from him.

"Oh—!" she gasped, her face showing fright until she recognized him. "Dutch!" she exploded, her voice filled with an odd mixture of anger and joy. Her emotion culminated in the act of swinging the sopping wet deerskin at his head.

His hand was quicker. He caught the wet garment and laughed as the water sprayed over him.

"Hey! I don't need a bath!"

The use of the word 'bath' came unexpectedly, and he knew she remembered too, the way she flushed. But she refused to look away, her silent gaze burning messages into him as she slowly pulled the wet garment from his grasp.

"That's what you said last time," she taunted. Then she returned her attention to her washing, as if he weren't there. He eased forward, one knee on the ground.

"You don't act very glad to see me? I thought—"

Her sudden look stopped him from saying whatever it was he had intended to say. Her beautiful oval-shaped face was within six inches of his. He searched her face, eagerly reading her desire, savoring the want he saw in her eyes. As his face moved closer, her eyes closed, and he kissed her lightly on her slightly parted lips. She opened her eyes, showing a slight disappointment, then recovered. She made a half-hearted attempt to continue her scrubbing.

"Have you come back to live with us?" she said, her voice unexplainably cool.

He settled onto his heel again, puzzled. "Yes...for a short while. You will come to my lodge again? As before?"

Her hesitant, short silence hurt, even before she said, "I cannot. I work in lodge of Black Dog now."

Tahchee felt an icy chill, especially when she kept her face averted as if ashamed. Then renewed hate surged through him. He seized her arm, forcing her to look him the eye.

"What's he done to you?" he demanded, his voice strained, harsh. He did not want to hear, but he had to know the truth.

Her dark eyes glistened. She ducked her head. "He comes to my sleeping robe. He makes me do things I do not want to do. His woman of many years hates me. She beats me when he is gone. She makes me do all the work."

He tried to imagine, but his sensibilities wouldn't allow it. He felt cheated, angry, frustrated. That man again! He stood, yanking her to her feet.

"I'm taking you away from here—now"

She pulled free, backed away, shaking her head. "No! His woman will tell. Black Dog will find you and will kill you!"

"Let him try!" He reached for her. "You're coming with me."

She yielded to his pull, but begged, "No, Tahchee! Black Dog has many warriors. You must leave Pasuga and never come back. Go to your own people. Forget Little Tassel. I am no more."

"You are to me!" he snapped, his soul burning in fire. He tightened his grip on her arm and began dragging her with him. "We're leaving here. Now!"

She still resisted, her tone plaintive when she said, "I can't. I belong to Black Dog."

"Like hell, you do!"

He headed for the village, pulling her along, taking long, angry strides. Little Tassel had to run to keep up, her efforts to pull free getting weaker.

People gathered, watched silently as he lifted the girl into his saddle. He vaulted on behind her, reaching around her to seize the reins, only to be stopped by a ring of angry-faced Osages pressing closer. He lifted the Henry, leveled it at the nearest warrior and thumbed the hammer back. The ominous click stopped the man.

"Out of my way," he said, hoping his clumsy Osage words carried the determined anger he felt. The warrior shook his head.

"Cherokee no take Black Dog second woman."

"Chief Clermont gave this girl to me when I saved his son from the flood. If Black Dog wants to take my woman, tell him to come and get her!"

In the tense moment that followed, he tightened his finger on the gun's trigger. He knew there was no way out but to shoot the man and make a break for it. But just then Old Hop came elbowing his way through the ring of people.

"Brave Cherokee speak truth," he said, holding up one hand. "Let him return to his people with his woman. If Black Dog no like, let him go find Cherokee and get his woman back."

The dark eyes in the huge head atop the spindly body of the old man burned from face to face around the ring. Tahchee could sense the will of Old Hop suddenly dominating. Old Hop sensed it too, for he spoke again, this time with authority.

"Many have said to Old Hop, we are tired of war. They say, lead us to join our brothers in north country. Now, I say I will lead. Go tell your women to make lodge ready for journey."

The low murmur in the crowd rose to excited talk. Tahchee relaxed as the people melted away, leaving Old Hop and the glowering warrior. Tahchee lowered the hammer on his long rifle, then motioned to the warrior with the gun barrel.

"You go find Black Dog. Tell him I took his woman. Tell him I go to my home on White River in Arkansas. He knows where it is. Tell him when he comes, I will be waiting. Tell him that I—"

He started to say, "Tell him I am the son of Song Bird," but checked himself in time. He wanted to see Black Dog's face when he heard those words.

The warrior spun and stalked away in silence. Old Hop came to stand beside Tahchee's horse. He held up a hand to shake, white man style.

"We part, my friend. Our eyes will never see one another again, but our minds will long remember."

Tahchee leaned down to shake the gnarled old hand. He knew the old man was right. He forced a tight smile.

"May our people find peace," he said. He hoped his remark sounded more sincere than he felt. Old Hop nodded.

"Our people will tell many stories about brave Cherokee who came to live with the Osage. They will tell about how he fought the mighty flood to save Chief's son. They will tell how he fought by the side of the Osage against his own people."

Then he patted Little Tassel on her thigh, adding, "Old Hop is proud brave Cherokee take beautiful Osage girl to be his woman."

His woman? That wasn't exactly what he had in mind as he reined the horse about, leaving the old man standing alone in the center of the soon-to-be abandoned Osage village.

He headed east, toward the old home place in Arkansas. As he rode with his arms about Little Tassel, he could not help but wonder if he'd make it…with Black Dog and his warriors on his trail. Or, if he did, what was Laura going to think when he came riding in with…his Osage—squaw?

CHAPTER 23

Tahchee rode hard, trying to put as much distance as possible between them and Pasuga before bedding down for the night. He cursed himself for leaving in such a hurry. The least he could have done was pick up a couple of sleeping robes. He dismissed the thought of building a fire when darkness closed in.

It gave him a peculiar, upside down feeling being hunted instead of being the hunter. With the feeling was also the tight fear of knowing Black Dog, a woman killer, would never consider coming at him single handed. Tahchee wouldn't have a chance against a dozen or more Osage warriors. His best bet was to keep going as fast as he could until somehow, someway he would be able to reverse the chase again. After securing his tired horse, he found a bed of leaves in a depression and wrapped himself and Little Tassel in the saddle blanket.

They shared their warmth through the long night. He slept fitfully, careful not to alarm her by submitting to his passion, for fear of reminding her of any sexual abuses she may have suffered from Black Dog's demands. In fact, he didn't think he slept at all until he awoke the next morning and saw her sitting not far away, pulling at the tangles in her hair.

"Are you awake?" she asked, smiling.

"I'm not sure." He sat up. "I may be dreaming I'm awake."

Her soft laughter was refreshing. "Like the butterfly?" she asked.

"What butterfly?"

"The butterfly the old women talk about. He was a very large butterfly with beautiful black and yellow wings. He fell asleep and dreamed he was a mighty warrior. When he awakened, he did not know if he was a butterfly who fell asleep and dreamed he was a mighty warrior, or a mighty warrior who fell asleep and was dreaming he was a butterfly."

He laughed, loving the story. He loved her cheerful attitude. Come to think of it, he wasn't quite sure about himself at the moment—was he the butterfly or a mighty warrior? He didn't care. He pulled on his boots.

"Dutch?"

He looked up at her, saying nothing, and waited for her to continue. She said, "I love being your woman. It is different sleeping with you. When can we see one another like that day in the river?"

His heart began to pound, his face growing hot. He saw her naked body again in his mind, floating before him in the sun splashed water. He killed the vision by getting abruptly to his feet and shouldering the saddle. Without answering, he headed for the horse. She followed, watched in silence as he geared the animal for travel. When he turned to lift her, she grasped his arms, forcing him to look at her.

"You already have a woman, don't you?"

She may as well know; be prepared. He nodded. "She's waiting for me. We have a child. A girl. But that doesn't mean I don't want you...as before. As a—"

He was unable to say what he meant, because he wasn't sure what he did mean. He saw the hurt in her eyes when she pulled away.

"She's that soldier's wife, isn't she?"

"Yes. But the soldier was killed. She and I knew one another a long time ago. I promised to take her to Texas—a far away place. You can go with us. Live with us until you find a man."

"You act one way, talk another! I want to go back to my people!"

"You can't. If Black Dog returns..." he paused, noticing her shiver. He stepped near, reached out and pulled her into his arms. "It'll be all right, Little Tassel. I promise. You'll like her...and the baby, too."

She wilted against him and he held her tight, feeling like a noble son of a bitch.

"I'm glad she's pretty," Little Tassel said. Puzzled, he held her back to look for an answer in her eyes.

"What's that got to do with it?"

"If I was prettier than her, she would never let me stay."

Then he understood. She was consenting to be wife number two. He knew he was digging a hole too deep to climb out of. He reviewed the conversation, trying to pin-point what he had said to lead her to believe he wanted her as a second wife.

"We'll see," he said, not liking the vague answer himself. But it was the best he could do. One thing he did know, they'd better get going or get caught and killed here in the wilderness.

Near the end of the week, Tahchee sighted the cabin. In a way, he was mildly surprised to see it still standing. He was more surprised, however, when he noticed the thin wisp of smoke drifting skyward from the chimney.

Laura?

Black Dog sat his pony staring down at the depression in the bed of leaves. His men waited, impatient to renew the chase. They weren't prepared for the order when Black Dog said, "We will sleep here tonight."

The Osage warriors obeyed, went about cold camp duties talking in undertones. Many were unhappy the way they were traveling, making very little attempts to hide their trail. Soldiers would follow. But this chase was serious, and they all knew it. Those closest to Black Dog had a feeling there was more to finding the Cherokee than there was to getting the girl back, for the leader seldom mentioned the girl. And Black Dog kept turning his gaze to the east, regardless of which way the trail of the pursued appeared to be heading, as if knew their destination. The older ones remembered the days they followed Black Dog east and waited in the mountains when he went on alone to spend the night.

The Osage warriors stacked their guns, military style, and sought comfortable places to sleep.

Major Benefield, walking and leading his horse, held up a hand to stop his platoon when he sighted the ghostly figure of Johnny Jumper materializing out of the dawn's weak light. The Cherokee tracker, wet to the waist from dew on the high grasses, pointed in the direction from which he came.

"Osage in there," he whispered. "Fifteen, maybe twenty. All asleep. Guns stacked. No guards."

The Major turned, motioned for his men to gather around. He spoke in a hushed tone.

"The tracker found them. They're all asleep. I want you men to spread out. Circle them. First man to make a sound gets court martialed. Understand?

"Now, listen close, men. According to that old Chief leading his people north, this has to be Black dog. He's mean and full of tricks. I expect each of you to be in a position in ten minutes. I'll fire the first shot. Shoot to kill. Any questions?"

"Does that mean we take no prisoners, sir?" a corporal asked.

"Absolutely not! We're not butchers. We're soldiers. If any man gives up—raises his hands in surrender—take him. We can hang 'em later."

Several men smothered their laughter and Major Benefield, grim faced, waved them away. He watched them fade into the fast-graying night, expecting to hear a twig snap under somebody's clumsy foot. Soon, he stood alone with Johnny Jumper and noticed the strange look on the tracker's face.

"What's the matter, Jumper? Scared?"

Jumper shrugged. "A little. I—"

He appeared hung up on the long pause, and the Major gave him a nudge. "You what?"

"I no understand. I know this is Black Dog. I track him before. But this time, he does not seem to care. He is following one horse carrying two people, a man and a woman. But sometimes he leaves their trail and heads east, as if he knows where they are going."

"You think this is a trick of some sort?" Major Benefield asked, concerned that he might be leading his men into an ambush.

Jumper threw out both hands, palms up. "No. They all there. Sleeping. But that another thing that bother me. Black Dog not posting watch like he always do."

Major Benefield considered the information, then discarded it. He'd already made his decision. His men were in place, and it was time to go.

"Let's move in," he whispered to the perplexed Cherokee tracker.

They worked their way through the dense underbrush growing profusely in the marshy bottoms along the Verdigris River. Johnny Jumper led the way to a slight knoll. Major Benefield crept forward to a tree, peered around. He was able to make out the Osage camp, just barely. He thought it peculiar the way they had stacked their guns. Evidently, they thought the military way was a good way to do it. Whatever. At the moment, he was glad. In addition to having the advantage of total surprise, he would also have a couple of precious seconds it would take for the Osages to get to their guns and start shooting back. He checked his watch.

Time. He raised his rifle, sighted on a light piece of cloth and squeezed the trigger. The gun boomed, kicked his shoulder. The dawn exploded. Flame lances cut the gray gloom, all pointing toward the sleeping Osages.

Major Benefield concentrated on inserting his next paper cartridge and ramming the ball home. He wished now he'd assigned his men to fire by odds and evens, for the sudden silence during the reloading process seemed an eternity. He sighted again, saw the surviving Osages snatching at the gun stacks. He selected one, fired. The man fell.

Another fusillade. Silence. Grunts and curses. The Osage guns answered. Balls whizzed, ricocheted off limby undergrowth. Major Benefield was ready again. He could see nothing. He searched for some movement beyond the pall of smoke. He saw a man running, sighted quickly and fired. He missed.

The gunfire became sporadic. In less than three minutes, it was over. Major Benefield cupped a hand near his mouth and bellowed, "Hold you fire!"

Cautiously, he approached the camp, his finger on his trigger and Johnny Jumper backing him up. His initial exhilaration of success with the ambush was quickly replaced by a sense of revulsion. He saw dead Osages sprawled everywhere. A hardened sense of reasoning set in. It was a military decision. You kill to save lives of innocent people, many of them women and children. If this was the only way to stop Black Dog, you had to do it.

"Hey!" someone yelled. "I got one!"

Major Benefield, nerves still taut, leveled his gun at the sound, expecting a trick. Many Indians could speak English, too. He relaxed when he saw his corporal approaching, prodding an Osage ahead of him. The light was stronger now. He could see the man's face, noticed the scars on his cheek— as if someone had scratched him.

"Dacy!" Laura screamed and left the frying pan on the stove as she hurried to stop Dacy before she pulled everything from the table. She swatted Dacy's hand. "Stop that! You hear me?"

Dacy let go, her lips puckering, threatening to cry. Laura pointed a finger in the child's face.

"No! No! No!"

Dacy sat down hard, whimpering, her moon-shaped face wreathed in heart-broken sorrow.

Laura turned back to the stove, her thoughts on the baby already dissipating. She was still angry over Tahchee not being here, nor any sign that he had been; angrier, still, that he had insisted she bring Dacy. She had debated about leaving her with her father and mother, but decided against it. Her father had accompanied her to the Taylor home. No one was here. It was risky even telling her father Tahchee was coming, since the army was after him. So was the Cherokee Lighthorsemen, her father told her. The Council wanted to put him on trial for fighting on the side of the Osage. Treason, they called it.

But she had to confide in somebody. William Rogers didn't approve of her running off to Texas with a wanted man, but, as usual, he let her have her way.

"At least leave Dacy with us," he had begged.

"No, father," she said. "You know as well as I do, Dacy belongs to him. It's only right we stay together as a family."

"I'm glad to hear you thinking like that, Laura. There's been times your mother and I worried about you. The way you liked boys and all."

"Oh, father!" Laura scolded gently. "I can take care of myself. You go on back home."

When was leaving, he told her she was welcome to come back home and live. "Clancy will be leaving home before long, I suspect. You and Dacy can have his bed."

"I'll wait here a few days," she told him. "If Tahchee doesn't show up, I may be home. But don't count on me staying long, if I do."

He looked disappointed. She didn't tell him that Major—Tom—Benefield was interested in her. He wouldn't understand. A woman, especially a widow with a child, had to grab at every chance she had getting a man or wind up starving to death. And Tom wasn't just any man. Not by a long shot. He was a Commanding Officer. The thought of marrying him had a strong appeal, very strong appeal. How would those high-handed army wives like that? Having an Indian the top ranked woman on the post?

Two more days, she vowed. She'd give him two more days. If he didn't show up...

Back at the stove, she reached for the skillet handle, scooted the pan to a cooler spot on the cooking surface and made a face at the smell of the burned bacon. She could never cook, hated trying. She picked up a fork to turn the meat, but froze when she heard voices outside.

Tahchee? No! He'd be alone. The chill stiffened her spine as she stepped quickly to the fireplace and snatched her rifle, a modern army issue designed for using paper cartridges and percussion caps. Dacy whimpered as she cocked the gun and leveled it waist high at the door, her finger tightened on the trigger when somebody knocked.

"Hello!" a man's voice called as the door creaked open. A familiar voice. A soldier from the army post? She wouldn't trust a soldier any more than she would a savage Osage. She lifted the rifle and sighted.

A head appeared, eyes trying to adjust to the gloom of the interior. Her heart skipped several beats, then raced madly.

"Tahchee!" she shouted. She lowered the gun and ran across the room. He flung the door back.

"Laura!"

She fell into his open arms, crushing the rifle between them, one finger still on the trigger.

The gun boomed, sending its ball ripping through the roof. She staggered back, stunned and surprised. Time stopped for an eternity.

Had she shot him? Shot herself? She saw his eyes focus on the wisp of smoke curling from the gun barrel.

Suddenly, he was laughing and Dacy was crying. Then it all came together, and she let her own relief spill out in hysterical laughter. He pointed at the still smoking gun.

"Put that thing away before you kill someone?" he mocked.

She made a move to stand the weapon against the wall, but held onto it when the beautiful Indian girl appeared at his side and seized his arm.

"Dutch!" Laura heard her say, but was unable to understand the rest of the question. She saw him nod and pat her hand. Then she recognized the girl—it was that Little Tassel.

An uneasy hurt squeezed her heart, and kept squeezing with increasing pressure as she watched Tahchee slip an arm about her trying to calm her. She wasn't such a little girl, not by a long shot!

She *was* his squaw! A flare of bitter anger caused her to tighten her grip on the gun. Unconsciously, she had the muzzle pointing at the two when Tahchee explained.

"Laura, this is Little Tassel. Remember her? She's the orphan—"

"Orphan?" Laura blurted, unable to contain her bitterness. "Do you take her with you everywhere you go?"

Dacy's cries were getting louder. She waited a full second watching Tahchee's mouth open and close as he tried to say something. Then, disgusted that he might even come out with a weak explanation of some sort, she whirled and went to see about Dacy. She propped the gun against the wall and stooped to get the baby just as Tahchee gripped her arm.

"Laura!"

She refused to look at him, concentrating instead on settling Dacy down. He forced her to face him.

"Will you listen to me!" he said, his voice brusque, full of anger.

She lifted her gaze slowly, experiencing a mild shock seeing him so close, as she'd longed for so many times.

"I'm listening," she said, surprised at the calm coolness of her own voice.

"She's just a girl—"

"And you're so *much, much* older," Laura mocked. His face reddened.

"What I mean is she was given to me—I mean assigned by the Chief to keep my lodge clean and do my laundry..."

"You told me that before. Keep talking. This is getting interesting, *very* interesting!"

She enjoyed watching him in misery, for he deserved it, bringing that— that backwoods tramp home with him. He frowned.

"Make up your mind," he said sharply. "Do you want me to explain, or not?"

"I said keep talking, didn't I?"

She watched him trying to get control of himself. God, he was handsome! She'd almost forgot. Even the strength of his voice was thrilling.

"I went back to try and get Black Dog one more time. He was gone. He'd taken her into his lodge—"

"So you thought you'd get even by running away with his wife?"

"No! She said he was doing awful things to her."

She laughed. "Like dragging her up a creek and throwing her down on a mud bank!"

He fell angrily silent, glared. She wished she hadn't said that, at least the way she said it. It was a beautiful memory, one that she cherished. She tried to apologize, but couldn't. She faced him defiantly and said, "I certainly wouldn't have risked my life helping you get away if I'd known you were going back after her!" She jabbed a finger at Little Tassel.

"I didn't go back after her, dammit, Laura! I went back to get Black Dog! You didn't let me finish. Her people are moving to Kansas and I decided to bring her here. She can stay with us...help with the housework. Take care of the baby. Give you more free time. she'll find a young man someday."

Such innocence! She didn't believe a word of it. There was more, had to be. She took a long look at the girl, standing over there pretending she had no idea what they were talking about. Of course, she'd be beautiful. He wouldn't have it any other way. Her cold reasoning returned.

So? I'm beautiful, too. She held Dacy back, cooing at her softly, thinking. She'd show that little savage a thing or two! In a sudden shift of emotions, a tactic she'd learned long ago in dealing with men, she held out the baby.

"Do you want to hold her?" she asked, her voice, she hoped, now normal. When he hesitated, she said, "She's your daughter, you know."

Although she was pleased at the mild shock he showed, she was disappointed when he quickly smiled and took her.

"I wondered if you'd ever tell me," he said.

It was her turn to be shocked. She hadn't told him. Had she? "How—did you know?" she stammered.

"It was the last thing Daniel said to me. Dacy is yours, he said. Of course, I didn't have the slightest notion what he was talking about until you told me what her name was. Then I knew."

"Daniel—?" She was still stunned. "How did he know?"

He shrugged. "I'm finding out Daniel knew everything there was to know."

She felt she was losing mental contact with him again as he kissed Dacy lightly on one cheek and began trying to make friends with her. She decided to wedge her way back into their love.

"She has your eyes, don't you think?"

"My eyes?" he questioned, suddenly interested and curious. "Really? I've never seen how my eyes looked. Are they slanted like that?"

Her old feeling of conquest was coming back. She smiled. "They are. That's what attracted me to you so much that first time in the grist mill."

"Oh, Laura—"

She forced a smile and gestured toward the girl.

"Does she speak anything other than Osage?"

His crooked grin showed a trace of embarrassment. "I taught her a little English," he said.

What kind of English words? she wanted to ask, but didn't. She went to the girl.

"My name is Laura," she said, speaking slowly and pointing to herself. "Laura," she repeated.

"Laura," the girl said, nodding her understanding, then added in bad

Cherokee, "I am called Little Tassel."

Laura disguised her jealousy with a smile. She extended a hand.

"Yes, I know."

The first thing to do when you want to get rid of somebody is make them your friend. So when Little Tassel took her hand, she squeezed and patted it with all the affection she could muster.

CHAPTER 24

A strange, uneasy truce settled over the cabin. Tahchee went about the daily chores of chopping wood and carrying water. He kept a constant lookout for any signs of Black Dog or the U.S. Army. Laura never mentioned going to Texas and, from the way she acted, seemed content getting better acquainted with Little Tassel. Also, he noticed with amused detachment, Laura appeared overly dramatic when she made all the sleeping arrangements. She insisted Little Tassel have a room of her own—the lean-to which Daniel had added for him. Laura took over his mother's bedroom, "—so Dacy wouldn't bother anybody if she woke up and cried during the night."

Then she pushed Tahchee toward Daniel's room. "You sleep in there," she said, then added meaningfully, "I want you to be close enough so I can hear you if you get up roaming around at night."

Her inference angered him at first. Then he laughed. "You're not a very trustworthy soul, are you?"

"I know men."

What was she up to? He decided to wait her out—for a few days, at least. He went out of his way to make Little Tassel comfortable and accepted

Laura's friendliness with equanimity.

Dacy enjoyed herself immensely showing off for the three adults. Evenings, after supper, Dacy would goad him into frightening her. He would jump at her and shout, "I'm gonna get you!" and Dacy would run squealing into her mother's or Little Tassel's arms. Laura would usually be the first to tire of the game and go to her room "to work on her hair," leaving him and Little Tassel to romp with the baby.

Dacy took turns sleeping with each, not because of any pre-arranged plan, but because she favored whomever would stay awake the longest and tell her stories. She would listen just as intently when Little Tassel told her stories in Osage as she did when he told her stories in English or Cherokee.

Late one night when Dacy was sleeping with Little Tassel, he awoke with a start, sensing a presence close by. He made a quick move for his gun, but froze when he saw Laura. She was standing over him, her beautiful naked figure ghost-like in the darkness, her long hair covering her breasts.

He felt suddenly hot, wanting her and remembering the time when he had her. He lay quiet as she settled slowly onto the bed, her breathing like the whisper of an owl's wings. Darkness blanked out her expression, but her movements spoke a thousand words.

An invisible force closed his throat, and he kept swallowing repeatedly to clear his breathing passage. His hand moved as if it had a will of its own, floating up to finger aside the long strands of hair, fully exposing one lovely, perfectly formed breast.

His hand trembled ever so slightly as he stroked the firm flesh, purposefully letting the tips of his fingers brush her extended nipple.

His passion for her deepened when she reached across to pull the blanket from him. Tingling sensations fanned out from his groin to all parts of his body. The feeling magnified a hundredfold when he felt her fingers curl around his turgid erection. He responded by taking her hardened nipple between his thumb and forefinger, rolling it gently as he pulled and pushed. She rocked on her knees, back and forth, establishing the intensity and rhythm of his pull on her breast.

His breath caught when he felt her finger tips dancing about on his most sensitive spots, as if she knew exactly where each was. Her bold exploration sent surges of intense heat through him. His lungs sucked air in short, sporadic intakes. Her aroma filled his nostrils, inciting an increasingly strong desire to seize her and pull her down beside him and plunge himself into her, by force if necessary.

He could stand no more. The world ceased to exist. There was no Dacy, no Little Tassel, not even a Black Dog. Or for that matter, he no longer existed himself. He was someone else, filled with nothing but lust and want. He reached for her, clutching her bare waist. She resisted his attempt to pull her to him. Instead, she lowered her head, her long hair covering his body from his chest to his knees. He felt her lips, her tongue.

Blinding passion exploded in his brain. He was unable to breathe, didn't want to, didn't need to. His muscles tensed, took over, arching his back. She was in total control now, working silently, destroying his being, fueling a maddening desire to end it all with one fierce thrust. He groped for her blindly, pulled on a fistful of her hair.

"Laura!" he whispered hoarsely, warning her.

She refused to be pulled away. Her refusal to leave him was too much. He erupted, not knowing where, not caring, not believing, not himself any longer. He heard a muted groan rising from deep inside his own being, and the low sound in the stillness helped reduce his muscular spasms to weak tremors. She was gentle using her long hair on him.

He lay still, swimming back to reality, stunned. Both surprise and wonder laced his feeling of shame. He wanted to apologize, finally, and circled her waist with an arm. He tugged weakly to get her to stretch out beside him so he could whisper his love for her between warm, thankful kisses. But she wriggled from his hold, rose silently to her feet and vanished into the darkness.

Weak and puzzled, he lay limp and exhausted. Soon, he drifted into a troubled sleep.

When he awoke, gray light of dawn was outlining the windows, stealing into the room. He lay on his back, remembering. Had it been a dream? He felt about cautiously, searching for the usual embarrassing wet spot.

Nothing. He thought of Little Tassel's butterfly and smiled. Had he been asleep and dreamed, or was he asleep now and only dreaming? Then he heard a voice. He sat up. He could hear Little Tassel talking to Dacy.

Dream or not, he hurriedly slipped into his trousers and went into the main room.

Little Tassel was up busy preparing a pot of coffee and carrying Dacy on her hip. He returned her pleasant greeting and eased into a chair at the table, admiring how easily she handled the baby. When the coffee was done, she poured him a cup and set it on the table. He sipped the hot liquid, his gaze following Little Tassel and Dacy, but his mind reviewing last night's experience.

Laura swept into the room with barely a glance his direction as she gave her bubbling attention to Dacy while treating Little Tassel with cool politeness. He watched her closely, wanting to catch her eyes, wanting some indication from her that they had shared a wonderful experience. He saw none.

He felt less than a man. An odd sense of disgust seeped in. When Little Tassel left the room to straighten up the beds, Laura brought Dacy to the table to feed her oatmeal. She glanced up at him, gave him a quick smile.

"You're sure quiet this morning," she commented. "Didn't you sleep well?"

The sarcastic pretense of innocence irritated him. He searched for signs in her face, reading it both ways. He cleared his throat.

"No," he said, finally. "I didn't sleep well...Did you?"

"I slept like a baby, for a change. Your problem must be the sleeping alone. Why don't you get rid of the girl. Then you can sleep with me."

He searched for words which he might use to express his old, his honest feelings for her. "Laura—"

"Oops!" Laura interrupted as Dacy spit out a spoonful of cereal. She wiped the baby's mouth, apologizing to the child for nothing. He had a feeling she was provoking him, on purpose. When she resumed feeding, she glanced his way and said, "Excuse the interruption. You were saying—?"

"Nothing."

Silence, then she said coolly, "When are you going to keep your promise?"

"Promise? What promise?"

"You promised to take me—us—me and Dacy to Texas."

"Oh, that?...I'm going to."

"When?"

He gave her a tight, triumphant smile. "I don't believe I promised 'when'."

"No, you didn't," she flung back without hesitation, her voice sharp. "But don't forget, I'm still a soldier's widow. I have special privileges at the fort. I'm needing a few things from the sutler. Somebody might ask me about you when I go back." She paused, her gaze leveling on him. Her veiled threat was unmistakable. She smiled sweetly. "Of course, I'd never, ever tell them you were living with me here, at the old home place."

His gaze locked with hers. He felt a smouldering anger toward this witch. Yes, witch. A witch who'd sneaked into his life and stolen his decency. He shifted his attention for a brief moment to the squirming Dacy. Was the baby really his? He studied Laura. Yes, she was a witch who'd learned how to unlock the dungeon where a man kept all his wild demons imprisoned. She had the ability to turn those demons loose against a man and all his goodness, reducing him to a state below animalism.

At long last, he added with a very restrained effort, "No. Of course, you wouldn't do that."

He detected a fleeting second of shock at his own veiled challenge. Then he saw the anger before she snapped, "But you'll never know for sure, will you?"

"Quit bluffing, Laura. We're all going to Texas. You, me, Little Tassel, and the baby. We have no choice."

"I'm not going a step with that squaw of yours."

"Then stay!" he flung back, angered by her put-down. "I'll take my daughter and my *squaw* and go without you!"

He waited for a sharp retort, watching her face closely as she kept her attention on Dacy. He felt sorry for being so brutal, then relented by suggesting, "You can't be jealous, Laura. Little Tassel can't begin to do things to a man you do, nor ever will."

Her gaze whipped to him. "What makes you think I'm jealous?"

"Something's changed you."

"You're absolutely right about that! I don't intend to share my husband with any woman. And, in case you don't know it, that's not jealousy. That's common decency!"

He tried to keep his own anger in check when he said, "You're forgetting something. One, I'm not your husband. Not yet, anyway. Two, what gave you the idea I'm—as you put it—sharing?"

"You may not be my husband according to recorded law, but you sure are according to *this* law," she said and lifted Dacy for emphasis. Then she motioned toward the bedroom where Little Tassel was working. "And don't try to tell me you haven't had her."

He gestured at the baby. "I'd be proud to claim Dacy. But, knowing you, she could belong to any man, even the soldier you were legally married to. As for Little Tassel...No. I haven't, as you say, had her."

"Do you expect me to believe that! No man can travel across the country with a girl and not share sex."

"It's the truth."

"I don't believe it."

"Of course. *You* wouldn't."

"What do you mean, 'I wouldn't'?"

"I think you know."

"Tell me."

He hesitated. Maybe he was getting in too deep. Then, still wanting to hurt her as she had hurt him, he plunged on. "You're obsessed with sex!"

She choked on a strange little laugh. "You're talking about what I did last night?"

"Partly."

"Don't sit there and tell me you didn't enjoy the way I pleased you?"

"It's not that. You enjoyed it more."

"So what?"

"So—" he broke off when Little Tassel reentered the room. He returned Laura's silent, hateful stare. Little Tassel apparently noticed, for she began flustering about, obviously embarrassed. She began to make too much noise banging pots and pans around. Laura spoke up boldly, asking, "Are we going to Texas or not?"

"Just as soon as I find Black Dog and kill him. Not one day before."

Laura stood. "Talk about being obsessed! You're the one who's obsessed...over killing a man who killed a woman who was too scared to give him what he wanted in the first place—a little sex!"

"God damn you to hell!" he said with a deep, intense hate. "Only a person like you would think like that!"

Laura turned to Little Tassel.

"Little Tassel, take care of Dacy for me for a few days. I need to go to Fort Gibson and pick up a few things from the sutler."

Little Tassel shot Tahchee a quick, questioning glance. He nodded, and she followed his unspoken suggestion.

"Yes. I keep." she stammered in clumsy English.

He added. "We don't mind a bit. You run on. We'd be glad to keep the baby."

Laura spun on him. "Well, you should once in a while. After all, you're her father!"

He watched her closely as she got ready to leave, trying to tell himself this wasn't happening; and, if it was, why? A new insight made her beauty ugly, like a poison flower begging to be eaten. This new perspective hurt. When she rode away, he stood with Little Tassel in the doorway, holding Dacy in his arms. Dacy whimpered and Little Tassel took the child from him, bounced her gently into a contented silence.

He murmured, "Now what?"

Little Tassel glanced up, a puzzled look on her face. He gave her a reassuring smile, but feeling no assurance himself.

There was a distinct possibility that she would tie up with that Major. And if she did, would she turn him in? He decided to go after Black Dog before he got taken in himself.

"Pack some things for the baby," he told Little Tassel. "We're going on a short trip."

The Rogers' place had changed considerably since the day he was here during the cabin raising over two years ago. More rooms added on, more outbuildings, a corral. And he guessed the awkward looking boy standing on the porch staring at them when they road up had to be Clancy. The boy called to someone inside the cabin.

William and Ellen came out on the porch. "Tahchee?" William called. "It is you, isn't it? Get down. Get down. And come in this house. Lord-a-mercy! It's good to see you!"

The way they made over Dacy filled him with an odd sense of satisfaction and pleasure that he'd never experienced before. He was proud.

"Where's Laura?" Ellen asked.

"She made a trip back to Fort Gibson," he explained. "Said she had to pick up some things."

He introduced Little Tassel, telling them only enough to make them comfortable with her presence. Then he added, "I need a favor of you folks. I have some unfinished business to take care of and I wondered if you would put up with Dacy and the girl a few days until I get back."

"Of course," Ellen said, acting hurt that he was being so apologetic about it. "She's our first grandchild, you know. We just might keep her."

"We tried to get Laura to leave her last week when she came by," William said. "I was worried then, with Black Dog still on the loose. But now that the army's caught him, we don't have to worry anymore about him burning us out."

"What—?" Tahchee blurted, not believing.

"We heard just this morning. Isn't it wonderful?" Ellen said.

He could only nod, dumfounded. "Yeah..."

That changed things. If the army hanged Black Dog, he would feel cheated. There was another way, however. Go back to his cabin and wait. If he knew Laura like he thought he did, she'd fix it up for him to meet Black Dog.

He barely heard when William was saying, "They say we can all start moving over into Indian Territory anytime we want now. The government's already started buying us out. You sold your place yet?"

"No..." he replied, letting his voice trail off because his mind was elsewhere.

William acted excited about the move and Tahchee let him ramble on. From the way he was talking, he estimated he could get more than enough to pay his debt to that trader. But the only debt he wanted to settle right now was with Black Dog.

After a decent interval, he took his leave and Little Tassel followed him out to his horse.

"You come back?" she asked, a worried look on her face.

"Yeah. I'll be back. These are nice people. They'll take of you."

"I no want to be with anybody but you."

The longer he stood there looking down at her, the more he realized how much he wanted to be with her, too. He glanced toward the house, saw Clancy standing on the porch watching. He didn't care. On impulse, he folded her in his arms. Her upturned face waited. He kissed her, hard. Then turned, vaulted into his saddle and rode away.

CHAPTER 25

"Dutch!" boomed the voice from outside. "United States Army! Come out with your hands up, or we'll burn the cabin down!"

Instinctively, Tahchee scrambled for his gun at the first word, then he relaxed, grinning. He was, however, slightly put out with himself for letting them surprise him like this.

"Dutch! We got you surrounded. We know you're in there—with the woman and baby. We don't want to hurt them, but we will if we have to."

He peeked out, saw the Major's head protruding from behind a tree. It would be easy to drop him with his new Henry. He was tempted to take a shot, just to scare him. But the stupid soldiers might go crazy and burn the house down out of spite. He needed it to pay his debt to the trader.

"Dutch! You got one minute! Come out with your hands up, or we fire the house!"

He leaned the gun against the wall, waited a few more seconds and eased out the door with his hands in the air. Soldiers materialized from cover, came at him from all directions, guns ready. Major Benefield halted a few feet away, his pistol pointing and a satisfied smile on his block-like face.

"Keep 'em high, Dutch. I'm making damn sure you don't get away from me this time."

"How'd you know I was here?" he asked, already knowing the answer.

The officer smirked and said, "We have our ways. I heard you were looking for Black Dog. Thought I'd help out. I'll take you to him. You can both hang together."

That confirmed his suspicion. There was only one way the Major could have known about him wanting to find Black Dog. Laura.

The Major gestured toward the cabin. "A couple of you men go get the girl and the baby."

"There're not here," Tahchee said.

"Where are they?"

"None of your damned business. You got me, and that's what you came for, isn't it?"

The Major glared, then shrugged and said, "I'm not interested in Osage women." Then barked to his men. "All right, men. Tie him up, and tie him good!"

The sun was down and full darkness was gathering momentum when Tahchee rode into the post compound with Major Benefield and the others of the escort trailing behind.

A curious crowd of soldiers appeared from the early evening shadows as they jogged to the stables and dismounted. The soldiers had to untie Tahchee before he could swing a leg over and slide to the ground. He rubbed his freed wrists and eyed the ring of men as they edged closer.

"Hot dog! Now we got two injuns to hang tomorrow!" said one. Others laughed.

"None of that, men," the Major growled. "Return to your quarters. This is none of your business."

The soldiers ignored him and pressed nearer to get a better look.

"So that's Dutch?" one said. "He don't look so all fired mean to me."

"Don't see why they bothered to bring him in atall. Whyn't they just shoot him and be done with it?"

One spat a string of tobacco juice at Tahchee's feet. Tahchee spit back, right in the soldier's face. The stunned soldier recovered quickly, shouting, "Why, you son of a bitch!" He leaped.

Tahchee stopped his charge with a balled fist to his face, smashing his nose. Blood spurted. The other soldiers surged forward, their combined weight too much. He went down under flurry of pounding fists and churning knees to his groin. He fought back until he hit the ground. Heavy boots thudded against his head, his arms, his ribs. Someone stomped on his stomach. He saw brilliant flashes of light and tasted his own blood.

The sharp crack of a pistol echoed off the stockade walls.

"Halt!" the Major roared. "The next man who lays a hand on the prisoner will be shot!"

The surly men back away, some licking their lips, anxious to get a chance to stomp a man to death.

Weak and dazed, Tahchee tried to get up, almost blacked out. He rested on one knee, breathing heavily, blood dripping from his nose and mouth. A sergeant stepped near, took hold of his arm to help him to his feet. He flung the hand away. He didn't want their help. He stood, finally, on trembling legs and faced his attackers, full of contempt.

"You're a bunch of shit eaters!" he spat, his own blood spewing from his mouth.

The largest man shouted another curse and charged, but Major Benefield caught him across the temple with his pistol. The burly soldier dropped. The Major stepped between Tahchee and the group, his pistol menacing.

"The next man who tries that, dies!"

The men stared at the fallen soldier, then at the resolute Major, their looks sullen. Major Benefield motioned toward his sergeant.

"Let's go," he said.

The sergeant shoved Tahchee to get him going, and the two fell in behind the officer. The ring of soldiers parted as they stalked through, heading for the powder magazine. Beyond, the golden glow of the sunset held the shadows back far enough for him to see Laura standing on the board walk, a satanic smile on her face. Major Benefield slowed when Laura stepped off the walk and came to intercept them.

"I see you got him," she said. "Have any trouble?"

"Not a bit. It went just like you predicted. When we threatened the girl, he marched right out. Meek as a lamb. But the girl wasn't there."

"She wasn't?"

"No. Least he said she wasn't. I didn't bother to look."

"Oh, she was there, all right," Laura said, then nodded Tahchee's direction. "I'd like a word with him. May I?"

The Major chuckled. "You won't slip him a knife this time, will you? You nearly got me court martialed over helping him escape that last time."

Laura flashed him a sweet, knowing smile and said—intending for her words to be for the Major's ears only, but Tahchee heard—"But I made up for it by helping you get him back, didn't I?...That and other things?"

He could see the expression on Major's face change to helpless pleasure, and he knew what Laura was talking about. The officer gave his permission by nodding Tahchee's direction. Laura came closer.

"I remembered what you told me, Tahchee," she goaded. "You said you'd like to be locked up with Black Dog. Now here's your chance. I hope you're happy. You threw away your life looking for him. Now you have him. Good Luck!"

"Thanks," he said, wanting to spit more blood, but swallowing the sweet fluid instead to keep her from having the satisfaction of seeing him hurt. "I see you found yourself another soldier."

"Not just another soldier this time. Tom is the Post Commander. As soon as we're married, I'll be the top ranked woman here."

"That means a lot to you, doesn't it?"

"Yes, it does—if I can't have you."

"Then it's my turn to wish you good luck. After him, there'll be another, then another, until you get too old for anybody. You'll wind up one day emptying chamber pots for young white wives on some god forsaken army post. You'll be the fat squaw walking around with a silly grin on your face—"

He saw her hand coming, but made no attempt to duck. The sharp slap echoed in the stillness of the parade grounds, sent blood droplets flying from his mouth. Something snapped in his mind. He grabbed her by the throat, all his senses screaming "KILL HER!" There was no fear in her face as she fought back, clawing to get his hands loose.

He never saw the pistol descending. There was an eruption of stars. As blackness closed in, he fought to hang onto her throat determined to pull her into oblivion with him. She kneed him in the groin, the sharp pain stealing the last ounce of his strength as he sank to the ground, unconscious.

Awareness sneaked back, fluttering in and out. Soon it was all there. He lay on his stomach, his cheek in a pool of blood, a terrible pain in his side. A broken rib? He pulled in a cautious, deep breath. The pain jerked at his spine like a giant hand pulling.

He opened his eyes, the puffiness making it difficult. The first thing he saw was the chain coming in one hole and out the other. He knew instantly where he was.

Black Dog!

His breath caught. Was he in here? He lay still, collecting his thoughts and getting control of his emotions. Soon, he rolled over, sat up, glanced around the large room.

Empty. But a sixth sense told him to look again. Then he spotted the man, standing in a far corner, only a darker blob in the deepening gloom.

His blood raced, his head felt light. At long last! But he clung to reason. He didn't mind being hung for violating a treaty between two nations, but he didn't want to be hung for killing Black Dog. It would defeat everything.

Wary, he struggled to his feet. He limped to the tiny window and looked out. Fireflies streaked through the brush beyond the perimeter clearing. Daylight was all but gone from the western horizon. He waited until his heart quit pounding before he turned slowly to face the dark pillar in the far corner.

"Black Dog?" he asked, speaking softly so none would hear outside the room.

No sound came from the shadow.

"I am the Cherokee who saved your nephew from drowning."

A long silence, then, "I know."

"I came to help you escape."

Black Dog grunted.

"Tonight," Tahchee added.

He tensed when Black Dog moved from the shadows, coming closer, his bulk noiseless in his moccasined feet. He paused a few steps away, the dying light sifting through the window, highlighting the scratch scars on his face.

"Cherokee lie," Black Dog accused, his voice low but strong. He raised a hand, brushed the scars with his fingers. "You are the son of Song Bird. I wear her scars on my face."

Stunned, Tahchee tried to catch the gasp before it cleared his throat, couldn't. Then anger blinded him. He beat it back, the supreme effort leaving him weak and trembling.

How—?

A sudden, blind rage exploded his being. "Woman killer!" he heard his own voice scream.

The big man lunged. Tahchee leaped sideways, then, cat-like, onto the man's back when he went by. He whipped an arm around the Osage's neck and threw all his strength into the hammer lock.

Black Dog pulled at Tahchee's arm with both hands, wheezing. Tahchee worked for more savage leverage. He felt his forearm sink deeper into Black Dog's adam's apple.

Just when he could feel the Osage's strength ebbing away from lack of air, he heard the chain rattle. He had to break his hold and be ready when the two guards rushed in to break up the fight.

He ploughed head first into one man and carried him stumbling backwards until he crashed into the far wall, his breath whooshing out. Tahchee considered breaking his neck, but knew he had no time. He swung a tight fist, feeling it smash into the man's temple. The guard's eyes rolled upward, showing all white before he wilted.

He spun, ready for the other guard. Black Dog had him down, belly first and had a knee in the soldier's back with one arm under his chin. Tahchee winced when he heard the young man's spine crack. He was thankful when the boy fainted.

Black Dog let go and leaped to his feet. His gaze burned into Tahchee, questioning. Tahchee gestured toward the open door.

"Let's go. I intend to kill you with my bare hands. I don't want to kill you here. You're not worth hanging for."

Black Dog laughed, a low, throaty laugh of contempt. "If Cherokee think he can get out of here and not get shot, Black Dog will follow. Black Dog be happy to fight son of Song Bird to the death."

Tahchee heard a shout.

"Follow me," he challenged and bolted out the door. He turned right, using his momentum to grab the porch stringer and swung his body, feet first over onto the porch roof.

Black Dog tried to imitate Tahchee's move, but failed. He hung by his hands, digging his toes into the log wall. He struggled to get his huge bulk over the edge of the porch roof. Doors started banging open around the compound. Tahchee seized handfuls of Black Dog's loose deerskins and pulled him rolling over the edge. There was another shout, then another. A gun flashed, cracked, and he heard the whoosh of a lead ball.

He spun, leading the way. He bounded over the low parapet and raced across the slab shingles toward the stockade wall.

The shouts behind and below grew louder. Guns barked in sharp staccato. Tahchee expected one of the lead balls to tear through him. But he made it to the stockade wall.

The tops of the sharpened logs were higher than he expected. He turned, braced his back against the wall and formed a stirrup with his hands.

"You first!" he commanded.

Black Dog made a running leap, stepped into Tahchee's hands and reached for the sharpened points above. Tahchee boosted with all his pained strength. A bullet exploded bark not six inches from his ear, then zinged away. The Osage looped one leg over, straddled the wall, and dropped out of sight.

Tahchee backed away a few steps. He made a running leap, literally running two steps up the vertical wall high enough to hook an elbow around one of the sharpened points. As he pulled himself up, he felt a sledgehammer hit his cracked rib, knocking the breath from him.

His arm hold on the log began slipping. If he fell now, he would die and Black Dog would go free. He gritted his teeth and fought to get his numbed lungs back into action.

I will not die! I am the son of Song Bird!

An unseen force tugged. He struggled higher, until, like Black Dog, he was able to hook one leg over the wall. He dangled on the outside, kicked away and dropped.

Free falling, he braced for the ground shock he thought would never come. He saw gun flashes coming at him from a corner tower. He hit hard, one foot striking an uneven spot. His ankle twisted, sending sharp pain stabbing up his leg.

Broken? There was no time to think. He tested the ankle by running. It held. Tahchee felt the wind burning his face as he raced after the ghostly form of Black Dog just now disappearing into the black curtain of the forest.

Rifle fire punched through the darkness from behind. Singing lead balls tore into the ground, their explosive impacts kicking up geysers of mud and dirt.

Tahchee crashed into the brush thicket, his super charged mind playing tricks. Was he dead and just imagining he'd made it? Then he spotted Black Dog. He was waiting at the edge of a high river bluff, undecided.

"Jump!" Tahchee shouted.

The man refused to move. Tahchee didn't slow down. He crashed into the Osage at full speed. They tumbled over the edge into space.

He gyrated both arms as he tried to keep himself righted so he'd hit the water below feet first. He kept going down, and down, and down into the blackness. Was there even any water down there? He hit leaning forward slightly. The water slammed into his chest and face, stunning him.

He fought to hold his breath as the sharp cold closed over him. Some of the water surged up his nose and forced its way into his lungs. He had to cough, but couldn't. His downward momentum slowed, stopped, and he kicked upward. When his head broke surface, he sucked in great lungfuls of the night air.

His wet woolen clothing pulled him under. He stripped, resurfaced and treaded water, naked, listening for Black Dog.

Had the Osage made it? Then he heard splashing close by. He swam to the sound. He seized the wet deerskins and tugged.

"This way," he ordered.

They swam with the strong current. Tahchee kept to the center of the swirling river by using the open sky above framed by the black wall on either bank. They bobbed together through a stretch of tumbling rapids. The rushing water banged them mercilessly into sharp rocks.

Tahchee lost sight of Black Dog, and the wild rush of water swallowed any sounds of his splashing.

The current pushed him into a quiet pool. When his hand slapped into the rough bark of a floating log, he hooked a lead-tired arm over the slippery surface and hung on.

He rested a second to catch his breath. He heard Black Dog.

"Over here," he called and began kicking himself and the log toward the sound. Soon, he felt the log twist and jerk, as if some giant fish had bitten into it. He hand-walked down the log until he could feel Black Dog's arms reaching over from the other side. He tangled his hands in the wet deerskins so they would both be able to relax, one on one side of the log and one on the other.

A sudden wave of nausea churned water from his stomach. the uncontrolled retching causing sharp pains to his damaged rib. When it was over, he lay his head against the log's cold surface. He felt more dead than alive.

But they were free.

He let Black Dog kick and maneuver the log. He kept it in the current as the night hours slipped away.

He heard crickets calling, a rain crow whistle, a bear coughing. A blood-red moon popped up from nowhere on the eastern horizon, brightening as it climbed higher in the sky.

Tahchee, his strength slowly returning, spoke to the invisible man on the other side of the log.

"There's an island where the Grand empties into the Arkansas. Head for it."

Black Dog grunted his approval.

CHAPTER 26

The river current slowed where the smaller stream widened to empty into the broad Arkansas. The moon, now full above, illuminated the forest on the island. Tahchee worked with Black dog to guide the log toward the foreboding land mass.

He felt weak from the beating, the exertion of the escape, and the long hours in the cold water. The chill drove deep, causing goose bumps and violent spasms of involuntary shivering. Would he have strength to fight? Had he lost his quickness? If he were less than perfect, so was Black Dog.

The island drifted closer, the frog grumps grew louder. The silent trees would be their only witnesses.

The baleful glare of the moon washed the sky clean of all but the brightest stars. The shadowy trees leaned over them. The log bumped the soft bank, rested in the eerie silence.

Tahchee could feel the muddy bottom with his bare toes. He untangled his hands from Black Dog's deerskins and waded toward the bank. On the other side of the log, Black Dog was doing the same, but he was still fully clothed, his deerskins soaked and dripping.

Black Dog scrambled up the bank, but Tahchee had a problem. Not only was the bank steeper and higher on his side of the log, it was muddier. He pulled himself up by grasping handfuls of grass and trying to find a toehold in the muddy bank. He heard a dead limb snap and Black Dog taunt, "Need help, Cherokee?"

"Not from you," Tahchee threw back. He was almost up.

Low laughter came from the darkness above. Tahchee found a toehold, finally, and reached up to grasp an overhanging bush. His foot slipped, but he clung to the bush, dug for a new toehold. He heard a movement and glanced up just in time to see the huge bulk bending over, bringing the club down with enough force to crush a bear's skull.

He lurched sideways. The club glanced off his head. He felt no pain, just a jarring sensation that traveled downward through every bone in his body. Then bright, brilliant colors filled the universe as he tumbled into a black hole.

He plummeted downward, ever downward, sometimes spiraling, sometimes floating. Suddenly, he was immersed in water. The warm liquid caressed his skin. He wanted to lie in it forever. Then he saw a light, bright as the noonday sun, and swam toward it.

"Tahchee?" he heard Song Bird call.

She was somewhere in that bright light. He tried to answer, but seemed locked in a frustrating muteness. He shaded his eyes, trying to see into the blinding glow. Nothing. Not even a shadow. He ceased trying to swim to the light.

"Dutch!"

That was Little Tassel calling! She must be somewhere in the bright light with Song Bird. He renewed his struggle toward the light.

"Dutch," Little Tassel called again, her voice softer, more endearing, encouraging.

He was in the swimming hole again, underwater, the sun flecks breaking through the overhanging trees, dancing across the bottom, forming bright patterns over Little Tassel's nude body. Odd, there was no need to hold his breath this time. He could breathe water as easily as he could air. He swam lazily toward Little Tassel, savoring the view of her bare beauty. She kept receding. Frustrated, he swam with increasing effort until his arms turned into leaden weights and refused to move at his will.

He rested, afraid she would disappear, but unable to do anything about it. Little Tassel stopped receding and beckoned, her arms waving silently, like long strands of underwater plants. He tried to will his own arms into action.

He could lift neither. He kept sinking, slowly, deeper into the water. His knees scraped bottom. He dug in his toes and kicked himself toward her. She held out her arms, her bare breasts erect, her long black hair floating about her head.

If only he could get to her! He managed to get one dead arm to respond. He reached for her. The instant his fingers touched her, she vanished. The dancing sun spots disappeared, and the pool of water around him turned into a murky cloud.

Instead of Little Tassel's hand, he was gripping something slimy and cold. He worked his fingers around the object to get a firmer grip and pulled, sliding himself across gravel on his belly. He collapsed, totally exhausted, not caring anymore.

His eyelids were too heavy to open. But he had to see. He struggled to lift his lids. He saw moss-covered rocks close by and a wall of deep green beyond. Everything was bathed in a pale light. He felt totally numb, and was lying on his stomach, half in the water and half out—if he were still in human form and not a butterfly. Without moving a muscle, he shifted his gaze cautiously, decided he was alive.

Where was he? Black Dog? A wave of nausea hit him. His stomach churned, then sent a gush of foul tasting water up his throat, out his nose and mouth.

He gagged, gasped for air, only to have it cut off with yet another eruption of bitter water. He struggled to his knees, the effort sending him into a fit of uncontrolled coughing. Water tickled the inside of his lungs and he fought to clear them. Each cough caused a stab of pain to his damaged rib.

He clung to more and more of each successive wave of reality until he had enough presence of mind to lift his head to see where he was—more important, to see where Black Dog might be.

Nothing. Nobody. Where had the Osage gone? Only when he realized the gray light around him was daylight and not the moon, did he know the answer. Black Dog had clubbed him, thought he was dead. Why he wasn't, he could only guess, for the dream remembrance told him nothing, only added to his confusion. He dragged himself across the rocks and into the underbrush, out of sight, he hoped. He lay still, breathing slowly and deeply, his mind busy.

If he were still on the island, so was Black Dog. He found it difficult to reason. His head pounded. He felt gingerly. The huge lump high on the side of his head burned at his touch. But he could feel no broken skin.

Then he walked his fingers along the sore rib. The spot where the ball hit was too painful to touch, but he pressed anyway. The bone seemed to be still in one piece, at least as far as he could tell. He glanced down, surprised to find the skin over the rib had not been broken. An ugly red and blue welt was the only visible sign where the ball had hit, obviously its charge insufficient or its energy spent in a ricochet. Whatever. But it couldn't be any more painful than if his rib had been broken. He sat up, rested his elbows on his knees, holding his head in his hands.

He had no weapon, not even any clothes. somewhere near was the man who killed his mother, the man he'd spent an eternity, it seemed, pursuing to kill.

No matter, he had to do it somehow...or die trying.

When his strength ebbed back, he stood to test his legs, flexing his knees carefully. Cautious, he moved about searching for something to eat, anything. He found a crab apple tree and chewed handfuls of the tasteless, cherry-sized fruit. He spit out the seeds and husks. He found a blackberry patch. The brambles scratched unmercifully as he worked his way among the vines, picking the ripe, seedy berries. He spotted a small black snake lying on top of the briars, lying in wait for unsuspecting birds to come feasting on the berries. The snake made a quick move to get away, but was not quick enough. Tahchee caught its tail and popped its head off with a quick whip-like action.

He found a sharp rock, slit the snake and peeled out pieces of its fish-like flesh. He forced himself to think of other things as he chewed the raw meat, trying to take his mind off what it had been.

The food made him feel better and he began searching for a healthy sprout. When he found one, he used the sharp rock to dig it out and trimmed away its branches and excessive root structure. Finished, he tested the war club for balance. He made a few swipes through empty space to get the feel of its swing. It was not as good as the one which Chief Cahtateeskee had given him that day they were chasing the Osages, but he was satisfied.

Now he was ready.

Wary and keeping a tight grip on his war club, he commenced his search of the island, only vaguely aware of the sun's increasing heat. His head throbbed with tom-toms of pain. He felt the massive lump again and speculated that Black Dog's club may have cracked his skull. The thought drove him into a state of desperation and filled him with a sense of urgency which corroded his caution.

He began making noise on purpose, hoping the sounds would bring Black

Dog out of hiding—if he were still on the island. Then it occurred to him that this might be the second or third day after Black Dog clubbed him. If so, the Osage might already be gone from the island.

Suddenly a chill raced up his spine. His scalp tensed, making each hair feel as though it were trying to stand erect. He sensed he was being watched. He crouched, club ready, his gaze sweeping the underbrush. He heard a laugh break the dead silence. He tightened his grip on the club, fixing his eyes on the spot. A bush moved aside and Black Dog stepped into the open, not ten paces away.

"So the son of Song Bird lives?" Black Dog mocked, an unpleasant smile on his scarred face. "This time I will make certain."

"Try it," Tahchee croaked. "I am waiting." He hefted the club. Black Dog sneered.

"The Cherokee needs a weapon?" he asked, expressing disdain. He spread his hands, palms up. "I have none. Can it be the son of Song Bird is no more than a rabbit?"

The scratch scars made the sneer more grotesque. The sight inflamed his raging hate. He tossed the club aside.

"Black Dog's death will be slow and painful," he taunted, his stilted Osage words sounding strange to his own ears, as if he were another human being.

Black Dog laughed softly and moved forward, hands out, his fingers in a tense curl. Tahchee's breath quickened, sending pain knifing through his side. The pounding in his head made weird spots dance before his eyes. Black Dog's huge bulk kept growing.

"Song Bird was my woman," the Osage boasted. "She came to me many times in the forest."

Utter disbelief and confused doubt chained Tahchee where he stood. He blinked rapidly, stunned. The image refused to go away. Black dog stopped.

"I see surprise in face of Cherokee rabbit. There is more to tell. When you leave cabin with uncle, I go to Song Bird. I say, the white soldier will send us to separate lands. Come live with me in my lodge forever. She say no. I cannot help myself. I want to take her anyway. She fight me. Black Dog anger make him crazy. When I chase away anger, Song Bird is dead." He touched the scars on his face. "My face bleeds from her last kiss. I am proud to wear her scar—"

"NO!"

Tahchee's fury tore away the chains. He leaped at the hated figure, his fingers clawing to rip the scars from his face.

Black Dog's rope-like arms wrapped him in a bear hug. Tahchee's breath went out in a cry of pain from his bruised rib. Black Dog lifted, then slammed the helpless him downward to meet his rising knee. The shock of the knee buried in his groin forced yet another cry of pain from Tahchee's burning throat.

Tahchee, desperate, jabbed fingers to gouge out the Osage's eyes. Black Dog turned his face away, then quickly shifted his hold to a hammerlock to protect his eyes.

Tahchee clawed at the huge arm crushing his neck and jaw, cutting off his air. The tom-toms pulsated, thundering commands for him to give up.

Never! He planted his feet and shoved. Black Dog lost his balance and, falling, beat at Tahchee's face with his fist. Tahchee, his head in a vice, was unable to avoid the blows. A fist smashed bones in his nose just as they hit the ground.

Black Dog kept his hammerlock and kept pounding at Tahchee's face. Salty flesh pressed against Tahchee's mouth and nose. He spread his mouth wider, then clamped his jaw shut, burying his teeth. Blood spurted.

"Ah-a-a!" Black Dog screamed in pain, involuntarily throwing Tahchee away and rolled.

Tahchee, free at last, leaped after Black Dog, landing on the Osage's back. He slipped his arms under Black Dog's arms and locked his fingers behind the big man's head. Tahchee threw every ounce of his strength into the hold, forcing Black Dog's head down, ever down until the Osage's chin touched his chest and he was wheezing for air.

He strained to break the man's neck, sensing victory. But his own blood dripped from his nose and wet his interlocking fingers, weakening his hold. He moved his head to one side. Too late. Black Dog felt the slippage and renewed his effort to break the hold.

Tahchee watched in helpless rage as his blood-wet fingers edged apart. Wild thoughts played tag with the throbbing pain in his head, brought back the vision of Black Dog snapping the spine of that soldier. He had to stay out of Black Dog's powerful arms. He let go and scrambled to safety, turning, ready to meet Black Dog's charge.

Instead, Black Dog lunged for the war club Tahchee had tossed away. He stood waving the club, a grotesque leer in his face.

Fool! he cursed himself for tossing the club aside. Blood pumped from his nose, filled his mouth as he gasped for air. If he would die, he would die as he lived. He spat red spittle at the armed Osage.

"I see the woman killer has to have a weapon!"

Black Dog pointed with the club. "There is one more thing I want Cherokee rabbit to know before he dies...The reason I go to get Song Bird, she carry my son in her body."

Tahchee's world exploded. A bloody bellow erupted from his throat as he leaped. The descending club was not quick enough, its balled end sailing past his head, its momentum pulling Black Dog's arm over his shoulder.

He threw an elbow, plunged its point into Black Dog's throat with the full force of his charge, driving it deep. He felt the mass of cartilage collapse.

Black Dog's eyes bulged as he dropped the club and stumbled backward. He made coughing sounds, clawed at his throat with both hands. Fear showed when he realized he'd never feel air in his lungs again.

There was no room in Tahchee's raging emotions for exultation nor pity. He snatched up the war club and charged, letting go with another wild yell. But he stopped himself from smashing the hated man's skull at the last instant when Black Dog dropped to his knees and reached out with one hand, his eyes pleading for help.

Sudden tears filled Tahchee's eyes, tears of hurt and anger. He dropped the club.

"You lie!" he screamed.

Black Dog's mouth worked but no words came out. He groped for Tahchee's hand, his face purpling, his silence infuriating. He grasped the big man's deerskins and heaved him to his feet, spat blood in his face.

"You lie!" he screamed again, then saw the death glaze forming in the Osage's eyes. He shook him violently.

"TELL ME YOU LIE!!"

Black Dog's head, eyes still bulging, became too much weight for the limber neck and lolled. Tahchee felt the dead weight pulling on his arms, but he still held on.

"Tell me you lie," he murmured, and begged, "Please, tell me you lie!"

Only forest sounds answered in the stillness. He let go. The body piled against his legs. He backed away, staring down.

The tom-tom beat swelled, became unbearable. He snatched up the war club and beat the body with uncontrolled fury, each sodden impact traveling up his arms and into his soul.

"You lie! You lie! You lie!"

His wild screaming disturbed a rookery of crows. The black birds swarmed skyward, cawing raucously.

Still the wild man beat and beat and beat until the blows weakened to nothing and the bloodied end of the club rested on the battered corpse. He stood transfixed, wanting desperately to reverse his life while angry sobs shook him. Soon, he released his grip on the club and staggered away, not knowing who he was, where he was, nor why.

CHAPTER 27

Brown, greens, reds, and yellows painted the hills with beautiful fall colors. An occasional purple of a tall, slender sweetgum tree provided the exclamation marks. V's in the clear blue sky pointing south sent down faint honkings from geese waggling goodbyes. A weak sun, at mid-morning, glistened off the overnight dew as the man, woman, and child paused where the faint trail left the river's bank and angled across the meadow toward the two-story log structure.

The woman sat astride the horse, her deerskin dress pushed high on her thighs, her moccasined feet dangling well above the stirrups. She held the sleeping baby in her arms. The tall man, wearing deerskins himself and a floppy brimmed hat, walked, holding the reins, sometimes leading the animal, sometimes at the side with one hand resting on the saddle's cantle, where it lay now.

Neither spoke as their dark eyes studied the building. Neither had ever seen an orphanage. Neither knew what to expect. The woman glanced down at the man, waiting for his decision. Without looking up at her, the man kissed air, urging the horse forward.

Where were the children? The man's questioning gaze raked the area, missing nothing, then centered on the building again. He had visualized an orphanage being alive with boys and girls chasing one another, screaming and laughing. Had the war touched this place, too, closing the orphanage? The somber quiet ahead depressed him. He trudged on, cautious, his own footsteps soundless beside the plodding horse.

A mousy-looking man emerged from the front entrance of the building and stood, a smile on his face, waiting for the visitors. He stepped from the porch to greet them.

"I'm William Lovely," he said, introducing himself, extending a hand.

The tall man grasped the offered hand. "Taylor. Daniel Taylor," he said, his voice soft, but firm.

"I expected you folks yesterday," Lovely said. "What happened? Run into trouble?"

"A little," answered the one who called himself Daniel Taylor. "The government men were half a day late getting there with our money. Time we got signed up and paid off for our place, it throwed us behind. On top of that, the trader I owed money to over in Indian Territory made a big fuss over the interest and I had to rough him up a little before he remembered our agreement."

Lovely shook his head in disbelief. "I hear the same story over and over. They're not even supposed to be doing business in the territory," he said. "I wish the army would do what they're supposed to do and run them out. According to the treaty—"

"Where're the children?" Taylor broke in, not interested in the treaty in the least; anxious, more, to get the boy and get on his way.

"The wife took them on a picnic," Lovely said with a wave toward the creek bottom behind the building. "The boy wanted to stay here and wait for you. But since you failed to show up yesterday like you said in your letter, I told him you might not be here for several days." He smiled at the woman still seated on the horse. "And this is Mrs. Taylor, I presume?"

The tall man nodded. Lovely pursed his pale lips and said, "I could hardly believe the things I read in your letter, Mr. Taylor. A Cherokee couple wanting to adopt an Osage boy! And one which most couples would consider too old to adopt in the first place. On top of that, you already have a child of your own, I see."

"The boy we want to adopt is special," Taylor explained. He had no desire to get into a deep discussion on the family situation.

"There should be more folks like you two. Seems to me that's the trouble with the world today. Groups hating groups instead of people loving people. Indians fighting Indians, Indians fighting whites, soldiers making war—"

And government men coming in to interfere in everything, he felt like adding, but didn't. Instead, he said, "That's why we're heading for Texas. Maybe things'll be different down there."

"I hate to see good people leave the United States," Lovely continued. "This is a great country...as soon as we get our problems worked out. Never before in the history of man have so many different races of people tried to live under one government."

"We'll see how it goes in Texas. We might come back someday."

"Wish you'd reconsider. Things are going to be all right now that the army's sent a new commander out here. General Arbuckle was bad enough, but that Major Benefield caused more trouble than he was worth. He couldn't even hold a prisoner when he caught one. And those last two he let get away, Black Dog and Dutch, were the worst of the lot. Then when he up and married that Cherokee woman, all my work on the treaty almost came unraveled. The Osages thought the army was taking sides with the Cherokees...and they had a right to. You may not think so, being Cherokees and all."

"No. I'd have to agree," Taylor said. Although he was impatient to get going, this was one subject he was interested in. "I haven't heard. What happened to the Major and his new missus?"

"He got transferred to Washington."

"Sounds like a promotion, to me."

"Quite the contrary. That's where they send all officers not suited for field command. Desk work is miserable duty for senior officers and their wives, especially lower echelon senior officers. Out in the field, they're gods. In Washington, they become nobodys."

Finally, some good news for a change, Taylor thought, smiling grimly. Serves her right. Of course, she might wind up snagging a high powered politician...

His thoughts strayed from her, for he really didn't care anymore. However, even knowing the army had made a change of command, he couldn't help glancing anxiously over his shoulder from time to time, his gaze searching the colored hills for any sign of riders. Especially ones wearing uniforms.

"Come on inside and refresh yourself," Lovely said. "The children will be back anytime now."

Keeping his impatience in check, Taylor helped the woman from the horse. They followed their host inside. Two white ladies were working at a quilting rack by the south window of the large sitting room where they could get plenty of light for their stitching. When Lovely offered chairs, they sat down; she rocking the baby gently in her arms and he on the edge of his seat, tense. One of the white women laid her thimble and needle aside and brought fresh water for them to drink.

The baby whimpered and the young wife bounced her gently until she quieted down. The lady serving the water asked, "Is she your little sister?"

She glanced at Taylor, perplexed. He answered for her. "The baby is her daughter."

"I'm sorry. She looks far too young to be a mother." When she noticed Taylor's frown, she offered a quick apology. "I meant it as a compliment; she's such a beautiful young girl."

"Elizabeth!" Lovely scolded softly. Then apologized. "Please don't be offended, Mr. Taylor. sometimes we white people have difficulty understanding Indian families and how they're formed—"

He broke off at the sound of laughter and yelling, growing louder. Lovely went out to meet the returning children. In a few minutes, he came back, leading a boy by the hand. When the boy saw the tall man, he bolted across the room.

"Dutch!" he yelled, plunging into the waiting arms.

Taylor, smiling broadly, returned the tight hug, enjoying the squeeze of the small arms about his neck.

"Dutch?" Lovely asked, a puzzled look on his face. "Why'd he call you that? I heard Dutch drowned escaping from a Fort Gibson prison."

Taylor glanced up. "He did," he said firmly.

Lovely's frown faded. He nodded, understanding.

Taylor returned his attention to the boy, held him back to get a better look. The boy, grinning sheepishly, glanced sideways at the woman.

"Don't be bashful, Honekahsee," he said. "You remember Little Tassel, don't you?"

Honekahsee nodded, but still held back. He pointed at the baby. "Where'd she get that?"

Taylor and Lovely exchanged looks, then both laughed.

"Her name is Dacy." Taylor said. "She's your new sister. Run along now and get your things. We have to go."

Honekahsee backed away, still staring at the baby, then turned and raced from the room. Taylor faced his host, extending his hand.

"Thanks, Mr. Lovely...for everything."

Lovely waved aside the thanks as they shook hands. "I only wish I could do more for your people. Perhaps, Mr. Taylor, when we get the Osages back to Kansas, the white settlers out of Indian Territory, and the eastern Cherokees to move out here and settle down with you Arkansas Cherokees..."

He paused, shaking his head, seemingly overcome by the enormity of the people-moving problem required in the treaty bearing his name. There was a disparaging note in his voice when he finished with, "Surely, there's some way to bring peace to the frontier!"

Taylor patted the bureaucrat on the shoulder. "Don't worry about it. It'll work out. No use beating on the bodies of the dead."

"Beating on the bodies of the dead? That's a new one on me. What does it mean?"

Taylor waved. "It's an old saying. I—"

Just then Honekahsee returned carrying all his possessions under one arm, wrapped in a newspaper and tied with a string.

"I'm ready," he said, his voice bubbling with excitement.

Lovely smiled, patted the youth on the head. "You be a good boy, you hear? And come see us when you grow up, will you?"

The boy made no reply, for he was already tugging on Taylor's hand, anxious.

The one calling himself Daniel Taylor yielded to the boy's pull. Little Tassel carrying the baby followed. He helped her into the saddle, the baby in her arms still sleeping. Then he took the reins in one hand and Honekahsee's hand in the other.

And the new family headed the way the V's in the blue sky overhead pointed...south toward Texas and a new life.

Printed in the United States
46786LVS00004B/31-81